Spartan Beast
Book Two of the Hellennium

by
P.K. Lentz

P.K. Lentz

PART 1

ATTICA

1. Scream for Me

Acharnia, Attica
The month of Thargelion
20 days after the fall of Athens
(May 423 BCE)

On a mountain trail in western Attica walked a man who once had been a general of Athens, the hero of Pylos and Amphipolis, but who now looked a vagrant, his clothing soiled, his beard unshorn, his sand-colored hair falling in matted locks. He shuffled toward the oncoming Spartan Equal, and he hummed. The tune was cheerful, giving no outward indication that he who hummed it inwardly seethed.

The crimson-cloaked Equal was unhelmed, long black hair falling down his back, and his sun-bronzed chest was bare. Like all full-blooded male citizens of Sparta, he was a beast born and bred for war, yet presently his only battle was with a bound lamb bleating and squirming as he carried it under one arm.

On seeing the shaggy, oblivious stranger in his path, the Equal barked, "Stand aside!"

Appearing to notice the Equal for the first time, the former general halted his steps, ceased his humming, and called out amiably, "Hail, Spartan warrior!"

"I have no quarrel with you," the Spartan said, continuing to close the distance between them. "Clear off and do not give me one."

"I shall give you no cause for quarrel, sir, I assure you," the other answered, stepping off the trail into the tall grass. His speech was the drawl of a high country dweller. "Diomedes is my name. I live in these mountains. A simple hermit. I offer no creature any harm."

Eyes narrowed in a threatening glare, the Equal passed him by.

The other drew up to walk alongside him and said, fawningly, "I am a great admirer of Spartan ways, sir. I would not scorn the chance to talk of them with you while you go on your way."

The Equal ignored him.

"Your unit intends to offer sacrifice?" the other persisted.

"Aye," the Equal grunted.

"You took the animal from this farm yonder?"

"Bought it there," the Spartiate corrected him.

"*Bought it!* Such magnanimity in victory." The hermit chuckled dryly. "Although, I suppose that since your people mint no coinage, it was Athenian silver you used."

The Spartan stopped and whirled, the lamb bleating renewed protest. "Leave me alone, you sack of goat shit," the soldier bellowed, "unless you wish to become a sacrifice yourself!"

"Apologies!" Freezing in his tracks, the shaggy one hoisted his hands in mock surrender.

The Equal growled, resuming his walk, while behind him, the mountain man cast doe-eyes to the roadside in search of a stone of a certain size. Spotting one as big as two fists, he moved swiftly.

The stone came down hard on the Equal's unprotected head just as he was turning to investigate the sudden flurry of motion. The soldier went down, and so did the trussed lamb. The former was silent, the latter not, and for a few loud seconds, the attacker stood monitoring the more dangerous of the two for signs of movement, of which there were none.

The Equal lived, breathing under the cover of his cape. Blood-smeared rock still poised, Demosthenes of Athens considered whether or not to bring it down and crush his helpless victim forever. A part of him wished to, but another part had a purpose for the man. It was this other part which Demosthenes desired to nurture, and so the Equal's death was to be delayed.

The lamb, on the other hand...

Kneeling, Demosthenes relieved the enemy of his short sword and turned it on the animal.

"I'm sorry if you thought this was a reprieve, friend," he said to it. "The gods have no use for you. But I am in need of food." Clamping a hand over the bleating lamb's face, he slit its throat, silencing its cries and sending hot blood spurting onto the hard-packed trail. He used the rope from the creature's legs to bind his human victim's wrists, then worked on finding the best arrangement by which to carry both burdens away into the mountains.

* * *

The Spartan stirred in his bonds.

Lifting the hem of his chiton, Demosthenes took aim, and the captured enemy completed his return to awareness choking on a faceful of piss.

Once Demosthenes had fully unloaded his bladder and the Spartan had finished coughing and sputtering, Demosthenes addressed the prisoner he had staked out spread-eagle on the forest floor.

"What is your name, Equal?" he asked.

The Spartan did not answer, rather just tested his bonds, which were rawhide strips. Unable to free himself, he relaxed well-muscled limbs onto the leaves, leveled his captor with a lion's glare, and he roared.

"Calm yourself," Demosthenes cautioned. He sat on a fallen trunk and laid his sword across his lap. "I have questions for you, and I recommend you answer them all. So,

Equal, what's your fucking name?"

"You think I have not been pissed on before, Athenian?"

"I have no idea what you Equals do to one another," Demosthenes said, "and I don't care. What you need to know is that, as of now, the only thing that you are *equal* to is horse shit. So what's your name, or shall I just call you Horseshit?"

The Spartiate growled, but yielded: "Arkesilaos. What do I call you, besides *dead man*."

Demosthenes toyed with the sharp blade in his lap. "I will ask the questions," he said. "Here is a simple one. Were you present on the first day of the siege of Dekelea?"

Arkesilaos tugged at his bonds again for good measure. "What if I was?"

"If you were, then you might remember a pregnant woman whose throat was cut by Brasidas." Such a matter-of-fact account of the event, coming from his own lips no less, prompted a cold sweat on Demosthenes' brow and an upward surge of acid from his stomach.

The prisoner sneered. "I remember the cow," he said. "Before the march, we passed her around like a whore and fucked the daylights out of her."

Demosthenes' fingers tightened on the grip of his sword. "You lie," he said quietly, hopefully. "But whether you are or not, I'm going to cut your balls off for saying it." He drew a breath and restored a degree of calm.

"She was the wife of some cunt. Demostratos, was it?" Arkesilaos laughed. "Is that you? No wonder she begged for it, being married to half a man!"

"She was the wife of the cunt Demosthenes. Which is me. When I kill Brasidas, I am considering making her name the last word he speaks. And since your present and final purpose in life is to help me practice for when I kill him, slowly, I want you to say it: Laonome."

"Laonome," the Spartiate said obligingly, but by no means submissively. He added: "the fat, slippery whore."

The words stung, but Demosthenes forced himself not to react. To claim his vengeance, he would have to be cold. "I thank you," he said. "You are making this much easier."

He stood, set down his sword and picked up a large, flat rock which he slid underneath Arkesilaos' bound right hand.

"I've killed plenty of men," Demosthenes said, conversationally. "But until recently, they were all trying to kill me at the time, which means I have done my best to make it quick. That is a hard habit to break, I have found." He shrugged. "I realize now that I dislike the sound of my wife's beautiful name on your lips. You don't deserve to say it, and neither does Brasidas."

With the first rock in place on the ground, Demosthenes picked up a second. Seeing his captor's intent, Arkesilaos clenched his fists, and the muscles of his arms bulged in a vain attempt to break free. "No!" he cried out, Spartiate discipline failing him.

The rock slammed down onto the Spartiate's right hand, smashing the bones of his fingers with a sickening crunch, sending a spray of blood onto the dried leaves underneath. Arkesilaos screamed, a nasal sound on account of his refusal to unclench his jaw, a sound that was half pain and half rage.

Demosthenes spoke calmly over the Equal's lingering groan. "Now, even if you escape me alive, you will be a cripple. You will never bear a spear for Sparta again." He threw down the bloodied rock and squatted to pick up another so large it required both arms. "This one will ensure you cannot escape at all."

Arkesilaos' next scream was more of a shriek. It began moments before the giant stone came crashing down on his right knee and lingered on long after the stone had settled. But the stone did not long rest, for Demosthenes retrieved it and repeated the process twice more, so as to thoroughly pulverize the man's left leg.

Famous iron discipline abandoned, a Spartan sent an anguished wail up over the tall pines: "*Help me!*"

"It is unlikely anyone will hear," Demosthenes said, "much less find you in time. I am afraid the best you can hope for is that they capture me after I finish. But I have a good hiding place, and don't think I am so stupid as to have brought you to it. So scream if you want to. *I* want you to."

That was a lie. In fact, this was sickening work, and he wished it would be over with, just as he had felt and wished the previous six times. But it had to be done. He needed to inure himself to the screams of the helpless. He had to learn to feel nothing.

He picked up his sword. "What next?" he asked of himself and his victim, who was quiet now but for sharp breaths drawn to combat the pain. "Your eyes?" He leveled his blade there, then shifted it down three feet or so. "Balls? Or your shield arm?" He directed the blade accordingly. "Which of those last two is more important to you? I know what my answer would be."

"Coward," the Spartiate rasped. Involuntary tears welled in his eyes. "Untie me and we will see who's still the better man!"

Demosthenes sighed and sat. "I hardly enjoy this," he confessed. "Not at all. But it has to be done. Do you have a wife, Arkesilaos?"

"Yes, yes!" the Equal answered, perhaps sensing, incorrectly, an opportunity to save his life. He gave her a name: "Kleora. And a son, Antikrates."

"Good," Demosthenes said. "I want you to know that they, too, will die soon. Every Spartan man, woman, and child will. For that is my sole purpose now: to obliterate your people from this earth, that none might ever walk it again who can rightly claim Spartan blood. I have the weapon which can accomplish the task. For now, it sleeps, but soon it shall wake. Soon..."

Arkesilaos groaned through clenched teeth, eyes shut tight against his pain.

"Shut up," Demosthenes said. "I've heard women giving birth behind curtains who make less noise than that." Likely driven by pride, the Equal quieted, and Demosthenes went on. "Do you know that you are not the only Arkesilaos? Of course you don't. But I do not mean other men bearing the same name. I mean others of *you*, for this world in which we dwell is but one of a myriad of copies. There are many more of Demosthenes, too, in these other worlds. They exist alongside us, invisible to us. She... *it* taught me that. My weapon.

"I suspect... nay, I am certain... that no other twins of me do what I do now. This world, this one layer of the many-layered cosmos, stands changed forevermore, made different from all rest. It was largely by my hand that this occurred. And my hand will alter it yet more, by ridding it of you and your kind."

Demosthenes brought his sword to bear, its tip hovering over the helpless Equal's nose.

"Take heart. Your wife and son will live on in other worlds. Better still, they will not have lost their husband and father, who dwells with them still, with two good hands and two legs on which he can walk. As for this world's Arkesilaos..." He rose from his seat one last time, touching the blade to Arkesilaos' throat. "I am tired of torturing him, and his time now ends. His family will grieve. But not for long."

Arkesilaos, the one belonging to this particular world,

raised a prayer to Zeus. The god did not answer, could not hear. Demosthenes drove his sword point down through the Equal's neck and into the forest floor. A spring of blood gurgled around the blade of hard Athenian steel, and the victim uttered a choked moan before descending into the black, godless silence of death.

2. Agis

The King was coming. One of Sparta's two kings, anyway. Agis the Second was the better of them, most would say, for his not having spent two decades in exile and disgrace like his counterpart. Agis was due at Athens's harbor town of Pireaus by midday, and Styphon stood on the beach at the head of ten Equals tasked with escorting him the five miles to the conquered city, where he would meet with its conqueror, Brasidas.

On schedule, or near enough, the royal ship *Archegetas* appeared. No special decoration made the trireme royal; the quality of its construction and identity of its trierarch were enough. New and better vessels existed now, thanks to the witch Eris, vessels equipped with complex rigging and triangular sails that allowed them to tack against the wind. The ones used a month ago to seize Athens with a surprise seaborne assault, had been converted triremes. Now, the new ships were being built to purpose.

In shipcraft, as in all things, some inevitably would reject the new and cling to the old ways. Styphon was uncertain where he fell. Perhaps somewhere in between blind adherence to tradition and blind longing for the new. Fortunately, one of his middle rank was rarely called upon to make such decisions, but only follow those who did.

When *Archegetas*'s crew had eased her into the dock and moored the ship, Agis and his entourage disembarked and strode the planks down onto the beach where Styphon waited.

"Lord King." Styphon and the men behind him all fell briefly to one knee and then rose. Spartans were no Persians who bowed and scraped the earth before royalty. True, Agis was a blood descendant of Herakles, and thus of Zeus, but he was still yet a man.

Agis was handsome and just under thirty, with bright, honest eyes and dark locks that tumbled over both shoulders. As an heir apparent, Agis had been spared the harsh training regimen prescribed to all other Spartiate boys from the age of seven, and thus his limbs were leaner than the ideal, his skin thinner and lacking in scars, yet none could accuse of him of putting on aristocratic airs. He wore a plain wool chiton bound by a leather belt, and the crimson cloak on his shoulders bore the white salt streaks of a sea voyage. His sole adornment, the only declaration of his royal birth, was a ring of plain iron set on a finger of his left hand.

The king smiled, acknowledged and dismissed the bows with a wave of his hand, which he then extended to clasp Styphon's. "What is your name, soldier?" he asked.

Styphon's heart froze. Since his shameful surrender at Sphakteria two years prior, his name had been a curse in Sparta, its taste often foul even to his own lips. But he spoke it anyway, with scant hesitation. "Styphon, sire."

The king's smile vanished. His open eyes hardened, and shrugging his cloak from his right shoulder, he drew his short sword. Styphon held his ground, unflinching even as the blade's point came to rest in the hollow of his neck.

"I have heard you called a *trembler*," Agis said. "Are you?"

"That is not for me to judge, sire."

"But it is." Agis poked him with the blade. "If you were raised well, then you are your own harshest critic. So tell me, Styphon, why did you bring shame upon yourself by surrendering so many Equals under your command to Athenian irons?"

Despite his best efforts, Styphon let his own black eyes fall from the king's penetrating, regal stare as he replied: "I believed it best for Sparta, sire."

"You mean you deemed the outcome of the war more important than that of a single battle, is that right?" the king offered. "And also more important than your own honor?"

"Yes, sire." Styphon began to sense that this was not a true interrogation at all, but something else. A performance...?

"What right-minded Spartan could argue that the opposite was true?" This question was rhetorical, but the next —directed not at Styphon but at the Equal to his right—was not. "What is this place where we stand, soldier?"

"Piraeus, sire," the Equal answered eagerly.

"And where are your unit's barracks?"

"Athens, sire."

"Athens, hmm?" Agis raised a brow theatrically. "Then I dare say we must have won the war, did we not?"

"Yes, sire," the man replied. This answer was less enthusiastic, as the Equal perhaps realized he was being patronized.

"And I hear that the man who led the force which broke down Athens' gates was this very man whom some have called a trembler, this *Styphon*." The king removed his sword from Styphon's neck, but kept it aloft and shook it while he raised his head to address all present. "Let any Equal who would question Styphon's honor be prepared to back up his words with hard evidence, or else face this blade!"

Styphon's face flushed, but not with pride. It was without question an honor for any man to have a King of Sparta proclaim his worth, but it was also much better that a disgraced man earn back his countrymen's respect by his own deeds, not be given it back by decree. But once spoken, Agis' words could not be unsaid. How they fell upon the ears and hearts of the six Spartiates behind him, and those of the six times six whom those men would tell of this moment, and so on until all the army knew, was for the gods to decide.

13

Right now, the six gave no indication of their reactions, and even Styphon had no time to ponder his own before Agis sheathed his sword and took long strides up the beach, forcing the escort detail to hurry after him. The king's small entourage followed, too: five bodyguards, and walking in an empty space all his own, a small man in a black robe who was well known to any who knew Agis. The little man's brown head was shaved bald and his delicate features refused to give away his age. The tall staff he carried, topped with a fist-sized, opal-eyed bronze figure of a bull's head, flicked sand with each step. His name was Phaistos, but most men called him simply the Minoan, and he was said to have been found alone as an infant in the foothills of Kythera, the last son of a civilization long dead. The Minoan was a seer and diviner, and Agis, like the king's father before him, never went abroad without this black shadow a few steps behind.

The combined party made its way from the harbor to the nearby shrine of Poseidon to let Agis pour an offering of wine as thanks for safe voyage, after which they passed through the still-splintered gate which once had barred the way inland to Athens. The soon to be razed Long Walls, which had sheltered a generation of Athenians from their enemies, rose up twenty feet on either side of them.

Agis eyed with curiosity the Athenians who passed on their daily business to and from the harbor. The few looks which came back were fleeting; most wanted nothing to do with him or any Spartan.

"Has there been any sign of resistance to our rule?" the king asked Styphon.

"I would not wish to preempt the polemarch, sire."

Agis looked crosswise at his escort. "Brasidas will tell me what he tells me. Right now I am asking you."

Styphon remained quiet, considering his reply.

"I can surmise the answer by the way you and your men watch the crowd," Agis remarked. "So you may as well tell me, phylarch."

"It's enomotarch now, sire," Styphon corrected.

"Congratulations," the king said. "Last I checked, my rank was still somewhat higher." Putting aside for now the matter of Athenian resistance, he laughed. "An unenviable position, to be torn between superiors. Do you bow to seniority or follow the chain of command? It is a choice that the Lawgiver in his wisdom left for each Equal to decide for himself, when and if the moment comes." He flashed Styphon a smile. "Very well," Agis conceded, "I will hear the answer from Brasidas. You might tell me one other thing, though."

The king's heavy pause hinted to Styphon that the question to come would be even more sensitive than the last.

"The witch, Eris," Agis began. Her very name was a thorn in Styphon's ear. "What became of her?"

Styphon despaired to speak of the she-daemon. In their first encounter, he had watched Eris slaughter a dozen veteran Spartiates as if they were children wielding birch whips. Even now he wondered if Eris would not swoop down from the Long Walls and take his head if he misspoke. But the asker was Agis, and he dared not try the king's patience or spoil his evident good will, mixed blessing that it was.

"She was felled by Athenian spindles at Eleusis," Styphon reported. "After slaying her rival, who fought for Athens."

"So I was told. But what became of her corpse?"

"It lies in Apollo's sanctuary, a cave on the north face of the acropolis."

"Curious," the king said with obvious interest. "Why has it not been buried? Or burned?"

With only slight hesitation that he hoped was not

detectable, Styphon lied, or at least withheld the truth from his king. He had to, for Brasidas had sworn him, and a very few others, to secrecy on the matter of his witch's apparent ability to shrug off death.

He thus answered with a refrain which almost qualified as a Spartan nursery rhyme: "It is not my place to question my superior's will."

Agis accepted the deflection. "It matters not. Merely a curiosity." His words lacked the ring of truth and clashed with his dark tone of moments ago. "It is not in every war that we see a goddess fighting on our side. Or whatever she was."

They walked the rest of the way to Athens in relative silence. When they reached the broken gates which had hung open since their breaching forty days ago, the gazes of Agis and his royal guards were on the crowded city beyond, particularly the white crags of its temple-crowned acropolis. They were laying eyes on these homes and holy places of their intractable foe for the first time, and they could hardly help but be struck with either awe at its grandeur or disgust at its prodigality. Maybe a mix of both.

The king, for his part, took on a philosophical air and lamented idly, "Perhaps it would be best not to tear down the walls which shield such beauty."

They continued on past the fire-blackened hillside which had been the seat of Athens's toppled democracy. It was near there that bald Phaistos the Minoan, with a rapid *thump-thump* of his bull staff, caught his master up and asked, "Lord King, might I go offer sacrifice at that shrine of which we earlier spoke?"

"Hmm? Yes, by all means," Agis answered him distractedly. "Take my guards with you. I am well protected, it would seem, against this Athenian resistance which may or may not exist." He shot a sly smile at Styphon, and then his gaze flicked to a wall nearby where two Helots had just begun to paint over graffiti of a giant capital letter Omega.

Flashing his own toothy smile, the Minoan seer bowed his hairless head, waved his staff at Agis's five spear-wielding bodyguards and scurried off ahead of them, virtually swimming in his black robes.

* * *

Brasidas had made his office in the red-roofed Tholos, the administrative headquarters in which Athens kept its civic hearth. Standing to either side of the cylindrical building's stone steps were larger than life-sized marble figures of the goddesses Hestia and Peace. Styphon paused beneath the latter and yielded so that Agis might mount the stairs first.

But Agis, whose eyes had not stopped taking in the sights and passersby the whole of the trek, likewise halted. He drew Styphon aside and leaned in close. "There is a special task with which I would charge you once this meeting is done," he whispered.

"But name it, sire."

"These Athenian women interest me," he began, leaving Styphon with little doubt as to where he was headed. "Find one—no, two—and bring them to me tonight, dressed in fine silks and jewelry as is their custom, hair piled in curls." He raised a cautioning palm and added, "Not virgins, and not by force, mind you. Find some wives or widows who will come willingly, in order to secure their property against seizure or win their families favor in the new order."

Styphon was careful to remain stone-faced, as though the perverse request were perfectly natural. When the king was done, he whispered back, "That may prove difficult, sire. Athenians keep their citizen women locked away. Particularly these days."

Agis turned away, dismissive of the excuse. "I have faith

in you, Styphon," he said, and clapped him on a thickly muscled arm before mounting the steps.

Styphon and the escort detail followed in his wake to the open double doors of the Tholos and proceeded into the round central chamber. Athenians, like most men outside of Sparta, were overly fond of embellishing their halls of government. Here in the Tholos, that tendency was illustrated, almost literally, in the murals of great Athenian triumphs from the mists of time, or ones they claimed credit for: over the Amazons, over the Centaurs, over the Persians. At the center of the tiled floor stood the perpetually burning civic hearth from whose embers all hearth fires in the city were lit. The priestesses who tended the flame, one of whom was stoking it now and glanced up blankly at them as they entered, had not flagged in their duties during the city's transition to new leadership.

Lining the Tholos' rounded walls were couches where the elected public officials of Athens' defunct democracy had taken their meals when on duty. Currently occupying one couch was a group of Athenians whom Brasidas had appointed as minor bureaucrats in the transitional government. The arrival of a party of Equals silenced their hushed conversation. They looked over and offered respectful nods.

Had Agis worn anything about his person to indicate his status, they likely would have raced over and competed with another to lick his cloak clean of salt. Instead, he was just another Spartiate, an object of fear.

The office of Brasidas was in a sub-chamber which once had served some or other official of the abolished democracy. Before they reached it, the polemarch appeared in its open doorway, sank to one knee in keeping with custom, and then came forward, smiling, extending his arms for an embrace.

Agis accepted the greeting and, at least for those few moments, they appeared as Lykourgos intended, as brothers, instead of what they truly were: a young king who had not yet managed to inscribe his name alongside those of his esteemed predecessors in the annals of history, and the older man of lower birth whose name already was spoken in Sparta with great pride.

Their rivalry had come to a head some months ago when the Elders had voted to put Brasidas in command of the invasion of Attica, rather than Agis, who in line with tradition had led it the three years prior. Some number of the Elders on the council would have seen tradition upheld, but enough were either afraid of Brasidas and his white witch or enamored of the pair's promises to strip Athens, by means of technology, of her twin advantages: control of the seas and her Long Walls.

Not even Agis could argue that Brasidas and his false goddess had failed to deliver.

Right now, as they broke off their embrace, whatever tension there was between them remained hidden.

"The sea god treated you well, sire?" Brasidas asked cordially.

"The god, yes, and your man here, too," Agis answered.

Once more, Styphon wished the king would hold his tongue, however good his intentions. Indeed, Brasidas used an instant when Agis's eyes were not upon him to cast Styphon a glance which held the promise of questions to come.

Spartans were not ones for small talk. These were two of the most powerful men in Sparta, and thus in Greece and perhaps the world, and there remained unfinished business in their city's recent victory: resistance in Athens and, of course, the thousand or so holdouts still under siege at Dekelea. The door shut behind them so they might discuss such matters, while Styphon's mind set to work on a problem of his own: how in the name of Apollon's asshole was he to find a pair of Athenian wives willing to whore themselves?

3. Aspasia

Before long, Styphon settled on an answer to his question, or least had decided where to go in the hope of finding one. Although plenty of Athens' many brothels, almost exclusively owned and staffed by foreigners anyway, had welcomed and even competed for Spartan business since the conquest, one in particular had emerged as the conquerors' favorite. It was the one run by Aspasia, an Ionian woman who was the former consort of late Perikles, and some said co-leader of the city with him by means of nocturnal whispers in his ear. So well-known had her name become that it was even known to all in Sparta.

This fame, one might say, had ensured her downfall, for to Athenians, even more than most Greeks, a famous woman was an infamous woman. Since her influential lover's death, Aspasia had become mistress of a brothel renowned not just for the quality of its girls but also its ability to accommodate nearly any price range. Spartiates, of course, being forbidden by law to possess currency and only able to scrape up a coin here and there in a city which was not to be sacked, favored cheap whores over refined *hetairae*. Aspasia had been among the first to offer discounts to Spartiates, a wise move which accounted for her establishment's present popularity.

Styphon knew the location of Aspasia's den, despite having never been a customer of it or of any other brothel in Athens. Going there, he entered, and the sight which greeted him within the parlor was that of a pale, nude brunette reclining on a couch alongside an Equal from his regiment, an under-thirty by the name of Geradas. On seeing Styphon, his immediate superior, Geradas quickly pushed the girl's hand out from under his chiton hem, threw his crimson cloak over her and cast eyes down in shame. By law, Equals were expected to exercise utmost physical discipline, but in practice, particularly when on campaign, a blind eye was turned to small vices.

Caught with chiton raised, Geradas doubtless hoped for leniency, even if he had no right to it. His hope was granted, and Geradas' only punishment today would be the scowl of mild disapproval leveled at him by his enomotarch as he passed. Styphon's priorities lay elsewhere. It was better that no one even knew he had come.

A white-skinned woman, all assets visible through her drape of pale blue silk, sensuous smile on her painted lips, approached and laid her hand on Styphon's collarbone, grinding her thinly veiled sex on his thigh. "Let us fuck like beasts," she said in a breathy approximation of the Lakonian dialect.

Styphon pushed her away—gently, since, after all, he was here to ask a favor. "Where is Aspasia?"

"The Lady does not see clients personally," the girl answered. Her affected dialect had vanished, replaced by Ionian, which she spoke with some island accent. "And if she did, you could not afford her." She pouted. "Am I not good enough?"

"It is not my own need which brings me here."

The prostitute sighed, then reluctantly turned away to vanish through a purple curtain at the parlor's rear, one of its scant few surfaces not adorned with pornographic paintings. Foremost among these was the mural on the coffered ceiling depicting a giant Aphrodite with a phallus penetrating the chasm between her splayed legs.

Standing in this place of decadence, which was perhaps not the lowest point to which a free woman could fall (that being street-walker) Styphon thought of the daughter he barely knew. Andrea was, what, eleven now? To avoid the bleak fate of children whose fathers were deemed cowards in Sparta, Andrea had been removed to Athens by Thalassia and Alkibiades, in whose care she had lived for more than a year. Styphon had asked Thalassia for that favor in return for the promise of reciprocation one day, the granting of some future favor unknown.

He could not know whether he would one day regret the bargain.

Now that her father's fortunes were turning, Andrea could safely dwell where she belonged, and so Styphon had sent her back to Sparta with a letter placing her in the care of neighbors and distant relatives. Seeing as he was standing under naked Aphrodite's gash, Styphon spoke a short, whispered prayer to that goddess to keep Andrea from harm and one day to give her a good husband and fruitful womb.

As he finished, Aspasia appeared from behind the curtain. The one-time most powerful woman in Athens was past the prime of her womanhood, a fact that her minimal application of cosmetics made no attempt to hide. She wore her age well, but it struck Styphon, as it must have struck many who met her, that regardless of her years she was a plain woman, round of face with mousy dark hair divided into thick plaits. Her expensive embroidered garments by no means lacked modesty. Without knowing otherwise, Styphon likely would never have marked her as a courtesan.

Aspasia smiled warmly. "What can I do for you this fine day, Spartiate?"

Her tone and the sparkle in her brown eyes were such that one could easily see why she was proficient at her trade: she could make a man, even one who looked down on her, feel as though pleasing him was its own reward.

"A superior bids me obtain two girls," Styphon said, avoiding mention of the king. "But not just any." He described Agis's request.

Aspasia's plump lips, subtly painted, pursed in thought. "Tricky," she mused. "Many women are worried what will become of their men and homes in the new tyranny. I may be able to find some takers. But if not, I have girls who can look and act as citizens easily enough. I doubt that your superior, whoever he is, could tell the difference."

"Deceive if you must," Styphon said. "Just do not make me party to it. What is the fee?" He suspected that tradition dictated some sort of dance take place over price in a place like this, but he was no dancer.

If he violated custom, Aspasia took it in perfect stride. "If I can fill the request as made, the bill will be but a drachma," she said. "My reward will be helping two women make their way in these troubled times. But if I need to pay my own girls, the cost will be twenty."

Styphon, being little used to coinage, did not even know how much silver was in the pouch of official funds he carried as a privilege of rank in Brasidas's temporary regime.

"Agreed." He started to empty the purse into his palm, but Aspasia's gentle hand came up and stopped him. "The bill is not yet known," she said with her disarming smile. "Come back and pay after your mystery man is satisfied. *Fooled*, if need be."

Something in her speech suggested she knew the customer was someone important. Perhaps that much was obvious, since the client otherwise would have come himself. But could she suspect it was the king? His arrival was not not quite common knowledge, but neither a secret. More likely, she thought the client Brasidas, although if she had known the polemarch, she might have realized Brasidas was well-placed enough in Athens by now to get what he wanted himself instead of sending a proxy to beseech an aging courtesan.

Letting her think what she might, Styphon instructed her on where and when to dispatch the women. Then he gladly made his leave, noting as he passed the empty couch which shamed Geradas had already vacated.

4. Discord

From Aspasia's den, Styphon returned to the Tholos in time for the evening mess, which was to be attended by Agis, the members of Brasidas's and Styphon's own units, and a handful of Athenian collaborators being groomed for positions of power in the soon-to-be-installed tyranny. Styphon's late arrival was scarcely noticed by the crowd of forty or so. Taking a spot against the wall (the Spartan attendees reclining on the bare tile, the Athenians on cushions), he ate cheese and bread and cold barley, and laughed along with all at a few pasty Athenians' attempts to choke down Spartan 'black broth,' the nearly sole ingredient of which was pig's blood. He listened to Equals compete to tell stories of their battle prowess in the hope the king would overhear and invite them to join the royal guard.

Styphon kept quiet, for he had no particular desire for more attention from Agis. He did not receive any. In fact, for some reason Agis seemed distracted and in a foul mood, almost a different man than the personable king Styphon had escorted from the port. Perhaps his mood was foul, or perhaps it was by some sort of strategy that Agis seized on an opportunity, opened by someone's tale of bravery in battle, to ridicule a particular proposal that Brasidas was purported to have made privately to Sparta's five supreme magistrates, the ephors:

"We shall need courage like yours when Brasidas has us charging an enemy phalanx without our spears," the king remarked, directing a humorless glare at the man in question. "Actually, what we shall need are prayers and bandages!"

A few present chuckled, but they stopped quickly for lack of company. Agis himself did not laugh. Brasidas produced his sharp smile, hawk eyes levelly meeting the king's gaze.

"My grandfather never would have believed Sparta would exchange bronze armor and encompassing helms for leather and bare faces in the battle-line," the polemarch returned. "Yet we did, and still we persist in winning battle after battle against men wrapped in metal. My father would have laughed at the idea of a ship that can sail into the wind, yet we took Athens with such vessels. Just the same, our sons will win battles with arms and tactics which today we find laughable."

"Hmm," Agis intoned, but the sound was ominous rather than thoughtful. It seemed to Styphon that the dearth of laughter scored by his last remark was perversely driving the young king to redouble his attack. "Well, then, why don't we all agree to ride chickens into the battle at Dekelea a few days hence and see who winds up laughing?"

This line scored him a few more chuckles, but they were nervous ones. Fully half of the men present were the members of Brasidas's own mess, and they remained stone-faced. Though they might savagely tear one another down in private, mess-mates did not look well upon one of their own being mocked by an outsider, even a king.

Brasidas's composure showed no sign of strain. He casually sat on the tile with his back against the wall. His smile patronized Agis, and any who laughed, as feeble-minded inferiors.

"By all means, laugh," he said. "I welcome it. But a man should know what he is laughing at, so let me explain. Yes, I do believe the sword should be our primary weapon, but not only that. The phalanx should be put to rest, too. Currently, when a unit's cohesion is broken, the battle is lost and no choice remains, even for the bravest of men, but to flee the field or die. Worse still, what can turn even the most disciplined hoplite regiment into fodder for light infantry? *Some trees. A swamp. A stream!"*

Brasidas shrugged. "I risk droning on, when we should be eating, but I only mean to say that it makes scant sense to me that a Spartiate should be the ultimate instrument of war, yet remain vulnerable to far lesser men on any terrain other than clear, level ground. We are missing something, and if you listen carefully enough, you can hear the laughter of those who truly have a right to laugh: the gods."

By now, there was no thought of laughter among the crowd, nor of eating. All eyes went to the king in anticipation of his rebuttal. But Agis, being an astute enough observer of his surroundings to ascertain that the time for mockery was done, changed his tone.

"Quite right," he said, in a way which made it clear he had no plans to concede the argument. "Change is inevitable. It can bring improvement or it can bring disaster. But tradition is the foundation on which positive change must be built." He sounded as if he were quoting some childhood tutor of his, but not for long. "I wonder whether most here would count the freeing of the Helots—all of them, as I understand is your advice to the ephors—as a positive or negative change?"

The king furrowed his brow and fixed Brasidas with a look of exaggerated interest. The position of which he had just accused the polemarch of holding was a new one to Styphon, as indeed it must be to all present, for all eyes—not least those of the Helot slaves serving the meal—joined those of Agis in demanding from Brasidas either confirmation or denial.

For the moment, Brasidas gave neither. "At Amphipolis, the battle during which I was captured two years ago"— doubtless, this reminder of his defeat was intended as a show of humility, which in turn proved his confidence—"I led a force of Helots who gave their service on the battlefield in exchange for freedom. They were no Equals, naturally, for how could they ever be? But they fought well, were loyal, and in the end they died for each other, for me, for Sparta, and for their families. I was glad to count them on my side and not the enemy's, for at present, are the Helots not as much our enemy as Athens was? Every year we renew our declaration of war on our own slaves, and when we fight wars abroad, we are forced to leave garrisons behind to guard against rebellion. Our Helots are a resource, yes, but at the same time they are a drain."

Brasidas might have intended to finish there, or might have gone on, but he was forced to stop: Agis, who thus far had only provoked others to laughter, began himself to laugh. He did so alone, and made a convincing display of amusement which he surely did not feel.

"And I suppose after freeing our slaves," the king taunted, "you'd have Equals give up training for half the year to push a plough and harvest wheat?"

There was no reaction from the forty-plus diners. Styphon wished the king would find a graceful exit from this conversation, but that seemed less and less likely. There was no doubt in Styphon's mind that Brasidas had a ready and convincing answer—regardless of whether he had come to it himself, or been fed it by his star-born ally Eris.

"Perish the thought," Brasidas answered. "Spartiates are born and bred to war, and it would be criminal to suggest it become otherwise."

Brasidas knew, better than any speaker whom Styphon had heard, how to ingratiate himself to an audience, even when speaking unwanted or unpleasant truths.

"I would dare not suggest we do without slaves," Brasidas continued. "I simply think that our slaves ought not also to be our neighbors. We should import them, as most do, from conquests abroad. We could do with far fewer, then, since their labor would be solely for our benefit, and not also for their own families and communities."

Abruptly, Brasidas abruptly threw a hand in the air and smiled. "Come now, Agis, serious talk like this has its place, and that place is not the mess! Doesn't anyone have a good joke?"

No one spoke. Agis smiled intelligently. "I could say that you just finished telling a joke yourself, polemarch," the king said. "But instead, I yield. I can see when I have been out-tongued. Really, if I did not know better, I would swear you were one of those Athenian demagogues sitting over there, looking pale for fear of giving anyone offense." Agis gestured at the future tyrants and laughed, amiably. "Or maybe the food is just not to their liking. I admit my error. This is not the place for such debate. But I can see you have taken it in the spirit in which it was intended," Agis doubtless lied, "that of brotherhood. The traditions we share are only strengthened by the raising and rejection of new ideas. Whichever side one takes, whether that of reckless change or respect for tradition, and no matter what one's rank, we in this room remain, forever, *Equals*."

The king raised and drank from his clay water-cup, no different than that used by anyone in the room. Amid a muttered chorus of agreement, or more likely plain relief at the easing of tension between the two leaders, the forty or so Equals and Athenians lining the walls gladly followed suit and drank.

Brasidas was last to raise his cup, in silence, hawk-eyes watching Agis.

* * *

After some reasonably good wine and brief entertainment presented by the future tyrants, when about half the diners had filed out, an Equal entered the mess fully armored with sheathed sword on his hip. He was Therykion, one of Brasidas's trusted lieutenants, and ignoring all others he made a line straight for the polemarch. His breach of protocol in wearing arms into the mess hall, Styphon assumed, would share its explanation with the half-dried blood which stained the lower half of his face.

On seeing his aide arrive, Brasidas rose and went to him without bothering to excuse himself from the cluster of messmates with whom he conversed. Agis, seated on the wall opposite in a similar cluster, watched the pair closely. The look on the king's young features, if Styphon was any judge, seemed one of worry, not of the general kind, but a more pointed variety

Therykion spoke emphatically and with urgency, but since he did so in Brasidas's ear, none of it could be overheard, not even when the whole room fell silent in the pretense of ignoring what was clearly a sign of some developing emergency.

Styphon's first thought, which must have been shared with others present, was that the Athenian resistance, led by a man known only as Omega, had added another Equal to the list of five whom they had murdered thus far, one here and one there, typically with arrows from the dark.

Others in the room might have persisted in that belief, but Styphon dismissed it when he saw Brasidas's sharp eyes dart to the king during Therykion's report. He knew that look, and grasped, too, Agis's apparent agitation.

Whatever had transpired, Agis was involved.

Brasidas gave his aide a brief, inaudible instruction, after which Therykion raced out.

The polemarch proceeded to the center of the room. "Matters of governance beckon," he said tersely to the crowd, for whose attention he had no need to ask, for he had it. "Fortunately, I am blessed with the presence of our king, with whom I shall now consult in private. Good evening."

The silent crowd caught his true meaning: that all but the two leaders should excuse themselves from the hall. A prompt evacuation ensued, in which Styphon took part. Unlike some others, perhaps, he understood that in the private meeting soon to take place, Agis and Brasidas would not be partners in tackling some emergency; they would be open adversaries.

Just before he left the chamber, Styphon turned at the sound of Brasidas calling his name.

"Stay near," the polemarch commanded.

Styphon acknowledged with a nod. Outside the Tholos, under the orange sky of early evening, the dismissed crowd dispersed quickly. Though doubtless curious, Spartiates were perhaps the least prone of any men on earth to indulge in gossip and rumor; they would know what they needed to know when and if their superiors deemed it necessary. Given his rise from accused trembler to Brasidas's 'dog' and partner in the recruitment of the she-daemon Eris, to leader of the marine assault which had taken Athens, then finally into the polemarch's inner circle, Styphon was likely to learn the truth sooner than most.

While the rest went to retrieve their arms and report back to their various duties in the occupation of Athens, Styphon took up a position around the corner from the mess.

Within a quarter hour, Agis strode out. Crimson cloak billowing, he walked with purpose. Styphon pressed closer to the wall of the alley in which he hid to avoid the king's notice. It was hardly necessary, for Agis evidently saw nothing but his destination, whatever it was.

When the king had gone, Styphon reported to Brasidas's

office in the Tholos.

The polemarch stood in his open doorway, and the look he wore was one Styphon knew: behind his hard eyes, flanked by the scar on his temple received at Amphipolis, where Demosthenes had dealt him his greatest defeat, a keen and vindictive mind was in motion.

The target of his fearsome mental energy, Styphon knew without asking, was Agis, their own king, the product of a dynasty which stretched back into the mists of time to a demigod's seed and which had emerged unchallenged through twenty generations of Spartiates.

With a flick of his head, the polemarch beckoned Styphon into his office.

"Agis sent his guards and his seer to the sanctuary of Apollo," Brasidas began bluntly when they were alone behind the closed door.

The explanation caused Styphon to curse himself. The king's black-robed Minoan, Phaistos, had not left to pray or sacrifice, but to visit the corpse of Eris. And Agis has sent his royal guardsmen not to protect the seer, but to aid him in whatever was his purpose.

"Apologies, polemarch. It was I who let slip her location," Styphon said swiftly, choosing to take a lesson from Brasidas himself in taking quick responsibility for failure.

With a wave, Brasidas silenced him. "It is not your place to suspect and second-guess your king. Under most circumstances."

A sharp look accompanied the latter remark. Styphon understood it: such things now *were* to be his place.

"Clearly, their intent was to steal the body from the cave. Fortunately, brotherhood prevailed. My men and his refrained from drawing weapons on each other. They fought fist and shield instead, and Agis's party was beaten back."

Brasidas chuckled darkly. "They are lucky that *she* yet remains dormant. They might have met a far worse fate."

No men knew better than the two present in the office what superhuman violence Eris was capable of, for they had witnessed it first-hand on meeting her. Fourteen Equals had gone into the woods a year prior on the mission to persuade her to aid Sparta. Twelve had not returned.

"Naturally, the incident will be kept silent." Brasidas tapped Styphon's 'loose' lips with a rough fingertip. He walked a small circuit around his office, appropriated from some Athenian democrat, and came to stop behind an overly ornate writing platform. "Agis has taken a liking to you," he observed. "The clash at the cave notwithstanding—after all, it did not happen—he leaves tomorrow to command the operation at Dekelea." He laughed. "By *command*, I mean he will take credit for success I have already ensured. He asked to take you with him, and I of course agreed. It is an excellent opportunity for you to further win the confidence of your king, don't you think?"

"Aye. Thank you, sir."

The polemarch searched Styphon's black eyes for evidence that he understood the unspoken purpose of gaining Agis's confidence. Styphon did.

"One last thing," Brasidas added, leaning on the writing platform. "I am sure I need not remind you what is the single most important object inside Dekelea. Whatever it takes, I want it."

"Sir," Styphon ventured reluctantly, "what if it... *lives*?"

The polemarch scoffed, then chuckled darkly. "Well, you have a special relationship with her from Sphakteria, do you not? She was ready to help Sparta before you, in your vast wisdom, turned her down." He smirked. "Maybe you can talk her out of her alliance with that cunt Demosthenes."

5. Inglorious Conquest

Leaving the Tholos, Styphon went to the place just off the agora where Aspasia was to send Agis's entertainment for the night. The two women were there waiting, standing arm-in-arm in the lamp-glow, flashes of finery showing underneath brightly colored, unblemished cloaks. Their pale faces, which were unpainted—women of standing in Athens, as in Sparta, used no cosmetics—bore looks of concern. Their presence in this spot was conspicuous, for even prior to the occupation, Athenian men never let their female relations venture out alone in the night.

That the two looked worried even before they saw Styphon approaching hinted that they were the genuine article, although possibly they were just highly accomplished professionals. Either would do. The real thing was cheaper by twenty-fold, but then, the coin was the enemy's anyway.

Awkwardly, Styphon spoke exactly the words that Aspasia had instructed him to: "It is a fine evening. I will take you to your appointed place."

The women gripped each other's arms more tightly and lowered their gazes to the stone-paved street to let themselves be led to their unknown client. With no more words shared, Styphon guided the pair to the seized mansion which once had belonged to the Athenian general Nikias, slain at Eleusis by one of Eris's unerring shafts. The garden gate was attended by two Spartiates of the royal guard, who leered and smiled knowingly, sharing a few lewd remarks before letting them pass. Another Equal at the door beckoned them into the house's megaron, where they were told to await Agis.

At the threshold, one of the women hesitated, and only crossed over in halting steps when tugged across by her companion. If she was not a real Athenian wife or widow, this *hetaira* had truly inhabited her role.

The expansive hearth chamber far exceeded anything to be found in Sparta. Its tables were polished, its couches gilded, its pillows embroidered, and its every wall covered with frescoes depicting pastoral scenes of men, women, and beasts. *Only two tools should be used to build a house*, Styphon's late father Pharax had been fond of saying, quoting one of the ancient kings, *An ax and a saw*. That king would have spat in disgust at the army of laborers and implements it must have taken to construct even the humble dwellings Styphon had yet seen in Athens, never mind an aristocrat's home such as this. As such, Brasidas's quartering of Agis in such a place might have been intended as an insult to the king's manhood. That Agis had not objected suggested he failed to see it as such.

In a far corner of the megaron, some local slave boy tended the hearth. Beside it, Agis's two remaining bodyguards sat scowling; one had his left arm bound up tightly in linens, and the other's lip was fat and purple, among other minor cuts peppering his flesh. On the floor elsewhere, in the dancing shadows cast by oil lamps, the Minoan seer Phaistos sat hunched with staff laid over crossed legs. Under the fold of his black cowl, a swelling around one eye was barely visible.

Presently Agis arrived from the back rooms clad in a plain, brilliant white chiton, his long hair braided. Shutting the door, he glanced at the two women and raised a brow. "I halfway thought you'd show up with nothing but excuses," he said. "And I would not have blamed you. But you came through! Good man!" Reaching him, he gave Styphon's arm a congratulatory slap.

The king then laid the same hand on the cloaked shoulder of one of the women, who flinched. He drew back his hand, pointed with it and said gently to both females, "Go to that writing desk. Record the names and demes of your husbands, and indicate whether or not they live. If you satisfy tonight, you shall get the promised reward."

Perhaps taking cold comfort in this early sign that the bargain would be honored and their virtue not given away freely, the two went unhesitatingly to do as instructed. While they were thus occupied, Agis drew Styphon so close that their foreheads nearly touched.

"I presume Brasidas told you what occurred," the king said quietly.

Styphon wanted no part in talk of the incident. He gave the most expedient answer, which happened to be the truth. "Yes, sire."

"I'll assume his account was accurate. My men went to seize Eris's corpse and obliterate it. Phaistos tells me its the only way to be sure that Sparta is permanently rid of the witch."

Whether he got his information from arcane lore, his imagination or, less likely, actual knowledge of these women from another world, the seer was right, Styphon knew. But he volunteered nothing of that.

Agis anyway expected no reply. He went on, "I apologize if you took any blame. Men such as you, fiercely loyal and desiring no part in politics, are the backbone of our state. Brasidas is right to put the faith in you that he does. Has he told you you shall accompany me to Dekelea?" Styphon nodded affirmative. "I look forward to having you by my side in battle."

"Thank you, sire." Styphon's gratitude was real; it was hard not to feel grateful for such a compliment from a king, even when the intent was surely to manipulate.

"Do you know why I consented to let Brasidas lead the invasion of Attica in my place?" Agis asked.

Styphon did not dare answer, not least because according to his understanding, Agis had not consented at all, but been ordered by the annually elected ephors of Sparta to stand down.

"Of course you do not know. Why would you?" Agis went on. "When the ephors voted three to five to give the invasion to Brasidas, the old men of the Gerousia, defenders of tradition, convinced me not to challenge the verdict. They had such little faith in Brasidas and his toys that they figured he would fail and we could get him exiled afterward, if not with the current batch of ephors, then with whatever five are chosen next year."

Agis scoffed and waved his iron-ringed hand. "But now that Brasidas has given us Athens, he's more popular than ever. The old … Bah! It's the old men who stand discredited! They managed to persuade the ephors not to renew Brasidas's forty-day command of the invasion force, at least, so that I might be the one to fight this, the war's final battle. But trust me, our internal war not over, not with the ephors still on the side of Brasidas and his reforms." The king accompanied his last words with a sneer, then leveled Styphon a dark look. "The coming year will determine our city's future, Styphon. Every Equal may be called upon to choose sides."

Stark warning given, Agis blew a cleansing breath, as if to banish matters of state from his body. He turned a fresh eye toward the women at the writing desk.

"It is an unpardonable shame to ask a brother to deliver a feast and then eat it alone," he said. "You will join me tonight?"

While Styphon pursed his lips and swallowed to delay his answer, Agis's arm snaked around his neck.

"You have a wife you aim to stay loyal to?" the king asked, sensing his hesitation.

"No, sire," Styphon answered. "She passed long ago."

"I love my wife," Agis said without pausing for the condolences for which Equals had little use. "I love *fucking* my wife. But Spartan women..." His nose wrinkled. "There is nothing truly *soft* about them. They are all sharp angles. And slaves are, well, slaves. Hardly satisfying."

Finished writing, the women looked anxiously over from the desk.

Agis's fingers pressed firmly into Styphon's neck. "You'll join me," he said. It was now more order than invitation. "And thank me later."

Releasing Styphon, the king advanced on the Athenians and offered to take their cloaks, which they removed and folded awkwardly before handing them over. Underneath, each wore a long chiton of supple, well-pleated linen, bound under the breasts (one pair ample, the other smaller) with a gilded cord. Unlike a Spartan woman's skirt, which was slit up the sides to facilitate sport, the hems fell to these more sedentary creatures' ankles, concealing their legs entirely.

Tossing their cloaks aside, Agis beckoned the women toward the back rooms. With one of Agis's hands set gently on each of their backs, they went, and Styphon followed. He caught a bitter look from at least one of Agis's guards, but then, any Equal who had had his shield arm bruised or broken in a fight with fellow Equals was bound to be in a bitter mood by day's end.

The windowless chamber behind Nikias's megaron was heavily curtained in shades of green, such that no trace of plaster showed. On the floor was a mosaic showing an olive tree wreathed with the leaves and fruit of the same. Soft couches lined the walls, and between them stood decorative glazed vases, the smallest of which stood half a man's height. The whole affair, which struck Styphon as modest by

Athenian aristocratic standards, was dimly lit by silver wall-mounted braziers shaped like iris blossoms.

By one of the couches stood a krater of dark wine and set of silver drinking cups. Agis ladled out two cups and held them toward the women, who accepted with downcast eyes but refrained as yet from drinking.

"You both look simply stunning," the king said to them when he had ladled two more cups and handed one to Styphon.

Agis drank, and the rest took their cue from him, for different reasons: Styphon because Agis was king, the women perhaps because they had not wanted to seem eager. They were eager, though. That much was clear by the speed with which the contents vanished, as if they were intent on drowning in advance, in a wine-dark sea, their memories of this night. It set Styphon to wondering once more about the women's origins, but he washed his curiosity away the same way that pair hoped to their inhibitions.

This drink, unlike that at the mess, he noted, was diluted more to the Spartan taste, which was to say barely. If Athenian women drank wine (and Styphon could not imagine such miserable creatures did not) they would not be accustomed to it at this strength.

Sipping from his cup, Agis raised a hand to touch the oiled, elaborate curls of the woman nearest him. She managed not to flinch, if just. Agis, with gentle voice and soothing smile, elicited both their names. He repeated each and commented on their pleasing sounds, matched by their owners' shapes. He poured them more wine and made one-sided conversation (if the girls were Aspasia's hetairae, they must have worked hard to suppress their certain talent for the latter).

Styphon said nothing, or gave minimal response when

forced to by Agis.

When the women were on their second cups, Agis led them to a couch, where they reclined with the men flanking them on the floor. There they drank a third cup of the same courage which had helped their inferior men face a deadlier kind of Spartan spear, and they shielded themselves from more of Agis's stabs at conversation.

At length, with a sigh, the king remarked to Styphon, "I had hoped to make headway tonight by some method other than the same old frontal assault. But then I suppose some strategies see frequent use for a reason."

Taking the wine cup from the woman nearest him—was her name Epione?—whichever was the smaller-breasted one —Agis rose and used her now-empty hand to bring her to her expensively-clad feet. He raised the skirt of his chiton, and her empty, pale-skinned hand soon was filled again: with the stiffening cock of the twentieth Eurypontid king of Sparta.

She averted her gaze and kept her slender fingers in place, working them along the shaft under their own impulse when the king removed his guiding hand. Her eyes she kept firmly averted, jaw set tight with unpainted lips a bloodless line. The idle thought flashed through Styphon's mind that a professional probably would have yielded to an instinct to please her client at this stage by giggling or giving some other sign of enjoyment.

"Styphon," Agis said while he was pleasured, "do you now know it is bad form to remain at ease while your king rises?"

As Styphon made to climb to his feet, the king laughed. "You miss my meaning!"

Leaning over, Agis drew the second Athenian from the couch and compelled her to stand before Styphon and mirror the act of her countrywoman. Thence, on Agis's direction, the males occupied the couch while the Athenian wives went to their knees and opened, with reluctance, heretofore closed lips.

They were not particularly skilled, or they hid it if they were. Agis hummed faintly in satisfaction then looked to Styphon and asked casually, "So many widows left horny by the war, and you never thought to remarry?"

"No," Styphon answered. He had not spoken to a soul about such things in an age, not out of any sense of privacy, for all Spartiates' private lives were matters of state. Simply, no one had asked.

"You owe Sparta a son," Agis said. He toyed with the copious dark curls piled on the head that bobbed in his lap. "To the back of your throat, darling, the back," he said to the mass of hair, pushing on it with a hand until a gagging sound resulted. "When you return home," he continued to Styphon, "I shall have you meet a cousin of mine, Hippolyta. Tight and wet as they come, with just the right amount of fire in her. Who knows what may result?"

Evening wore into night, with plenty of wine and seed spilled down throats and elsewhere. A fair amount of the latter was Styphon's, though he did not share with his king the particular mania which left Agis insistent that his partner (and hence both women, since the pairs were hardly fixed) remain fully clad in their un-Spartan finery and dangling silver which caused her to jangle with each thrust. But the result was in Styphon's favor, for he had scant desire to see the two forced to undress, and in the females' favor, too, for they at least retained some shred of modesty while their virtue was taken.

Taken, yes, for Styphon met the women's glazed eyes enough times while taking it to leave him confident what would be the amount of Aspasia's bill.

6. Sleeper in Chains

23 days after the fall of Athens (May 423 BCE)

In the dark hole in the woods where he lived like an animal, the one-time general of a conquered city was dragged from nightmare-ridden sleep by the clink of metal. He knew of an instant what it meant. It was the sound he had waited for all these nights.

At last, it moved.

Pushing himself upright to what extent he could in the tiny cave he called home, he kicked away the brush that concealed the opening, letting in just enough pre-dawn light by which to see the whitish, human-sized lump which was the corpse of Athens' champion and destroyer, butchered on the plain of Eleusis by its star-born enemy Eden, whom the Spartans called Eris. In the days since, the body had exuded a white, pus-like fluid which hardened to form a flaky, irregular, semi-translucent chrysalis under which, day by day, its gruesome wounds healed.

This day, it would appear, the healing was complete.

The sound came again, the gentle clinking of iron, and this time he saw the accompanying stir of movement in the chain-bound chrysalis. Then again it stirred, the creature's limbs appearing to meet the resistance of its encircling chains. Then it fell still, and Demosthenes crawled closer, reaching out to begin clawing away the flaky white substance over its face.

Before he reached it, there was a sudden, jerkier movement, a louder, sharper sound—and the chain snapped. Demosthenes raised an arm too late to prevent its end grazing his cheek, stinging and perhaps cutting the flesh. He fell backward, but only a few inches before his shoulders pressed against damp, cold moss, and he rubbed the stricken cheek

43

whilst before him the once-dead form rose and twisted, its white second-skin sloughing off in sheets. A hand came up, tearing the stuff from its head, and in the bleak light of a ruined world, Demosthenes beheld again the living face of the inhuman thing with whose fate his own was now irrevocably entwined.

Jenna Ismail Cordeiro had been its name once, when it was born a human on some distant heavenly body far-off in one of many futures.

Geneva it had become on entering the service of the strange demi-god Magdalen, its body and perhaps its soul remade to meddle in the affairs of countless worlds, some of them Earth, a living weapon wielded by its dark mistress.

Geneva had betrayed that mistress—twice—including in coming here, to his world, where it had taken the name which Demosthenes and others knew, the name which meant *a thing from the sea*, because it had crashed there and washed ashore.

He looked into the living, wintry eyes of Thalassia, and they looked back at him with a seeming lack of recognition. The face in which they were set was hard of expression, with tendrils of dark, damp hair matted to its smooth, new skin, which was of Persian tones.

"It's me," Demosthenes said in a hoarse whisper. "Demosthenes. Do you remember?"

Its partly crusted lips did not crack to speak. It lifted a hand, and resting in its palm was a length of iron chain, which it looked down to regard briefly before its body fell forward, as if in exhaustion, onto Demosthenes. He caught it, its weight pushing him backward against the curved wall of his cave so that he looked upward into the creature's so-human face, just inches from his.

"Do you remember me?" Demosthenes asked again.

The wintry eyes, which had shut, now reopened, and so

too did its mouth open.

"What the..." it began.

It stopped. Thalassia retched, and what passed next between them was not words. From between its lips, spewing onto the lower half of Demosthenes' bearded face and filling his mouth before he clamped it shut, came a warm and copious wave of the white, pus-like substance which had formed her chrysalis. In revulsion, spitting what tasted like thick, vinegared milk, he averted his face even as a second wave of it coated his tightly shut eyes.

Thankfully, that was the final deluge, but sputtering Thalassia continued to spray droplets of it over him with no apparent thought given to directing it elsewhere. Keeping eyes shut, forcing all he could of the viscous fluid from his mouth, Demosthenes waited several moments until silence reigned and Thalassia's head had sunk onto his shoulder. Its form was naked, its linen chiton evidently having been dissolved or absorbed. The Amazonian armor Thalassia had worn in battle he had left behind in Dekelea as flight-slowing weight.

Wiping his face with a palm and spitting more forcefully, he shifted Thalassia into his lap so he might look down upon its face. The hard expression was gone, replaced by weariness.

"What do you remember?" he asked eagerly, the liquid assault having done nothing to dispel his feelings in this long anticipated moment. It was not happiness, not nearly, but it was something bright, when for so long he had felt nothing but grief and rage.

It drew a ragged breath and answered: "Of course... I f-fucking remember you. Idiot. I died for you. For... Athens." Metallic clinking drew Demosthenes' gaze to Thalassia's hand. "Chains?" she said in wonder. "Did you... really think..." It did not finish, but said instead, "Idiot. They don't... make 'em here... to hold me."

"It was a message," Demosthenes said. "Not to leave if you awoke while I was away."

Thalassia scoffed. "I know when you're... lying, remember? Anyway, you're literate, and I invented the fucking *pen*, so... next time, leave a note." It blew a tired breath and scowled. "Maybe I don't know you... You look like a goat." Its eyes took in the cramped, dimly lit cave. "Where are we? Shit... we didn't win."

Demosthenes stared emptily at her, a shade of the man he once had been.

"No," he said. "No, we did not."

The human-like being shut its eyes, tightened its lips, stilled its breath. It asked, as one who does not wish to hear the answer, "Laonome?"

The empty shade of a general stared yet more, giving no reply.

"Oh, Dee..." it breathed, opening bright eyes that shone in this dark place. They gave a look of pity. "I'm so sorry."

"Do not be. I made my own choices. I bear their consequences. I would not look back, only forward."

Thalassia, who read mortals well, knew better than to question him, even if it knew, as its eyes bespoke, that it did bear much responsibility for the disastrous outcome of their joint machinations. Surely it could tell that Demosthenes thought so, too, no matter what he might say aloud.

"Eurydike?" Thalassia asked of her friend and Demosthenes' devoted concubine before Athens' fall.

"I don't know," he answered blankly. "Alkibiades said she was taken away. Alive, last he saw her, outside the walls of Dekelea. Alkibiades is there now, with the remnants of our army, under siege, unless the place has already fallen."

"How did they take the city?" Thalassia asked.

Demosthenes told of what had transpired after Thalassia's death. He spoke of the ships which Eden had helped Sparta to build, ones greatly resembling drawings Thalassia had made almost two years prior, ships which could tack against the wind and outrace a trireme. But Athens was a democracy and proud of her navy; her shipwrights could never have been convinced to embrace such change. But in Sparta, it would only have taken an edict of the ephors.

He told of how such ships had easily evaded the Athenian navy to land a Spartan force at Piraeus, the harbor of Athens, and how that force had made its way inside the Long Walls to the gates of the city, broken them open and set fire to the Pnyx and other sites. He told Thalassia how, seeing the city ablaze on the horizon, the Athenian forces arrayed at Eleusis to meet Brasidas had broken ranks in fear as men raced home to defend hearth and family.

He told how he and Alkibiades, during the Athenian rout, had rallied the citizen cavalry and such other fighters as they could and led them to Dekelea, the mountain town north of Athens which a season earlier Thalassia had helped to fortify.

"A Spartan army came there," he finished. "Styphon brought us Brasidas's demand for surrender. Your Spartlet, Andrea, was with us. We sent her to safety with her father. That is when..."

He had no wish to speak of the incident, but Thalassia had to be told, as preface to his coming demand.

"To compel us to surrender," he resumed, "Brasidas executed Laonome before my eyes, though I begged to take her place."

On his lap, Thalassia's eyes had fallen shut, and it seemed for a moment that it slept—until a tear welled at the edge of its lashes and carved a wet path down its temple.

Demosthenes swallowed anger. How convincing was this creature's mimicry of humanity.

"You advised me to kill Brasidas when he was at my mercy in Amphipolis," Demosthenes said. "I refused. That is my failure. Had I only heeded you..."

She might be alive, and I might be human still, instead of like you, he did not finish.

"Never again will I err on the side of mercy. Neither honor, nor compassion. Even—"

"Dee..." it interrupted him softly, opening eyes filled with pity. "No, not like this. You will have your revenge, but —"

"Yes," he in turn cut the creature off. "I will. A thousandfold. You will help me see to that."

"Of course," Thalassia agreed without hesitation. "But first I need—"

"Your people ply the cosmos in metal ships," Demosthenes pressed on undeterred. "Yet what have you given us since coming here? *Stick-launchers. Grain grinders. Farming implements.* I think you play with us, handing us toys as though we were children. Your missions on behalf of Magdalen, by your own admission, included *extermination.* Such missions were not undertaken with sword and spear. No, you know of terrible weapons, ones more than capable of destroying a city. I would know of them. I would *use* them. To make of Sparta but a bitter memory. A city of ghosts, with not even a woman or child left alive to shed tears on the grave of the last man to fall."

As he spoke, his untrimmed nails bit deeply into his palm. He finished, "We will annihilate Sparta utterly, you and I. And before he dies, slowly, by my hand, Brasidas will witness it. So tell me, Sword of Magdalen, how may we achieve this?"

"It's... not that easy," answered Demosthenes' naked, exquisitely crafted blade. "If you were stranded in the wilderness, even if you had years, could you make an iron sword? A trireme? A temple? Yes, the Caliate has weapons that could turn a city to ash, but..." It sighed. "Dee, even if I could make them—"

"A plague, then?" Demosthenes asked, having anticipated such an answer to his prior question. "In Athens, you used chickens and their eggs to make me and others resistant to the plague which decimated our city. Is the reverse possible? Could you induce a plague at Sparta?"

The Sword shifted in his lap, raising itself onto two supple arms, then settling back to converse face-to-face in the faint, bluish light that filtered into the cave.

"Dee..."

"Stop calling me that."

"Don't call me 'Sword of Magdalen.' *Demosthenes*, have you given any thought to—"

"Answer!" he said. "Can Sparta be afflicted with a plague? It must be deadlier than that which we suffered!"

"The plague killed so many in Athens because you were crowded behind walls and under siege for years. Sparta has no walls. It's hardly even a city compared to Athens. A plague would not have the same effect. And... I have seen plagues used as weapons before. When they are effective, there is no controlling whom they kill, no stopping them even after the job is done. You don't want to be the one who does that... I won't let you be that."

"Poison," Demosthenes suggested next. He had spent long days and longer nights considering the instruments of his vengeance. "You know of substances which heal. You must also know those which kill. Could Sparta's water sources be poisoned? Their food?"

The look of pity, gradually fading from Thalassia's face until now, at last became purely a look of impatience. "Sparta's water comes from springs, not wells, so no, it could not easily be contaminated. Their food..." The Sword frowned in thought. "Possibly. A fungus could kill many without the source being discovered until it was too late, and then could be stopped when its job was done."

"You could do this?" Demosthenes asked eagerly. "You *would*?"

The Sword sighed. It looked tired. "It will take time to cultivate the right fungus. Months, maybe. If, by then, you wish to use it... then *yes*."

His Sword's eyes met his in the dim glow, and in its gaze he perceived that it spoke truly.

"In the meantime," it went on, "clearly you have not been bathing, but I would like to. We'll need a better place than this to live. A city, preferably. From there, we can locate Eurydike, rescue her, and plot to liberate Athens."

"When every Spartan is dead, Athens will be liberated," Demosthenes said.

"And Eurydike?"

"She is likely dead already. If not, then she too will be free when Sparta is destroyed."

"What if she's *in* Sparta? Will we poison her, too? And Andrea?"

"When the time comes, we will try to spare them," he said irritably, then pressed, "You will do it? Cultivate a fungus?"

Thalassia set fingertips on his unruly facial growth. "From this moment, no matter what else occurs, Sparta is doomed. By fire, sword, fungus, or whatever else it takes. Now..." The hand fell away, and Thalassia sank against him.

"I'm so fucking hungry, I'll eat a horse if you have one."

7. Meat & Philosophy

The skin on the underside of the roasting lamb had formed a blackened crust, the cracks in which showed bright pink. Drops of rendered fat fell and crackled in the flames underneath. Kneeling at the fire's side, Thalassia rotated the spit. It had freshly come from bathing itself in the stream nearby and dressing in the woman's chiton of white linen Demosthenes had thought to bring in his flight from Dekelea.

She hardly looked to be one of the three deadliest beings on earth. But she was. In many ways, and to *all* who encountered her, not only her enemies.

It, he reminded himself. *It* was deadly. A thing, not a person.

From by the fire, it smiled at him, warmly.

"Thank you for this," it said, meaning the lamb. "And the dress."

"I remember you saying once you that you are only ever hungry after you... die."

"Mmh-hmh." Its mouth was full with a chunk freshly torn with fingertips from the cooked side. Grease dripped from its chin. It looked down upon the breast of the white chiton it wore and, frowning, untied the garment's belt and shrugged it off so that it fell into a heap on the leaves around the wearer's ankles. It rose briefly to step out of the chiton entirely, then resumed squatting by the fire, close enough by it, by Demosthenes' reckoning, to have burned off its body hair, had there been so much as a strand of it anywhere on Thalassia's body.

Its body was so very, very human.

"No sense getting it dirty," it explained.

Demosthenes knew well enough that modesty was not a feature of the otherworldly culture which had spawned

Thalassia. Sitting on a large, flat sun-dappled rock, he shifted his gaze to the snatches of Attic countryside that were visible between the trunks and low hanging branches of the forested mountainside. Normally he built fires, when he needed them, far from the little cave in which he slept, in case the smoke drew unwanted visitors. Today, however, it no longer mattered; they would spend no more nights here now that Thalassia was mobile.

"I thought we might travel to Naupaktos," he said blankly. "It is the nearest staunch ally of Athens, and unlikely to capitulate easily. It will fall to Sparta... just not immediately."

"Sensible." Leaving the spitted lamb, naked, light-footed Thalassia made its way in near-silence across the leaf-strewn forest floor and mounted the flat rock to sit at Demosthenes' side. Its bare arm brushed his, and he moved it, muscles tensing.

"I know that I wrecked your world," Thalassia said. "All your pain comes from me. I deserve your anger. You should show it. Say what's in your heart. It's better than the way you've been looking at me. Or not looking at me."

Demosthenes took his eyes briefly from the distant hills to cast a sidelong glance at Thalassia, reconsidered, and looked away again. "I do not hate you. No more than I do myself. We deserve each other."

She set her hand on his.

Its hand. *It*. A thing to which death is a temporary impediment to spreading death and madness had no right to be called human. A machine, perhaps.

Demosthenes withdrew his hand from under hers and set it on his thigh.

Thalassia exhaled a little sigh. "I died for you," the machine said. "For Laonome. For Eurydike. For Athens. I could have left. I still could. But I won't. I'm with you until you're dead, a moment I will do all I can to postpone. Even when you're an asshole, like now." It scoffed. "Really—chains? Did you think could *force* me to agree to your plans? Why would you think you'd need to? I should be offended. You know, I'm glad I vomited in your face. I'd do it again."

Perhaps the machine hoped to make him smile. But he felt only contempt: Thalassia was as petulant as ever.

"Had I wished to force you," he observed, "I might have carved the remaining Seeds out of your flesh and hidden them somewhere."

He felt rather than saw Thalassia's flash of anger. "That would have been... very stupid."

"Or I could have butchered you a bit more and given you to Eden in exchange for Brasidas. I think it likely she would have taken that trade."

Thalassia's second flash of anger was yet more palpable. "*That* would have been..."

"But I did not consider it," Demosthenes said. "Not for more than an instant. You see? I accept that we are together until death. My death, anyway. Yours... perhaps a few of them, at this rate."

"Look," it said, "Dee... and I'm going to call you that until you learn to like it... I know where your head is. I understand. And believe me, I see the irony in my advising against rash action, but what you're doing, what you *want* to do... it's not the way. When I wanted revenge... no, needed it... I left the Caliate with a stupid plan. And now here I am. No turning back. But you know what the difference is between us?"

"There are fewer now, but still many, I hope," Demosthenes answered, though there had been no pause for reply.

"The difference is," Thalassia went on, "I had no one I trusted—no one who had *proved to me over and over again* that I could and *should* trust them. Never mind if they kicked the shit out of me now and then. I had no one to tell me I was wrong."

"You regret coming here?"

"I didn't say that. What I mean is that the road to revenge is rarely a straight one. You'll need your wits about you, and an open mind. It's not passion but calc—" Thalassia looked through the trees, frowning, and said, "Shit. Someone's coming. Four someones, in what they think is stealth." The unhuman watched and listened intently for another moment before adding, "Two... no, three of them... are Equals." Keen, pale eyes fell on Demosthenes. "Should we do this together, or would you rather I take care of it myself?"

"You are strong enough?" Demosthenes asked.

"For four? Always."

Scanning the trees, Demosthenes saw no trace of any presence, but that meant nothing. Thalassia's eyes and ears were not to be doubted. He answered her question by taking up his sheathed short sword from beside the rock and drawing it.

"There are two blades for you in—" he whispered.

"I saw." Still naked and unworried, Thalassia slipped down from the rock and moved in silence to the cave mouth, retrieving two short swords. That they were of bronze gave them away as Spartan in manufacture.

"You killed the owners?" Thalassia asked.

"Eventually."

A sword in either hand, Thalassia leaped onto the rock, having made no stop to retrieve her discarded garment from the ground. Demosthenes knew better than to suggest to the living weapon that it dress. After all, why let the enemy bleed all over a good chiton?

Soon Demosthenes, too, heard the crack of twigs and caught sight of movement through the trees. He stood by Thalassia in silence, awaiting the arrival of four men who probably had followed the smoke of the cooking fire. Just as probably, they knew of the Equals who had vanished in these woods and thus expected trouble.

Less probably did they expect the degree of trouble they were about to encounter.

Two red-cloaked Equals crept into sight, saw that they were being watched, drew their swords, and broke into a run toward the camp. Both Demosthenes and Thalassia stood fast and at ease as a third Equal appeared alongside a fourth man dressed in brown and green and carrying a strung bow. This was an Arkadian, more accustomed to creeping about in forests than Equals were, doubtless brought along as a guide or a tracker.

The party of four halted a short way off, standing apart at even intervals. The Arkadian nocked and arrow and drew back the string of his bow.

"Throw down your arms!" one of the Equals demanded.

"I am but a simple hermit," Demosthenes called back, without complying. "My companion and I were discussing some tenets of natural philosophy while we dined. You are most welcome to join us. For the meal, at any rate. I hear you Equals are not much for philosophy."

"It is you who'll be joining *us*, filthy one," the eldest Equal returned. "Equals have disappeared in these woods, and your bare-assed *companion*"—he flicked his sword at Thalassia—"carries two Spartan swords, if I am not mistaken. Surrender, and you need not die just yet."

Sighing, Thalassia said, "They decline to share our meal, my goat-looking friend. Shall we instead give them a taste of our philosophy?"

"I doubt it will be to their liking."

"Sir..." a younger Spartiate attempted to interject. "That woman... I wonder if she might not be—"

"Enough prattle!" the lead Equal barked, heedless of the youth's wisdom. He took a few more steps forward, brandishing his sword at his quarry, which stood upon the rock looking down on him "Come down from there!"

"Shall I?" Thalassia asked.

"Sir..." the youth said again, beginning to backpedal.

Dropping to a crouch, the Sword of Magdalen leaped up and forward from its perch in the direction of the Spartan leader. Seeing, he moved his sword in a small arc to aim it at his airborne foe, but it was scarcely enough; Thalassia parried his blade with one of hers even as the second came straight down into the crown of his skull, splitting it in two.

Demosthenes did not stand idle and watch, but leaped down, if less acrobatically, and charged the younger Equal, who planted his feet to challenge the certain doom which he alone had foreseen.

He forestalled Fate for but a moment, as his unwashed attacker dropped under his brazen stroke and cleaved his thigh with well-honed Athenian steel. Then, while the young man stumbled, bleeding and crying out, Demosthenes slashed his neck wide open, leaving his fleeing shade to lament that his grandfathers had traded the encompassing bronze helms of yore, which might have saved him, for those of stiffened leather, as he wore.

An arrow flew past Demosthenes' head, and he flinched, but turned to see that he was not the target; it was Thalassia, who at present advanced on the Arkadian woodsman in long, swift strides.

Turning, at the ready, Demosthenes sought with his eyes

the fourth assailant, the last of the three Equals, but he spied no movement. What he found instead was a crimson cloak spread out on the forest floor, its wearer already made a corpse by the machine which Magdalen had built to that very purpose. So quickly on the heels of Thalassia's first kill had this one been slain that Demosthenes had not even been aware.

The Arkadian whirled and broke into a frantic run, but behind him was the blur of honey-colored flesh which in no time caught him up. Instead of a fountain of blood erupting from him, however, Demosthenes was surprised to see him but tumble to the ground, and further surprised that no death blow swiftly followed. He ran to where naked Thalassia, her skin lightly speckled with blood, stood over the groaning Arkadian.

Reaching down, she picked him up by his vest of tanned hide and deposited him roughly at the base of a pine.

"Why did you spare him?" Demosthenes asked.

"Answers." Crouching in front of the Arkadian, Thalassia thrust one sword point-first into the ground and used the free hand to slap the man's cheek until he came to his senses and paid wide-eyed fearful attention.

"I know when men lie. Speak truly, and you will live," Thalassia said sternly to him. "Is Dekelea still in Athenian hands?"

"A-Aye! L-L-Last I knew... t-two days ago."

"Where is Brasidas?"

"A-Athens..."

"And a woman with long, blond hair? Scary, like me. You might know her as Eris?"

"I n-never laid eyes on her. She's not been seen s-s-since the conquest."

Thalassia asked next of Demosthenes, "Anything else

you would ask him?"

"No," Demosthenes answered. "Do you truly intend to let him live?"

"Yes! Yes!" the Arkadian implored. He leaned forward, only to be roughly shoved back by Thalassia.

"He could take a message to Brasidas," Thalassia suggested.

"I desire no contact with him until our last, when I kill him."

"Then it's your choice," Thalassia said, rising. "Someone once said to me that you might as well keep your word when it doesn't matter. That way, people will trust you when you really need to betray them."

The Arkadian looked up into Demosthenes' eyes, saw written in them what his fate was to be, and began intoning the prayers of the soon-to-die. The names of gods were thus upon his lips when Demosthenes put sword to his breast and ran him through.

"Who was it who said that?" he asked of Thalassia.

"Him," the Sword of Magdalen answered.

Demosthenes needed not ask who *he* was. It meant the enemy, and former lover, that Thalassia had come to this world to unmake by preventing his very birth: the man known to the fighters of the Veta Caliate as 'The Worm.'

Minutes later, Thalassia sat again upon the rock, still unclad, pushing blood-gloved fingers through the charred skin of a lamb leg to tear free dripping morsels of meat which she... *it*... stuffed into its maw.

"You should eat," Thalassia spewed. "Unless you only eat Spartans now."

After kicking out the remains of the cooking fire, Demosthenes did partake, accepting portions which Thalassia tore off for him. Blood and fat covered the lower half of her face and ran down her breasts. It had been Thalassia who told him, seasons ago, that humans had not been created in their current state but rather had developed slowly out of lesser forms. Demosthenes did not quite grasp the concept, as was the case with any number of her teachings, but it occurred to him now that here sat the very image of one of those pre-human predecessors.

"What are you looking at?" she asked of him eventually, when her mouth was clear enough of food to let words pass in the other direction.

It asked. *Its* mouth. The Sword, the machine.

Realizing he had been staring, Demosthenes averted his gaze. "Just... considering your many charms."

Thalassia shrugged. "I hear that a lot. Should we go to Dekelea?" Thalassia's transitions frequently were jarring.

"No," Demosthenes replied, angrily.

"It may still stand. We could break the Athenian force out and have an army. Maybe even kill Brasidas."

"No!"

"It's worth considering."

"It isn't! If Eden is there, will you fight her again? *Die* again, or worse? Then where would I be? No, I won't risk it. Now, might you be finished eating soon?"

After a few minutes, Thalassia did finish, wiped face and hands on the cloak of a dead Equal, and wore the white dress which, owing to her foresight, had remained clean. Thalassia did not need to be told that wearing a pair of swords as they traveled would cause her to attract rather more stares than she already tended to receive, and so, helping herself to the dead Arkadian's sailcloth satchel, she stowed inside it the two sheathed short swords.

"Let's move," she said when she was ready, although it was Demosthenes who had been waiting for her. "Ruthless plans to lay, killer fungus to breed, Naupaktans to charm, city to liberate, beards to shave and such. We'll be busy."

Only a few paces outside of camp, Thalassia stopped and whirled, putting herself in Demosthenes' path and forcing him to stop short. She laid a palm on his chest.

"Dee..." she said, the look in her wintry eyes growing suddenly earnest. "Thank you for keeping me safe. I know you didn't do it for me, but you did it, and I'm grateful. I'll make sure you don't regret it. We both have enough regrets."

The palm slid from his breast, and Thalassia turned and strode on, calling back, "What the fuck are you standing around for? Keep up!"

And so Demosthenes struck west and south for the city of Naupaktos following behind the Sword of Magdalen, the star-born creature of chaos, the deadly and beautiful machine who already was convincing him once more, against his better judgment, to conceive of her as a human... and a friend.

8. Ares Descends

The darkness was like that of Erebos itself, but the trek through the Parnes mountains under the new moon had gone without incident. Now Styphon stood, as daylight broke, among the silent ranks of Spartiates north of Dekelea, just out of sight of the town's walls. Each was panoplied for war: greaves of bronze, breastplates of stiffened leather, eight-foot ash spear in right hand, bowl-shaped, lambda-blazoned hoplon affixed to the left.

Ahead, on the broad north-south road, a detachment of Sparta's Theban allies wheeled as though to depart in the direction of the sea. They would march only a short distance, however, before halting and turning to pounce on the Athenians from the east, taking them by surprise.

Ambush was not a tactic to which Equals were accustomed, and none found it particularly tasteful, but most recognized the necessity of sinking to it from time to time. Not every battle could take the ideal shape, in which two sides squared off shield-to-shield while pipers played Castor's Air and the paean sounded, and when it ended, the gods who looked down upon the field were left in no doubt of which city was the more deserving. On the contrary, an unannounced assault represented, to most in Sparta, particularly the elders, the coward's path—the Athenian path. But times were changing, more rapidly now than ever, thanks to Brasidas and his blond witch.

The trap shortly to be sprung had been conceived and laid by Brasidas, but King Agis, thanks to his traditionalist supporters on the Gerousia, would be the one to spring it. Ten days prior, in the deep of night, an Athenian citizen, a tribemate to Alkibiades, had been allowed to sneak up to the walls of Dekelea. Easily confirming his identity, the Athenians inside had hauled him up and over the walls, where he had delivered a story: the Athenian general Kleon had rounded up a force of allies which he planned to land on the nearby shores of Oropos. From there, he would relieve Dekelea and perhaps even march on occupied Athens.

When it came, Kleon's force would set ablaze a signal fire in the mountains to the east, and thence begin its advance. On learning of the new threat, the Theban allies of Sparta, in charge of maintaining the northern half of the siege of Dekelea, would have little choice but to march out to meet it. This was the moment when the Athenians trapped inside Dekelea were to move, bursting out from the town's northern gate to attack the Thebans, catching them from behind and in disarray. The terrain around Dekelea, being mountainous, scarcely allowed for quick reinforcement from the Spartan forces to the south, thus allowing the Athenians to make their escape and join up with Kleon's army.

Kleon's army, however, did not exist. It was the invention of Brasidas, who had supplied the story to the Athenian messenger by means of turncoats, who had also been the ones to convince the messenger to accept this task. Being known to Alkibiades, the man was an obvious choice, since his word would be trusted. Moreover, he had no inkling of the deception, thus foiling Thalassia's ability to separate truth from lies, if she remained inside Dekelea and had recovered.

What would in truth await the Athenians, if and when they burst out from Dekelea's northern gate, was not only a Theban force ready and waiting for them but also a phalanx of Equals under King Agis, who had spent the night slowly advancing from the south over treacherous terrain

Agis had offered Styphon a place near to him in the ranks, an honor so great that only a fool would accept it. None but the champions of festival games were afforded the privilege of defending their king's life in battle, and there were more than enough such champions present to do the job. The name Styphon had only just risen above the level of curse; no need to cast it back down into the depths by taking honors which he had not rightfully earned.

That offer, and Agis's behavior toward him, suggested that the king was courting him to some end. Spartans would be called upon to choose sides soon, Agis had warned him. It was easy enough to see how winning over a close associate of Brasidas would mark a coup for the traditionalists in Sparta who supported Agis and opposed Brasidas's reforms.

But now was not the time for such distant concerns. A lookout on a nearby hill signaled to the waiting Spartan army: the gates of Dekelea were opening. The bait was taken.

The air vibrated with the shock of hooves pounding earth, the Athenian cavalry taking the lead, and it did not move tentatively but galloped boldly into the unknown. The Spartan phalanx behind the hill held, every man's limbs tense and ears alert for the command to advance.

At last King Agis gave it, and as if the six hundred men of the phalanx were one body, they got underway. Across the broad north-south road, the Thebans sounded their own command, and their formation, four thousand strong, halted its false march to the sea to face an imagined challenge, and it turned (with rather more chaos and confusion than the same number of Equals would have produced) to face its true target.

Wheeling left, the Spartan phalanx cleared the hillock which had concealed it. The mountain road leading into Dekelea came into Styphon's sight, and then so did the Athenian cavalry, until then nothing more than an invisible thunder. The horsemen's gallop slowed to to a canter, and then they stopped at the wildly waved command of the hipparch at their head. The momentum of a charging body of cavalry was difficult to break, and therein lay its strength, but the Athenians, renowned as skilled riders, managed it.

They stood still, unsure what to do next on their two hundred or so snorting, restless mounts, staring down a slope at two armies, Spartan and Theban. The latter was far larger in size, but the former was arguably more deadly.

Behind the Athenian cavalry came the first of the thousand or so Athenians who had followed, having crossed by means of a pre-built plank bridge the encircling siege-trench which the horses preceding them had simply leaped.

The Athenian hipparch, a man in armor polished so brightly it rivaled the white sun which was just rising, made no move. Either he was carefully studying his options or was so struck with fear as to be completely at a loss for what to do. One option he might consider, it occurred to Styphon, was to lead his cavalry into the still sizable but shrinking gap between the two enemy forces. He might just make it, but the men on foot would doubtless be left behind to surrender or die.

The Theban force let loose a cheer as if they had already won, and Agis ordered the Spartan phalanx to tighten its ranks against the possibility of a suicidal Athenian charge, while on the road the resplendent hipparch—Alkibiades, almost certainly—hoisted his lance and addressed his men in inaudible speech.

Turning his mount, Alkibiades led the charge along the road, on course for the open space between the two opponents. He had made his choice. He would leave his unmounted countrymen to face their fates, it seemed, and without hesitation or protest, the two hundred riders fell into formation behind him. Little surprise such treachery, given what every Spartiate boy was taught about Athenian society: the cavalry of Athens was made up of men from its aristocracy, whose very existence came at the expense of the common man. It was only natural that such men would feed the less fortunate to beasts when the need arose.

There was no possibility of closing the gap between the Theban and Spartan forces in time to block the escape, not without breaking ranks, and so Agis ordered the pace held, and the Spartan advance continued steadily over rocky, rolling ground which might have broken the cohesion of lesser infantry. Meanwhile, the four thousand Thebans opposite, in spite of their commanders' loud entreaties, moved more like a horde of half-civilized plainsmen than a disciplined army.

Unopposed but for an erratic hail of javelins from the Theban side, which flew far from true, the Athenian horse threaded the needle and made good its escape. There was yet a good chance they could be stopped: a hundred and twenty Theban cavalry, which was by many accounts superior to a greater number of its Athenian counterpart, lay in wait to the north against just such a contingency.

Again, the plan of Brasidas.

Boldness, if unmixed with caution, might make disaster of any triumph, or so the Spartan saying went. Thus did Agis order the Spartan left to turn and face its shields to the passing enemy cavalry. Styphon was on the right, and did not turn his head to watch the horse flee, although while it was in his line of sight, he did scan it unsuccessfully for any sign of a man riding with a corpse slung over his saddle.

The two attacking forces joined up, the Theban right lapping like waves on the cliff which was the Spartan left, and together they advanced south along the road, reaching in no time the crest on which the Athenian horse, minutes ago, had paused in shock. Dekelea was visible now, and before it a shallow bowl of grass and crags in the middle of which a thousand Athenians had formed a ring of spears. Behind them the gates of Dekelea stood shut, and blocking those gates were the ones who had shut them: fifty Theban cavalry that had raced in behind the Athenian breakout to cut off any quick return by the enemy to the safety of the walls.

On the crest, Agis's trumpeter called a halt, which the Theban general echoed, and both armies stood united and facing the circle of trapped Athenians. King Agis broke from his place in the second rank and went forward to address them.

"Athenians, we give you one last opportunity to yield! I know you have refused terms from Brasidas already, but now you face Agis! If you will not trust a polemarch, trust a king! Your own leaders have left you! Throw down your weapons now, and you may return to your homes and submit to your new leaders. But if you resist, the family of every man identified as being present on this field today, whether he lives or dies, will be reduced to—"

A lookout bellowed from a hill to the north: "Cavalry! Cavalry!"

The air and earth began to vibrate with the familiar thunder of hoofbeats. Aborting his speech, Agis raced back to his place in the ranks, shouting orders for the rear three ranks of the six which made up the Spartan phalanx to turn to face the new threat from behind.

The rearmost ranks of any army were made up of its lesser troops, which in Sparta's case meant men at the beginning or end of their military careers, men of twenty years or sixty, and it was they who now were to face the returning enemy cavalry.

This was not the best choice, Styphon knew, not while

67

there remained ample time to shift the best men rearward. The Equals surrounding Styphon in the first rank, still facing Dekelea and the lesser enemy, realized it, too, and they threw him questioning glances. As enomotarch commanding the thirty-six men on the formation's extreme right, his duty was to relay orders from above, not give his own.

There was no time to ponder, barely to act.

"*Cycle!*" Styphon screamed, and in the space of seconds, the neat six-by-six square of hoplites over which he presided disintegrated, its rows shifting out and back in a dance of spears. Just as quickly, the body reassembled, and when it did, Styphon and the men of what had been the front two ranks facing Dekelea stood facing down the more immediate threat from behind.

Formed up in a wedge, the Athenian citizen cavalry charged full tilt around the base of the same hill which had earlier concealed their ambushers. At the tip of the wedge, shining Alkibiades raised his lance high overhead, its point agleam with the pink of daybreak. There was no telling just where on the Spartan line they would strike, but all along its length a double row of spears were set and ready. The Spartiate to Styphon's left, Diphridas, cackled with black delight at the coming massacre of beasts and men.

"Shut your hole," Styphon snapped at him.

A roar, a chorus of battle cries, erupted from the east, followed by a roll of thunder that eclipsed the pounding of the horses' hooves: the Thebans' patience had run out, and they were attacking the encircled Athenian infantry.

And Ares, the lord of slaughter on high, descended shrieking upon Attica to slake the mountain plain with blood.

The Athenian wedge entered the final approach, its target picked: Styphon's right-wing-turned-left. Mere instants from certain death, the hipparch at its head lowered his lance and veered abruptly. Spear blades barely grazed the horse's flank, but that hardly mattered, for its rider did something almost unthinkable. He threw himself to the ground, straight at the enemy line, three men down from Styphon.

The mad Athenian tumbled in a clatter of polished bronze, and before any Spartiate could bring his unwieldy eight-foot spear to bear, Alkibiades' lighter cavalry lance was swinging. He slashed two Spartiates behind the knees, and they stumbled back onto their comrades, even as the Athenian's blade swept upward into a third Equal's groin.

Styphon's mind filled with curses, and not a little admiration, for he saw Alkibiades' deadly purpose. His mad assault had opened a gap in the front rank, just three shields wide, but enough for the horseman following just seconds behind him to hit the phalanx without being skewered.

The second rider slammed into the Spartan line, then another and another, side-by-side, the thin end of a widening wedge. The third row of cavalry hit within spear's reach of Styphon, and his blade found the rider's neck. The man tumbled into the press of horses and hoplites to be trampled.

Styphon's spear was hardly righted before he felt the crush of the assault on his shield and was thrown back, back, heels digging in. Only Diphridas, the Spartiate who had laughed, stood to his left, the phalanx's edge, and ever more horsemen were pouring in, the wedge growing wider and wider until it spilled over the edge of the phalanx, forcing its second and third ranks to come forward and add their spears and bodies to stopping the charge. Horses screamed agony as their throats were cut or bellies ripped open, and men screamed, too, as they were crushed beneath hoof or skewered with lance or spear. The Athenians worked their long swords like scythes, and it was one of these which sent Diphridas to the unnameable realm. But he was avenged: his killer followed him below, Styphon's own spear blade having pierced him through the soft underside of his jaw, opening his skull like a blossoming flower.

The slaughter of Spartiate and Athenian alike was great, but Styphon's feet gave only a few steps, and these came early on. By the time the full weight of the Athenian cavalry had landed, its failure was sealed. It broke like water crashing on a seaside cliff, causing great spectacle but achieving nothing. The stone of Sparta's sons today had held fast.

But not at little cost. The price was yet being paid, with men on both sides continuing to fall as the futile assault persisted. Styphon killed at least three more himself before the weight on his battered hoplon subsided and he was able to move forward behind the Athenians who had begun to turn tail and flee, some on foot, others on their mounts. If the Theban cavalry were not just now arriving from the north to ride them down, they might have been allowed to escape with their lives, for Equals never gave in to the folly of pursuit. They never cheered, either, for celebration implied surprise, and victory must never come as a surprise. And so the Spartan army was silent.

The exhilaration of slaughter leaving him, Styphon wasted no time pushing through the packed hoplites to where he had last seen Alkibiades.

"The hipparch!" he cried, shoving Equals out of the way and searching the mounds of dead and writhing men and animals. "Where is their hipparch?"

"Here," someone said, and kicked something near his foot, which turned out to be the still, gray hulk of a dead horse. Pinned underneath, the carcass covering him from thigh to shoulder blades, a man laid on his stomach in the churned soil. From atop the once-bright helm still covering his head, a once-white plume snaked away into the mud.

Kneeling, Styphon gripped the plume and yanked off the helm. Chestnut curls spilled out, and Alkibiades stirred, barely, alive but insensate.

Nearby, King Agis sat upon the ground, unhelmed, head held in hand, amid a cluster of his guards. He had sustained some minor, bloodless injury.

A fresh cheer filled the air, reverberating off the walls of empty Dekelea, in front of which the Theban infantry and cavalry, outnumbering their foe by four to one, had overwhelmed a shrinking ring of Athenians. A small number of the latter still fought valiantly on—enveloped and offered no quarter, they had no choice—but their annihilation was at this point a certainty. Hence the Thebans' celebration.

While other Spartiates found and tended to their wounded brothers, Styphon searched the faces of the enemy dead for that of Demosthenes, but none were he. The absence ascertained, Styphon left his gear with a Helot and made haste across the field toward the gates of Dekelea, passing the heaped bodies of the Athenian infantry intermixed with plenty of Theban corpses. As he went, he absently scanned the lifeless faces over which he stepped, but did not linger to look, for it seemed unlikely that Demosthenes would have been among that group.

By now the town's gates had been opened to allow the Thebans to enter and search for any remaining defenders, while women and children and old folk cowered in their homes. Entering, Styphon searched with a growing sense of futility for the pair he sought.

Within a quarter-hour, a Dekelean town elder had handed over a corselet of leather and bronze. Shaped for a woman, the armor was pierced and rent with gashes. Styphon had not witnessed the clash between Thalassia and Eden at Eleusis, having been miles away commanding the marine landing which had captured Athens and thrown its defenders into disarray, but he had heard it told by those present that the two women had cut each other to ribbons like frenzied Maenads setting on a hapless intruder into their sacred wood.

The same Dekelean elder told Styphon that Alkibiades had been in command of the town for some days now, since Demosthenes had vanished.

Styphon rewarded the old man by finding the Theban general, grabbing him by the throat, and instructing him to make sure that his half-civilized horde showed some restraint whilst in Dekelea.

The news that Demosthenes and his witch had eluded capture failed to surprise Styphon, even if it did disappoint. Brasidas would not be pleased, even if he surely had anticipated and planned for such a possibility.

Styphon returned to the field of battle to find that Alkibiades had been extracted from under the horse carcass. His eyes were open but glassy, and his head lolled as Styphon inspected him for injuries. He had suffered a deep scratch above the greave of his left leg, and a dent in his helmet likely explained his semi-consciousness. Perhaps a bone or two was cracked.

He would live. That was fortunate, for although as a prize he ranked third in Brasidas's estimation, the polemarch would undoubtedly find a use for Alkibiades.

9. Hand of the seducer

Styphon knew the Athenian jail compound well, having spent more than a year of his life in it, held hostage with two hundred of his countrymen, until Brasidas had arrived and organized escape.

This time, Styphon was on the other, preferable side of the bars, and had come to fetch an Athenian prisoner—a man, in fact, who once had come to visit him during his own imprisonment. He had a private cell, so as not to allow him the opportunity to plot with his fellow prisoners, potentially accomplishing the mirror image of Brasidas's own feat of mass escape.

That prisoner, Alkibiades, sat on the straw-covered floor of his cell, his bandaged leg stretched out. He saw his visitor through the cell door and smiled. "Styphon," he said, sounding truly pleased by the sight. "How is your girl?"

Although a victor owed the vanquished no reply, Styphon gave one: "Andrea is well, last I knew. At home."

"In Sparta," Alkibiades said approvingly. With some difficulty, he stood and limped the short distance to the door with its small, barred portal. The last time Styphon had seen Alkibiades in this prison, when their roles had been reversed, the preening blatherer had been immaculately groomed. Now, after a month spent under siege and a day in prison, his once proud waves of chestnut hair were oil-soaked tendrils clinging to his neck. "I am glad she will no longer find her father's name a burden. Congratulations."

To this Styphon did not bother to reply, but just unbolted the door and pulled it open.

Limping out, Alkibiades asked simply, as one pleading for some harmless bit of information to which he was not entitled, which was exactly the case: "Eurydike?"

The Athenian's grimy features showed that he expected the worst. And why not, for the last he had seen the Thracian girl was on the plain of Dekelea, where Brasidas had spared the slave's life, choosing instead to cut the throat of her mistress, the wife of Demosthenes.

"She is also in my household," Styphon begrudged. "Safe." The answer produced a look of relief on the prisoner's face. "Come."

With a bleak sigh, Alkibiades stepped out. "I do hope this is not an execution."

"An interview," Styphon said. Alkibiades preceded him down the dark hallway, the sandal on the foot of his wounded leg scraping along the stone.

"I've told your men all I know," the prisoner complained. "I know nothing about any resistance, or who this 'Omega' might be. I don't know any Sigma or Psi either, for that matter. And as for Demosthenes, he vanished over the wall one night with star-girl's body. He wouldn't tell me where he was going. I don't even think his mind's all there anymore."

"We know all that," Styphon said. It was not only the testimony of Alkibiades and others in Dekelea which bespoke Demosthenes' flight from Dekelea: his black scale armor and Pegasos-blazoned shield had been found on the corpse of another fallen Athenian after the ambush.

"So what is the purpose of this *interview*?"

"I am to take you to Brasidas," Styphon said. "What he wants is his concern."

Alkibiades laughed. "Maybe he wants to know how good his mother was at sucking my balls. I'll be happy to tell him that."

"Do not count on him having a sense of humor."

"Unlike you, hmm?" The Athenian scoffed.

Exiting the jail complex, Styphon and an escort detail of two more Equals, forced to match the snail's pace of their captive, walked an agonizingly slow path from the jail to the nearby Tholos, the administrative center of Athens. It was mid-morning and Athenians thronged the streets. Their lingering, surreptitious stares said they well knew the identity of the man marching in irons past the columned law courts of the fallen democracy. If they felt admiration for him, they kept it to themselves.

At the Tholos, the escort fell away, leaving Styphon to help the hobbling prisoner up the steps and inside to the commandeered office of Brasidas.

The polemarch stood behind the heavy oaken table which looked once to have been part of a trireme's deck, silently gazing down at an assortment of parchments cluttering its surface. Styphon stood silently awaiting acknowledgment. Somewhat surprisingly, Alkibiades possessed the wisdom to do the same.

At length Brasidas looked up and smiled less than convincingly. "Please, have a seat." He gestured at a cushion beside a low table. "Will you drink some wine?"

In spite of his wounded leg, Alkibiades made no move to sit. The offer of drink was likewise declined with silence.

Brasidas's smile faded into a reflective frown. "A Lakonic reply," he said. "Suit yourself."

Unaddressed and apparently unneeded, Styphon stepped back to excuse himself.

The polemarch stopped him by saying, "Styphon, you may remain. Shut the door."

Styphon did so and then resumed his position a pace to the Athenian's left.

"If we may speak as one commander to another," Brasidas began, and set his hand on a marked slip of paper, "I have here the final tally for the action at Dekelea. Would you care to hear it?"

Alkibiades returned quickly, "Just assume I gave whatever answer shuts you up the fastest."

Styphon saw anger behind the polemarch's smile of forbearance. "Your cavalry attack killed fourteen Equals," Brasidas said. "The wounds of another eight will probably consign them to the reserves. And although you pretend a lack of interest, I know you wish to hear how many Athenians fell."

He paused as if waiting for Alkibiades to urge him on, but resumed anyway when the latter refused.

"Four hundred and ninety-two dead. Half again as many wounded. Nearly six hundred captured. Thirty-six of the dead were of your cavalry, by the way, which means your horsemen managed to kill one Spartiate for every of two of their own who fell." He raised his scarred brow. "Which is rather impressive, to my mind."

Alkibiades cleared his throat, as if his pride had lodged there on the way down, and he said dryly, "Commander to commander, polemarch, I request leniency for all those captured but myself. They will settle back into their lives and obey your laws. I will instruct them thus myself."

With a shrug, Brasidas dismissed the matter as unimportant. "My post as governor is temporary. In a few days' time I will leave, and a government of your own people will take over fully. It will be up to them to decide what to do with your men. My guess is that most will be pardoned. They will if we have chosen our administrators well from among your people."

"You mean your *tyrants*," the Athenian scoffed.

"Most will call them that. Should angry words become actions, there will be a garrison of Equals here to help them maintain order. But then, you are not likely to witness any of that."

Alkibiades turned to Styphon at his side and smirked contemptuously. " So it is an execution after all."

"No," Brasidas inserted over a reply that Styphon had no intent of making. "You misunderstand. You are coming with me to Sparta. I have heard men say that you have a fondness for our values. Well, you shall get the chance to experience them up close. Without a spear aimed at your throat, so to speak." He smiled again, more genuinely. "So long as you behave yourself."

The smile fell. Brasidas rapped with a bent knuckle on the tabletop. "Now on to other business. You have been cooperative in answering our questions, I hear, even if you had nothing to tell. However, I should like to ask a few of them just one last time, with a certain witness present."

Puzzlement showed on the Athenian's face as the latch sounded on the door behind him. Styphon had a sudden inkling of who was shortly to appear, and it caused his muscles to tense. He turned his head, and so did Alkibiades, to join Brasidas in casting an eye upon the opening door.

There was no urgency in her step as she slid in through the widening gap, a pale shade possessed of a grace which only bolstered the aura of strength she exuded. Her long, silken locks of gold were twisted into braids that were gathered and fastened to her head with onyx-head pins. No respectable woman of Sparta would ever wear her hair thus, lest she be the target of scornful stares from men and women alike, but Eris was no Spartan woman. Perhaps she was not even a woman at all, in spite of appearances. When Styphon saw her, as he was now for the first time since her demise a month prior in a whirlwind of mutual slaughter with Thalassia, he could not help but see the nightmare-fiend which had slain a dozen Spartiates before his eyes with little more effort than it took a farmer to stick a pig.

The smile Eris wore now, as she glided in and shut the door behind, hem of her long white chiton grazing the straps of high-laced sandals, was one which other men might find disarming, but Styphon saw in it only a fearsome grin to rival that of any hound of Haides. Likewise her dark blue irises were eddies in the water of Styx, her flawless, alluring skin the surface of a bleached skull long ago picked clean by crows.

"Styphon," she greeted in her lilting, barbarian accent.

Even her sweet voice, as she spoke his name in cordial greeting, became in his ears as the scrape of talons on bone.

Thankfully, her attention did not linger on him. She instead looked to Alkibiades, who quickly averted his face.

"Did every hair on everyone's body just stand on end, or only mine?" the Athenian asked in a whisper.

A smile creased Brasidas's angular features. "Eris is... an acquired taste," he said. Eris gave a thin smile of her own, without removing her eyes from Alkibiades.

Straightening himself and banishing unease from his expression, the prisoner faced her.

"Eden," he said curtly, addressing her by her true name, which Styphon had heard only once or twice, many months ago, and only in private. To all who knew her in Sparta, she was Eris.

"Alkibiades," she returned. The name dripped from her rose-colored lips and even seemed tinged with a hint of awe. She raised a soft, deadly hand and stroked his fuzz-covered jaw, which twitched subtly in response. "What did the Wormwhore tell you about me?"

"Little," the Athenian answered. "I learned late of your existence, only when it could no longer be hidden from me. Thalassia keeps her secrets well." He gave a conspiratorial half-smile. "Fortunately for me, in some respects. If she was forthcoming with anyone, it's Demosthenes." His bright eyes shot to Brasidas, to whom he said, "She is no goddess, you know. She comes from another time and another world and doesn't give a centaur's balls about Sparta."

The Athenian read Brasidas's faint smile and sighed, concluding, correctly, "You do know that. Not outside this room, though. Everyone else actually believes she's Eris."

"Their idea, not mine," said the pale witch. "Who am I to deny men their little fantasies?"

Alkibiades continued to address the polemarch: "She will lead your city to ruin, as Thalassia did mine."

"Blame Geneva, then," Brasidas returned. "As I am accustomed to thinking of her. Or Demosthenes. I only did what was necessary to level the field for Sparta. I use Eris, as she uses me. I suffer no illusions."

Alkibiades chuckled darkly and returned his gaze to Eris. "You will suffer, all right."

"I presume you know of Geneva's ability to discern truth from lies when any man speaks?"

In Alkibiades' hesitation, Styphon saw the Athenian's answer and further sensed him reliving a hundred conversations, a great many lies told. "No..."

"It is an ability she shares with Eris here."

"When I met him, Demosthenes knew," the false goddess intoned very near to the Athenian's ear.

"So much they neglected to tell you," Brasidas lamented.

The Athenian scoffed. "I see your aim. You won't turn me against them."

"You overestimate your worth," Brasidas said. "But then, I have been told that about you. No, as I said, I only wish to question you in the presence of my witness, who possesses a rather useful ability in that respect. It will not take but a moment."

The polemarch proceeded to ask Alkibiades whether he had communicated at any time with the resistance currently operating in Athens; whether he knew the identity of Omega; whether Thalassia had been conscious when last he saw her; and whether he had any knowledge of the whereabouts or intentions of Demosthenes.

Alkibiades answered all in the negative.

When Brasidas signaled he was finished, Eris, whose piercing witch-eyes had remained locked on the prisoner throughout the questioning, put one bare arm affectionately at the base of the Athenian's neck.

Styphon shuddered at the thought of being the recipient of such a touch.

The Athenian did not appear to relish it either, his head subtly craning away from her.

"He speaks the truth on all counts," Eris announced. "He is a good man. I should know." She faced Alkibiades. When next she spoke, her breath must have licked the Athenian's neck. "Did the Whore tell you anything of what would have been your future, but for her meddling?"

It was clear that this piqued the prisoner's interest. He shot the pale enchantress a brief, sidewise look as he answered: "Thalassia said there was no recorded mention of me in history."

Eris's free hand rose to stroke the Athenian's shoulder over his soiled prison smock. "She lied. As she does so well. You were to have been a hero. A legend. In fact, now that I stand so close to you..."

Her hand slid down the length of his arm and across to his abdomen. Alkibiades raised an arm as if to check her, but evidently thought better of it and stood still as Eris gripped his manhood through the fabric. Brasidas looked on with a smirk which soon spread into a grin.

Styphon hardly envied the Athenian. Far better and less dangerous to have unwanted attention from a king—or even a venomous adder—than from this silken witch.

After a few moments being held thus, Alkibiades expelled held breath when at last Eris withdrew her hand, by which time the fabric of his garment stood propped up from underneath.

"Release him to my custody," Eris said to Brasidas, though her strange eyes remained on her prey whose scruffy beard she scratched with a fingertip. "Let me groom him, tend his wound, and take him about his city to show him how well it has been treated. And I can tell him of the future out of which Geneva cheated him."

"I... would prefer my cell," Alkibiades pleaded hopelessly with the polemarch.

Brasidas, furrowing his scarred brow in feigned consideration (feigned because surely he and Eris had planned the whole affair) before granting consent. "I cannot conceive of safer hands," he declared. "Just see that he understands the consequences of trying to escape you."

"I can see in his eyes that he does." Eris stroked her charge's greasy locks then wiped fingers on the waist of her chiton. "Even if he behaves, I imagine he will soon enough be begging for release."

She took the silent, erect prisoner's hand and led him from the office, a wolf leading the sheep to his not unpleasant fate. Satisfaction permeated the gaze with which Brasidas watched them leave.

* * *

When they were gone, Styphon began to address his superior: "Polemarch, if I might make an observation which may have some bearing on the whereabouts of Dem—"

An abruptly upraised palm from Brasidas silenced him.

"You will return to Sparta with me, naturally," he said. "Are you pleased with that news?"

The question was strangely informal, and caught Styphon by surprise. He gave the safest reply any Equal could, one which paraphrased Lykurgan code: "It is not my place to be pleased or displeased with an order."

Brasidas laughed a genuine laugh, if a brief one. Styphon had on occasion seen Brasidas appear to relax his ever-heightened guard in private, but rarely to this degree.

"You should be pleased, Styphon," he said. "You are not my dog anymore. We conquered Athens together. You have a bright future now. It could be that one day, when I am an old man in the reserves, and you are a general, I will serve under you. I want to be sure you remember me well. So relax."

Styphon did not, but pretended to. Brasidas's smirk implied that he noted the difference as he fell to silence and looked to the door, as if waiting.

"I think that ought to do," he said quietly, at length. "She has incredible hearing, you know. If you mean to say what I think you do, best she remain in the dark. Report."

Understanding, if barely, Styphon proceeded. "Perhaps it is nothing, sir, but the timing given by Alkibades and others for the departure of Demosthenes from Dekelea coincides with—"

"The disappearance of Equals in the hills of Parnes?" Brasidas finished for him.

"Aye, sir." Styphon suppressed mild disappointment.

Brasidas tapped some parchments on his writing pedestal. "Three more Equals of late," he said. "And an Arcadian. I believe you are correct, Styphon. If she knew of the missing soldiers. She surely would have drawn the same conclusion." Styphon noted the perhaps deliberate avoidance of Eris's name, as if her sensitive ears might be attuned to its speaking. "But she is only freshly awakened, and I would as soon have her back in Sparta before she learns and elects to give chase."

"Forgive me, sir," Styphon inserted, "but might it not be for the best if she found and killed them?"

"It would be," Brasidas agreed. "But is that outcome so certain? And if she did succeed, what cause would she have to return to us? There is a third she-daemon, you know," Brasidas added almost in passing. "Sleeping under a mountain in the far east, beyond Scythia. The eldest of the three, it seems. Once vengeance is claimed, ours may simply opt to join her sister."

With a nod, Styphon conceded the point, endeavoring to put from his mind the blood-chilling notion of a third Fury akin to Eris and Thalassia.

Brasidas thumped his writing pedestal. "Ah, I'll be glad to see the end of this administrative shit! It's all tally-sheets and numbers and money. And dealing with these Athenians —gods, is there even one man in this marble rat's nest who won't do anything for a few silver obols?" He snorted. "Then again, I suppose those are the only type of men who will serve their country's enemy."

"No, they are all like that," Styphon joked, and was proud to make the polemarch flash a smile.

It swiftly vanished, and Brasidas said, "Just one more thing before I dismiss you, Styphon."

There was nothing especially ominous about the polemarch's tone—if anything, since Eris had left the room, it had been ominously friendly. Still, something made Styphon dread whatever might follow.

"I must congratulate you on having gained the king's favor," Brasidas said. "It will certainly boost your career." He gave a half-shrug of humility. "As you rise, I hope you will not forget who it was that dragged your name from the mire in the first place."

Feeling relief that this was all Brasidas wished to add, Styphon reassured him, "I shall carry that debt unto death, polemarch."

"Good." Brasidas smiled. "Thank you. And merely out of perverse curiosity," he chuckled, though his sharp eyes were intense, "has Agis had you procure whores for him?"

Though momentarily taken aback, Styphon considered no answer but the true one: "Yes, polemarch."

With a satisfied smirk, Brasidas asked, "Where did you go? Aspasia's?"

"Aye."

"Only the best for royalty, eh?"

With some hesitation, Styphon agreed, "Aye, sir."

Brasidas flicked his fingers in a friendly wave of dismissal.

"Go on," he said. "Leave me to a few last hours of this mind-numbing shit before we sail."

With a final, curt, "Aye, sir," Styphon ducked out of the office. He chose simply to be grateful for the change in Brasidas rather than expend thought on what, if any, dark motives might lurk behind it.

The life left unanalyzed was a happy one, someone had said, or should have.

10. Walking to Corinth

They walked to Corinth like two itinerant beggars, possessing nothing in the world except what they carried. Only one of them looked the part, gaunt and ungroomed, while the other suffered little more than hair which was limper and less lustrous than once it had been. On the first night of their journey, spent encamped in the hinterlands of the Attic-Megarian frontier, Thalassia partook of another Cyclopean portion of the cooked lamb, borne over her shoulder in a sack made from the cloak of a dead Equal, before declaring her post-rebirth hunger sated. Demosthenes nibbled, and they slept on separate beds of brush. Under normal circumstances Thalassia slept only one night out of six, but these were not normal times for her; she was yet weak.

Deep in that night, Demosthenes sobbed in his sleep from a dream which often plagued him, that of Laonome pleading with him from a field of asphodel to eat of the Sad Queen's fruit that he might join her. How he tried and tried to take the fruit from Laonome and crack its red shell and pluck out and swallow its sweet seeds... but ever did the fruit, and she, remain just out of reach.

He was halfway between worlds when, from one realm or the other, arms encircled him, pulling his cheek against a soft, linen-clad breast while warm lips pressed to his scalp and whispered soothingly, "Shhhh...."

Surrendering, Demosthenes accepted the embrace and wept into the softness for long minutes before he felt underneath him rough twigs, heard the cricket-song, realized that the scent filling his awareness belonged not to his wife but another he knew too well.

"No!" he hissed into the linen. Raising an arm between them, he shoved Thalassia and twisted away, scrambling on all fours in the dirt to put distance between them. She yielded, watching him go from where she knelt by his bed of brush.

"Dee," she said when he had sat huddled inside his cloak in the cold darkness for a while, his back to her.

"Don't speak to me."

She obliged. The hours seemed endless until dawn came. Even before there was light enough for mere mortal eyes to see by, they broke camp and resumed their journey. After a short while spent navigating wooded slopes in silence, Thalassia in the lead, she fell back beside Demosthenes and began speaking, aloud but as if addressing no one in particular.

"The scene is a stable in Athens. Two slaves make cakes from heaps of shit for feeding to a giant dung beetle. The slaves' master, Trygaeus, they say, begs daily of Zeus not to sweep Greece away with this war that turns cities into empty husks. So insistent was Trygaeus to learn the god's intention that he strapped together a bunch of ladders and tried climbing them, but he only fell and cracked his head. So instead he found this giant dung beetle, his Pegasus, on the back of which he means to fly up to Zeus and ask him face-to-face about his intentions for—"

"What is this? What are you talking about?"

"A play," she replied without looking at him or stopping. "It's called *Peace*. Aristophanes would have presented it a few years from now. He still might. No way to tell. I thought you'd like to hear it. It will pass the time, at least."

"A comedy is perhaps not what suits my mood now."

"You want more tragedy? I have those, too, but—"

"Why..." Demosthenes began, then hesitated, wondering whether he should engage her at all. "Why are you being so kind?"

She shot him a glare as they walked. "I've always been kind. You just never bothered to notice."

"On the day we met, you choked me near to death, kneed me in the groin and kicked me repeatedly while I lay on the ground."

"I didn't know you yet! And you stabbed me."

"Later, you dragged me up the stairs of my own home and threw me across the roof."

"I—well..." she hunted briefly for words. "I said I was sorry. And I paid the price. You hardly spoke to me for a year."

"That was for kidnapping the daughter of an Equal."

"Fine," Thalassia conceded. "This is all ancient history anyway. If you insist on dwelling on it, I'll have to bring up what you did in Amphipolis, and you don't need that now. Do you want to hear the fucking play or not?"

Demosthenes took a moment to consider, or rather just not to appear overeager, then answered, "Yes, I suppose. Your lips have been still so long, I would not deny you a return to running them nonstop."

Thalassia regarded him with raised brows, but smiled. "Now who's the kindly one?" she asked. "So Trygaeus comes out and starts talking to the beetle..."

Over the next two days, they crossed the Megarid and the Isthmus, and thanks to the traveler-out-of-time with whom he traveled, the ears of Demosthenes became the only ones in his world to have heard works which now were as likely as not never to be written. During the comedies, he failed to laugh as he surely would have a year ago, but still, intellectually he appreciated the humor and was grateful for the diversion. Surely that was Thalassia's motive, for she was intimately familiar with those dark paths down which his mind, if left to form its own thoughts, would otherwise travel.

They were the same paths on which Thalassia was a tool to be used by him, a thing instead of a companion who cared for his welfare. Did she know that, and was her behavior calculated to steer his mind in the direction most beneficial to her? That would hardly surprise. So often, it seemed that she could see his very thoughts, even if she claimed such was not among her powers.

She was a woman, though. Perhaps that was enough.

Before reaching Corinth, they bathed in a stream and washed their clothing, for what good it did. For lack of a razor, Demosthenes' face remained covered in wild growth. That was perhaps for the best given that Corinth was a Spartan ally, and her authorities might be on alert for a fugitive Athenian general and a Persian witch. Fortunately, if any city existed besides Athens where it was possible for strangers to pass unnoticed, it was the bustling port of Corinth, where ships put in every day carrying visitors who had never set foot in Hellas, and never would again.

Reasonably confident of anonymity, they passed through the gates and made straight for the crowded docks that sat on the Gulf to the west which was named for the city. By late afternoon, Demosthenes had secured passage for them on a Zakynthan trader that planned to depart in two days' time for Naupaktos. For payment he handed over the only coin he possessed, since his nighttime flight from Dekelea had not allowed for a purse full of clinking silver: he spent his death-coin, a Mysian gold stater depicting Pegasos, intended as his payment for the boatmen should he fall in battle.

Except for the simple fact of its beauty, it bothered him little to part with it. There was no room for fanciful beliefs in Thalassia's universe, the cold, rational one which he had little choice but to accept as his own. Her universe had its own gods and monsters which were human, or had been once.

Demosthenes convinced the captain to begrudge him a few silver drachmae back from his gold, and these coins he pressed into Thalassia's palm.

"They have nice things in the markets here, and they're cheap," he said. "This should buy you a better dress and maybe some beads or something shiny. Just don't wear it until we board the ship."

Thalassia looked down at the coins and back up. "Are you saying I look awful, are you trying to make me happy, or do you just think I'm vain?" she asked. "Keep in mind that you can't lie to me and that I'll take the money regardless of your answer."

"I barely understand the question. But the choices are not exclusive of one another, so my answer is all three."

Her lips parted in offense. "You think I look awful?"

Exhausted, Demosthenes shrugged. Her fingers enclosed the silver, all but one finger, which she put on his chest.

"I understand," she said, and her pale eyes said she did. "Thank you. I'll make it go as far as it can."

"I believe it," Demosthenes said. He had never shopped with her, but Eurydike had on many occasions, and according to her, Thalassia had a way of getting whatever she wanted for any price she named. If sailors were more like market stall vendors, he might have let her negotiate their passage to Naupaktos.

Thalassia went and did her shopping and by nightfall kept their arranged meeting at the steps of a temple on which men and women copulated, some for love, some for money. It was not for nothing that Corinth had the reputation it did.

Thalassia watched the couples appraisingly as she and Demosthenes left for the place he had meanwhile selected for them to pass the night: a grassy, vacant lot just inside the city wall. There was little chance that the Corinthian authorities, who were rather tolerant of vagrancy, would give them any trouble. The greater risk was from robbers, although more accurately, in their particular case, the risk was *to* the robbers.

They settled down in the grass, Thalassia with her tightly wrapped bundle from the agora. Her eyes were on a lamplit street in the distance, well populated with milling crowds in high spirits. They seemed headed nowhere in particular, perhaps just anywhere but home. Their voices were a dull cacophony lapping at the nearby city wall.

"Corinth seems nice," Thalassia observed, not so idly.

"I know what you're getting at," Demosthenes said. "You want to have fun. Go."

"Not without you."

"Really, just go. You deserve it. Enjoy being alive."

"You're alive, too," she said. She nudged him, pale eyes pleading. "Come on. I don't mean sex. Let's just take a walk, see what there is to see. Street performers, anything. I don't care."

Demosthenes gave some honest thought to her proposal, and within seconds rejected it. "I'll stay here." He pointedly met Thalassia's eyes, wintry portals behind which all lies withered to dust. "I would not say this to you if I did not mean it. Go. Enjoy yourself. I want you to."

The piercing eyes tasted his words, accepted and swallowed them. Thalassia frowned disappointment, but she conceded and stood.

"Don't sleep until I come back," she said. "It's not safe. I won't be long."

"I don't need your protection," Demosthenes returned acidly. "I've killed dozens of men with my own hands. Hundreds as a general."

"I know, I know," Thalassia said. "But I'm leaving my stuff. I just don't want it stolen."

She turned and headed toward the crowds, but Demosthenes did not track the progress of her plain white chiton through the grass. He laid his head on whatever finery his death-coin had bought her and stared at the twilit clouds and wrestled with shades.

Truly, it was but one shade which gave him grief. Its fingers were perpetually wrapped around his heart, ready to squeeze whenever darkness fell or he found himself with more than a moment's quiet. There was far less of the latter now that Thalassia was around, but Laonome seemed to be countering whatever relief that gave by making the pain burn even more intensely at the times it did flare.

He scoffed at himself. It was hard to stop thinking of the world in terms of shades and unseen forces, even though they had no place in his new universe of lines and layers and suns and planets, and men and women whose machines made them the equal of any god.

Laonome was gone. She was not a shade and could not haunt him, which meant that he haunted and punished himself. Even knowing that, he could not stop. The universe around him was a cold, sterile void; if only he could swallow a portion of it to inhabit this husk that was forced to go on living.

But then, no, no one was forcing him to live. It was his choice, and men could always change their minds.

He shut his eyes and steeled himself to watch his love die nine or twenty times.

Something stung him on the crown of his head. He started and flew onto one knee, sword in one hand, the other on his scalp, where he quickly realized he had been pelted with a stone. How long had Thalassia been gone? An hour? He had claimed not to require her protection, and he did not, but... her presence in a fight was comforting.

He had risen, aiming his sword in the direction from which he presumed the rock to have come, but the moonlit space was empty. He turned left and right, and in the latter direction saw his assailant: Thalassia, who could pass for a shade when she wanted to. She crossed the final few feet separating them and sank gracefully, cross-legged into the grass. She reached over and picked up the missile she had flung at him, a marked ivory cube, which joined a duplicate already in her palm. Dice. Under her other arm was a thin, rectangular board, painted with colorful squares and Egyptian markings.

She set the board on the grass in front of her and emptied onto it a canvas pouch of small game pieces of painted clay.

"I don't know what the fuck this is," she said. "Hopefully you do."

"It is... Senet," Demosthenes said, sitting and laying his sword in the grass. By setting it to racing, the scare had actually done his heart some good. "It's Egyptian."

"I got that much. Can you teach me how to play?"

"I could," Demosthenes halfway agreed. "How did you get it?"

"I asked," she said, giving no indication that she saw the question for the accusation it was, even though she surely did. "I promised to return it when we're done."

He stared blankly at a bright purple hieroglyph of a bird. "I told you to enjoy yourself. This is not your idea of a good time."

"Fortunately for you, I rarely do what I'm told." Thalassia smiled and extended the dice to him on her open palm.

Demosthenes breathed a sigh. It was one of relief, even if he did his best to make it seem one of annoyance. "I would have to be the one born yesterday, not you, to be so foolish as to roll dice against you."

Back in Athens, he had had occasion to witness Thalassia's ability to ensure that whatever numbers she wanted would more often than not be the ones to come up. It had to do with things called *angles* and *force* and *trajectories* that certain types of philosopher were always on about.

It just now occurred, in his present penniless state, that such an ability might be useful to one in want of money. With no gods to punish the wicked for such sins, what was there to lose but a little integrity?

"I'm three days old, thank you, and you can roll for me." She pushed the dice into his hand. "Will you teach me, or what?"

He did, and by the time the noise of the crowd had faded into cricket song and he surrendered his bleary eyes to sleep, he was fairly certain that, in spite of her concession to fairness and profession of ignorance, Thalassia was letting him win.

11. *The Nymph's Tit*

The next day, at Thalassia's urging, since their ship did not depart for another day, they made the strenuous hike (for mortals, at least) to the summit of Corinth's monolithic acropolis, where stood what was perhaps the greatest temple to Aphrodite in all of Hellas. Business there appeared slow today for its state-employed prostitutes. Unsurprising, perhaps. Most of Corinth's famous temple whores these days worked at other sanctuaries down below, since it was a rare man who could make this climb with desire and stamina intact in the early summer heat, like that which bore down now. The temple itself had wares on hand, of course, mostly to accommodate passers-through coming to 'see the sights.'

The two arriving now with that very purpose had no intention of offering their patronage to the temple, but truly had only come for the view. Demosthenes himself did not see a great deal immediately on arrival at the summit, for his head hung low, while fat droplets of sweat falling from his brow made dark spots on the stone underfoot. Unflagging Thalassia, meanwhile, proceeded to a western outcropping and perched on its edge with her gaze upon the blue, tranquil Gulf of Corinth which they were soon to cross, and where crying gulls circled the square sails of ships crewed by men from cities near and far, Greek and barbarian, heard-of and unknown.

Demosthenes had not seen one himself, but the sails of the new ships which Eden had designed for Sparta, the ones used to conquer Athens, were triangular. When eventually he got up and joined Thalassia, though not as near the edge as she, he looked for any such sails on the Gulf, but found none.

Thalassia drew back from the precipice to stand by his side.

94

"It's pretty," she said, an inane but honest observation. "Thank you for bringing me."

Demosthenes scoffed. He did not bother to explain why her gratitude was absurd; there were any number of reasons.

She raised one of them. "I know, I've seen a lot," she said. "It doesn't mean I can't appreciate this. It's all I've got now."

Such words as these might have been spoken with bitterness, but were not. Her voice held acceptance of the exile which, after all, was self-imposed.

"I've told you of Spiral," she went on, a touch wistfully.

She had. Spiral was a floating city among the stars, Magdalen's base and headquarters of the army Thalassia had betrayed.

"In the Veta Caliate, after the first time we die, for training purposes, Spiral is where we awaken and meet Magdalen for the first time. It was just the two of us, alone in a room. We exchanged some niceties. She was very kind and sweet. Then she took me out and let me see where I was."

There was a substantial pause during which the pale gaze aimed out over the Gulf seemed to envisage, temporarily, sights far different than ship's wakes and sea birds and cliffs awash with bright morning sun.

"Spiral sits on the edge of a nebula," Thalassia went on. "You don't know what that is. It's what's left after a sun explodes. Think of the most incredible sunset you ever saw and, well, make it fill a thousand skies and give it colors so deep and rich that even letting them share the names of other colors would be a gross insult. Set the hidden faces of all the gods into the swirling clouds, each eye big enough to fit a thousand suns, and..."

The trance into which Thalassia had inadvertently slipped suddenly broke, her impossibly distant vision shattering. Her head sank.

"Well, I was never a poet in any language," she confessed. "When I stood on Spiral, my new body just ten minutes old, and I saw that sky for the first time, I laughed. It's what everyone does, apparently. Then it turns to tears, and you crumple in a heap at Magdalen's feet. That's what I did."

She laughed. "And then you get used to it. You stop appreciating things, or appreciate the wrong things. So..." She turned her head toward him, wisps of her plainer-than-usual hair licking her cheek. "Thank you for coming up here with me. I appreciate it."

Demosthenes could summon no reply. He had pictured the things she asked him to picture, or tried, but he knew in his heart that his earthbound, mortal mind's eye was utterly insufficient to begin painting the vistas which inhabited hers. He could never know Spiral, or a nebula, or any more than the one sun which felt far too close at the moment. Maybe he could never even really know one who did know those things.

He knew one thing, though: Thalassia had changed. She was not a new person—hardly—but just a few months ago, it would have bordered on unthinkable that he might spend three days alone and in close contact with her without experiencing moments of discomfort or embarrassment or even fear for his physical safety by her hand or tongue. There was no evidence now of the volcanic temper of her past. The change, he recalled, had begun in the days before she had died, but perhaps death had caused it to crystallize.

It seemed strange now, too, that he had mistrusted her. Now... there was no other hand than hers on this earth in which he would more willingly set his life.

But then, his life was not worth as much today as it once had been.

"Sorry for the pointless babble," Thalassia said after

receiving no reply for some time. "Stop me next time."

"Half the good things in the world likely began with pointless babble," Demosthenes philosophized.

With a vacant half-smile, Thalassia silently agreed. She walked away from the monolith's edge and toward Aphrodite's temple. "You should rest for the climb down," she said. "I'll just look around. I promise to stay out of trouble."

* * *

She kept her promise. On their descent to the lower city, they wandered a bit before coming upon the street opposite the harbor, where among the stalls selling food and trade goods they found boisterous crowds gathered around tables where men played games of chance overseen by spear-bearing city guards looking outward and keen-eyed watchers with arms as thick around as some men's waists looking in.

They watched the games for a while, moving from table to table until Thalassia made the inevitable suggestion.

"We don't need coin," Demosthenes countered.

"We don't *not* need it."

The discussion persisted at low intensity until Demosthenes let himself be convinced, and they selected a game. None of the gamblers they had seen so far had been women, and so to avoid undue attention, he would take part, allowing his slave and 'good luck charm' roll the dice on his behalf. It seemed the kind of eccentricity that Corinthians could understand.

One problem remained, a mildly revolting possible solution to which Thalassia whispered in his ear. Reluctantly, he presented the proposal to one of the guardians, who approved it: instead of five obols, his opening stake would be fifteen minutes of Thalassia's services in private.

He took his seat, and Thalassia's roll won the pot for

him, and so he fortunately never learned whether she would have gone through with payment had they lost.

Her control of the dice was not absolute, but any control at all was more than others possessed, and enough to ensure she won far more than she lost. After twenty rounds or so, she tapped Demosthenes' shoulder as a signal that the overseers were getting suspicious, or at least annoyed, and it was time to move on. They went to another game and another, doing the same; five in total, not counting the one they left immediately when Thalassia informed him that the dice were loaded. She could have compensated, but out-cheating cheaters seemed a risk hardly worth the payoff.

By evening's end, when Demosthenes declared the time ripe to quit, they carried silver coin amounting to a month's wages for a skilled laborer in Athens. As they walked away from the waterfront, Thalassia took the lead and stopped them in front of a certain establishment they had passed numerous times. The sign in front, illustrated by a crude pictogram, was *The Nymph's Tit*.

Demosthenes asked her with a silent, frustrated look what on earth made her believe he would want a whore.

"Just wait right here," she instructed, and she went inside, returning a smile from the armed, well-groomed man leaning by the door. Minutes later she emerged, but not alone. Beside her was a young woman dressed in an over-short chiton of pink linen, her lips painted, flowers wound into her ash blonde hair.

"This is Ammia," Thalassia said, coming up to him. "She has strict instructions to clean you up, cut your hair, shave you and get you looking respectable again for Naupaktos, and not to try to sell you anything else. Right, Ammia?" The girl nodded, smiling warmly. "In fact, she won't speak unless spoken to."

Demosthenes' eyes fell away from the prostitute's in mild embarrassment while Thalassia rounded behind him and set hands on his shoulders.

"Come on," she said, pushing. "If you decide you want to be filthy and hairy again, that's easily achieved."

He allowed Thalassia to guide him into a tastelessly decorated foyer, where Ammia took his hand in hers to lead him through a lavender curtain.

"What about you?" Demosthenes asked Thalassia, who made no move to leave.

She just smiled and patted her bundle from the agora, and then was out of sight.

In a tiled bath chamber, Ammia spent the better part of an hour performing the tasks she was paid for, and performing them both clothed and wordlessly. She was good with a razor, and left his cheek smooth and devoid of stinging cuts.

A cut would have reminded of him Eurydike. Well-meaning, life-loving, easily distracted Eurydike who was now a slave to harsher men.

He repelled that guilt-inducing incursion on his thoughts; there was no choice.

At one point, a fresh white chiton and blue cloak were delivered to the room, and at the conclusion of her services, Ammia made to help him dress.

"These are not mine," he protested.

"Your nice Persian said they were," Ammia explained. Her voice, unheard until now, proved her to be no Corinthian but some child of the far north, doubtless a slave for some portion of her short life.

Demosthenes thanked the girl, who kissed him lightly on his freshly bared cheek and assured him Thalassia had already handled the bill.

He came through the curtain into the parlor and stopped cold at the sight of a witch.

He had seen this witch before, back when Attica was free, in Dekelea when she had stayed there helping to build the walls. The walls from atop which he had witnessed...

No. It was an avenue of thought which must be blocked in waking hours. Laonome haunted him enough in slumber.

This witch wore black, as witches would, and her ebon locks hung in damp curls that would flatten into sinuous waves when dry. Bronze hoop bracelets adorned her wrists, a multitude of copper rings her fingers, charms of bone and bead the bare expanse of honey-gold skin, which her ankle-length black gown left exposed, above her breasts.

Then there were the eyes which she, or one of Ammia's colleagues, had rimmed with blackest kohl, driving any beholder's gaze into pale blue irises which few men were likely to prove able to meet for more than an instant. A shame that her sandals were the same well-worn pair she had been wearing since Athens' fall.

A shame because so many men would ultimately find their gazes forced there.

Indeed, the only other time he had seen Thalassia thus, he had averted his eyes as though from the sun and found himself fumbling for words.

He did better this second time. After a moment's stunned silence, he said, "When I sent you shopping, I had in mind something less... conspicuous."

Thalassia, who surely had anticipated his reaction, smiled. "We can afford another dress," she said. "If you insist."

He looked her up and down a few more times, pondering. Thalassia seemed both unbothered by the scrutiny and unworried about the verdict, presently delivered.

"Keep it," he declared. "If I am to travel with a barbarian, I may as well travel with a barbarian. It's not as if I will be standing for elections anytime soon."

He quickly regretted those last words, which potentially revealed him as not only an Athenian but a prominent one. Evidently they were shedding their physical disguises as of today, but still, there was no need to invite scrutiny.

Thalassia noticed the slip and reassured him, with a look, that no harm was done. She seemed to be right, since beside him, Ammia's reaction was a smile and quick round of quiet, girlish applause on behalf of a fellow female who had just won the approval of her presumed master.

They left *The Nymph's Tit*, rested the night near the harbor, and with the dawn they set sail for Naupaktos—though not before having procured for Thalassia a plain, hooded gray cloak she could keep tightly clasped during the voyage, lest the Zakynthan sailors balk at transporting a witch.

12. Agathokles

Founded by Helot slaves fleeing the yoke of Spartan domination, the young city of Naupaktos had proved a natural and steadfast ally for Athens since even before the latest, just-ended war. Naupaktos's legendary shipyards had constructed thirty-three triremes for the Athenian navy, and two years ago its Messenian leaders had sent troops under Demosthenes' own command to free their enslaved Helot cousins at Pylos.

Demosthenes had until now, as he came ashore this day, never set foot in the place. It was a small city, barely a city at all compared to the likes of Athens, but then few were. It was more a town with walls, and its seat of government was not hard to find; it was, as with most cities, near the agora. Leaving Thalassia outside, he entered the compound alone. When he saw no faces that were familiar to him, and no one seemed to recognize him (the latter he reckoned a blessing), he pulled aside a clerk and asked him the whereabouts of Agathokles, who had led the Naupaktan contingent at Pylos.

Armed with an answer, he returned to Thalassia, who waited in her encompassing, hooded gray cloak at the bottom of a set of stone steps built into the uneven ground on which much of Naupaktos sat.

"Agathokles is presently the most senior of the city's three strategoi," he informed her. "Not only that, his opinion would appear to hold more weight than any other in the democracy. He is bound to show himself in this place before the day is done."

They sat on the stone steps and commenced waiting.

"What will you ask of him?" Thalassia asked.

"A roof," Demosthenes said. "Secrecy. Whatever aid he can render to our cause."

"And by cause, you mean ravaging Sparta with a fungal plague."

"The means of destruction is of little importance."

"Right," Thalassia said. "The Naupaktans might disagree. Chances are high we'll be killing lots of Messenians, too, so... you may not want to mention that."

"Agreed."

They fell into a brief silence, into which Thalassia said, "Senet?"

"No."

More silence, which Demosthenes sensed would not endure.

It did not. "I enjoyed killing those Equals back at the cave," Thalassia remarked conversationally. "I'd like to do more of that. I never did much wetwork with the Caliate, and never with fucking *swords*."

"'Wet' work?" Demosthenes asked. As usual, he allowed himself to be drawn into her bizarre orbit rather than following his better judgment and shutting both mind and mouth.

"Bloody," she clarified.

"You mean to say you are new at killing?"

"Relatively. From up close, anyway."

"Were you never trained at wielding a blade? Blades?" he corrected himself, for Thalassia fought with one in either hand.

"A bit. But my body just does it. Like yours sweats when you're hot." She ran a fingertip across his temple.

"That's... horrifying, I suppose."

"We'll have a lot of free time waiting for fungi to grow. We may as well go to Athens, you and I, and kill Equals. We might even end up liberating it."

"Only the two of us?"

"It's better that way. If the Naupaktans sent men with us, some would die or be captured, and give away our location."

Demosthenes shook his head. "It's too great a—"

"Just think about it," she interrupted calmly. "You want to kill Spartans. I want to kill Spartans. So let's go kill some fucking Spartans. And Eurydike may be there. Don't you miss her?"

"I..." Demosthenes began. "I miss the existence of which she was a part. Times have changed."

He swallowed a pang of mourning for the man he once was, a man who could feel things other than grief and rage. Whatever was her fate, laughing Eurydike surely did not deserve it, but such small wrongs would be righted with his righting of the greatest wrong: the existence on this earth of a city called Sparta.

"I will consider it," he concluded.

Thalassia leveled him a look which assured he communed now with the more serious self which she so frequently concealed under layers of frivolity, glamour, or hedonism. She set a hand on his knee and said, earnestly, "Good. I hope so."

As if she knew it was what he desired, which she probably did, she ceased speaking for a while and let him seek to empty his mind. That she read him thus was enough to set him wondering idly, as he had once or twice in the past, whether Thalassia herself were not a figment of his imagination, visible only to him.

But she could not be. Far too much death and tragedy were attributable to her for that to be the case.

Though they sat shoulder-to-shoulder on the steps, they shared no further word or glance in the hour it took for Agathokles to show himself. He arrived with a rapid-moving crowd of men whose importance, in their own eyes if no others, was evident by the way in which they bore themselves. Agathokles walked at the crowd's head, looking considerably better groomed than he had when Demosthenes had fought with him in besieged Pylos.

Flying to his feet, Demosthenes put himself in the group's path on the top stair, where Agathokles' gaze swiftly found him. His eyes narrowed and pace slowed, forcing two men behind him to stumble, and then his eyes went wide and he grinned through his short beard.

Quickening his pace, Agathokles reached the summit with arms spread for an embrace which Demosthenes gave, if less wholeheartedly than the Naupaktan. Several others in the party recognized Demosthenes, too, as the Athenian commander under whom they once had served, and they joined their leader in demanding a warm greeting. Demosthenes obliged them all, and managed to convey some false impression of good cheer, but not before hushing the first few who uttered his name aloud.

"If you must use a name, call me Diomedes," he said. Perhaps because their fathers and grandfathers had been fugitive slaves freed by Athens from Helotry and transported here to turn a conquered, formerly hostile city into a friend, all quickly understood his need for discretion.

After his wide grin had lingered for just the right amount of time (the ability to gauge which was suggestive of a skilled politician), Agathokles put on a graver look in acknowledgment of the sad event which could not but be the immediate cause of their reunion: the fall of Athens.

"May I speak with you in private?" Demosthenes asked.

Agathokles readily agreed and bade his comrades continue on without him as he accompanied Demosthenes to a less well-traveled space to one side of the stone steps.

"I heard just yesterday of the fall of Dekelea, my friend,"

Agathokles said.

That came as news to Demosthenes, but not as any surprise; he suppressed any reaction.

"Such a pity," the Naupaktan went on. "Thank Zeus you evaded capture. It is an honor that you would make your way here. If you have come seeking sanctuary, you need not even ask. Consider it granted."

"Do not let custom put words in your mouth that are better left to measured thought," Demosthenes warned.

It was ironic advice, perhaps, coming from one who had very recently rejected Thalassia's counsel against rash action.

"Nonsense," the Naupaktan protested. He paused, pursed his lips, flicked a glance downward and seemed to reconsider. "Well, perhaps I should hear you out." His well-trimmed beard, tinged with gray, framed an apologetic smile. "This city is a democracy after all, thanks to Athens. At least, for now it is." Leaving his last, cryptic comment unexplained, he continued, "Make your request and be certain it shall be looked on with favor."

"I am certain of it," Demosthenes said. He gave a friendly smile, which quickly faded as he began steeling himself for the necessary task of recounting the tragedy which had left vengeance his only reason to continue living.

He opted against preamble.

"On the first day of Dekelea's siege, Brasidas slaughtered my wife before my eyes." The statement had its intended effect; Agathokles' features went slack in horror. "Had she lived, I might at this moment be holding my firstborn instead of standing here with no possessions except what I can carry."

Agathokles gave a long look of abject pity, then hung his head and said quietly, "Your grief must be impossible to bear. I shall pray for her, friend."

Demosthenes forwent telling the Naupaktan not to

bother. Neither did he take time to indulge in that grief of which Agathokles spoke.

"I shall have my day with Brasidas in due course," he pledged. "Before that, I will slaughter as many Equals as I can, by any means necessary. You will not likely want Naupaktos implicated. But perhaps, as a private citizen, you might give Diomedes a place to stay for a short while."

Before Demosthenes had even finished the request, Agathokles was shaking his head. "You have not heard, my unlucky friend," he said. "No wonder, given your recent ordeal. Sheltering you can hardly make us a target of Sparta's wrath, for we already are one." The ever cheerful Agathokles grew utterly serious. "Not a week ago, a Spartan herald came bearing a demand that we dissolve our democracy and accept a new regime of Sparta's choosing. If we refuse, and they conquer us by force, every man woman and child of us will be put to death or returned to the slavery from which our fathers escaped, our city returned to the Lokrians from whom Athens seized it on our behalf."

Demosthenes muttered under his breath a curse learned from Thalassia. "How long did they give you to decide?"

"Naturally, our assembly asked the herald that question. His answer was that we had however long it might take for Sparta to decide it was convenient to attack us, absent our submission."

"I take it by your words that a decision has yet to be taken?"

Agathokles frowned. "It needs proper debate, and to be honest, while Dekelea yet held out, we had hope Sparta might yet be struck another blow that would cause them to forget about us for a while. Now our last, slim hope lies with Argos, which has received a similar ultimatum. They have yet to give any response to our proposal of forming a league with them."

He sighed and shrugged. "No one in this city has any love for Sparta, and even less faith that they would uphold any agreement. My own inclination is toward resistance, but what's certain is that our little town stands no chance alone. It may be that soon you shall be forced to flee to another city. But until that time, you are welcome."

Demosthenes hung his head and allowed a tiny, aggravating thought in the corner of his mind to swell first into an idea and then into words. Still, he hesitated to speak them, for they represented a distraction from his only true purpose.

"I may be able to give your city a fighting chance," he said to the troubled Naupaktan. "In truth, not me so much as... *her*."

He turned and indicated the cloaked figure standing halfway down the staircase, who threw her hood back in response to the unplanned signal.

Agathokles' brow furrowed as he gazed at her until recognition dawned and he smiled. "I saw her in your bed at Pylos!"

"Yes," Demosthenes confirmed. "That was the day I met her. My life has not been the same since. Tell me, do the accounts you have heard of the battle at Eleusis include stories of two witches or goddesses joining the fight on either side?"

Staring at Thalassia, Agathokles answered, "They do. The slaughtergod's sister for Sparta, and for Athens, the last of the Amazons. Like most educated men, I did not count it as a literal truth."

"It is true," Demosthenes revealed to his comrade. "More or less. The woman you see is no Amazon, but she is a warrior, and a strategist and inventor, among many other things, and she did fight for Athens that day."

Dividing his gaze between his friend and the cloaked

figure, Agathokles adopted a puzzled expression. "Those same accounts say that both women fell with horrific wounds."

"That, too, is true," Demosthenes said. "Yet both live. I would not see this one fall in battle a second time, but perhaps she might be of help in devising some means of defending your city."

Momentarily, the Naupaktan's ponderous look broke, and he laughed. "Although I cannot think of why you would deceive me in this, forgive me for saying I am unconvinced. However, lacking any other source of hope, I would be a fool to decline." He clamped a hand onto Demosthenes' shoulder. "So the answer is yes, my friend. Please do lend us the aid of your Amazon—or whatever she is!"

Thalassia ascended the stair toward them, the hem of her gray cloak sweeping the stone. Agathokles offered her a warm smile which was met in kind.

"Modest Diomedes leaves out the other asset he brings to Naupaktos," Thalassia said upon arrival, "which is the mind of one of Athens' greatest generals."

For the sake of politeness, Demosthenes stopped short of scoffing. Perhaps, if nothing else, he was the best general ever to lead Athenians into a siege before slipping over a wall and leaving them to their fate.

Agathokles nodded agreement with her assessment, while a new light in his honest eyes hinted at rising hope.

"Can you give us a navy like theirs?" he asked directly of Thalassia. In spite of its strangeness, he showed no discomfort at addressing a female thus, in the presence of a male peer, on matters of war. "We have yet to see these new vessels, only heard stories of their matchless speed and maneuverability. It is said that Sparta only sends them out in numbers, lest one be captured and copied by enemies. Can you build us such ships?"

Surprisingly, Thalassia cast a glance at Demosthenes, seeking his assent before answering. Silently, he gave it.

"I can show you the design and methods. But building the ships and and training men to crew them would require more time than you are likely to have. More urgent will be establishing a defense against invasion."

"You mean machines, like Brasidas' katapeltai, or these bows I hear you used at Amphipolis."

"Machines are a crutch for unclever men," Thalassia said, sounding surprisingly like a Spartan. "Depending on them instead of brains and flesh and bone is a mistake. However... yes, machines."

"And will you take the field for us, as you did for Athens?" Agathokles pressed.

"No," Demosthenes swiftly answered on her behalf. "If she is lost, there will be nothing to stop the Spartan beast from devouring all of Hellas. The freedom of Naupaktos means as much to me as it does to you," he lied well, "but that freedom will never be assured unless that beast lies slain forevermore. That, and no less, is my current purpose. And hers."

"Aye," Agathokles said softly. His look was one of sympathy. "Countless of my forefathers have wished the same. Revenge... *justice*... was for them but a dream. Perhaps now..."

He did not finish, but merely looked at Thalassia. The look was not a hopeful one.

"There is support for both sides," the Naupaktan continued, "resistance and capitulation. The outcome of an eventual vote is uncertain. What might tip the balance is some proof that you two can deliver on your pledge of aid. The thinking is that Sparta cannot consider moving against us so long as Argos yet stands in defiance. Should Argos yield or fall, however, it becomes a near certainty that our assembly will vote swiftly in favor of surrender."

"Somehow, we will tip the scale," Demosthenes said. "Naupaktos will fight and keep her well-earned freedom."

"I pray so, friend." Agathokles' smile lacked its former cheer, but surely not because he knew that his friend's pledge was an empty one. "In the meantime, by nightfall, I shall have a suitable bed ready for my two honored guests to share." He laid a hand gently on Demosthenes' arm and said somberly, "Such tragedy, this shameless murder of your wife." He tilted his head at Thalassia. "Thank the gods you have this one to ease the loss."

PART 2

RETURN TO ATHENS

1. Homecoming

36 days after the fall of Athens (June 423 BCE)

At Gytheio, the port of Sparta, some five hundred Equals and as many Helots walked the gangplanks down from lumbering troop ships to set foot for the first time in months on Peloponnesian soil. Since the port lay some twenty miles from Sparta herself, a considerable march yet remained before most of the travelers truly saw home.

Home. The place, the idea, had never held much allure to Styphon. It was thus for most every Equal, for whom campaigns were an opportunity to escape the tedium of a strictly regimented existence of constant drilling. Home was a patriotic ideal, a place in the heart, more than it was a country filled with friends and family, as it was to Athenians, Argives, and the rest. For the part-time armies of other cities, the departure to an uncertain fate in war abroad was a dark and ominous thing, while a return home in victory was joyous. To Spartiates, the opposite was true. There would be no triumphal parades, no flowing wine, for those Equals who had returned from war with their lives, only an absence of the shame which would have accompanied defeat. For that reason, the river of men that now overflowed the winding road from Gytheio to Sparta for the better part of a day flowed somberly.

Sparta was not even a city at all, by the standards of many men, but rather a union of five neighboring villages which, as a matter of pride, lacked defensive walls of any sort. There was therefore no single moment of return marked by a pair of massive gates like the ones Styphon had helped to batter down at Athens. Houses, each on an equal plot owned by one male citizen, simply began to appear on the roadside where before there had been none, at which point women, children, Helots, the old, and those younger men unfortunate enough to have remained at home emerged onto the twilit roadside to witness the homecoming.

The only voices raised in joy or otherwise were those of children who knew not that the sight of an army returning from battle was no more a thing to be celebrated than if the men had been farmers trudging back from a day's labor in the fields. For where other men made their living in the latter way, and bore arms only on command, war was a Spartiate's livelihood.

The first Spartan village on the route of return was Kynosoura, where the column began to shrink as men who made their homes there broke away to rejoin their families for muted public displays of affection that were sure to grow more intense in the privacy of their simple homes. Styphon saw the reunions in the corners of his vision but paid them no particular heed as he continued his own march. Shortly, the houses of Kynosoura thinned out and vanished, and after a short stretch of desolate scrub, Sparta's acropolis broke the horizon. It was modest compared to that of Athens, which seemed to sprout marble columns as a swamp did reeds, but the difference was only fitting: where Athenians, and a majority of Greeks with them, placed value in pomp and wealth and display, Sparta favored simplicity in all of life's aspects.

Styphon's house, in the village of Mesoa at the foot of the acropolis, was like most, a single-room dwelling of unpainted wood, topped by a sloped roof of reeds. He came upon it as night fell. His feet and back ached, though he would not dream of letting it show in his gait as he walked the straight dirt path to its door.

To one side of that door there stood the slight figure of a female. Not his daughter, he knew right away. The month since Styphon had last seen Andrea was a short spell compared to the usual stretches of half a year or more, and so her form was fresh in his mind. No, the female by his door was the other whom he had shipped here from Athens twenty or so days prior, alongside Andrea. She was Eurydike, the Thracian slave of Demosthenes, captured by Brasidas and given into Styphon's keeping on the polemarch's whim.

Eurydike's tattooed arms were bound behind her back, and the thin iron collar which permanently encircled her neck was at present tethered by a cord to the roof's eave. Whoever had put her there certainly intended the rope to have been stretched taut, forcing the slave to stand on tiptoe to prevent hanging; instead, Eurydike's bare feet were flat on a rounded stone tall enough to let her stand in relative comfort.

As Styphon drew up in front of her, the slave turned her head aside with lips drawn tight in an angry, prideful frown.

"Who put you here?" Styphon demanded.

Defiantly, she refused to look at him.

"I am not a master who looks for any excuse to beat a slave," Styphon said. "But do not test me."

It was harsh, yes, but expected of him, and besides, Eurydike was new to his household. Who knew how well the soft-bellied Athenians did at breaking in their servants.

"A neighbor saw her spill water at the well."

The familiar yet unfamiliar voice that turned Styphon's head came from behind the woodpile on one side of his house. The speaker, Andrea, stepped out of the shadows there. The eleven-year old's long brown hair was tied back, and the black eyes she shared with her father caught the first twinkling starlight. She had been hiding, watching him since he came into sight.

"He was right to punish her," Styphon lectured. Like all goods in Sparta, slaves were communal property, and every citizen therefore had the right to discipline one. "How long has she been thus?"

"Six hours," Andrea answered with a vague note of disapproval. "He said he would return to let her down. I'm sure he's forgotten."

Styphon growled. Such domestic nuisances as this one to which he had returned were perhaps part of the reason Equals were forever eager to set off on another campaign.

Fortunate, then, that wars never seemed to be in short supply.

"Did you put the rock under her?"

Far from assuming the cowed demeanor of a child caught in transgression, Andrea held her head high and narrow shoulders back to answer without shame: "Yes."

"Then you should be punished, too." It was another lecture, not a threat. "How will this one learn her lesson if you interfere?"

Willful Andrea held her ground. "She was my friend in Athens, and remains so here."

Styphon stepped closer to his daughter, looming over her. She did not retreat but only stared up.

He scoffed. "Seems that preener Alkibiades and the rest failed to make an Athenian out of you," he said. "You are a Spartan girl. Now get her down and come inside."

"I'm not tall enough."

"Then be resourceful enough."

Passing strung-up Eurydike like the object that she was under city law, Styphon entered his house. The hearth burned gently in one corner, and the simple floor of planks was clean, the earthenware neatly stowed. The hard pallet on which he slept when not on campaign was made up with its single blanket and pillow of straw. The two smaller, softer beds by the wall opposite had not been there on Styphon's last visit.

Then, Andrea had been in Athens, kidnapped and taken there. Prior to that, she had dwelt in the home of her dead mother's now-dead sister.

Thalassia was responsible for the kidnapping, and the death, but Styphon could hardly bear a grudge. He bore partial guilt himself, having asked the witch to protect Andrea, back when his daughter seemed destined for the miserable future that awaited any Spartan child whose father was marked as a coward. It would have been a decent choice, had his fortunes not turned.

Styphon set down his pack, removed his cloak and lowered himself to the floor by the crackling hearth. He rested his head in one hand and nearly began to nod off. He would have, had not Andrea entered, alone.

"Where is your *friend*?" He teased, rather than mocked.

"She will come in when her tears run dry."

Andrea seated herself cross-legged on Styphon's pallet. The short skirt of her chiton barely covered her. Athens had not infected her with modesty. Neither had it changed her speech, which was proper country Doric.

"Are you two living here alone?"

"Yes."

Another domestic nuisance. He had sent instructions to Andrea's mother's cousins to have them looked after. He told Andrea as much.

"Lost, I guess," the girl said dismissively. Then, "Eurydike is eager for news of Demosthenes. And Thalassia. And Alkibiades."

"The first two she can request of me herself," Styphon said. "As for the third, are you sure it is *she* who wishes to know?"

Once more Andrea, when caught, made no excuses. "He might be your enemy, but Uncle Alki was good to me. He never tried to make me Athenian. He taught me our laws and the life of Lykurgos. His wet nurse was Lakonian."

Styphon suppressed a fresh growl. "Be that as it may, I do not wish to hear him referred to as *uncle* under my roof. Understood?"

Now Andrea looked more like a child ought to when scolded. "Yes."

"Yes, *father*," Styphon corrected.

"Father," she added blankly.

In a silence filled by no more than the crackle of flames, Styphon considered deceiving his daughter, telling her that Alkibiades was imprisoned in Athens or some such. Not dead, for that would cause her needless grief. But the chance she might learn the truth from other sources was too great, even were she not half as clever as she truly was.

And so, sighing, he surrendered the truth: "Alkibiades is here in Sparta, a prisoner. He recovers from a wound."

To her credit, Andrea's reaction was suitably Laconic, showing neither joy at the good news nor grief at the bad. She asked with apparent disinterest, "Will he be tried?"

"That's up to the Gerousia," Styphon said. More likely up to Brasidas and Eris, he did not add, even if rightfully the decision did rest with the elders.

Andrea nodded, grateful acknowledgment of a favor rather than approval of the statement. Styphon met the opaque eyes that were so much like his, and he marveled at what went on behind them. He had scant experience of eleven-year-old girls, but surely this one was wise beyond that age. She had always been to some degree, but he noticed it more now that she was his responsibility and not some little creature hiding behind the skirts of female relations.

"Put away what's in my bag," Styphon said to her. "And I'll tell you what the *slave* wants to know."

His emphasis on Eurydike's proper role in his household was deliberate. No good could ever come of a citizen befriending a slave.

Andrea rose to accept the bargain, and while she knelt and opened his pack, Styphon fulfilled his end.

"Eris slew Thalassia, then Eris herself was slain," he reported. "But they are immortals, or something like it. My own eyes have since seen Eris walking again, and I am all but certain the other does, too. As for Demosthenes, he escaped from Dekelea and is at large. Presumably he is with Thalassia."

Placing Styphon's threadbare bedroll in a bin for laundering, Andrea froze and said mournfully, "Brasidas should not have killed the wife of Demosthenes."

Eurydike had witnessed the woman's death and nearly shared her fate. Doubtless the slave had already spoken of that event to her 'friend.'

"She had his baby in her," Andrea went on, returning to Styphon's pack. "It was not an honorable act. It was murder. He is unclean."

"That is no matter for a young girl to be concerned with."

There was acquiescence in Andrea's nod as she next pulled from his pack an item he had bought in the agora of Athens with an obol coin found underfoot in the street: a short length of red silken ribbon. She raised it between thumb and forefinger.

"What's this for?"

"You're cleverer than that."

"For me?"

"Unless you think it would suit me better."

Andrea draped the frivolous adornment across two open palms for examination.

"No doubt your *uncle* provided you with better," Styphon said, suddenly embarrassed by the feeble gift.

"I always dressed as a Spartan," Andrea snapped, then added by way of apology, "...*father*. His house was full of silk and gold, and I could have indulged, but I did not."

Grunting his approval, Styphon removed his sandals, crawled onto his hard pallet and stretched out upon it to welcome sleep.

Andrea looked thoughtfully at the ribbon. "If I wore this, I would get a beating from the other girls."

"Then I suppose you must not let them see you," Styphon replied absently. His lids were heavy, but he kept them aloft just long enough to see Andrea tie the ribbon into her hair.

"No," she said. "I want them to try."

2. Gerousia

Leaving morning mess on the third day after his return, Styphon heard his name called and turned to find that the caller was no less than a king.

Halting, Styphon waited patiently for Agis to catch him.

"You are wanted before the Gerousia," the king declared.

Such a summons was rarely occasion for the smile with which Agis delivered it. The disparity gave Styphon pause.

Agis clapped him on the shoulder. "I know. Since when do the old men send a king as their page? I volunteered for the task. Come!"

Together they walked the arrow-straight, stone-paved Hyakinthian Way, through crowds of thronging Spartiates emerging from mess. All parted readily for Agis.

"You shall meet my cousin today," the king said en route. "Two days since your homecoming, and she tells me you have yet to call on her. Hippolyta is not one whom a man should keep waiting."

"Apologies, sire."

"Be sure you do not apologize to her," Agis scolded. "If I know her, and I do, the silence has only made her wetter."

Styphon gave the king a half-hearted smile which faded at first opportunity. Hippolyta, who was no mere woman but a cousin to the Eurypontid king, would be Styphon's second unplanned encounter of the day, after the Gerousia. And the day had scarcely begun.

He was not sure which appointment caused him the greater concern. He had begun to picture Hippolyta as an ill-tempered dog-face. Agis swore to her beauty, but then he was her blood.

The crowd thinned, and conversation became easier as

they left the Hyakinthian way and found the well-pounded dirt path to the agora, where sat the meeting hall of Sparta's administrators, the ephors.

"There is a matter you might help me with, sire," Styphon ventured en route.

"Name it," Agis said with enthusiasm. "And stop calling me *sire*. Zeus willing, we might be family in a month."

"Zeus willing," Styphon echoed faintly.

Knowing that it could only increase the pressure on him for a successful match, he stamped down pride and doubt to pose his favor.

"My daughter, Andrea, excels in her learning," he said, "so much so that her teachers dissatisfy her. Yet they will not allow her to study with the older girls. I am loath to ask, but for her sake—"

"Say no more." Agis raised a hand adorned with its plain iron ring of kingship. "I shall find her a private tutor myself if need be. She studied in Athens, did she not? I should hate to see her run back there at first opportunity claiming that we stifled her intellect. Our system works, but allowances must be made from time to time."

"Thank you, si—" Styphon began, and corrected, "Agis."

A pity the gods could not hear silent prayers, or Styphon would have sent them one just then that at least one or the other of Hippolyta's face and personality proved not to be completely objectionable.

* * *

The administrative building in which the elders of the Gerousia convened was, like all the structures of Sparta, a plain thing. The laws laid down long ago by Lykurgos forbade grand, columned halls of government full of gilded statues that might distract those within from the vital business of running a state. The ephors might not have met behind walls at all, but beneath the open sky as did the citizen assembly, the Apella, which elected them, except that the Apella gathered out in the country. Here in the bustle of the agora, walls were a necessary evil.

Well, that and the fact that the governance of Sparta was perhaps not always as transparent as the Lawgiver intended.

They reached the whitewashed box at the agora's edge, with a single door and small, high windows set, likely not by coincidence, well above the height of prying eyes. The unarmed Spartiate at the door, more gatekeeper than guard, waved them inside.

Arranged in a single row on a slightly elevated platform at one end of the single chamber were the current crop of twenty-eight men of the Gerousia, all past the age of sixty and serving until death. With the power to overturn the decisions of kings, it was effectively the highest law-court of Sparta. In the current contest for power underway between the reform-minded supporters of Brasidas and the traditionalists, the Gerousia was strongly on the side of Agis and tradition, but a shift was not out of the question. In the past year, two elders had died of natural causes and been replaced by men who showed signs of favoring Brasidas.

Brasidas already had on his side an arguably more important ally in the form of three of the current year's five ephors, the annually elected magistrates who reigned supreme in the affairs of the Spartan state. Since they reached decisions by majority vote, the favor of three was as good as that of all five. It was those three votes (or one vote, it might be said) which had stripped command of the attack on Athens from Agis and placed in Brasidas's hands.

As one of Sparta's two kings, Agis was counted a member of the Gerousia regardless of his age, and so after arriving in the hall with Styphon, he went to take his rightful place on the platform.

Sparta's second king, the bland and unpopular Pleistoanax, was present, too. He stood as far apart from Spartan public life in spirit as he stood physically now from the body of elders. His father had been a disgraced traitor, and Pleistonanax himself had been convicted and sent into exile twenty years earlier for accepting Athenian bribes. But the Gerousia, on the insistence of a vaguely worded Delphic oracle, ever wary of inviting the gods' wrath in the form of an earthquake or a Helot revolt, had lately reversed the exile. Since then, Pleistonanax had been a king in name but in practice a pariah, arguing for peace with Athens now and then, lest Sparta suffer a defeat and decide to blame it on him.

Since Sparta was not that big a place, Styphon also recognized nearly all of the other men packed into the room, conversing in clusters. Most were from prominent families, since it naturally was such men, here as in other cities (democracy or not) who dominated affairs. In those other cities, such men would possess wealth and be called aristocrats. Here, they were just men to whom others chose to yield out of respect—until some relative disgraced his family name and another rose to replace him. Although one Equal was not supposed to be more equal than the next, the reality was different.

Several of these men, strangely, nodded to Styphon and greeted him by name, almost as though he were one of them.

Absent from the hall's audience of fifty or so men were Sparta's five most powerful and prominent, the ephors themselves. Technically, the five magistrates presided over all gatherings of the Gerousia, but in practice they only made an appearance when the matters under discussion were particularly momentous. Evidently, this day's meeting did not qualify.

The man who had the favor of three of the sitting ephors, Brasidas, who once had been an ephor himself, was present. Styphon had not seen Brasidas since their return from Athens, but now the polemarch treated him to a raised hand and welcoming look from across the room.

The chairman thumped a ceremonial staff on the wood to bring the room to silence, a prayer to Zeus was invoked, and the gathering commenced. Matters that were perhaps important, perhaps not, were raised, discussed, and finally dismissed, referred to the assembly or the ephors, or otherwise deemed worthy of action. Even if he grasped the necessity of such proceedings to the healthy function of the Spartan state, Styphon could hardly help but allow his ears to fall halfway shut. If the higher-born for some reason wished to claim that their birthright included having some additional meetings to themselves, that seemed just fine.

Styphon's ears opened again at the sound of the word, *"Lastly..."* It was spoken by the elder who kept charge of the agenda, and Styphon gave the man his focus.

"A commendation is to be handed down this day," the old man said, "to an Equal who distinguished himself in battle."

Hearing no more than that, Styphon flushed with the realization of why he had been summoned today.

"Styphon, son of Pharax, in battle against the last Athenian holdouts at Dekelea, took it on his own initiative to shift the ranks of his *enomotos* to ensure that his best men, and not ones as old as I, received an enemy cavalry charge. Five of those best men were fortunate enough to give their young lives in stopping the charge cold, and it is thanks to their sacrifice that the enemy's hipparch now sits in a cell just yards from this place.

"Outsiders are fond of saying we have a system which

rewards only obedience, but we know this is not so. Sparta prizes quick thinking and the taking of risks, too, and these qualities are what Styphon displayed at Dekelea. For that, following the recommendation of Agis, who held command that day, Styphon hereby receives official commendation on behalf of the Gerousia of Lakedaimon, along with the thanks of all Sparta."

The few eyes which had not already turned upon Styphon did so. Styphon did not acknowledge the attention, did not smile or speak words of gratitude, and no round of applause filled the small chamber. Nor would there be any tangible reward apart from this brief recognition. The white-bearded elder lowered his hand, and Styphon's moment in the sun reached its end.

Shame in Sparta lasted a lifetime, glory but an instant.

But the elder was not done: "However much we value quick thinking," he went on, "the fact does remain that Styphon acted without orders, an offense punishable according to its severity and the history of the offender. The sanction decided upon by this body is a fine of ten *medimni* of barley per month, for six months, over and above his normal contribution to the mess. I have no doubt that as an Equal in good standing, he shall make the payment with pride."

The staff thumped wood, a clerk at a writing desk in one corner entered a final note on parchment, and the meeting was adjourned. As all began to stand and file out into the midmorning sun, Styphon found himself the recipient of not a few subdued words of congratulation. Just outside the door he found Brasidas, who managed to seem as though he had not been waiting for him.

"Well earned, Styphon," the polemarch said, and appeared to mean it. He smiled his thin smile. "The award, if not the fine. I consider you to be my protege, and I could not be prouder if I had received another commendation myself today."

Brasidas, of course, had been the recipient of countless honors throughout his adulthood, and would receive yet more for his victory against Athens. Those would come from the ephorate, however, not the Gerousia which, if Agis was correct, had expected Brasidas to fail. Some elders might even have *hoped* thus, but to ever admit such a thing would be highest treason.

Moments after Brasidas made his leave, Agis found Styphon and aimed a look of distaste at the departing polemarch's back.

"The fine came as news to me," the king said. "I just now finished arguing to have it overturned, but no luck. I will pay it for you, if need be."

"It is my honor to contribute," Styphon said, and it was. At worst, it did not matter much.

"You only say that because you have no wife to feed," Agis returned with a grin. "Speaking of which, if you are quite done having your head swollen, let us go see if my cousin doesn't swell your cock!"

3. Hippolyta

Hippolyta dwelt in the home of her mother, Agis's sister, in the village of Limnae, but it was not there that the two men called upon her. Instead, Agis led Styphon east into the woods through which flowed the River Eurotas, on small trails that the king seemed to know well.

"Sire," Styphon addressed Agis humbly as they walked. "I mean, Agis..."

He wished another favor of sorts from his king, this one for himself rather than Andrea. He might have thought twice of asking were it not a simple favor which he was almost duty-bound as a well-bred Spartiate to ask.

"It is open knowledge that an army will march in the coming days to recapture Pylos," Styphon said. "I hear that it is you who is to lead it." He added, transparently, "As is your right."

Agis glanced back over his shoulder, as one in no doubt of what words would come next, and he prompted, "Yes?"

"I only wish to express my hope that my unit will have the honor of accompanying you."

The king's snort said he was unsurprised. "You know there is not a man in the city who does not share the same hope. If there are any who do not, they daren't admit it."

"Aye," Styphon said, sounding suitably chastised.

"Your request is noted," Agis said formally, pushing aside a shoulder-level branch across the trail. "And it will be given favorable consideration. Now, silence from here on. We come upon her."

Hope renewed where he had counted it lost, Styphon was glad to obey.

They heard evidence of Hippolyta's presence well before they saw her, as through the sparse wood came a strange, high pitched sound, part grunt, part war cry. Seconds later, it was followed by a sharp, resounding crack, like the fall of a woodsman's ax on timber.

"She gathers firewood?" Styphon guessed.

Agis only chuckled, and his laugh was punctuated by another iteration of the same *groan-thump*. As they continued along the trail, they heard the sound twice more, nearer each time, before Agis halted, ducked low to the ground and put out a hand with two fingers raised in the signal for stealth, which Styphon heeded. The sounds came again, their origin now identifiable as a space just ahead, past a green thicket. The two men hunkered down, Styphon confused and Agis smiling knowingly even as he reached out with one hand, grabbed a leafy branch, and gave it a shake.

"Who's there?" a female voice demanded sharply. "Show yourself like a man or die like a pig."

Styphon could not but look to Agis for guidance, and thus he followed the king's lead in rising from his concealing crouch with open palms upraised.

"No need to stick us two pigs, cousin!" Agis said. "You are in no danger!"

In the clearing stood two women clad in the plain long dresses of citizen women, with slits to mid-thigh on either side so as not to restrict their freedom of movement. Both were armed with javelins; one brandished hers almost like a sword, showing she could not have been serious about running the intruders through, while the other crouched with a whole sheaf of the missiles slung over her shoulder. It appeared that this latter had been collecting the shafts from the vicinity of a birch which, judging by the state of its trunk, had seen much service as a target.

Styphon knew which of the two he hoped was Hippolyta. The one holding the sheaf was thick of jaw with a plain face and too-narrow hips, while the other, the woman aiming the iron-tipped shaft at Agis as though it were a blade, was fairer by far. Her black hair tumbled from a central part in free, natural curls—the only kind of curls found on Spartiate women—framing a tanned face which in spite of its smooth lines had just a touch of the masculine about it. Her plump lips were all woman, though, and of the kind that could give a man ideas even when they were, as now, twisted in a sneer of exaggerated contempt. Sharp shadows lined the contours of her biceps as she snapped the javelin to vertical and swung it round to rest it across her shoulders behind a strong but graceful neck. Agis had just called this particular woman *cousin*, but then he undoubtedly had more than one of those.

Styphon's uncertainty ended when Agis strode up to this woman, laid an affectionate hand on her cheek and said warmly, "Hippolyta."

Hippolyta responded by swinging the javelin from her shoulder in a telegraphed arc that forced Agis back several steps. When the stroke was complete, her eyes found Styphon's. "This is him?"

"It is," Agis answered. "I hope you have not already repelled him."

"He's got to be braver than that." She inclined her chin at Styphon. "Have I put you off, Styphon?"

Styphon considered his reply, settling on, "Not yet."

Hippolyta aimed a smile at him. To his own surprise, that victory inspired in him his greatest sense of achievement thus far on a morning in which he had been singled out for honor before kings and elders.

Agis gave Styphon a wink of encouragement. "He may yet be the one who breaks you, *theria*," he said to his cousin. He waved Styphon closer and put an arm around him. "Hippolyta has thrown off all her other would-be riders.

130

Lately she has devised a test which I am sure you will have the indignity of facing. She expects you to beat her in a contest with this so-called *weapon*."

The insult prompted her to brandish the 'weapon' again at Agis. Smiling, the king disengaged from Styphon's side.

"Now that introductions are complete," he said, "nature must be allowed to have its way with you. Perhaps your companion will allow me to escort her home."

That was just what happened; Agis left with the plain girl, leaving Styphon alone in the clearing in the company of the prospective bride to whom he had yet to speak more than two words.

With the removal of Agis's powerful presence, Hippolyta seemed almost to shrink, her manner becoming instantly less confrontational. She threw Styphon fleeting glances, every third one or so of which found his eyes and caused her to smirk. This went on for some time before she laughed.

"How long do I have to stand here acting like a girl before you say something?"

The question was not laced with scorn, as it might easily have been. It was playful, meant only to defuse the tension before it built to breaking.

"Not much longer." It was the first answer which came to Styphon's mind.

That mind was serving him well today, it seemed, for Hippolyta said amiably, "Just let me know when you are ready." Her thumb picked at an imperfection on the smooth ash shaft of her javelin.

"Am I really to beat you with that thing?" Styphon asked.

She raised a brow. "You are to try," she said. "But only if you're interested in courting me. You may wish get to know me first."

"At which point, if I were to fail in the contest, we would have wasted a great deal more time. Not to mention that one or both of us might be disappointed. Better to get it over with."

Styphon put out his open right hand, and with a pleased smile, Hippolyta set the javelin into it. He tested its weight, shifting his grip along the length of the shaft, searching to restore some connection with a weapon he had not picked up since childhood.

"That trunk?" he asked, indicating the already splintered birch, which at its widest point was scarcely the breadth of a man's hand with fingers fully outstretched.

"That's the one."

Judging by its current state, the target posed little challenge to Hippolyta, and perhaps her friend. Concentrating intently, Styphon raised the javelin to his ear, adjusted once, again, and then once more. Finally, he put one foot forward in the bed of dry needles and poised for the throw. After a deep breath in which he endeavored, and failed, to clear his mind of all thought and forget his audience, he drew back and released. Shaft spinning, the iron-tipped javelin sailed up into a shallow arc on course for the mark.

Styphon knew it, and doubtless Hippolyta did, too, well before the javelin's tip began to fly off true, that the shot would not land well. The loud crack that sounded on impact was that of wood-on-wood as shaft struck bark, iron head biting only air, and then the leaves of the forest floor.

Avoiding his audience's gaze, Styphon cursed and set himself to receive some manner of rebuke, whether gentle or mocking. But Hippolyta said nothing. She merely continued staring in the direction of the missed target while chewing the inside of her smooth cheek.

"There are some obscure rules in this contest," she said at length. "One of them applies to men who have just earned commendations."

Styphon looked at her in puzzlement. "How do you know of that?"

Hippolyta made a little face that gave the answer and made Styphon feel the fool for asking. Agis had told her, of course.

"The rule allows you to call in a substitute to throw for you," she went on. "And it need not be a man."

Her meaning could not have been clearer: this courtship was not to be a battle at all, at the end of which one party would wind up broken. She wished for him to succeed.

"It hardly seems fair, but if that is the rule..." Styphon said, "then I exercise my privilege and call Hippolyta."

"An excellent choice," she said with every appearance of seriousness. "I hear she is the best."

Hippolyta fetched a new shaft from among several leaning against a nearby tree, and she poised herself for the throw. The tanned, athletic body which was a thing of beauty while standing still was only more breathtaking to behold in motion. From somewhere within that graceful form came the shrieking grunt he had heard earlier, and the javelin flew, but Styphon's eyes did not follow it. They stayed fixed on her body so that he did not even see, but only heard, the iron tip strike home, gouging a fresh wound into the tree's well chipped skin.

She turned, caught him staring, and met the attention with a smile of satisfaction. "Shall we take a walk?"

* * *

They took their walk by the Eurotas, and then the next day took another walk, and the next another. Before the third was done, Hippolyta's arm had quietly wound itself around

Styphon's, and their conversations strayed into ever more intimate territory.

"As a girl, I caught the eye of an ephor's wife," Hippolyta revealed. "She took me as a lover for a few years. Her husband was none too happy, but what business of it of his what his wife got up to while he was too busy for her? He came and complained to my father, but my father, bless his buried heart, sent him packing."

Styphon did not have much to say in answer to that. It was an open secret that Spartiate women got up to such activities while their men were away on campaign, which was often. That certainly did not qualify as a flaw in her. In fact, the more he came to know Hippolyta and find no flaws, the more he wondered whether he was not missing something.

"How is it you have not already wed?" he asked.

"I am only twenty-four," she complained. "We're not Athenians, you know, marrying girls off before they even have hair on their holes."

"What I mean is—"

Seizing on the chance to torment him, Hippolyta pressed, smiling, "Yes, what *do* you mean?"

Styphon returned a good-natured growl. "You know."

"Hmmph," Hippolyta snorted. "I think I do. You want to know what's wrong with me. The answer, at least the one I'll admit to, is that I cannot stand the idea of marrying some under-thirty who still lives in the barracks and only comes home to stick his cock in me now and then."

Styphon nodded silent understanding.

"Is that how it was with your wife?" Hippolyta asked, without preface or apology. Now it was Styphon's turn, evidently, to share intimate details.

"Yes," he confessed. He had known and loved Andrea's mother, but not nearly so well as he might have had she lived past his thirtieth birthday, upon which he would have been permitted to dwell in his own home with her.

Hippolyta rubbed his arm in a brief offer of sympathy and let the subject pass.

They had walked the same course through the wood each day. This day, near the end of that course, Hippolyta disengaged her arm from Styphon's, ran toward the river and stood with her back against a tree, facing out across the splashing current. Naturally, Styphon followed. When he came round, Hippolyta declined to look at him, but only stood with her arms at her sides. She licked her shapely upper lip, bit the fat lower, pursed them, pressed them together—doing anything with her mouth but let it be still, while her eyes likewise lighted everywhere but his face.

Her intention was not hard to ascertain, yet Styphon held back several beats, until he became certain. Once he was, he acted.

Inserting himself between her body and the river, he pressed up close to Hippolyta, set his palms on the bark of the tree at her back, trapping her. He lowered his head until her upturned nose nearly met his twice-broken one. Her eyes finally found his, and the excitement he saw in them erased all doubt as to her desire.

That spurred him on. He kissed her, delicately at first, and then with the force and vigor that her eager response seemed to demand. Living up the affectionate nickname by which her cousin had called her, *theria—wild girl*—she seemed to wish to devour him.

Suddenly, her lips slammed shut. She twisted her head, breaking off the kiss. Her hand came up and slapped his cheek, not hard, but enough to sting. Stunned, Styphon froze, only to find his face struck again, and again, and again.

"What—" he began, but was cut short by another slap.

Then a sixth, and still without explanation.

The seventh landed, but on the eighth he caught Hippolyta's wrist.

"Why?" he demanded angrily. He could not have misread such signals as she had given.

The playful smirk which appeared on her face caused his annoyance to melt. "Why?" he demanded again, now likewise smiling.

"Ask your daughter when you get home."

The question thus dodged, Hippolyta yanked him into her to resume the kiss as though there had been no interruption. She panted like a beast, and her throat hummed moans of pleasure which after some minutes of passion became words.

"Lower," she breathed over the gentle rush of the Eurotas. "Lower, kiss me lower. I'll return the favor."

There was no cause for refusal, and less for delay. Sinking to his knees as she hoisted the skirt of her long chiton for him, Styphon tongued the folds of her womanhood. Her hand found the crown of his head and clutched a handful of his long hair and used it to guide him. After some minutes, his effort paid off: Hippolyta's hard thighs tensed and she bucked and spasmed and cried out much like she had when throwing the javelin. Finally the tension left her and she slid down the tree trunk, took his face, slick with her sex, between her hands and briefly resumed their kiss before shoving him back onto the tree's thick roots, where with ample skill she lived up to her promise of fair exchange.

4. Uninvited

With unsanctioned reluctance, Styphon parted with Hippolyta to return to his mess for the midday meal, after which he made his way home to Mesoa and pushed open the door to his simple home.

He froze in the doorway when too many eyes met his in cold greeting. Four too many: two male and two female, even if neither of their owners met the strictest Spartan definitions of the words 'man' or 'woman.'

"What are you doing here?" Styphon asked. He hoped that neither his rage, nor the fear which checked it, entered his voice.

Ghostly Eris rose from where she sat alongside Andrea on the floor. A smile curled her bloodless lips, long flaxen locks trailing down over the breast of her simple Spartan dress.

"Apologies for not seeking your permission, Styphon," she said. There was no apology in her icy tone. "You were unavailable."

"Answer the question," Styphon said firmly. He sent a stone-faced look around the room, stopping at each of the other three present. First his daughter, who met it sheepishly, with guilt in her black eyes. Next Eurydike, who was defiant, daring her master to remove her from the lap on which she sat, the lap of the second unwelcome guest and final recipient of Styphon's glare: Alkibiades.

The Athenian smiled pleasantly back. Dressed in fresh clothing, face neatly shaven and clean hair tumbling around his ears in sweeping curls, he looked far better than he had when Styphon last saw him.

Eris went on in the accent of whatever part of Hades had spawned her: "Alkibiades expressed a desire to visit your slave and your daughter, and his behavior warranted the reward."

She spoke as one who felt no need ever to explain herself, Styphon thought, but who did so now and then out of imagined magnanimity.

"Andrea tells me she is unsatisfied with the course of her learning," Eris continued. "I have agreed to become her tutor."

"That will not be necessary," Styphon said hurriedly. "I have arranged for her needs."

Eris stepped forward and placed a palm lightly on his chest. "You are a good father." Styphon's ears imparted menace even to those flattering words. "So you know you must do what is best for Andrea. Having been student to my inferior in Athens, she knows what I can offer. Do you not want great things to lie in her future?"

Styphon fumed, but looking into the deep blue eyes of Eris he recalled his first, bloody meeting with her in Arkadia and knew the futility of opposition. There was no doubt that this was just the intended result of her hard look, the look of an eager killer. Eris delivered it with ease, and in such a way that it was invisible to all in the room but its recipient.

So instead of protesting further, Styphon nodded assent to the she-daimon's tutelage of his offspring. Equals were brave, but they did not throw their lives away in vain. In shame, he broke Eris's gaze.

Andrea rose next from the floor, came forward and slid her arms around Styphon's waist. He looked down upon a red ribbon binding the tight braid in which her brown hair was bound.

"Thank you, father," she said, and looked up at him with more happiness in her eyes than he ever remembered seeing there.

It was said that what made a child the happiest was rarely the best for him. Or her. And proximity to Eris was surely not the best for any child. But Eris could not simply be denied. Were he to try to keep Andrea from her, whatever the witch's designs were, there was little doubt he would ultimately wind up on the losing side, perhaps dead. At least this way, he might remain alive to attempt to counter her dark influence.

That matter resolved, at least for the present, Styphon turned his attention to Alkibiades and the Thracian slave whose arms were wound possessively about the preener's neck. Clean tracks in the grime on her cheeks attested to recent tears.

"I'm sorry to have barged into your home, Styphon." Unlike that of his warder, Alkibiades' apology actually sounded sincere. "These are my two favorite girls in the world. I could not pass up the chance to check on them."

Styphon's mind filled with harsh replies which he stifled in favor of a more measured response. Strong evidence suggested that Alkibiades was being courted to Sparta's side by order of Brasidas. Why anyone should deem such a thing necessary was beyond Styphon, but then plenty of other matters of state were also beyond him. It was not his place to sabotage such plans. Besides, perhaps there was a way he could use the Athenian to his advantage in controlling his household.

"My daughter cares for you," Styphon said. He was sure to make it clear in his voice that the admission came grudgingly. "The slave, too." He grunted a sigh. "So, as much as I loathe the sight of you," — that was rather an exaggeration — "as long as the girls' behavior justifies it, and you arrange it with me, you may continue to visit them."

The preener's eyes lit and he grinned, appearing

genuinely astonished. Eurydike ventured a tentative, disbelieving laugh. Her fist went tight in hope around a handful of the loose, pale blue chiton draped over Alkibiades' hairless chest.

"Well done." Eris looked at Styphon, and addressed him, as though he were some animal whose owner had trained him to speak on command. "An arrangement which benefits all involved," she observed, condescendingly.

She signaled to Alkibiades, who gave a servile nod. Reluctantly, with a final brief but intense kiss on his lips, Eurydike removed herself from his lap and let him rise. To reach Eris, the prisoner walked a circuitous course which took him past Andrea, whose hair he tousled before departing the house in Eris's ice-cold wake.

After the pair left, Styphon made no mention of the visit. He only reminded the two females of their chores and went about his afternoon. That night, when all were in their beds, Styphon, not a little self-consciously, posed a question of his daughter.

"Why might a woman invite a man to kiss her, only to slap his face?"

Andrea giggled softly. "Why would you want to know that?"

"I'm asking for a friend. If you know the answer, just tell me."

"Fine. It's a silly superstition that some girls have."

"Explain."

"If a woman slaps a man during their first kiss, the number of times he allows it before stopping her is—" She scoffed gently and finished, "It is the number of babies they'll have together."

Styphon stifled a sigh, lest he betray that his interest was more than casual. He just said curtly, "I see. Thank you."

"Were you kissing a twelve-year old?" Andrea asked. "Because no one else believes that stuff. I think she was just playing with you, whoever she is."

Styphon grumbled, "Go to sleep."

This offspring of his was too perceptive for anyone's good.

After a brief round of maddening giggling, Andrea fell silent, letting Styphon hope she was done. Moments later, her voice sailed again through the darkness.

"How many times?"

After some hesitation, Styphon gave up the charade and confessed, "I lost count."

"That many?" Andrea said. "It's going to get crowded in here."

"Go to sleep!"

5. Half-dead eyes

"Dee... Wake up! Dee! Demosthenes! Enough of this. Move."

Laying in his borrowed bed near the shipyards of Naupaktos, Demosthenes groaned and swatted the air in the direction of the insistent voice.

"This makes five days you've been drunk, Dee," Thalassia said. "No more."

"Go away!"

"We've got shit to do. This ends now. Get up."

A hand gripped his arm, and Demosthenes was dragged from the bed. He fell clumsily to the plaster floor, which tilted lazily under him like the deck of a galley under sail. Shifting to sit with back against the solid bedpost, he set bleary eyes on the face which had come to dominate his rather miserable existence.

"What's it matter?" he demanded. "You don't need my help to glow... grow your fungulus. When that's done, no more Sparta. And Demosthenes can..." With some difficulty, he linked his two thumbs in front of him and flapped his hands like the wings of a bird. "...go to the crows." He cawed twice, but the second caught in his throat and prompted a fit of coughing.

When it had run its course, Thalassia gripped his jaw in her strong, feminine fingers and said in a tone just as firm, "No, Dee. *We* have work to do. We will convince this town to resist, and help them succeed at it—which, if you recall,was your idea. We will go to Athens and do whatever we can. And we will try to find Eurydike, who trusts us and loves us. Is that understood?"

"You are such a bitch." Demosthenes shut his eyes as he spoke, so as not to witness her reaction to the words, although he knew he might well feel it.

"Oh, come on," was her mild reply. Rather than squeezing tighter, her hand slipped from his jaw. "You've seen me when I'm a bitch. This is not it. I'm *kind* now, remember? But what I'll be soon if you don't get sober is *gone*. I won't do this alone, and if you're just going to give up and die, I won't stay and watch."

"Go, then!" Demosthenes said. He dragged up his eyelids to meet the wintry stare he found was upon him. "Your work here is complete. You ruined me. You ruined my city. You ruined my world."

Thalassia quickly returned, "I want to help you reclaim all of those things."

"Your *help* is toxic!" He scoffed bitterly. "Fitting then, that the last thing I ask of you is to poison a city."

"If I leave, there will be no *fungulus*, you drunk idiot. You'll be on your own, and from where I stand, that doesn't look like a threat that anyone should take seriously, much less Sparta." She leaned close and laid a hand on a cheek which he had allowed yet again to become covered in a fuzz of growth. "You have one day, Dee. I'll be back tomorrow at this time. If you're drunk, or sleeping it off, you'll never see me again."

"I wish—" Demosthenes began acidly.

Thalassia touched a fingertip to his lips. "Don't," she said gently, "say anything you'll regret. We'll talk tomorrow."

Standing, she spun and silently departed the room, leaving Demosthenes to ponder the choice between drowning himself in a sea of dark wine or seeing his vengeance realized. There was only one answer, he knew, but it could not be made in earnest until after a few more hours spent in the bed onto which he presently hoisted his tired carcass.

Around midday, he stepped out into blinding daylight and walked the unpaved road down to the harborside ship-sheds where labor was underway to construct new defensive weapons of Thalassia's design. She was not present there when he arrived, but he had not come to seek her. Finding the craftsman in charge, he merely offered his assistance, and was given tools and a job to do.

He worked there all afternoon, sweat pouring from limb and brow, and he took a meal with the friendly Naupaktans, meeting their requests for tales of Athens' fall with polite insistence that he wished to feel as one of them for the day and put such things from mind.

Such was hardly possible, of course, for the memories were everpresent, but the men honored his wishes and let him be silent. It was that evening that Thalassia, the architect of their endeavors, returned to inspect and further guide their work. She paid Demosthenes no special heed, apart from a brief look conveying her cautious approval.

The look which Demosthenes returned conveyed, or perhaps failed to, that he did not give a fuck about her approval... or wished he did not have to.

That night he returned to the same bed where he had previously slept off vats of wine and instead slept off a half-day's work. The bed was sized for two, on Agathokles' assumption that they were accustomed to sharing one, but Thalassia had not been spending her nights with him—he did not know where she went. This night was no different; he slept alone and woke alone, and he had just washed and dressed when she made her promised return.

"Good," she said on seeing him. "Come with me."

"Where?"

"Just come. Trust me."

Sighing, Demosthenes made for the door. "There are none on earth I trust more. It is my special madness."

Thalassia smiled and took his hand as they exited into the street, where she tugged him along with purpose. At some point in their residence here in Naupaktos, she had obtained a long, pleated chiton of her favored color, the green of sea-foam, and it was this which she wore. Though they were strangers in this place of exile, passersby gave them not a second glance except perhaps for men committing Thalassia's form to memory for later recall.

He had acted as a child, and now here he was being treated like one, drawn by the hand to some unknown destination. It was only after some time had passed that it occurred to him to reclaim his hand. When he jerked it free, Thalassia gave a backward glance as if to be sure he was not attempting escape, and then returned her gaze forward.

Heading west with the morning sun at their backs, they walked until the buildings of the waterfront gave way to empty fields of tall grass and wildflowers, and still they kept on going.

"It was on a whim that I pledged our aid to Naupaktos," he said as they walked. "Your aid. But why do you care whether some little shit town ends up paying tribute to Sparta?"

"Pride," was Thalassia's swift answer. "I'm sick of losing. And there are probably other reasons."

"Probably?"

"I admit," she said, "I sometimes act without thinking very far ahead. It's one of my very few flaws."

"Astonishing."

"That I have flaws? I know."

"That you would admit to having one."

"Humility is just one of many qualities that makes me near-perfect."

Demosthenes scoffed lightly and pondered whether to let the conversation end. As was often the case in her presence, he concluded that silence was likely the best course before proceeding to speak.

"You needn't pretend arrogance with me," he said. "In truth you despise yourself, a trait which we now both possess."

Thalassia halted, causing Demosthenes to do likewise, and she turned on him first with a look of irritation, then melancholy. "I'm not ready for a suicide pact just yet."

She resumed walking on a path which gently inclined and followed the Gulf coast.

"And if you believe your pledge of aid to Naupaktos was a whim," Thalassia said next, "you're only fooling yourself. That was the old Demosthenes showing through. The one I knew before I died. I miss him. So maybe that's another reason why I give I shit about this town."

On this, Demosthenes belatedly clamped his lips shut, and so had no need of the admonition Thalassia next delivered:

"Let's not speak until we get where we're going. You'll ruin the surprise."

He stayed quiet as long as he could, which was about a dozen paces, before letting out an observation which could not go unspoken: "I don't like your surprises."

After that, they walked in silence, always uphill and away from human habitation, along the rocky coast. Sunlight warmed skin which was swiftly thereafter cooled by gusts of sea wind.

Eventually, Thalassia slowed and halted and announced, "We're here."

They stood in tall grass near the land's edge. All that lay ahead was a sheer drop of at least sixty feet into foaming waves.

"A dead end." Demosthenes observed. "Why does that strike me as appropriate?" It was with some annoyance, but also rising trepidation, that he asked, "Why have you brought me here?"

Thalassia turned to face him, putting her back to the cliff. The wind made of her long hair a writhing gorgon's crown, and a devious light shone in her pale eyes.

"I've brought you here—and by *you*, I mean this Demosthenes with half-dead eyes who treats me like I'm his possession, some magic sword he can use to pretend that he's strong instead of weak—I've brought *that* Demosthenes here so that he can throw himself the fuck off this cliff."

6. αἱ τοῦ σώματος ἡδονή

Demosthenes scoffed. "Fuck you," he said, using her own classless vocabulary, and he spun to begin the return trek to town.

"I thought you trusted me," Thalassia called after him. "What is it you think you have to lose? You're already dead! Coward!"

Demosthenes slowed and halted, but did not turn.

"We both died fighting for Athens," Thalassia went on. "I had my rebirth. You need yours. Let me help you."

"If you want to help me," Demosthenes said, still giving her his back, "you know the one and only thing I want."

"You can have your revenge," Thalassia said, coming nearer. "But the path to it is not the one you're walking."

As he felt her presence at his shoulder, Demosthenes sighed angrily. "I don't understand," he said. "You're a hundred-something years old and all but immortal. You've seen a thousand worlds, of the endless number which comprise the cosmos. How can any of this matter to you? How can I matter?"

"Other worlds are in my past," she said. "I'm probably stuck in this one until I die. That may be a long time, and I'd like it to be enjoyable. Something has to matter. Something other than trying to right a past mistake."

"And you choose Athens? Naupaktos?"

"No, Dee, you fucking idiot. As you've observed once or twice, I'm mildly... unbalanced."

"What I have observed," Demosthenes corrected her, "is that were there a goddess named Madness, she would kneel at the altar of Thalassia."

"Fair enough," Thalassia agreed, perhaps flattered by the appraisal. "I don't know what this is that we have between us. You hate me, but you don't. You want to leave and never come back, but you don't. You're intimidated by me, like any sane person should be, but you're also not. And me? Most of the time I want to rip your fucking skull out through your face and stomp it to dust. But I also don't. Whatever it is, I know I'd miss it if it went away. You would, too."

Instinctively—defensively—Demosthenes scoffed, even if he sensed in his heart that she spoke truly. Her madness had penetrated him, infecting him as any plague might. Now, contaminated as he was, what other company could he keep but her? She was as his shadow. A shadow with whom he could converse as he could with no other and which was capable of cutting down men by the score on his behalf.

Of cutting him down.

He knew. She was a part of him now. If Thalassia were to leave, and he did not die soon thereafter by his own hand or another's, he would spend what remained of his life trying to find her again.

The way her pale eyes shone hinted that Thalassia knew what thoughts dwelt behind his half-dead ones. Surely, she did.

"If I smash my head on the rocks," he observed, "I will not grow a new one."

"It's safe," she assured. "I've done it."

"*You* are not normal."

"I'll go first and be in the water if you need help. Just trust me." She turned from him and ventured closer to the cliff's edge with purpose in her step. As she walked, her chiton fell discarded, so that by the time she ran out of earth on which to walk, she stood unabashedly naked but for high-laced sandals. Many times had he seen that flawless form unclothed, but never once had he truly felt desire for it. Yes, in one drunken, shameful night in Amphipolis he had forced himself on her, but fear and resentment, not lust, had driven him to that. Out of spite she had allowed it, that he might be be left with his well-earned regret.

Demosthenes followed her to the land's edge and stood by her side looking down. The sight made his stomach lurch: far below, waves slapped jagged boulders, sending white spray skyward. It was beyond madness to elect to throw oneself from such a height into raging sea. But the one standing naked at his side had filled his existence with madness to such degree that perhaps it was his own standards which stood in need of adjustment.

Thalassia turned her head to look at him, the dark corona of her hair, the only hair on her smooth body, fluttering in the breeze, and she said without smiling, "I'm going. I hope you follow."

Without awaiting his reply, she dove off: head first, arms down, legs pressed together, her nymph's body a golden javelin which the sea lord could only welcome with open arms.

With barely a splash, she pierced the waves a fair distance from the nearest rocks and vanished for several seconds before her head emerged, dark hair clinging tightly to her skull and bare shoulders.

Demosthenes stood with clenched fists, staring at the ground at his feet and the open space one step beyond.

Was that step, as Thalassia claimed, the necessary next step on his path? A step into rebirth instead of failure, defeat, death?

Rebirth as what? A creature of vengeance? If anyone should know that path, it was she.

She had asked him what he had to lose by jumping. That answer was clear. Not much at all. Within seconds of Thalassia's dive, he had known that walking down from this place the way he had come was no option.

The way was forward. Down.

He stepped back several paces, putting Thalassia and the sea out of sight. Then, throwing off his chiton, he strode once more toward the cliff, swiftly lest he give himself time to change his mind. Strong wind at his back, he timed his steps so that his final stride landed right at the cliff's edge.

Without looking down, he launched himself into void.

His stomach, and other organs besides, seemed to remain on the cliff whilst the rest of him plunged relentlessly down, down, sea and rocks rushing up as if with the sole intention of ending his life. Though it lasted just a few seconds, packed into that descent was an eternity's worth of regret that his feet were not still planted firmly on earth.

There were other regrets, too, which tried and failed to coalesce, largely for lack of time.

He arrowed his body just in time to strike the shield of waves feet-first. Still, the waves won: the waters of the Gulf of Corinth pummeled and tossed him, dragged him under and stole his breath, a precious gift which could not be replaced until mouth found something other than brine to gulp.

Water-bound limbs working too slowly, at last he broke the surface, where as if to add one final insult, a wave slapped him square in the face. He wiped his eyes, opened them and cast stinging eyes around to gain his bearings.

He had missed the sea-worn rocks at the cliff base by a wide margin. Thalassia had been right; it was safe, and not just for a near-immortal. He looked up, and there was her sleek head, watching. Over the crash of surf and through the water in his ears, he heard her scream in triumph on his behalf.

As if the sea which shoved him rudely from side to side were nothing but a tranquil pool, she swam in his direction.

"The beach!" she called, gesturing east. "Can you make it?"

He was breathless, shaken, his limbs almost numb with cold, but there was not a chance he would allow her to carry him to shore.

The long swim to land was far harder than the leap, and made the whole experience far less pleasant. By the time he could reach bottom and crawl the remainder on hands and knees, his body ached all over. That Thalassia arrived at the same time as he left little doubt that she had held back to keep pace with him. He was used to such gestures from her and had learned to suppress the natural humiliation they inspired.

A few yards before the shore, her magnanimity ended and she waded rather than crawled. Where Demosthenes collapsed on the beach with chest heaving, she lowered herself with perhaps marginally less grace than usual.

Side-by-side and naked, they lay on the white sand, hearing the surf, looking up at a cloud-streaked sky, saying nothing for a time while wind and sun dried brine-soaked skin. Eventually, Demosthenes' panting gave way to controlled breath.

Thalassia broke their silence first. "Ready to go again?"

"Just give me a year or two on this spot first," Demosthenes answered.

"I could do that," she agreed. "Thank you for trusting me."

"It's less a choice than a compulsion."

"You're alive," she returned. It was a plain statement rather than any defense of her influence on him. After a few moments of silence she repeated, "You're *alive*. So be alive, Dee. If revenge is what you live for, so be it. But live."

"Is that what you live for? Revenge?"

"No," she answered slowly. "It's always there. But no. If it were, I'm reasonably sure I would not be cliff diving with a sad vagrant this morning. I would be out in the world making it a worse place for a lot more people than just you."

"And every other Athenian," Demosthenes reminded her.

He had spoken absently rather than accusingly, but Thalassia's reply was unusually earnest:

"I tried," she said. "I want to try to make it better."

Lying on his back, Demosthenes let his head fall sidewise to face her. He found Thalassia lying fully on her left side, cheek resting on the back of one hand. Her pale eyes were on him in a strange way, like one might look upon a grave of a friend, a friend put under the cold earth not by tragedy but by his own foolish action. It was sorrow mixed with disappointment, but not pity for either the living or the dead.

He had been about to say something the moment before he looked at her, but he forgot what it might have been. While his mind flailed in search of the lost thought, he kept his eyes locked eyes with hers for too long, leaving him no graceful way to disengage. The result was an uncomfortable silence.

Thalassia oftentimes could be relentless, unforgiving, but she was capable of mercy. She showed it now by averting her eyes.

"You should stay and rest and enjoy this place," she said faintly. "I'll go, if you'd like." They were hollow words, spoken without meaning and showing no sign of reflecting true intent. She stayed where she was, warm and naked and inches away.

For two years, Thalassia had been his guiding star and his madness. Yet, at present, she was all that anchored him to the firmament. Her mad voice somehow had become the voice of reason, and it had kept on speaking to him even as he refused to listen. Thalassia knew him better than any man or woman ever had, well enough to know what it would take to force him to cease pitying himself and see the way forward.

It had taken a leap from a dangerous precipice, a leap which part of him, he realized, had not survived. A new man had indeed emerged from those waves, still bent on vengeance but rid of those soft, unneeded things which held him back. Despair. Hopelessness. Self-pity.

He was a new man, and this new man began to experience thoughts which the old one had not dared entertain. Laying here in the sand beside him was one who had ushered him through darkness and into new light. He stared at her silently and had these new thoughts, yet remained uncertain of what to do with them.

Thalassia's pale eyes flicked down the length of his body, as his had not yet done to hers, but wished to. They flicked back up with sure knowledge of at least one thought of his new self, for there existed some secrets which the male anatomy was scarcely capable of keeping.

Thalassia touched his wrist, tentatively, with the tip of one finger, setting the hairs of his arm on end. "The thing you're thinking of doing," she said, "you're welcome to do it." Hopeful eyes backed up the invitation. "Very welcome."

For days now, another, weaker Demosthenes had taken perverse pleasure in disappointing this one being on earth who truly had faith in him. Now, he did not even consider letting her down. Rolling over so their bodies faced, he laid his left hand upon Thalassia's cheek and kissed her.

It was not the first time he had tasted her lips, but the first time in which all four lips both gave and received. Hers were softer than they looked, and touched with brine that only enhanced their flavor. She tasted, above all, so very human.

Grains of sand found their way between them but were

ignored as Thalassia kissed back gently, unaggressively, deploying the tip of her warm tongue between his open lips. Her hand slipped behind his head, fingers nesting in his sodden hair and applying just enough inward pressure to make clear that she was in no hurry for the engagement to end.

Demosthenes gladly obliged. He wrapped an arm around her torso and pulled her star-born body close. Her leg enveloped him, the touch of her flesh everywhere warming his, and for long minutes their lips never parted for more than the instant needed to find a new angle and press home again.

During those minutes, her hot fingers and soft palm found his cock, from which the adverse effects of the frigid sea had long since fled. She stroked it with skill, and he repaid in kind with a finger slipped into the folds of her hairless cleft. Her hips reacted eagerly to the pressure. Before long, the light touch with which she pleasured him became a firm grip used to tug him into her parting thighs. Just when he felt the first trace of wetness, she sprang up from the sand and mounted him as gracefully as any Scythian might an unsaddled horse. The maneuver put Demosthenes on his back as he entered her, again not for the first time, but for the first time sober and with neither party acting only to diminish the other. This was pure, wild lust with no thought devoted to anything but gratification and release.

After some time spent underneath her, the mount heaved and toppled its rider, throwing her to the sand with an impact that would have taken the breath from another woman. With one knee braced in the moist sand, he became a farmer and she the mired plough he struggled to drive upfield. Thalassia wore her pleasure openly, intensely, on her face but rarely met his eyes, nor he hers. Pulling him into her with an iron hand on the back of his neck, her other rubbing their point of union, she achieved shuddering release. Then she expelled him into the cold air, but for barely a second while she rolled onto her shoulders and knees, head down, showing him her sinuous panther's back. He reentered from behind, her rounded backside grinding against him in movements which led her to another climax, and then him to his. He took no care to withdraw, but just spilled seed inside a womb he knew to have been rendered barren, lest Thalassia and her kind criss-cross time and space spewing out bastards.

Spent, he lowered himself atop her back, careful to remain inside of her and enjoy the lazy back-and-forth motion by which she continued to softly milk him. He set his cheek on hers, shut his eyes and tried not to let the imminent, inevitable end of what could only ever be a fleeting, Lethean interlude spoil the warm tingle of her flesh against his.

But ending was inevitable. At some point they would have to speak again and leave this beach and find ways to interact when fluids were not being exchanged. He would have to go back to feeling hatred and rage and regret and annoyance and confusion again, day in, day out, instead of the freedom and contentment he felt now.

Thalassia became the first to speak, in words slightly distorted by the compression of her jaw between his weight above and the beach underneath. "Tell me we'll do that again," she said.

"I'll need a small amount of time," Demosthenes answered.

A brief, nasal laugh stirred grains of sand under Thalassia's face. "Not what I meant. But definitely, as soon as you're ready again and I scoop the sand out of me. What I meant was … tomorrow. And the next day, and after. Do you want that?"

With that question, the poised ax fell, shattering the

dreamworld into which the sea had expelled him.

On its surface, the question required little thought: of course he wanted that. But there were other things of which he was equally certain he wanted no part.

He rolled off of her to lay on his back, while she remained on her stomach, looking over at him expectantly.

"The day you died," he said directly, for his new self was direct. "Alkibiades told me you loved me. Do you?"

He did not watch Thalassia's face while she considered her answer. Perhaps he should have, but in the end, Thalassia was, among many things, a consummate actress: he would never see on her face anything but what she wished him to see.

"Alkibiades," she began softly, but with emphasis, "is full of two things. Himself, and shit." After a brief pause, she said in more subdued tones, "I don't do love anymore. Not ever."

Unsurprisingly, as he looked into them, Thalassia's wintry blue eyes told the same story as her pleasing lips.

"Nor I," Demosthenes said. As he made the assertion, it occurred to him that although it was no lie, neither could he be certain of its truth. Perhaps, one day, he would feel love again, after vengeance was taken. If he lived through its taking.

But he could not love *her*. The sight of her reminded him too much of what he had lost. If he was to love again, it must be someone new, he thought, someone who had naught to do with all this devastation and death and torment, someone who could make him forget for more than just the span of a kiss or an embrace.

"Good," Thalassia said. "Sad, but good. Then we'll do more of this?"

"When there is time. We shall be busy."

"Doing?" She slid closer, crossing his thigh with hers, setting fingers on his sandy chest.

"Sinking every ship that Sparta sends toward this town. And going back to Athens to kill some fucking Equals."

Thalassia laughed a wicked little laugh, and her hand slid down his torso to a place which soon began to feel rebirth of its own. "Let me just remove that sand for you..." she said, and proceeded to do so in a manner which precluded further speech.

7. Abduction

50 days after the fall of Athens (July 423 BCE)

In the black of night, unannounced, Styphon came to the shuttered window behind which waited the object of his hunt. By his side was the assistant to which tradition said he was entitled this night. In his case, the man fulfilling that role just happened to be a king of Sparta.

Agis set his back to the wall of unpainted clay brick at one side of the window. Styphon did likewise on the other. Sending one hand overhead, up past the window sash, the king slipped a finger behind the closed wooden shutter and exerted slight outward pressure. It moved, and Agis withdrew his hand, conclusion drawn: it was unlocked.

The king gave a sly smile, knelt before his subject and put both hands near the ground with fingers interlaced for use as a step. Being the one who was to proceed alone through the aperture, Styphon did not return his smile, but just drew a quiet breath and set his sandal into the king's hands. Agis boosted him up, and when Styphon had his balance, he carefully opened both shutters and crept through.

He did not go silently. That was impossible, particularly when the only covering sounds were the calls of crickets and night birds. But then, utter stealth was not required. For all that his entry was surreptitious, it was expected.

Styphon lowered himself into the enclosed candlelit space on the window's other side. He had been in the house before, a few days prior, but not this corner of it. The furnishing was plain and sparse, of course, as it was in the dwelling of any Spartiate family desirous of a sound reputation, consisting of just a sleeping pallet, large wicker basket for storage, and a woven mat to cover the floor of hard-packed earth. Near the pallet, a candle burned in a clay stand, its flickering light illuminating a human-sized lump covered entirely by a wool blanket. It was to this lump that Styphon walked. Crouching by the bedside, he gripped an edge of the blanket, and with a heart that quickened in expectation, he threw it back.

The sight revealed was that clothes wadded up in a surely deliberate imitation of a sleeping form. Styphon stood and turned toward the only remaining place where his quarry could hide. Setting his gaze on the wicker basket, he searched for signs of movement and listened for breath, detecting neither, then walked slowly in its direction. He reached it and stopped, set fingers on its worn handle, and pulled.

Inside, curled up tightly, looking up at her discoverer past brows crumpled in anger and up the short length of a dagger held tightly in both hands, was Hippolyta.

A little puzzled, Styphon froze and gave her a questioning look which might have been lost in the darkness. Had she had second thoughts?

She growled at him, softly, then whispered through grit teeth, "Don't touch me!"

Styphon's eyes flew to the curtain behind which likely slept, or sat awake, any or all of Hippolyta's parents and siblings. Whose side would they take if tonight went wrong?

"I won't let you," Hippolyta promised, again keeping her voice low. It seemed she had no wish to see her family rush in to her aid. "I will *not* let you take this knife from me, drag me to my bed, force your cock in where none has been before, pound me until I quiver and melt underneath you, surrendering what I've saved for my husband. I may not have the strength to stop you, but I shall not go easily."

Looking into Hippolyta's eyes, Styphon saw the gleam there and felt relief. This was a game. From what he knew, most Spartiate women underwent their bridal abductions eagerly, or at least passively, and why not?—the groom was a man of their choosing and the night of his coming known in advance.

Hippolyta was eager for her abduction, too, but pretended otherwise. The tradition, after all, could only have arisen in less civilized days, when wives had been taken by force.

Styphon knelt by the basket, and Hippolyta's eyes and dagger tip followed him. She gave him another low snarl.

"Theria," he addressed her firmly but affectionately, "I shall take what I want, and what I want is your stain on that sheet." He put his palm out. "Hand me the knife."

She stabbed in the direction of his face, not enough to make him flinch. Styphon sent his other hand over the basket rim, behind her head, and clutched a handful of her hair. It had been cut short in preparation for this night, the shorn locks dedicated to Artemis. What remained fell barely to the nape of her neck. He pulled and twisted, forcing her head back, palm still open near her chin to receive the weapon.

Her lips curled in pain and defiance. She made no effort to use the knife, but did not surrender it either, and so after several seconds Styphon grabbed the blade by its flat, wrenched it from her grasp and laid it gently on the floor. He stood, dragging her up with him by the roots of her cropped hair. She twisted her body as best she could and took some deliberately ineffectual swipes at him. Taking no notice, he started toward the bed, leaving his bride with little choice but to step out of the basket.

With her fingers clawing not too hard at the skin of his forearm, he brought her to the foot of the sleeping pallet. She had worn a short, loose shift of bright white linen, but now he stripped her of that, the garment coming away easily with the yank of a single tie at the shoulder. Keeping his grip on her hair, he cleared the wadded clothing and blanket from the pallet, revealing a clean white sheet spread over a thin mattress. He forced her down onto that, finally released his grip on her hair, straddled her naked, writhing body and batted away the flailing arms she endeavored to put between them. After a brief struggle, more show than substance, her arms were pinned to the bed. Styphon's own long hair fell down to frame a bride's features twisted in faux defiance even as her body fell still.

"It is no use fighting," he said, having no trouble playing the part assigned him. "It will only hurt more."

Hippolyta chuffed at him like a trapped beast. It was a fighting sound, but her eyes held invitation. Holding her wrists together over her head in one hand, Styphon employed the other to forcibly part clamped thighs. They slipped out of his grasp a few times, but eventually he caught her, she yielded, and his groin settled against hers. A few flicks of his hand pushed his chiton clear and set their parts in alignment, making all ready. Only a thrust was needed now to couple them in the one manner they had not yet enjoyed, for she had preserved it through twenty-four years until this, her wedding night—not so much to honor any goddess or moral code as to prevent her becoming a mother before her time.

Still restraining her, Styphon pushed his way inside. The first stroke met with resistance, but in drawing back and renewing the assault twice more, he broke through into a slick, warm haven. Hippolyta yanked her hands free, and they flew to his back, clawing. She held her breath. Pretended defiance faded from her face, and replacing it was genuine uncertainty, as if she had yet to decide whether or not the new sensation was a welcome one.

Styphon stayed still inside of her, holding her, awaiting the verdict. She gave it to him with a hand at the back of his head, pulling his face down into a kiss.

"Fuck me," she breathed into his ear, and her new husband complied.

* * *

They finished, or Styphon did at any rate, but they could not linger. This was, after all, an abduction. Were he under thirty, he would return now to the barracks, but he was four years past that and the master of a house to which his wife must now be taken. Rising, he pulled Hippolyta up behind him,pausing as she used the bed's white sheet to wipe his genitals and hers. On rare occasions (Styphon knew thanks to Andrea's mother) the bridal sheets would wind up stained with blood. More often than not, though, a Spartan woman had broken her own barrier by phallus or finger or exercise long before her wedding night.

The abductee quickly dressed herself and let her abductor lead her to the window, where with bare foot planted in his hand, she climbed up. Her royal cousin helped her down, and when she was clear, Styphon hoisted himself by strength of arm alone and joined them outside, just as the cousins were finishing an embrace.

"Will you run, or shall the lucky groom carry you over his shoulder?" Agis asked. Some men, half in jest, were known to carry their new wives all or part of the way home. Most weighed less than war gear, so the challenge was not great.

Hippolyta answered by grabbing Styphon's hand and pulling hard to force him into a run. With a last look at Agis, Styphon let himself be led a few strides before, as a matter of pride, he overtook her.

They reached his home, the size of which had expanded of late by the addition of a separate bedroom for Equal and wife. To build it, Agis had summoned some members of his guard who had completed the task in two days, not begrudging Styphon the favor a bit. It was to this newly built room which Styphon took his bride, passing first through the larger main chamber, where Eurydike slept by the hearth. Andrea was elsewhere, in quarters arranged for her by Agis on the reasoning that her absence helped to ensure that the introduction of daughter to step-mother waited until daylight, when circumstances ought to prove rather more favorable for all involved.

There, in Styphon's new bed, which differed from the old one not only in size but also in having some padding and being raised off the ground for greater warmth, they conjugated their union again, held each other for a while and finally slept, limbs entangled, as husband and wife.

8. Piss & driftwood

On the day of his rebirth, Demosthenes had sought out Agathokles to present him with his intention of journeying with Thalassia to occupied Athens. The Naupaktan, not unexpectedly, had tried to dissuade him.

Demosthenes had held fast: "I must return. I know not even whether my wife was laid in a proper grave or if my father yet lives. Thalassia tells me there is resistance in Athens. If our aid can be of use to this so-called Omega in the liberation of my city, then we must offer it, as we have to Naupaktos."

Still, Agathokles had argued against their going.

"Athens is ruled at present by a pack of tyrants under the leadership of some weasel named Isodoros," he said. "They treat the city harshly in response to every act of resistance. The jails are full of the innocent and the streets full of informers eager to collect the generous reward that would surely be theirs for turning you in."

"It is a risk I must take," Demosthenes had said, making it his final word on the matter. "We will be gone but a few days, and Thalassia has given your craftsmen and engineers more than enough to do in her absence. When we return, we will help rally your countrymen to ensure the vote on Sparta's ultimatum goes in favor of war."

In conceding, Agathokles had cast his eyes on Thalassia and implored her, "Bring him back alive, good witch."

"More alive than he is now," she had pledged in reply.

The following day had seen them boarding a trading ship bound for Corinth to repeat in reverse their earlier voyage to Naupaktos. A day later, Demosthenes sat with reins in hand atop a horse bought in Corinth for the overland leg to Athens. Thalassia sat in front of him in the saddle, her black, jasmine-scented single braid bouncing in time with the galloping hooves, and the warm flesh of her buttocks rubbing his groin, maybe not always inadvertently. The riding gear they had brought from Naupaktos lacked stirrups, of course, those being an innovation of Thalassia's which had never spread beyond the now-disbanded citizen cavalry of Athens. They were useful, to be sure, but he had ridden most of his life without them and did not regret their absence. At any rate, they would have brought unwanted attention, and to the right observer, revealed the riders' identities.

Not that they could hope to go long unrecognized once they drew near Athens, where both were well-known. They would have to avoid public spaces, perhaps even moving only by night.

One thing he knew, or two perhaps: he did feel alive, and he was greatly eager to see his city again, even if only by starlight.

As they rode, he voiced this thought to her.

"You need another name for me when we're alone," was her tangential reply. "Like I have Dee."

"I wish you did not."

"I don't have time for four syllables. Neither do you."

"Thalassia," Demosthenes intoned. "Despite its length, I have no trouble wrapping my tongue around it."

"Well said."

"But if you insist, I could call you... *Lassie*," he suggested idly. "Or... this Omega fellow makes his name a letter of the alphabet. I could call you *Theta*. Or even just the sound *Th*. That would save a great deal of time."

Thalassia's neck twisted that she might regard the rider at her back with a look of surprise and amusement.

"First," she said, facing forward once more, "I like this new you. Second, *Thalassia* is just what some Spartans decided to call me two years ago. I like it, and it's who I am here, but it isn't actually my name."

"*Geneva* is scarcely shorter, and less... graceful."

"That's my Caliate name. You could call me by the one I was born with."

"Jenna Cordeiro?"

"Just Jenna. Sometimes. If you want."

Demosthenes gave no reply, only rode.

"But if not," she added after some time, "I'm happy to be Thalassia."

They reached Athens just before dusk. While on the road, Demosthenes had pondered which of the fifteen or so gates of Athens would be the easiest to pass through unnoticed. On arrival, he learned that his answer did not matter, for the walls of Athens were mostly dismantled. Already there were large gaps, and so it was through one of those by which they slipped into the city.

He knew where he must go: if there was one man in Athens whom he could trust not to turn him in, it was his cousin Phormion. Phormion's house was in the same deme as his own, where the likelihood of being recognized was greatest, but declining Thalassia's suggestion that he wait while she fetched his cousin to some safer location, Demosthenes insisted they go together.

He wished to visit his home.

Thalassia could see equally well by night as by day and creep as silently as any shadow. She would be his eyes, reporting whether the way was clear, and if it was not, clearing it.

She went ahead, cloaked and hooded, while he skulked in the shadows of a nearby alley until she returned to report a lone, unarmed watcher, disguised as a beggar, near the front. If Demosthenes merely followed a circuitous route and entered by a rear window, he could access his home undetected.

"Go make contact with Phormion," he told her. "I won't be long."

Nodding simple acceptance, she vanished into the twilight, and following her instruction, Demosthenes slipped like a thief into his own deserted home.

The megaron's floor was strewn with refuse, the plain walls and pillars inscribed all over with graffiti: Lakonian names and vulgar rhymes. The hearth sat cold and stained with a dozen spills never cleaned. The drapes were torn down and trampled. The air reeked of shit and urine.

Clearly, his home had seen use as a barracks—until fairly recently, judging by the state of some the more disgusting evidence.

There at the base of the hearth were the clay fragments of the pot from which Eurydike was ever digging out a bronze obol before running to buy a new spark from the priestesses of Hestia to rekindle the flame she had let flicker and die. Elsewhere, in splinters, lay the polished ebony table which had been the first item to furnish the house when it was built. In a small room off of the megaron, the recessed bath buzzed with flies on account of its having been used as a latrine.

He surveyed all this damage, these insults, and they bothered him little. He had not expected the place to look as he had left it on the day of Athens' fall. He had come for two reasons: one, just to show that it was his and he had the right, and two, in search of some sign of his wife's last days, some token left behind for him in the hope he would find it.

The light was failing; there was not long to look. He went to the most obvious place, a hollow underneath a floor tile in a storeroom where once he had kept valuables; not surprisingly, it lay open and emptied of its contents. He ascended the stairs, fighting off a tendency of his mind to drag him back to when he had been glad to climb them. The path took him through what had been the women's quarters, which had been sparsely furnished before Thalassia and Laonome had filled it with soft and shiny things, now all gone.

He went to his bedroom, which he knew with near certainty had been the stopping place of any number of whores, each of whom had taken away something of his wife's until all that remained was what he saw now. Just a stained, torn mattress on the floor, missing even the carved bedframe which had supported it. He gave the chamber a cursory search, but found nothing.

There was nothing to find. There never had been. What had made him think there might be? The universe which he now knew did not work that way. The slaughtered did not get last words or the chance to leave tokens behind for those who loved them. They simply breathed one moment and did not the next, their bodies banished into cold earth and their shades into permanent oblivion.

The last of the day's light nearly gone, he returned to the stairs. As he walked, his toe struck some item which skittered across the tiles. Stooping and sweeping his hand over filth, he found it and raised it into what light he could find.

It was a dolphin carved of driftwood.

Laonome had bought it in the agora in the first days after their wedding, a gift for Thalassia. It was a token of friendship, and a joke of sorts, since *thalattia* was what men sometimes called the smooth wood from which such carvings were made.

It was stained now, missing its dorsal and one flipper. Since it had been given as a gift, it belonged to Thalassia, not to him, but it had passed through his wife's hands. She had picked it up in a market stall, set coin into craftsman's palm, and carried it here.

It made a poor token of his wife, and certainly was no final expression of love, but it would have to do. Taking it, he stole out into the night the way he had come, knowing in his heart that this place would never again be his home, that he would never return, not even should Athens one day be restored to freedom. He was a citizen of Athens no more, except perhaps in some small corner of his heart. He was a wanderer and an exile now.

Like she who once had been called Jenna and made her home somewhere in the stars.

Driftwood.

9. Necropolis

Sticking to shadows, Demosthenes approached the home of his cousin Phormion. Before reaching it, he heard a low whistle which almost might pass for that of some night bird to one who was not alert for such a signal. Following the sound, he found Thalassia. Cloaked and hooded like himself, she was all but one with the night.

She put a hand on his shoulder and found his eyes with hers, which glowed like moons, and asked without words what his pilgrimage had yielded. He produced the dolphin. She saw it and smiled sadly. He tried putting it in her hands, for it belonged to her, but she pushed it gently to his breast. Accepting, he tucked the carving into the pocket formed by the fall of chiton over belt and let her lead him over a low wall into his cousin's garden.

Phormion stood waiting for them in the light of an oil lamp, where he wasted no time dragging his fugitive cousin into an embrace. "I was sure you had died," he said gravely. "Then I heard they were searching for you."

They separated, and Phormion, who was lame in one leg from a childhood injury, leaned on his walking stick as they retreated into the darkened megaron of his house.

"You are right to be careful," Phormion said. "Should you happen past the wrong eyes, you will find yourself in chains."

"They can try," Demosthenes said.

Phormion's gaze went to Thalassia. "This one is legend to the hundreds who saw her that day," he said. It was harder for him, apparently, than for slave-descended Agathokles to break the habit of speaking *of* females rather than to them. "Of the rest, some believe, others do not. What is she?"

"Difficult to explain," Demosthenes evaded. "Suffice to

say that with her nearby, I need have little fear for my life."

"I am glad to give you shelter. But the authorities may expect your presence here. It may not be wise."

"We need no shelter and would not endanger your house. My present desire is for information."

"Whatever I can provide."

Demosthenes asked, "Was Laonome given burial?"

"Aye. May the Maiden embrace her. The Spartans turned over her corpse, and I myself oversaw her placement in the family plot."

The pang of grief gave Demosthenes only momentary pause before he inquired, "What of Alkibiades and Eurydike?"

Phormion answered quickly, "The former is said to have been captured alive and taken to Sparta. As for your concubine, I have not seen her since the fall."

"And my father?"

Phormion's face was deep in shadow, but Demosthenes detected the change in its expression. "You have not heard," he said somberly. "Days after your wife was slain, Brasidas had Alkisthenes bound behind a chariot which was driven up to the walls of Dekelea. Not three days after your wife's interment, I tended to his."

A fresh pang of grief followed quickly on the heels of the last, and Demosthenes hung his head. Alkisthenes had been a harsh man of foul temperament, and scarcely in his adult life had Demosthenes ever enjoyed the man's company. Still, blood was blood, and the severity of the crime not mitigated by such details.

Thalassia's hand appeared on his shoulder. He shrugged it off.

"Brasidas has already doomed himself and his city," he said. "No act he commits now can worsen his fate."

"I, too, pray for justice, cousin," Phormion said. He had no grasp of the full meaning of Demosthenes' words, but how could he? No gods would have a say in events to come.

"Brasidas," Phormion said, and grimaced as though the name were rancid meat, "has left the city, leaving his sandal-lickers in charge, men whom any Athenian should be ashamed to share a tribe with. Chief among them is—"

"Isidoros," Thalassia finished for him. "We hear the new regime has not gone unchallenged."

Phormion nodded at her, but addressed his answer to his fellow citizen, whether out of persistent habit or intimidation. "The man called Omega and his followers have killed a small number Spartans and a few collaborators. No one knows his identity."

"Surely it is best that few know," Demosthenes said. "We need not know his name, or meet him, to aid his cause. But before we do, I must attend my wife's grave."

His cousin's face showed understandable concern. "It is certain to be watched."

"I know." Having obtained from Phormion all he desired, Demosthenes seized his cousin's hand. "I take my leave now. Know that there was no other man in the city I considered coming to first. I am in your debt."

He stopped short of promising repayment, for there could be no certainty he would ever see Phormion again. With a last embrace and good fortune wished both ways, the two visitors slipped over the wall into the night and set course for Athens' necropolis, the cemetery of Kerameikos on the city's outskirts.

They moved cautiously and kept once again in shadows. Minutes into their trek, at the end of a dark alley, Thalassia stopped abruptly, set her back to a wall, pulled Demosthenes' body and mouth in close to hers, wrapping a leg around him.

A sidelong glance told him why: a club-wielding Scythian guard patrolled the dimly lamplit street ahead. Athens had long employed the foreigners as police so that they might remain non-partisan and never serve as the private army of some tyrant or oligarch. It only proved how well the arrangement worked that the Scythians continued to keep order under the pro-Spartan regime.

The guard who squinted in their direction saw as Thalassia intended: a street-walker grinding her groin against a client. Before resuming his patrol, he waved his club at them in a warning to finish and move along,.

While their faces were close, Thalassia whispered, "Phormion was lying when he said no one knows who Omega is."

"Does he know?"

"I couldn't tell from what was said. But I suspect he's with the resistance in some capacity."

As the Scythian turned a corner, Demosthenes pulled back from the unexpected close contact and observed to Thalassia before they bolted across the lit avenue, "That guard might have asked to see your street-walker's permit."

"Fortunate for him that he decided not to."

* * *

Stealing up to a grave *stele* in Kerameikos cemetery was unlike sneaking into his house, for a stone which stood barely the height of a man's knees, surrounded by others of its like, was a rather more difficult thing to approach undetected. A different strategy was required.

There was a watcher posted here, swiftly located by Thalassia: another false beggar seated near the cemetery gate. They approached the man swiftly from two sides, shadows emerging from the night to loom over him. He yelped before Thalassia ordered him to hush or die and dragged him to his feet. Pushing him up against the gate's stone pylon by his throat, she relieved him of two objects which Demosthenes discerned in the darkness as a dagger and a syrinx. The latter, presumably, served as a means of signaling his masters in the case of just such an emergency as he now faced.

Thalassia cast his weapon into the darkness and slammed the reed pipes against the stone, smashing them. She asked her terrified prisoner, "How much will they pay you if you spot Demosthenes and he is caught?"

"H-half a *mina*," the informer rasped.

"Did you take the job for love of Sparta or of money?"

"Neither," he choked, clutching at the immovable fingers on his throat. "I... seek only... not to starve."

Thalassia released the man, and he slid heavily to the base of the pylon.

"Here is the one you await," she said. "You will sit here with me while he visits the grave of his murdered wife, as is his right. Give me no reason to kill you, and when he is done, you can run and tell your masters that Demosthenes has come. They will fail to kill or capture him, but perhaps you'll get your reward anyway. Does that sound a fair deal to you, shit-weasel?"

The breathless informer could scarcely nod swiftly enough.

"Go," Thalassia said next, gently, to Demosthenes. "Take as long as you need."

In silence, he left Thalassia and her charge and made his way past half a hundred graves to one which was not yet grown over, its soft earth yielding underfoot as he knelt to touch the engraved marble. It was difficult to discern in the darkness, but a combination of touch and fain vision told him that the relief on the *stele* showed a seated woman with one small boy in her lap and another standing behind the chair.

The former figure, though it resembled her not at all and was not meant to, represented Laonome; the latter would be her two sons by her first, deceased husband. The meaning was that the three now were reunited in Haides.

He knew, and could feel with his hands, that below the relief was an inscription, but neither eyes nor fingertips were up to the task of reading it in the deep of night.

He set his fingers instead on the face of the graven woman meant to be Laonome.

"How I have missed you," he said. "More than that, I miss what might have been. But I am no more the same man you knew. Part of him died when you did, and the rest... *drowned.* I have done things that would scarcely make you proud, and I shall do many more. I would tell you I intend to avenge you, and I will do that a thousandfold. I will make of Sparta a necropolis to dwarf this one. But not in your name, for I know you do not care. Even if you were in the arms of the gods, and not consigned to endless oblivion, you would not care for vengeance. You would only wish for me to be happy. Would that I could grant you that. But it will not happen. With luck, one day I shall be... satisfied. That is all."

The words had poured from his tongue with hardly a thought. Now that they trickled to a stop, there were but two things left to say, and one act to complete.

"I love you," he said to the stone profile which was not hers. "Goodbye, forever."

Removing the carved dolphin from his chiton, he dug a small hole in the soft, cold earth which held Laonome, set the token inside, and covered it over.

Wanderers and fugitives could have no possessions, least of all sentimental ones.

Rising, he turned his back on the grave and moved at speed to rejoin Thalassia.

She dragged the informer to his feet, gave him a shove, and bade him, "Deliver your message."

As he sped off into the night, rightly grateful to leave Karameikos with his life, Demosthenes said to Thalassia, "Please go to her grave and read it for me."

With no hesitation, no word or look of complaint, she disappeared into the necropolis. Knowing she would have no trouble catching up, Demosthenes passed through the cemetery gate and started on the path for their next destination.

Hardly a minute later, she was a black presence at his side.

Quietly, as they crept, she spoke the words that had been chosen by either Phormion or the gravestone's sculptor: "*I await having you by my side, husband, to comfort me. But please do not hurry, since where you are is the far better place.*"

Demosthenes' eyes stung as they watered briefly before the night air dried them. He had never managed to recall Laonome's precise last words to him, so these words which had never passed her lips in life would have to do.

"Thank you," he said to Thalassia, pausing beside her in a shadowy nook, their backs to a wall. "Now let us see to leaving this city bloodier than we found it."

He shared a look with Thalassia, and found a starlit grin and eyes that hungered for slaughter.

10. Twenty-Four

It was deep in the night that they killed their first Spartans in the city of Athens: a pair of them guarding the main gates of the jailhouse. Thalassia took one and Demosthenes the other, she cutting the throat of hers before the man even knew that death was upon him, while Demosthenes charged his, witnessing surprise light his face in the glow of a nearby oil lantern, while his hand went to his sword a scant second before he was run through.

By the time Demosthenes had pulled his blade free and spit in the face of the softly groaning corpse-to-be, Thalassia was vanishing over the top of the jail's perimeter wall. Moments later, there came from within the jail's courtyard the sound of the timber bar (which normally required two men to shift) being removed, after which one of the two bronze-clad wooden doors swung open wide enough for Demosthenes to pass through.

Inside, a dark form lay on the ground, Thalassia's second victim of the night: an Athenian guard with his neck broken. The sight caused Demosthenes no hesitation, no second thoughts. Whoever stood in their way would die. Those who remained could sort the bodies by citizenship later.

They proceeded to the jail's administrative building, where a kick from Thalassia quickly splintered the wood around the iron lock. The Athenian in the dimly-lit anteroom beyond appeared to have been half asleep, but at the sound of the breach he flew to alertness. He had no time to rise from the bench on which he had reclined before Thalassia was on him, straddling the bench with one immovable arm wrapped around his skull, her other pressing a blade to his throat.

"Quiet," she advised rather than commanded him.

Demosthenes stooped to face the guard, who had wisely

opted against resistance. "Every prisoner in this place will walk free tonight," he said. "You can help us open the cells, or we can leave you here choking on your own blood and do it ourselves. I will give you a moment to decide."

"Don't kill me," the man pleaded. "I'll help. I know who you are. I voted for you."

Demosthenes looked to the man's captor, who affirmed the truth of the speaker's assertion by releasing her grip. He sat rubbing the neck he had narrowly avoided having opened.

"What is your name?" Demosthenes asked.

"Karpos."

"Well, Karpos, tell us where the other guards are posted and who among them is sympathetic, and then lead the way."

* * *

Ten minutes later, three guards including Karpos were on their side, while five more lay bound and unconscious, their lives spared as a favor to the three who helped. The doors to every cell in every block of the compound were thrown wide, their occupants set free. Common criminals shared quarters with the political prisoners of the tyranny and innocents rounded up in mass arrests, men and women alike, and since there was no time to sort them out, all were set loose and directed to exits at the prison's rear.

"Leave the city if you want to stay free," Demosthenes told as many as he could, brushing off their expressions of gratitude. "Go to your kin in the country."

While the last doors were unlocked (or in Thalassia's case, broken) a trumpet wailed somewhere outside the prison walls. The cause was all but certain: someone had found the Spartiate corpses flanking the main gates.

"Everyone out!" Demosthenes urged the prisoners and cooperative guards alike. "Unless you're ready for a fight."

Everyone did leave, including Karpos, who wished good

luck to the last two who remained inside the prison walls, two who stood side-by-side, cloaks shed, swords drawn, in the prison courtyard just inside the closed but unbarred main gate.

"You said you don't fear for your life when I'm around," one said to the other. "I appreciate the sentiment, but some fear is healthy."

"Then I am plenty healthy," the other returned.

It was true: his heart raced at the knowledge that those bronze-clad doors, from behind which came the sounds of a crowd gathering, would shortly be thrown open, and in would charge some great number of armed and armored men, probably Equals. And here he stood in just a layer of linen.

"I'm not worried," Thalassia said.

"Death is but an inconvenience to you."

"I meant about you." She looked over at him, and Demosthenes saw lantern-light flicker over a network of black lines on her right cheek, her Mark of Magdalen, which had not been present moments ago. The blue eye at its center studied him, and her dark lips formed a thoughtful smile.

With a quick motion she tucked both of her swords under one arm and produced a small, round tin from which she removed the lid. Into it she dabbed the thumb of her right hand, which came out black with kohl. The hand went to Demosthenes' face, where it touched him above the brow and traced a downward path over his right eyelid, stopping just below the cheekbone. It repeated the motion on a diagonal over the same eye. The result, Demosthenes could only surmise, not having a mirror handy, was a black, Xhi-shaped analog of Thalassia's Mark.

"War-paint," she said approvingly.

With a final smile, she faced the doors and set herself, a sword in each hand, to meet the imminent attack.

Through the bronze-clad wood and over the prison walls, they heard a barked command to advance. The doors were shoved open by what turned out to be unarmed slaves, who immediately retreated into the night, leaving the way clear for what waited behind: a phalanx of Equals six men wide—as many as could fit abreast through the doors. The front rank bore their full panoplies of war: helmets and leather breastplates, lambda-blazoned shields, and eight-foot spears. Behind them stood six more, and six more, and six more just the same. Twenty-four shields, twenty-four spear-blades, twenty-four short swords hanging ready in reserve, arrayed against two with only swords and whose flesh was all but bare.

In the recent past, Demosthenes had joked quietly with himself or Thalassia about having gone mad. Here was sure proof that he had.

"I can take twenty," Thalassia said. "You all right with four?"

"Cocky bitch," he returned without rancor, knowing that her estimate was probably not far off. A man of excessive pride would be ill-suited fighting alongside Thalassia. He would kill himself trying to keep up.

Thalassia knew pride well, for she expressed a great deal of it herself, and could prod expertly at that of men who shared the affliction. She exercised that ability now, as the Spartan phalanx stood motionless, staring hard over their shield rims at the enemy revealed to them.

"What's the matter?" she taunted. "You bitches afraid you can't handle a little girl and a man wearing makeup?"

There was no movement in the phalanx but for the slight swaying which proved its component parts were flesh and not bronze. Then one man among them, standing in the second rank gave himself away as the officer present by bellowing in the voice of command: "*Eíphoi!*"

Swords. Covered by the protruding blades of those behind them, the men of the front rank laid down their spears, their wall of overlapped shields parting just enough to let the shafts pass, then filled their empty right hands with the drawn short swords which were better suited, or so they believed, for such close combat as was to come.

At a second barked command, the front six began a slow, steady advance, while behind them the second rank repeated the act of trading spear for sword.

"Let's do this," Thalassia said, and she launched herself into what for any other man or woman, not least one dressed in nothing but the flowing long chiton she had slit from hem to waist, would be a headlong charge into death.

But this day it was Death who wore the gown and bore twin swords wide in the shapely, outstretched arms of a demi-goddess ready to usher men's shades into Haides' cold embrace.

Death charged, and her chosen companion, Demosthenes, followed without hesitation or thought for the odds. He went without pride, too, a lack which kept his path firmly within her wake, since to strike off on his own and go right where she went left would have meant the end of him. Thus, from a few paces behind, he witnessed the first blood shed as Thalassia ducked under the strokes of the two Spartans at the end of the first rank, sprang up within arm's reach of either and cut their two throats above shield rims. They were dead but did not know it yet, still standing as Thalassia used their shadeless bodies as shields which hung from her arms as she charged on into the oncoming second rank, bowling two men over before crushing one's face with a planted heel and dipping her sword's tip into the other's heart as though his leather breastplate were a layer of tilled soil and her sword a planter of seeds.

She had already killed these four, leaving Demosthenes almost wishing he could stand idle and watch, such a sight was his partner to behold on the killing field, when he hit the bleeding phalanx in the same spot. The front line was turning right to envelop the intruder, even as she killed another, but two Equals stood ready and waiting, facing Demosthenes and separating him from his tiny army's deadlier half.

He had never before charged two ready hoplites, much less Spartiates, and much less in a battle he had picked, with a sword his only armament, wool chlamys wound around left arm in lieu of hoplon, skin all but bare, lacking even faith in Pallas as his armor. The Demosthenes who had died at Dekelea likely would never have conceived of such an act, but this one did, and in a black corner of his mind, the corner which celebrated slaughter and only fully brightened at the sound of death groans, he knew why.

He charged because *she* was on his side, and short of Eden, or overwhelming force, or a trap, or something more than these two dozen men could offer, Thalassia was unstoppable, and therefore so was he. Screaming the name of no goddess or city, but just letting loose a roar befitting those painted, unarmored warriors of the north whom he presently must have resembled, he joined the fray.

His sword batted aside that of one Equal, his whipped cloak entangling the sword arm of another, and he threw his weight into the joint where two bowl-shaped shields overlapped. The shields gave way just enough let him through, where he released his cloak and grabbed instead the long hair of the man to his right, whose sword arm posed the most imminent threat. Equals wore their hair thus as a deliberate insult to their enemies of whom they supposedly had no fear, and now it was used to its intended purpose:

Demosthenes pulled, and the man's head came back, exposing his neck, which Demosthenes hacked into once before sending his blade into a backhand swing that blocked the other's renewed attack. Whilst Athenian steel grated on inferior bronze, Demosthenes ducked close and shouldered aside the enemy's hoplon to deliver a fist to the face which sent the second man staggering back.

These two were not his only opponents, of course; more swarmed around him, even as Thalassia made more corpses of the rear ranks and drew the bulk of deadly attention to herself. But with the removal of those two—the second of which he finished with a stab to the groin as he fell—nothing else stood between him and Thalassia, whom he joined at the bronze-clad doors of the prison gate. Were he fighting alongside any other, such a position would be untenable: back to a wall and surrounded by a dozen men (for Thalassia's toll by now was at least ten).

With a flashed smile, Thalassia welcomed him to her corner of the small battlefield, then gave him her back, entrusting him with its defense. He accepted the task, and after blocking a few attacks with a hoplon plucked from arm of a slain Spartiate, he wounded a man in the knee, sending him back, then took the eye of the Equal who shifted into his place.

By now, some number of the still undaunted phalanx had seen fit to retrieve spears from the ground, thinking them the better weapon after all with which to hack down or stab a cornered foe, but they were wrong; Demosthenes, in a battle-induced state of hyper-awareness, found their spear thrusts even easier to anticipate and intercept, whether with hoplon or blade. By dropping to one knee with a spear blade hooked on the shield's bottom rim, he was able to pull its wielder off balance so he tumbled onto waiting sword, running both hands down the edges as he instinctively tried to ward off death.

Just in time, he saw the next spear-point advancing from above and sprang upright, deflecting it with his stolen shield and attacking low underneath. He drew blood in a glancing blow to the leg of his attacker, who drew back his spear for a fresh assault. As it passed his head, Demosthenes saw blood on the blade, and his stomach lurched. The swiftest of glances over his shoulder, all he could afford, told him why.

Thalassia's gown was torn and stained deep red just under one shoulder. The attack he had deflected had instead struck the back of she whom it was his duty to defend. It was no fatal blow to the likes of her, and she would not have felt its sting, but he cursed himself no less for the grave lapse.

He moved to take out his anger on the spear's wielder, but too late, for that Equal screamed as Thalassia hacked his spear arm clean off at the elbow, and then he was silent but for a gurgle as her blade lighted briefly on his neck before flying off to drink of more strong Lakonian blood.

Rededicating himself to his task, Demosthenes dealt with two more Equals, killing one and wounding the other with a hoplon rim to the throat followed by a slash which bit unclad thigh. Then, breath heaving, he reset his blade, scanned the space in front of him and realized there was no one left to kill.

The ground just inside the jailhouse gates stood littered with the dead and dying. Some of the latter were still, with only low moans to distinguish them, while other wounded men left trails of gore on the hard-packed dirt as they attempted to drag themselves to imagined safety. Four of the less wounded had regrouped beyond the threshold of the open gates. Demosthenes was mildly displeased to recognize three as opponents he himself had failed to kill. Two of the four were fully armed, while two bore only shields. Their faces were blank, but the eyes glittering in the lamplight betrayed an inner struggle: to advance and die in honor, or to keep their lives?

"They'll run," Thalassia declared quietly. She looked as though she had bathed in blood, her once-white chiton now slick and black and hugging every curve. Her face was spattered, and arms which still held swords ready for more were streaked red from knuckle to pit. "Shall we allow it?" this Fury asked. "Your call."

Surely she was right: the men would flee. The prospect of being branded tremblers held less fear for them in this moment than did the nightmare vision before them. Demosthenes felt vaguely that he preferred that they die, but the thrill of the fight was fading, A bare toss of his head communicated the decision.

Accepting it, Thalassia took a lunging step forward, brandishing blood-coated swords in a feint meant only to terrify. It worked. The makeshift wall of four shields crumbled as two of its members turned tail and ran, or rather limped toward the watching crowd of civilians and slaves which had gathered a safe distance behind. The two who remained gave one another a glance, pressed closer together and backpedaled in a more orderly retreat.

"Fuck off!" Thalassia yelled at the spectators, and many heeded the command. Throwing down one sword, she set her emptied hand on the great door of bronze-sheathed wood and heaved it shut, dragging with it a few corpses that were in the way. Then she did the same with the second door and barred the two with the ten-foot timber she handled as though it weighed no more than a spear.

"We should go," she said, retrieving her cloak from where she had set it before the battle.

Demosthenes, who had meanwhile found his own blue chlamys lying relatively unsullied by blood, followed her in the direction of their planned escape. Figuring the few exits would by now be watched, if not guarded, they instead went over the prison wall, Thalassia scaling it first and helping her less nimble companion to follow. They had partaken of a fair share of slaughter this night. Rather than invite more, they dropped silently into an unlit street, covered their bloodied clothes and skin with cloaks and stole away, hands clasped so as not to lose one another in darkness.

11. Blood & jasmine

Owing to the raised alarm and the sounds of battle which carried far in the quiet of night, the streets of Athens did not long remain empty. Men ventured out in search of what was amiss, and Scythian guards leaped at shadows, forcing the perpetrators of the prison break to move with extra stealth. After some minutes spent running in careful bursts, they halted their flight in a narrow alley between shuttered market stalls. Demosthenes leaned against one wall, Thalassia the other. So narrow was the channel that their knees touched. At first the only sound in Demosthenes' ears was that of his own heavy breath, but as he brought that under control, it was superceded by the drone of cicadas and the distant shouts of men.

Then an excited whisper from his companion. "You did so well."

Cloak thrown back on her shoulders, Thalassia was a dark, glistening shape against the moonlit gray-brown brick behind her. Pale blue eyes gleamed in a smooth, blood spattered face.

"I killed four," he said dispiritedly, remembering that this very number had been her prediction before the battle. "And wounded three. And allowed you to be wounded."

"This?" A supple, bluish arm decorated with irregular black smears came up, and a sticky hand touched his cheek. "It's nothing. And four is great," she said. "But you shouldn't be counting. Just kill until you win."

She breathed a contented sigh.

"You did *very* well," she repeated in a slower, more forceful whisper.

Demosthenes knew that tone. He knew the touch now, too, that of her hand sliding from his cheek down the side of his neck to rest on his collarbone. Both signaled what was coming next, and although a small fraction of his mind was disgusted for an instant, his body responded, and responded still more when Thalassia's wounded back left her wall of the alley so that her front might make tantalizing contact with his. Her breasts met his chest, pressing upon him through gore- and sweat-soaked linen.

"I love fighting with you," she said. The crown of her head rested on his temple, her breathy voice tickling his earlobe, her hair smelling of blood and jasmine. With a deft motion she unpinned her cloak and let it fall. Her pelvis pressed against his. "There's another thing I love doing with you."

"Half a city is hunting for us," Demosthenes protested, mildly.

"So?"

"We're covered with—"

"We're *alive*. We can do—"

Now it was Demosthenes' turn not to let her finish. If he was to be a dweller in her city of madness, a citizenship which he had accepted, then the new madness was to resist its rules.

Bringing hands up between them, he shoved her back against the brick of her side of the alleyway and followed her across, grabbing a handful of disheveled hair that had fallen loose from its braid, and he kissed her hard on dark, parted lips flavored with an unmistakable tang. She kissed back gratefully and entwined his waist with one leg, insistent on drawing him closer. His fingers traced her shoulders, found the wet fabric there and slid it aside so that her chiton, rendered useless by the battle anyway, slid down her arms and hung suspended on bent elbows until she dipped her hands and it caught on her raised thigh. Soon enough it fell from there, too, and the garment ended its useful life forgotten, blood-drenched, trampled underfoot.

He ran his hands, as sticky as hers with half-dried blood, down her bare body, over soft breasts with dark, taut nipples that gave way and sprang back with every passage of palms which left trails of other men's life essences on honeyed skin which, but for the lack of light, would have appeared pink with the same blood. One hand settled on her hip while the other traversed her flat stomach, with its bare hint of rippling muscle beneath, crested the low hill just south of it to advance into the unforested valley below where warm wetness refreshed the film of half-dried gore coating his fingers.

He rolled those fingers back and forth over the shrouded spot which she shared in common, as with all her outward anatomy, with women born of earthly seed. Like any of them would have in her place, in the unlikely event they were wicked enough not to mind the blood, Thalassia squirmed in response, raking his skin with crusted nails.

Soon her nails left his back, and the soft fingers appeared under the hem of his chiton, wrapped around his manhood, pulling it toward her with clear intent. He heard the sound of sandal hitting wall as she planted the foot of her raised leg on the wall behind him.

Her warm palm guided him to regions warmer still, and he thrust inside her, driving her back into the hard surface behind. She embraced him and moaned. Another scrape of sandal on plaster and Thalassia became weightless, holding her whole body aloft on spread legs braced between the two walls of the alley. Relieved of the resistance of her weight, each thrust up and forward became that much easier and more pleasurable.

After ten or a dozen such strokes, Thalassia came, with one hand on her sex, the other at the back of partner's neck, pulling his head against hers. Her more-than-human muscles tensed and shook, and from behind him Demosthenes heard a sharp crack which sent heart into throat and threatened to soften other organs now in use.

"Sorry," Thalassia whispered hurriedly in his ear. She was breathless now, something she had not been in the orgy of slaughter just before. "I cracked the wall. Don't stop."

He did not; the interruption only forestalled completion by seconds. With nose buried in black curls, inhaling death and nectar as she held him tightly, he let seed explode into the warm abyss of her womb.

They stayed thus for a very short while before Demosthenes unsheathed himself and fell back against the opposite wall. He looked behind him and in the dim starlight could discern a spider's web of black crevices in the plaster. He looked back up into another barely visible web, that of Thalassia's Mark. It reminded him that he, too, was wearing warpaint, and he scarcely wished to imagine his appearance below the neck.

"We will make grim sights come sunrise," he observed. "We must wash."

Thalassia clipped on her cloak, but left her bloody rag of a dress on the alley floor. "Phormion's?" she suggested.

"Our enemies will search there, and I would not see my cousin's life shattered like mine for aiding us. Nor anyone else's. No," he concluded. "A great many Acharnians sheltered in Lakiadai during the Spartan sieges of years past. Many of the temporary shelters built for them now stand empty apart from vagrants."

"Like us?"

"As you say. And should any eyes fall on us, the folk of that district are more hostile than most to Sparta. Collaborators will be few."

Keeping to the darkness, a cloaked shadow leading the

way, they crept away in search of shelter for the night.

12. Feel it

Navigating twisting back alleys, hiding from Scythian guards and clusters of bystanders awakened by the alarm, they reached the outskirts of of Lakiadai in inner Athens. The district's residents were Demosthenes' tribemates, and like him, cousins to the Acharnians, whose farms had been the most devastated by successive Spartan invasions. Thousands of Acharnians had sought shelter here, overflowing the homes of their relatives and necessitating the construction of temporary dwellings, since had fallen to disuse. They were ramshackle, single-room structures barely tall enough for a man to stand inside, effectively tents made of plank and plaster, not even worth tearing down to make fresh use of the materials.

Thalassia scouted the maze of these dwellings in search of one not presently occupied by beggar or vagrant while Demosthenes crept up to the community cistern with two pitchers 'borrowed' from a front garden. Minutes later, they met up again, and Thalassia led him to the shelter she had chosen.

Inside, she laid down her swords and let her cloak slide to the floor of filthy, matted straw. Blue light let in by the single, small window illuminated a ghastly, glistening wound on her upper back where a spear blade had opened her flesh. The sight of it made Demosthenes wince. Setting down the pitchers, he bid her crouch down so he might wash it.

Before commencing, he gingerly ran a finger along the edges of the wound, finding them slick with milky, translucent mucus, the same stuff which had coated her in death.

"You feel nothing at all?" he said, knowing the answer.

She half-turned to give him her profile, not her pale eyes.

"I choose what to feel."

That seemed not so much an explanation as it did, strangely, an apology.

"Does pain not have its uses?" Demosthenes contemplated aloud. "Does it not help us to know we are alive? And to keep us alive?"

"It does," she said. "I'm aware of the damage. It just doesn't translate to pain. The sensation is blocked. Or muted to near nonexistence."

"How long has it been since you felt pain? Physical pain," he clarified, for he knew she could, and did, feel pain of other kinds.

"Other than slight and consensual," she answered, not too cryptically, "a long time."

"You can remove the block any time?"

She threw him a glare. "What are you getting at?"

By her tone, she knew exactly what he meant.

"Feel it," he said quietly. It was a suggestion, not a command. "Just for a moment. Be one of us. Be alive. Be... Jenna."

Thalassia scoffed, abruptly turning her head to give the asker a faceful of hair. "What would be the fucking point of that?"

After a moment's thought returned no point he could articulate, Demosthenes joined her in scoffing. "You're right. It's foolishness. I apologize."

Lifting the pitcher, he poured water in a trickle over the wound while dabbing at it with the hem of his already bloodied cloak.

Suddenly Thalassia fell forward onto her knees and groaned sharply in an unmistakable way. Setting down the pitcher, Demosthenes pressed close and maneuvered to face her. She looked up at him with eyes narrowed and teeth clenched, emitting a low groan. Movement near the floor caught his eye, and he looked to find her fingers rapidly opening and closing in an insistent gesture.

He understood the request and set his palm into the clutching fingers, which Thalassia proceeded to squeeze so hard it seemed as though the skin of his hand must break open, blood and bone shooting out like pulp from a grape too long on the vine. Instinctively he wished to free it, but tempering instinct, he offered no resistance.

Whether from pride or some other motive, she had taken his challenge. The block was lifted, pain felt. The nasty, deep, gaping tear on her back was no longer just a cosmetic damage to her fast-healing flesh but a true wound of battle, the kind which made the bravest of grown men, Equals like tortured Arkesilaos, scream to the gods for mercy.

And so Demosthenes endured the crushing of his hand, knowing she endured far worse. Leaning close, he wrapped his free arm about her, set chin on her good shoulder and saw her face in starlit profile: eyes tightly shut, lips pursed as if in intense concentration. Her breaths came in short, sharp, irregular puffs.

"Enough," he whispered into her ear, but she showed no sign of having heard him. "Stop," he repeated. Again it was but a request, all he had the right to make. Thalassia's mind, like her body, was her own.

She remained thus, squeezing his hand, for the space of many more intense breaths. Then, at last, taut muscles fell slack and her iron hand opened. After a brief silence, she shrugged him away and looked up. He could see that the pain was gone, but her expression was bitter.

"Happy?" she asked.

"Likely never. But the gesture is appreciated."

The twist of Thalassia's lip, and his hard-won sense of

her, told him that she had intended to be angry at him but something, perhaps his choice of reply, had prevented it.

"That hurt like fuck," she said. "I know, that was the point. But from now on... just accept that I'm better than you, and be glad for it."

"I would not wish it otherwise," Demosthenes said, resuming washing her wound. "I merely thought to give you an experience you may have forgotten."

"What, of having an asshole enjoy seeing me suffer? I don't need that."

"I won't lie to you, since it's pointless to try," Demosthenes said. "I did not exactly *enjoy* it, but..."

"Yeah." She cut off his search for words. "I know. That's why I did it. Now, if your troglodytic little monkey-brain is done coming up with ingenious ways of interfering with me, you need sleep."

In that, Thalassia was right. He had not slept since Corinth, and there but briefly. "And you?" he asked, rinsing sticky blood from all her limbs.

"I have another three or four days before I need sleep."

"You'll heal faster."

"We need clothing," she said. "I'll get us some." While still in a crouch, she drew her cloak up around her and pinned it.

Demosthenes lowered himself onto his backside in the filth of the floor. "I would prefer you did not steal from my countrymen, if you can avoid it."

"I'll go to Alkibiades' house," she answered, rising and picking up one of her two swords. "If it hasn't been thoroughly looted, there will be something there."

Demosthenes accepted the wisdom of the plan. "Just that, then. Please do nothing foolish."

In the starlight, the purple shade looming above him

scoffed. "That was the old me," it claimed, not very convincingly. "Besides, a foolish act is just a clever one that didn't... something. Never mind."

She vanished, and in silence Demosthenes shed his own cloak and chiton and set to removing the gore from his own limbs and the warpaint of kohl from his cheek and forehead. Then, wrapping himself in his cloak and rolling his bloodstained chiton for a pillow, he laid down his head.

At first he tossed and turned, finding it difficult to sleep in spite of the exhaustion of travel and combat. If only, he thought absently—then balked at finishing the thought.

If only she were at his side.

Had he become so dependent on her presence? For protection. For distraction. Whatever else. The notion kept him awake longer still, fingers tensing on the sword handle at any sound sharper than that of a night bird's call.

"*Dee!*" he heard what seemed like seconds later, but surely was longer. He shot upright with sword in hand.

Of course, there was only one being in the cosmos who called him by that name, and so he quickly knew there was no danger.

Thalassia threw a heap of white fabric into his lap. The fresh garment which she wore glowed softly in the moonlight.

"Get dressed. We're going to meet Omega."

Demosthenes shook off the sleep which yet dragged at his eyes. "What? How did you...? But..."

"Save your poetry for later," Thalassia chided, jerking his arm.

"You did something foolish."

"It worked, which means it's... never mind. I had a conversation with your cousin."

"Phormion? You should not have—"

"It was pleasant and civil. By the time we finished, he

was even able to look me in the eye and not stutter much."

"And he knew? Of Omega? Why did he not tell us?"

"Simple. He swore secrecy. Even if he hadn't, someone like you, whom the Spartans can't wait to capture, is the last person they want knowing a secret like that. Now dress, will you?"

13. Huntress

One's wedding was hardly enough to excuse a Spartiate from the routine of morning mess, calisthenics, and drilling, and so Styphon awoke early the day following his abduction of Hippolyta.

When husband and wife had dressed, Hippolyta pushed back the plain curtain separating new construction from old. In the small megaron the hearth still burned, tended all night by Eurydike, who upon seeing them did as was expected of her, walking over promptly (if without enthusiasm) and putting knee to floor with head bowed before her new mistress.

Looking gratified by the gesture, Hippolyta set fingertips on Eurydike's matted, coppery curls. The hand then slipped under the slave's chin and tilted the downcast, freckled face upward.

"Eurydike," Hippolyta said. "Styphon says you are undisciplined. Are you?"

The former slave of Demosthenes answered hesitantly, "I do not know, mistress."

"You do not know? It seems you ought to." After a pause which went unfilled, Hippolyta resumed, "Have you had a mistress before?"

As Hippolyta's fingers fell from her chin, Eurydike slowly nodded. Her former mistress was, of course, the one she had witnessed executed by Brasidas. Before the deed, Eurydike had even done her best to see their places exchanged. But Styphon had not told his wife of those events.

Hippolyta went on, "It will be a new experience for me having a maid dwelling in the house. We Spartans are used to our slaves living outside the city with their families. Hence I cannot tell you precisely what sort of mistress I shall be.

However, I suspect I will be a strict one." She put a hand over Styphon's lips and asked the slave, "Does my husband fuck you?"

Eurydike answered dully, "No, mistress."

"Strange," Hippolyta said. "You are quite pretty, for a... what are you, a Thracian? Yes." She ran fingers over one of the dark bands of ink which ringed her slave's upper arms. "We don't get many of your kind here. In fact I've never seen another. So I suppose I could truthfully say you are the best-looking Thracian I have ever seen."

She chuckled; Eurydike did not. Unsure what to make of the unfolding encounter, Styphon only stood by and let it proceed.

"If you are undisciplined," Hippolyta observed, "then my husband must punish you. Does he?"

Dismay was evident in Eurydike's eyes, probably at learning (as Styphon himself was realizing along with her) that the new mistress of the house seemed inclined toward harshness.

"I try to give him no reason."

Hippolyta smiled. "Such a cute accent." The smile vanished. "But that was not an answer. What does he beat you with? There must be something. Bring it to me."

No such implement existed, and Styphon had not beaten or otherwise harmed her since her entrance into his household. Like his new wife, he was new to cohabitating with a slave, but evidently it had led him down a different path than she. It seemed to him that a slave who remained present while the master slept, so long as he or she was adequately obedient, was not one who should be needlessly embittered.

Eurydike's eyes went to her master for salvation which he declined to offer. She threw her gaze instead at her mistress' feet, letting silence be her reply.

Understanding, Hippolyta mused, "We'll go and fetch a switch today, then. I think walnut will do nicely." She stuck up her pinky finger. "About this thick. Yes, that should yield a satisfying stroke. But let's inspect the target. Stand up."

Eyes downcast and hidden by her hair, Eurydike became a statue.

"You like my feet?" Hippolyta asked. "If you would care to kiss them, go ahead. Otherwise, stand up, turn around, bend over and show me my target. I am curious if you have freckles there, too."

Keeping her face hidden, Eurydike dragged herself upright, her body a stiff, shadeless shell, and did as ordered. Hippolyta gripped the high hem of the slave's short chiton and flipped it up to expose rounded buttocks, one of which she passed a hand over before swatting just hard enough to make its flesh shiver. With her other hand, she tugged Styphon's belt.

"You tell me you never availed yourself of that?" she asked incredulously. "Why ever not?"

Styphon had no answer to give. It had not occurred to him to do anything of the sort. If he thought of Eurydike as a person and not just another object in his home, like a cooking pot or a table, then it was as his daughter's friend, or else a hostage entrusted to his care by Brasidas in case she proved of use someday against the former master who presumably gave a shit about her.

Eyeing the 'target,' which was indeed freckled, Hippolyta sighed petulantly. "That will do for now, slave," she said. "If I need you, I—"

What stopped her speaking was the faint sound of a stifled sob. After flashing Styphon a strange look which he failed to interpret, Hippolyta walked around bent Eurydike's still exposed rear to kneel by the slave's face and part its curtain of dirty red hair. Eurydike's next sob was louder, wetter, and still more poorly contained. Styphon saw a tear plunge from her cheekbone to form a dark circle on the floor mat.

Almost maternally, Hippolyta took the slave's head in hand and used an arm on her back to guide her to the floor, where Eurydike curled up.

"I am sorry," Hippolyta said to her softly, holding her. The apology must have surprised the recipient even more than it did Styphon. "I was only playing. It was in poor taste. I am not like that at all, I promise."

The soft, sweetly spoken words of comfort failed to silence Eurydike's sobs or stop her tears, but rather seemed to have the opposite effect: now she cried loudly and openly. Hippolyta buried the younger woman's face against her breast, rocked her and whispered soothingly into her ear, "Shhh. It's all right. I think we'll be friends. I really do think you are pretty, you know. That part was truth."

Eurydike continued to weep with undiminished intensity, surely not just over the cruel jest at her expense but other built-up sorrows besides. Over her red hair, Hippolyta delivered her husband a fresh, strange look.

He understood it, or thought he did.

Yes, she had been toying with Eurydike, but the tearful result was no mistake. The scene before him now, with slave curled up receiving comfort in her lady's arms, was exactly the ending she had desired from the start.

It was not for Styphon to imagine why that was, any more than it was for any man to imagine why women did almost anything they did. But if he had to guess, that guess would be that he had just witnessed the start of a seduction.

14. Blight

"You mustn't be late to mess," Hippolyta advised her husband while still comforting Eurydike.

Nodding agreement, Styphon started out the door of his house only to behold Andrea returning up the long, dusty trail that connected house to unpaved street. She had been running, but slowed to a fast walk on seeing her father. Caught, she surely saw no sense now in racing up to him for a scolding.

She met him with gaze averted.

"Where have you been?" Styphon asked.

"Where you sent me," she answered. Styphon lacked a witch's truth-sense, but native instinct told him this was a lie.

"Are you sure you were not with Eris?"

"I ran into her," Andrea confessed, or certainly only half-confessed. "I lost track of the hour. I apologize."

Since taking Eris as her tutor some ten days prior, Andrea had been acting strangely and telling what Styphon suspected but could not prove were small lies. Now, for example, the bedraggled look of her, short breath, and smell of fresh sweat suggested she had come from rather further away than the nearby house where she was to have lodged the night.

He was considering whether to bother confronting her or be on his way when Hippolyta came up behind him to stand in the doorway, forcing the moment of formal meeting between step-mother and step-daughter.

"Andrea," the new wife greeted. "You are as beautiful a girl as your father has said." Styphon could not recall having told her such a thing. "No to mention keen of mind and fleet of foot." These things he had told her. "I pray I prove worthy of membership in such a remarkable family."

Andrea only looked at her.

"Do you have nothing to say to your step-mother?" Styphon prompted.

"Thank you, ma'am."

"Pft," Hippolyta said. "I would hardly expect you to call me mother, but not that. Hippolyta, or Lyta, if you like."

"Thank her," Styphon said, nudging his daughter's arm. "And then apologize for your lateness. And your appearance, while you're at it. Is that blood on your dress?"

Looking down, at the spots in question, she thought a moment and said without looking up. "A girl I was wrestling with had her period."

"I did not ask you that, did I?" Styphon pointed out. "Apologize."

"I am sorry, Hippolyta," she said. Andrea's normally sharp wits must have mounted a recovery, for she looked straight up at Hippolyta and offered with some sincerity, "You will prove more than worthy. I can tell my father has done well for us both." Stepping forward, she lowered herself, took Hippolyta's hand and kissed the back of it.

"Add kindness to your growing list of blessings," Hippolyta observed. She touched Andrea's hair, then drew her into an embrace which was returned, if somewhat stiffly. "I have a wonderful idea," she said when they broke. "My wedding night has left me... salty. Eurydike's hair needs washing, and you've been menstruated upon, poor thing. Let us all three go to the river and bathe."

"A fine idea. In fact, Andrea," Styphon went on to decree, "you will become Hippolyta's very shadow for the next three days, helping her to adjust."

Andrea's face fell slack and for several seconds she appeared to ponder confrontation, but in the end she opted reluctantly to yield: "Yes, father."

To the degree which he could know his strange daughter's mind, Styphon understood her hesitation: she feared displeasing Eris. If only there were some way to break the she-daimon's hold on her. What interest did the witch even have in an eleven-year-old girl?

Leaving the females to embark on their outing to the river Eurotas at their leisure, Styphon hastened to morning mess.

* * *

Before and during the meal, word circulated that decisions were to be handed down this morning which units were to accompany King Agis on the expedition to subjugate and punish renegade Pylos, the city given its independence two summers prior by Demosthenes. Every Equal, naturally, was eager to find out he would get a chance at glory, but inevitably a large number were to be disappointed.

When dining was done, crowds clogged the open area near the foot of the acropolis, in sight of its golden temple, which was not by any means truly the center of the amalgam of five villages that constituted the city of Sparta, but was called a center and treated as such. (Neither was it a square, yet some called it that, too.) Styphon went to the place himself, and arrived at the back just as one of the king's men mounted the stout wooden platform which saw frequent use for announcements, speeches, floggings, executions, and the like—anything meant to be public, which was a great many things.

The king's man had no need to call for silence, for it was swiftly given. He unfolded a parchment and began to read from it, calling out a list of beasts and fearsome adjectives which were the adopted names of the 128-man *pentykostyes* to be called up for the campaign: Warthog, Python, Falcon, Fearless, Blood-slaked, Ironclad... the list went on. Styphon listened carefully for the name of his own unit, Scorpion, but the speaker fell silent without uttering it.

The men of the crowd finally broke their silence with words of muted celebration or congratulation, never disappointment, lest that be interpreted as objection to the will of a superior, in this case a king. Styphon, likewise, kept his disappointment private.

The king's man raised a hand, plunging the crowd back into silence for a final announcement, the time of departure for those named to bring doom to Pylos: tomorrow's dawn.

Styphon's men were sullen as he led them through drills and then accompanied them to a subdued midday mess, at the end of which a Helot messenger summoned Styphon to the king's presence at a corner of the red and gold painted temple to Apollo. Going there, he found Agis consulting with a cadre of advisers and the pentekosters of the units chosen to assault Pylos. Over the heads of those men, the king waved Styphon closer, interrupting his council of war.

"As most of you must know, Styphon last night became my kinsman," he said to all present. The small crowd raised a congratulatory murmur. "He now has the misfortune of staying home fucking my cousin instead of helping us bring Pylos to heel. Now, if you would excuse me a few moments while I have words with him."

Agis said to Styphon, "Walk with me," and together they set off into one of the many wooded areas which filled the spaces between Sparta's five villages. When no man was left in sight, Agis said, "Apologies for making light of your being left behind. I would like to say it's mainly on account of your unit being only freshly returned from Attica, and there is that, but I am only a man and cannot always put my own desires aside. The desire in this case is to see the gods plant a son in my cousin's womb before they make her a widow. A mere king cannot control Fate, perhaps, but he might give it a nudge." He rapped Styphon's upper arm with a friendly punch. "Offspring sired on her would have a valid claim on the Eurypontid throne, you know. Not a strong one, but a claim. Stranger successions have happened."

"It had not crossed my mind," Styphon said. Perhaps in truth it had, but only in the form of hope that it was not the case, since boys with tenuous claims to kingship often enough were the target of plots to ensure they never lived to see adulthood.

"Gods willing, there will yet be plenty of war to go around," Agis said. "Pylos is being offered no alternative to destruction, but surely at least one of those other towns who were sympathetic toward Athens will yet refuse to capitulate. With luck, maybe some few of them will even try to form a League against us and require some harsh lessons."

After traveling a few more paces in silence, Agis leaned close and lowered his voice. "I am told by those who were supposed to care for her that Andrea vanished in the night, not to be seen again. Did she return to you?"

"She did," Styphon said, declining to offer further detail.

"Good, good," Agis said, although strangely he sounded as though he did not quite mean it. "She is a fine girl," he went on, curiously, before arriving at what was surely his real point. "It is a shame to see her fall under such a malign influence as that so-called tutor of hers, the bitch whose name I prefer not to speak. Would that I could have provided her a tutor." He paused, then added, certainly not extemporaneously, "I still could, were the current one somehow removed. That would be a good thing for every man, woman and child of us, never mind your girl." He chuckled darkly. "Better for all excepting one man, perhaps, Brasidas, who then would have to stand or fall like the rest of us, on his own merits."

Without giving reply, Styphon listened to the king speak with a false casualness, as if these thoughts were just now entering his mind, of killing unkillable Eris. What reply could there be except to counsel him against such madness, and that was hardly an enomotarch's place.

As if echoing those thoughts, Agis mused aloud, "Alas, I suppose it could not be done, except by some ruse or ambush, and even then not without substantial loss of life and the promise of terrible vengeance upon all in the event of failure. Right?"

At least the question was an easy one. "Most certainly," Styphon answered.

"Unless..." Agis continued, as though the words were not prepared in advance. "Pah! No, never mind."

Styphon knew the next line scripted for him. His lips struggled against the sense of duty which would have him speak it. When Agis threw him a darkly disappointed look, Styphon's inner conflict was settled, and he surrendered the expected words.

"Unless what?"

The young king subtly smirked and wrapped a brotherly arm around Styphon's neck as they walked. "I am told it is not possible to deceive the witch," Agis said. "But if some close associate of hers were to pass along false information, believing it to be true, then there would be no lie for the witch to detect. A proper trap might thus be laid, yes?"

"Yes," Styphon was forced to concede. The identity of the proposed intermediary between Eris and her would-be assassins hardly escaped him.

"Look, Styphon," Agis said, lowering his voice further still. "I will not insult your intelligence any further. I know you know what I ask of you. You needn't give answer yet. I leave with the dawn not to return for some number of days. In the meantime, when you're not fucking your wife, give some thought to whether ridding your city, and your flesh-and-blood, of this blight is not worth the risk. Will you do that for me, Styphon?"

"Of course, sire. Agis."

"Good man." The king halted and let more space come between them. His hand came to rest at the nape of Styphon's neck, where it squeezed just slightly, his iron ring of kingship pressing into his flesh. "And should you choose to report what I've said to Brasidas, which I understand is a possibility, well, you will still be a good man. However, a misguided one, and one whose death I would soon regret having to cause."

The ringed hand affectionately patted Styphon's cheek.

"Now get off to your marriage bed and do your duty as a citizen," he said, smiling, not needing to offer reminder that it had been his guards who built the bed.

* * *

That night he performed his duty as many times as he could, and the following dawn he stood and watched the army set off. At the head of the column was Agis, flanked by his elite bodyguards and his bald, staff-bearing Minoan seer, and at its rear went the covered behemoths, the katapeltai, drawn by teams of oxen and accompanied by the men trained to operate them. These machines and their crews were the concession of Agis and his allies of the Gerousia to the majority of ephors who might otherwise have tasked their own favorite, Brasidas, with subduing walled Pylos. In the face of division, there had been compromise: king's leadership, polemarch's methods. For supporters of either side, there was advantage to be gained in victory and blame to be reaped in defeat, but when it came to one matter, no man of Sparta, not even Brasidas who argued for an eventual end to the institution of Helotry, disagreed.

Pylos, the city of slaves which two years prior, under the guidance of Demosthenes, had revolted and won its freedom, must be ground to dust. Its population, having proven its disloyalty, was to be given no second chance at servitude. Rather, its streets were to be emptied of living souls, every last one sent to the afterlife, their homes thereafter to be given over to other subjects whose loyalty was unquestioned.

15. Omega

They slipped out of Athens by the Itonian Gate, which now that Athens was a subject city was but a set of pylons, its stout wooden doors unhinged. The main streets were alive with Scythian police and armed collaborators questioning bystanders in the hunt for escaped prisoners, but by using patience and observation, they carefully evaded notice.

Dawn was breaking by the time they reached the appointed place outside the city, an old broken footbridge over the river Ilisos. They settled in a secluded copse on the riverside, in sight of the bridge, where Demosthenes sat on a fallen elm and ate from the bread and cheese which Thalassia had thought to bring him from Phormion's. Seated beside him, she flicked stones at various inanimate targets on the far side of the gently rolling current, hitting them every time.

Having eaten, Demosthenes found a place to rest his head whilst his partner's keener eyes kept watch. He kept silent and did his best to narrow his awareness in time and space, to think nothing of the past or future, or of gods that did not exist, or of multi-layered universes that did and were filled with pleasure palaces built on exploded suns. There was only the flesh on his bones, the one yellow sun that warmed it, chill mud under sandaled feet, fish grazing the rippled surface of the lazy river ahead. These things were real, and so was she beside him, Thalassia. Since her death, she had become more human and he less.

Somewhere in the middle, they had found a place of understanding.

"What are you thinking?" she asked, giving away that she could not, in fact, read minds.

He answered without delay: "I was thinking that I should very much like some roasted chestnuts once they're in season."

His companion saw it for the lie it was, of course, for even if she could not read minds, she did read fluently the unspoken language of deception.

She laughed knowingly and said without rancor, "That can probably be arranged."

As Phormion had not revealed Omega's identity, they were to know him by the fact that he would carry Phormion's cane, the Egyptian one of ebony which long ago had been a gift from Demosthenes to his cousin. Before much more time had passed, a lone figure walked cautiously up to the bridge from the direction of Athens, bearing the black stick in hand. At the river's edge he stopped and looked around, at which point Demosthenes stood, drawing the man's gaze. At this distance Demosthenes did not recognize him, if his face was a familiar one, but a short walk up the bank, under the man's watchful gaze, offered a better look.

Omega was a stout figure, thick of neck and limb, with a square chin, hard face, and closely-cropped hair, almost a stubble, that conformed to the shape of his skull... and Demosthenes did know him as an acquaintance, met on several occasions. He had been a trierarch of some repute during the war, winning the award for valor in the naval battle at Chalkis. His family was a wealthy and prominent one, and as a boy he had been close friends with Alkibiades.

"Greetings, Thrasybulus," Demosthenes addressed the younger man as they reached the bridge. Thalassia stood in his shadow a pace behind.

Thrasybulus—Omega—broke neither his silence nor the hard stare which he split evenly between the two before him.

Judging that the tone of the meeting was to be less than cordial, Demosthenes adjusted his own manner to match. "You know what we did," he said curtly. "We are in Athens one more night. We would see our time put to good use in your cause."

The man who had been a captain in Athens' now nonexistent navy scowled and grated, "Had you come to me yesterday and told me your plans, more men freed from chains might have retained their freedom instead of being recaptured by Spartans and their sycophants. We would have been prepared."

"We operate on instinct," Demosthenes said, knowing that Thalassia smirked inwardly, if not openly, at the borrowing of her sentiment. "Plans laid by us are not necessarily plans."

At length Thrasybulus growled reluctant approval. "An impressive feat," he said. A note of bitterness could not be concealed. "What else do you have in mind?"

"We come to ask that of you," Demosthenes answered. "Shall we walk?"

Together, the two men in front and Thalassia behind, they crossed the bridge, Phormion's cane tap-tapping on the boards. They continued onto the small, dusty track beyond.

"Even if you succeed in restoring the democracy," Demosthenes said, "Sparta will only send another army to subdue a city lacking walls. If Athens is to be free again, Sparta must met a broader defeat. That is what my companion and I work toward—on other fronts than this. But while we are present in Athens, I would see our actions coordinated with you, that they might not catch you by surprise... again."

Appearing skeptical, or perhaps just permanently annoyed, Thrasybulus slowly came to nod. "Last night changes things," he reflected. "We have yet to learn what Isodoros will do in response to your provocation. The greatest likelihood is a fresh round of mass arrests, perhaps killings, to prove to his patrons that he is up to the job of keeping order on their behalf."

"If I may?"

The interjection came from Thalassia, whose tendency in such encounters as had until now been to let Demosthenes speak for them both. He gave his silent approval, which was entirely for the sake of their audience, and she proceeded.

"Have the prior harsh actions of the tyranny diminished support for your cause?" she asked.

Thrasybulus lowered his brow and eyed Thalassia with suspicion. His gaze flicked to Demosthenes briefly, then back. Suddenly Phormion's Egyptian cane flew up in his hand and arced toward Thalassia's head. Demosthenes took a step back, surprised but not worried, while the blow's intended target easily blocked the attack with a hand that shot out from under cloak. A heartbeat later, she wrenched the stick from Thrasybulus' grasp and set its scuffed, tapered tip against his neck, where it settled into the hollow of his throat.

The resistance leader did not retreat, and his face showed no fear. "I only wished to see for myself what I had heard," he said. He hooked a finger over the cane to lower it, which Thalassia allowed him to do. Gracefully righting the stick in one hand, she offered him the jackal-engraved handle. Taking it, he asked of Demosthenes, "Is she what they say she is?"

"Yes and no. Ask the shades of the twenty Spartiates who died at the jail."

"*Twenty?*" Thrasybulus echoed incredulously, the first crack in his stony composure. "We had heard eight."

"Twenty," Demosthenes swore, "or may Zeus and Apollo wither me with plague. Only seven fell by my hand." He was sure Thalassia would not begrudge him the exaggeration. As for the two gods he had invoked, they could go fuck themselves. "Now, you might answer her question.

What has been the people's reaction to the tyranny's crimes?"

Thrasybulus pondered a moment, answered, "Every harsh deed of the new regime causes men's longing for the old ways to increase and our cause to gain followers. What of it?"

Demosthenes attempted no reply, but yielded to Thalassia.

"The tyrant's heavy hand speeds his demise," Thalassia said. "The more harm Isodoros inflicts on Athens to restore his image in Sparta's eyes, the more your own support will swell. In the short term, more Athenians may suffer, but ultimately when you make your move, greater numbers will be ready to stand behind you, or at least stand aside."

Omega absorbed her words before evidently rejecting them. "I won't welcome seeing more good men and their families lose their property, their liberty, their lives, for the sake of speeding a counter-revolution. I want my city back, not a ruin." His brine-worn features shook in an emphatic negative. "No. If you two truly wish to aid our cause, then kill Isodoros. The tyranny is not united behind him. There are at least two factions riven by various petty disagreements, who agreed only reluctantly to unite behind him. I'll wager that his removal would set them to fighting again. I have begun laying plans for his death myself, but I sense you are capable of achieving it significantly faster and with less... waste." His eyes were on Thalassia.

Demosthenes likewise looked to Thalassia, who barely flashed him a glance before answering on their behalf, "We shall do it tonight."

A smile cracked Omega's features, then vanished, replaced by his perpetual scowl. "Then my faction shall lay plans for the aftermath. And perhaps a small celebration. But..." He leveled an intense look at them. "I implore you to cause no more chaos until then. As I said, I desire freedom for our city and our people, not a shade-filled ruin."

"We shall spill no more blood but the tyrant's."

Their purpose discharged, Demosthenes was eager now to end this encounter,. Still, learning what he could of a friend's fate was worth a small delay.

"What news have you of Alkibiades?"

"He was taken to Sparta," Thrasybulus answered grimly. "For members of the Board of Ten, such a voyage was followed soon after by the return of their bodies for burial."

"They were *strategoi*," Demosthenes mused. "Alkibiades was—"

"Along with you, Alkibiades resisted them the longest," Thrasybulus correctly observed.

"Sparta will find a use for him," Thalassia interjected. "Alkibiades will make sure of it."

Knowing of Alkibiades what even a childhood friend such as Thrasybulus could not—his would-be future as a traitor to Athens in the same future, now unwritten, in which Demosthenes was to die in a ditch in Sicily—he readily accepted Thalassia's assurance. Omega seemed less sure.

"Who remains of the Board?" Demosthenes asked.

"But one," Thrasybulus replied. "Your fellow hero of Pylos, Kleon." He breathed a humorless laugh. "Last year, I regretted not having been present to see you bloody his fat face during the Spartan jailbreak. How little our old squabbles matter now."

"Where is he? Gone to ground, I imagine."

"No, in fact. He is presently in Corinth in the hope of pushing its democratic faction into a coup."

The news caused Demosthenes to share a thoughtful look with his partner. Perhaps, when next they passed through Corinth, they might test whether Kleon yet bore a grudge. For Demosthenes' own part, no longer was there room in his heart for petty hatreds—only that hatred which counted most.

"Thank you," Demosthenes said earnestly to Omega, halting on the trail and prompting the others to follow suit. "It is a noble task you have undertaken. This evening, my partner and I shall see to the matter discussed before taking swift leave from Athens. I hope we shall meet again one day."

"Aye," Thrasybulus concurred. "May Fortune bless your efforts this night, and all others."

"She will, friend," Demosthenes said. "I give her no fucking choice."

16. Tyrannicide

They reentered the city before the sunset curfew and hid until nightfall near the home of Isodoros. Then, in near total darkness thanks to a thick blanket of clouds hanging over Attica, their faces smeared with kohl, they crept into sight of the tyrant's residence.

Four Spartiates stood sentry on its front gate, the approach to which was lit by oil lamps, while two more walked the mansion's perimeter. The added security made sense in light of last night's events, but leave it to Equals to live up to the reputation they only partly deserved by assuming an attack would come in the form of a frontal assault. Equals by and large were no dumber than any other man, but what they were was obedient to a fault and obligated—nay, bred—to keep their mouths shut when given bad orders.

Frontal assault was surely an option, since Thalassia could dispatch them all with ease, but that was not their intent tonight. Rather, they surmounted the low garden wall at the rear of the residence, waiting until the two sentries were around corners. Once in, they took shelter briefly behind a pair of massive decorative amphorae, and when they were sure the coast was clear of slaves and any guards Isodoros might have posted within, they swiftly crossed the unlit garden of low shrubs to arrive at the smooth exterior wall of plaster. Yellow or some bright color by day, it presently appeared dull gray against the deep blue of night. Set into it above their heads was a small window, currently shuttered, which could only lead to one or the other of the master's bedchamber and the women's quarters.

Demosthenes crouched with back to the wall and let Thalassia mount his shoulders. Then he stood, putting her head above the window sash where she listened carefully for several seconds before using a thin piece of copper to gently open both sides of the shutter. She slipped inside and few seconds later sent down an arm, which Demosthenes clasped. She hoisted him, and he climbed inside as soundlessly as he could then crouched by the wall, letting his vision adjust while Thalassia carefully re-closed the shutters above his head.

"Women's quarters," Thalassia informed him in the lowest of whispers, her lips tickling his ear. "Five sleepers. Follow me." Her hand found his and clasped it tightly. Her vision, of course, required no time to settle, and she used that advantage now to guide him as they crept across the tile floor like the assassins they were to shortly become.

She stopped at the wooden door to the master's chamber. As was typical, it was equipped with a lock for such times as the man of the house required privacy with some flute-girl or concubine. Thankfully, at present, the door stood ajar. Thalassia pushed it open, producing a faint creak. When no sound of stirring or movement came, they pressed on into the room where presumably their target lay sleeping.

Thalassia pivoted to set the door back in place, at the small cost of another creak, then guided Demosthenes' hand to the lock and whispered in his ear, "If anyone makes a sound, bolt it."

He understood the reason for the instruction—for all of the second which elapsed before he was compelled to follow it.

"Who is there?" an occupant of the room called in a breathless whisper.

Demosthenes slid the bolt home, gently, while Thalassia vanished in darkness on a course for their target's bedside. A second later he overheard her say, in a sultry whisper, "I need your cock in me."

Either she meant to buy herself a few seconds of confusion or, more likely, she was toying with her prey.

To the sound of fainter, unintelligible whispers, Demosthenes ventured forward and perceived as he came closer Thalassia kneeling upon the bed alongside the chief tyrant of Athens, holding to his throat the dagger which was the only armament either of them carried this night. Her other hand held a silken pillow over Isodoros's face. His labored breaths hissed through it.

Demosthenes asked his fellow assassin in a whisper, "What are you waiting for? Just kill him. He might cry out."

"I told him if he does, his family dies, too."

Demosthenes chose to assume this was a bluff. "Just do it!" he urged.

"Sure, but it's your city. I thought you might want to yourself. If not, you could have waited a block away."

"Just—" Demosthenes started, but he finished with an angry sigh, drawing his own dagger. Coming up beside Thalassia and setting a knee on the bed, he aimed the tip of his dagger at the tyrant's throat, and with scant hesitation, drove it downward. A gurgle sounded as black blood rushed out, soaking the edge of the pillow which Thalassia pressed harder onto Isodoros's head.

His limbs flew in wild spasm before falling back lifeless on the bed, and in a swift motion, Thalassia was on her feet. She looked to the chamber door seconds before it shook gently with an attempt to enter from without. Then came a soft knock and a woman's voice: "Isodoros?"

Demosthenes did not wait to hear more, but went to the room's single window, identical to the one by which they had entered, and opened its shutters. Thalassia was right behind him.

"Isodoros?" the woman said again. "Are you well?"

As a freshly made widow pounded on the locked door of that room, the pair of tyrannicides vanished into the night, navigated a maze of deserted Athenian streets, mounted their waiting horse, and commenced the night-ride to Corinth.

17. Lord of Wind

The day after the departure of the expedition to punish Pylos, when no duty pressed and he was reasonably certain that Eris was out of the city, his daughter along with her, Styphon went to a certain dwelling near the center of Sparta. The estate on which it stood was state-owned, having been seized half a generation ago from the family of an Equal sent into exile for embezzling public funds. The exile's house, while no non-Spartan would call it a mansion, was rather larger and better furnished than was the standard to which more honest folk held themselves.

The dwelling had served a number of mostly diplomatic purposes over the years. Currently, it was where the captured Alkibiades was held under house arrest.

Oddly, at least to Styphon's mind, no guards were posted at the entrance. Eris, the prisoner's warder, perhaps was thought to be deterrent enough against any attempt to escape. Whatever the reasoning, Styphon was able to walk up the straight path to the door and hammer twice with the worn wooden knocker graven in the image of a gorgon.

Within a few moments, Alkibiades—Athenian, preener, last leader of his city's defeated army, and the man whom Styphon's own daughter called *uncle* for his having fed and sheltered and educated her for more than a year prior to Athens' fall—opened the door from within. Smiling as one who after too long had finally laid eyes again upon a friend, which Styphon did not consider himself, he came forward for an embrace not on offer.

Alkibiades' jaw was freshly shaven, and his oiled hair, worn long for an Athenian, fell in waves framing features which might have been carved in fragile alabaster. Gone were his jewelry and silken finery, but he had not bowed entirely to

Spartan tastes: evidently he had somehow come by a chiton, certainly not of local make, embroidered with a red geometric design at the collar and hem and in a vertical line connecting them. The battle-wound to his leg, which gave him a slight limp, did not appear to be seeping through its bandage.

Strange how the manicured hands of someone who would have looked more at home in the pavilion of a Persian king, if not his harem, than on a battlefield could acquit himself so well on the latter, wielding the weapons of a man.

But then, much the same could be said, and even more accurately, of Eris and Thalassia.

Declined an embrace, Alkibiades greeted cheerily, inaccurately, in his effeminate Attic dialect, "My good friend Styphon, to what do I owe the pleasure of your most welcome presence?"

In addition to continuing to dress frivolously, he apparently had failed to adopt a more Lakonian style of speech.

Styphon's reply, by contrast, was stripped to bare necessity: "I would share words."

"By all means!" the preener returned eagerly. As he stepped back to make way, Styphon noted the presence of a curtain just hanging inside the door, the only purpose of which could be to prevent guests seeing inside until such time as they were invited in. Pushing the curtain aside while Alkibiades stayed to close the door behind it, Styphon learned the reason for the foreigner's unseemly concession to privacy. In the megaron beyond the curtain, near the hearth, on one of many embroidered rugs that covered any trace of the hard-packed earth underneath, were two young Helots, one male and one female. The male stood upright with a water pitcher held in either hand while the female knelt by his feet. The evidence of the former's erection and the latter's placement relative to it lent itself amply to a conclusion of what activity they had been engaged in immediately prior to the guest's arrival. The significance of the pitchers, however, eluded Styphon.

Entering just behind, Alkibiades provided answer by addressing the pair.

"I don't recall telling you two to stop," he said. There was more playfulness than command in his tone.

On hearing it, the male hoisted the two pitchers in well-formed but trembling and unsteady arms above the female, who settled in to resume her prior activity of fellating him. It became clear to Styphon, though he wished it had not, that a game was underway, with the female engaged in a race to bring the man to release before his strength gave out and he was forced to douse her—assuming the spasm of climax itself did not achieve a similar result.

The male Helot's wet hair bespoke a round of the game recently played in reverse and lost. Or won. In this house, it seemed rather likely that the only winner was Alkibiades.

"You can stop," the pair's unrightful master told them a moment later. "Go into the back rooms and finish, or not, as you see fit."

Relieved, the male set down his burden and went with the female, who rubbed his arms for him with some affection as they walked.

"Husband and wife," Alkibiades explained in a low voice. "Ask them, if you want, whether they would prefer their usual labors. I'm sure they would elect to stay." He chuckled. "I punish them, but not as harshly as you lot."

In fact, many Helots of Lakonia were largely well treated, but it was ever the way of Athens to equate all Helotry with its more brutal Messenian incarnation. Nonetheless, Styphon had not come to correct his misconceptions. Nor had he come to find out how Alkibiades treated the sex puppets to which a prisoner ought not be entitled.

When they stood alone in the megaron, Styphon began to broach the one subject which did interest him enough that he willingly suffered his present company.

For caution's sake, some preamble was unavoidable.

"I would have this conversation remain between us." When Alkibiades started to offer assurances, Styphon cut him off. "They involve a certain individual whose name I prefer we not speak, one who evidently cannot be deceived. Thus I would not expect you to succeed in lying to her, in the event she were to ask you directly about our conversation. What I ask is that you not offer up such information to her willingly. Can you make such a promise?"

All trace of Alkibiades, self-important lover of excess, now vanished. In his place there stood Alkibiades, lover of being important. "I swear it," he said earnestly.

"Then I would have you speak to me on a subject in which I know you have an interest: my daughter, particularly with regard to the intent and motive of her tutor."

Alkibiades' look, especially his pair of expressive brows, said he was unsurprised by the request, but found it a difficult one. He gestured at a soft couch (another foreign indulgence), then walked there in his uneven gait and lowered himself upon it. Accompanying him, Styphon squatted to bring himself level, but declined to sit.

"I possess no sure knowledge," Alkibiades said. "But I can offer you insight and informed speculation. I will give it freely, too, with nothing asked in return." He shrugged. "*Although...* should you find yourself in a position to recommend me to anyone of influence, be it Brasidas or the king or some other, the favor would not go amiss."

Styphon cleared his throat loudly in the hope it might put the other back on track.

It did. "Forgive me if anything I may say is already familiar to you, but I shall start by telling you about Thalassia, since in at least some ways she and *the other one*"—he obliged Styphon's half-superstitious desire to avoid Eris's name—"are alike. They served in the same army, the Veta Caliate, which was led by a woman, and from what I understand, almost exclusively female in membership. They hail from nowhere on this earth or under it, but from other worlds among the stars, although they are humans, or claim to be. Their bodies and minds have just been *improved* in relation to ours on account of their also hailing from else*when*. What is the present and future to us is the past to them, already written."

"Andrea," Styphon interrupted, making of his daughter's name a command.

"I will get there," the blowhard returned, undaunted. "Our futures to them are written, but not immutable. Their actions already have changed the fates of our cities and all who dwell in them. Where our war was to have raged for another generation, instead it is already ended, albeit with the same victor. Thalassia lied to me about my own fate. She told me history was due to forget me, but Eden... *Shit!* Sorry, won't happen again... informed me I would have been a hero of my people, the last great champion of Athens, who failed only in the last days to turn the war around. Hektor, if you like, to my city's Troy. Achilles would have been—"

"I do not have all day!" Styphon snapped.

Alkibiades frowned and nodded, then continued. "I do not begrudge Thalassia the lie. We all need to look out foremost for our own causes. She never let me in on what hers was, but I can tell you it is not democracy, nor the welfare of Athens. Ede—I mean the one I will henceforth call Frosty, which is how I think of her—does not even know. I don't know that Thalassia's aims matter much to her compared to her rage at being trapped on our world because of her. Demosthenes knows her aims, I should think. If not, he is a far greater fool than me."

Of course, there was little chance Alkibiades actually believed himself a fool, or anything short of a demi-god, for that matter.

He might well be Aeolus, lord of winds, it seemed at this moment to Styphon.

"By Zeus, you blather too much, even for an Athenian!" Styphon grated. Surrendering to a longer stay than he wished, Styphon consented to sit, albeit on the floor rather than a cushion. "The next word from your lips had best be my daughter's name."

"*Andrea*," Alkibiades obeyed pointedly, but not fearfully, "was a pupil of Thalassia in Athens. And of Sokrates, may the Maiden shelter his gentle soul," he inserted, a brief shadow falling over his features. "I am not privy to what Frosty has in mind for your daughter, but I have at least a guess as to what Thalassia's intent was."

"A *guess*?"

"She never actually told me, but it is more than a guess. Having been the star pupil of Sokrates myself, I never *guess*, only draw reasoned conclusions based on the available evidence. Instinct, too, but mostly evidence. Now, may I continue?"

The preener had the gall to sound perturbed. Under Styphon's answering glare, he resumed.

"My reasoned conclusion is that Thalassia aimed to plant in Andrea, and the school for girls that she and I hoped to found, a seed which might grow over time into something not unlike her own Veta Caliate, an independent army of warrior-women with brains to match their blades. 'Pythagorean Amazons' one might say."

He seemed proud of the description, which did not mean much to Styphon.

"What end the existence of such an army might serve, I know not, but I can say with certainty that it would amount to a force for *change*. Even not knowing the aim, I supported the effort out of a personal fondness for Thalassia and a more general fondness for perverse ideas."

Styphon scowled in disgust that his daughter might have been used in the furtherance of what the preener correctly labeled a perverse idea. But he checked any other expression of displeasure and asked instead, "You believe that the other"—not being a child, Styphon refused to refer to Eris as *Frosty*—"may possess a similar intent?"

"I cannot be as sure as I was with Thalassia, for the simple reason that I have not"—quite transparently, he smirked—"been fucking her for as long. But it is my initial guess. I mean *conclusion*."

"Would that it had been your initial utterance," Styphon lamented aloud. Complaining was not the Spartiate way, but he could scarcely help himself. "Is that truly all you can tell me of that creature's designs on my daughter?"

"No," Alkibiades said coolly. "There is yet the matter of my instinct."

For the sake of dragging words, whatever their value, more quickly out of the man, Styphon played along. "And what does instinct tell you?"

"It tells me..." Alkibiades paused theatrically and smiled to himself as though at some inner joke. "It tells me," he resumed slowly, "that Her Frostiness *likes* Andrea. For one reason or another, she simply enjoys her company. Maybe she just likes being a teacher, and Andrea is the right student. Or maybe your girl reminds her of someone from her past, or herself a hundred years ago. Yes, she is quite old. She might even want Andrea as a lover. I just sense that where Thalassia took no particular pleasure in being Andrea's tutor, this one does." His exquisite brows rose in a facial shrug. "That's all I have, except for one last impression I will offer not knowing whether it is relevant or not." Again Alkibiades adopted his most serious look as he warned, "I would not envy the man who tries to insert himself between that woman and what she wants."

With that, the Athenian exhaled in a sigh and sat forward.

"Help me up, would you, friend?" he asked. Styphon got to his feet and offered the preener a thick forearm which Alkibiades used to rise. "I would ask you to stay and share wine and some more talk," Alkibiades went on, "but I have discovered that no one *ever* says yes to that in Sparta." He chuckled. "Or maybe just not to me. I will detain you no longer."

As they walked to the door, Alkibiades set a hand on Styphon's bicep, turning him.

"There is actually one matter I would put to you," the preener added. His bright eyes were sincere. "A request, in fact. You needn't reply now, merely keep it in mind. Assuming I am not executed, if one day I should be allowed a return to Athens, I should like to take Eurydike with me. I was never her master, but she and I do share a bond." He raised an open palm. "As I said, no answer is expected, and the day when one will be needed likely remains far off."

"Even if that day comes, the answer may not be mine to give," Styphon said, proceeding past the privacy curtain to the exit. Alkibiades hobbled along behind. "There are two others whose permission you will need. Brasidas... and my wife."

"*Wife?*" Alkibiades echoed after a moment. He laughed. "Congratulations!"

Without responding to the well-wishes, Styphon turned on the house's threshold and defied, just this once, his tendency to keep his thoughts to himself when they were unasked for.

"I will offer you an observation of my own. Call it instinct, or whatever you like." He set his hard, black eyes on those of Alkibiades. "When you lie with either of those two... you are not fucking *them*. They are fucking *you*."

Feeling a touch of pride that a Spartan had had the last word with an Athenian prattler, Styphon turned and departed.

　　　* * *

Returning to his home after evening mess, he found Hippolyta and Eurydike, mistress and slave, partaking together of a meal from the same platter, in breach of long-held custom. The latter looked up at him showing guilt mixed with fear for the instant before her gaze darted elsewhere. The former, his wife, smiled at him knowingly. Her plans, it seemed, were proceeding apace.

"Andrea has not returned?" Styphon asked.

She had not, and as night fell, that did not change. While Hippolyta was in bed, asleep after their obligatory, if pleasurable, efforts toward conception and Eurydike was huddled by the hearth, Styphon sat outside under a swath of stars, watching for a small shadow on the long path to his door.

At last Andrea came, walking the final stretch with her head bowed in one or all of shame, annoyance, or fear on discovering that her father had waited up. Styphon had never beaten his daughter, but plenty of fathers did, and most would for this offense, even here in Sparta where boys were expected to be boys and girls could be boys, too.

Styphon stood to meet her. "Tell me all you did with your tutor today, Andrea," he demanded as she drew up in front of him, avoiding his gaze. Her bowed head gave him a clear view of the red ribbon, his gift to her, that spiraled down the length of a thin braid hanging amidst the locks of her long, straight hair.

"Lessons," Andrea said lamely.

"On what? Loosen your tongue or have it loosened. I will have details."

"Nature," she said, avoiding her father's gaze. "Mathematics... cosmology ... anatomy."

"Those are subjects, girl. What did she actually teach you?"

Shifting uncomfortably, Andrea offered nothing.

"If you are too ashamed to repeat it," Styphon lectured, "then it was not worth learning. Now, swallow your shame and answer."

"I am not ashamed," she said quietly, and Styphon believed her. "Please just let me be, father," she begged. She had yet to meet his gaze.

"*Leave you be?* You are my blood. That means something to me. Does it to you?"

She came back quickly, resignedly, "Yes, father."

"If I ordered you to stop seeing your tutor," he asked, "would you heed me?"

Head hung, she said nothing.

"The truth, girl! Would you obey me, the one who put life into your flesh?"

"No!" Andrea came back, raising a face in which fire suddenly burned alongside fear. "I could not. Eden teaches me what no other man or woman on earth could. She teaches me Truth, about this world and others! She cuts a trail for me through the mire of ignorance and lies in which we wallow, every one of us in every city!"

Looking down upon his daughter, Styphon listened calmly to her passionate, un-Spartan outburst and what followed.

"Thalassia... *Geneva* started me on the path, but she held back," Andrea said. "She concealed things. Eris does not. She trusts me. She sees greatness in me. She wants what is best for me, and I..." Suddenly the fire in her flickered, still burning but with reduced intensity as she said to the earth, "And neither will I settle for anything less than what is best for myself."

Styphon let silence fall as he continued to regard her, considering the path of which Andrea spoke, as well as his own path.

"Step closer," he commanded her at length.

To her credit, his daughter did not hesitate, even though she may have believed his intention was to bring her within arm's reach for a blow. Instead he took a matching step, bent down and drew her into an embrace. He kissed her hair, adorned with its red ribbon. "I, too, want what is best for you," he said.

After some hesitation, Andrea brought her arms up to return the hug, stiffly at first and then melting into it. Styphon let the embrace endure for a few shared heartbeats, then broke it and stood over her.

"You may continue to see Eris." He forced past his lips the witch's name, the borrowed name of the goddess that she was not. "With the understanding that you do so under my authority and not against it, and that you are still bound by the rules of this house. Is that understood?"

As if scarcely believing her luck, the eleven year-old who was wise beyond her years returned wide-eyed, almost incredulously, "Yes, father." She gave him a little smile, stepped forward and sent her thin arms once more around his ribs. "Thank you, father."

Styphon remained a statue. "Now get to bed."

Disengaging, Andrea complied, opening the door and creeping into the unlit, silent house. Instead of following, Styphon remained outside a moment longer. Sleep was far from his mind, for he had in the preceding moments reached a decision which charted a dangerous path for himself, for his family, and for Sparta.

He would risk them all and use his own daughter to lay a trap which, if the gods willed it, would ensnare Eris and leave her dead. This time for good.

Zeus help them all if it failed.

PART 3

THE BATTLE OF NAUPAKTOS

1. Waking up in Corinth

Demosthenes tried in vain to open leaden eyes. Failing, he rubbed them instead. During the night, if night it was, since he had no idea of the time, someone seemed to have replaced his head with a replica formed of wet clay.

"Good morning," said a woman. He did not instantly recognize the voice, which bore some foreign accent.

He dragged his eyes open, shut them again under a deluge of light and blinked forcefully until he was at last able to peer out at reality through narrowed slits, putting face to unfamiliar voice.

Almost.

"Do I know you?" he asked the blurred impression of a female hovering over him. All he could tell was that she was pale of skin with ash blonde hair.

And she was in bed with him, and naked.

She laughed. "I should think so." She shifted her position on the soft mat, forcing him to roll his dully aching head to keep her in view. "It will come back to you," she said sympathetically. "If not, you can ask your nice Persian when she returns. She knew me a few times last night, too."

A name drifted into reach of Demosthenes' mossy tongue. "Ammia," he said. She had made him look human again after his brief stint as a cave-dweller.

"Mmm-hmm," the northern prostitute confirmed.

The realization that he was in Corinth spurred more memories. Yesterday, he and Thalassia had come from Athens to learn that the ship on which they had intended to make their return to Naupaktos had sailed early, without them. The next was not due to depart for three days. They had argued mildly about whether to wait or just make the two- or three-day trek overland. He could not recall who had argued for what, but evidently waiting had won, and they had wound up back at the *Nymph's Tit*. That was where this room was, he felt sure. On the floor, near a window which seemed to look out from a second story, sat a wine krater painted with images of a Dionysian orgy. A clay cup floated in the dregs of purple wine that remained at the broad vessel's bottom.

Under the blanket, a hand appeared on Demosthenes' cock, calling to his attention that it was erect.

"I'll take care of that, no extra charge," Ammia offered.

"No." Demosthenes hand covered hers and started to remove it, but he lost the will, which made her smile.

"Your Persian's gone to get food," Ammia said, subtly stroking him. "And anyway, she will hardly be jealous. The four of us were as one last night."

Something in that statement struck Demosthenes as odd. "Four?"

Ammia sighed plaintively, hand still teasing him. With a smirk, she lamented, "You really cannot hold your wine, can you? So charming. You saw another client, Menandros, passing by and invited him to join."

"I did?"

"Aye." The prostitute shrugged. Her palm ran up and down the length of his shaft which, partly thanks to her, showed no sign of flagging. "I can't just leave this here," she said of it. "Call it pride of profession."

With such warning given, and no argument offered by the recipient, Ammia proceeded to lubricate palm with tongue and commence a skillful massage which within a short span saw the matter tended to.

While she wiped her fingers on the blanket, Demosthenes' eyes went to a rustle in the curtained doorway. Carrying a platter piled with bread and various relishes, Thalassia took no pause to survey the scene on the bed, but only walked to its edge, where she placed the tray on the blankets.

The timing of her arrival was rather too perfect to be coincidence; more likely she had returned moments earlier and chosen to wait outside rather than interrupt.

She spared a quick, serious look for Demosthenes which, if he read it correctly, had nothing to do with Ammia.

Sitting naked on her haunches on the bed, the latter twisted to face Thalassia and smiled. "Hi," she said, and no more. There was something of the smitten adolescent in her manner.

Withholding return of the greeting, smiling back distractedly, Thalassia said, "Ammia, sweetheart, would you excuse us? Take some breakfast if you like."

Looking disappointed, the young Illyrian (as Demosthenes by now had uncertainly marked her) slid off the bed.

"I will see you again?" Ammia asked hopefully. She set fingers gently on Thalassia's cheek.

Thalassia took the hand and kissed it in a manner that was only subtly dismissive. "We are in Corinth another night."

With a sigh, Ammia leaned in and kissed Thalassia's cheek before throwing a silken gown over her shoulders. "I will miss my new friends."

She left the room, though not before blowing a kiss to Demosthenes which went unreturned—an omission she did not pause long enough to note.

"You make friends easily," Demosthenes remarked, dragging himself upright in the bed.

Thalassia took the spot that was still warm with the prostitute's indentation. "It's a nice change for me."

Her look became serious as she announced, "There's

news. Agis left for Pylos with an army. By now, it has probably already fallen."

Half-covered by a blanket rank with stale sweat and fresh semen, Demosthenes stared at the platter of bread and olives and various accompaniments Thalassia had brought. The thought of eating turned his stomach at the moment, and he labored to think past a fog clouding his mind. Reading what were doubtless unsubtle clues, Thalassia removed the breakfast from in front of him and set it instead by the window.

"Shit," Demosthenes muttered under vile-tasting breath.

Just prior to his departure from Naupaktos, he had advised the Naupaktans to deliver a message to their cousins in Pylos advising that they abandon their city entirely and seek refuge in Naupaktos. It was implausible that such a mass exodus of man, woman, and child could be safely undertaken, by land or by sea, but stripped of the Athenian support which had won the city its freedom, Pylos was doomed to fall. They had decided, both before and after Demosthenes' briny rebirth, against voyaging to Pylos to help defend that city. Given its location deep in Spartan territory, it would be more difficult to defend than Naupaktos, and chances were high of their becoming trapped there if defeat came.

Equally as certain as the defeat of Pylos was that its conquerors would show their rebellious slaves no mercy.

"An army under Agis?" Demosthenes asked, the ache in his skull rather hindering the speed of his thoughts. "Why not Brasidas?"

"Maybe he's fallen out of favor. Maybe Eden snapped his neck. Maybe he knows a king's thunder is best stolen one bolt at a time. It doesn't matter now. What does is that—."

"The fate of Brasidas is of utmost importance to me," Demosthenes chided. "But yes... a great many good men, and even more innocents, will suffer and die. It pains me."

It pained him rather less than it should, he knew. Less than it would have a year ago.

"They will be avenged."

"Of course," Thalassia said. "But before that, it may impact our plans. The Naupaktans may be cowed and vote to capitulate."

Demosthenes sighed, forcing himself to rise from the bed. "Then I suppose we had best set to finding my fellow Athenian, a man most gifted in delivering speeches that goad men to war."

"I've asked around and have an idea where to find him."

"You are busy while I sleep," Demosthenes observed as he hunted down his clothing.

"You should sleep less."

"I should *drink* less. You pulled me from one lake of wine. Why did you allow me to fall into another?"

Thalassia smiled warmly. "Simple. There is drinking because you want to die—and drinking because you want to live."

2. Kleon

The northeastern quarter of Corinth was known by all to be a stronghold of the democratic faction, a place where the enforcers of the ruling oligarchy dared not venture for fear of igniting a fresh civil war sure to decimate both sides, as had occurred in the past. The information obtained by Thalassia got them to a certain street, where they simply began asking after Kleon until they found a man who answered, according to one who knew the difference, them with a lie. Under threat of violence, he admitted knowledge of Kleon's whereabouts and took them there.

The ruling faction in any city expected to be the target of plots, and ever allowed those making them to walk about with some degree of freedom, hoping that their plans would never gain momentum, or else would be defeated when the time came. Kleon, wanted not by the Corinthian oligarchs themselves but their Spartan patrons, was a special case. His capture was likely to bring the man who delivered him fortune and favor, along with minimal risk of revenge attacks, since he was a foreigner lacking blood ties in the city.

Fittingly, Kleon's hiding place was a room tucked behind a butcher's stall in the small agora built by the democratic neighborhoods to sustain them when the main market was made inaccessible by open war between the factions. The blood-spattered butcher, a thick-set, cleaver-wielding man, eyed his three visitors with suspicion and curled his lip while the unwilling guide explained that his two captors had come to see 'the Athenian.'

"Kleon!" Demosthenes called into the shop, past the hanging corpses of sheep and birds. "It's your ally from Sphakteria come to see if we cannot call ourselves the same again!"

The stall fell silent. A moment later, there was a rustling at the back, and a curtain was gently pushed aside.

The face which next appeared was scarcely recognizable. Kleon had grown a beard, full but well-trimmed, to cover his perpetually rosy cheeks. The face had less meat in it, too, as did the rest of his form, which had grown decidedly less stocky in the time since their city had fallen.

However much he had changed, two shrewd eyes forever casting about in search of advantage gave the demagogue away.

"Let them through," he said to his Corinthian hosts.

His invitation was reluctant, as was the subsequent wave of the stall-owner's iron cleaver as he bid them pass. Less reluctant was their unwilling guide's disappearance into the street the instant Thalassia's firm hand was removed from the back of his neck. Making their way between the carcasses, they reached the curtain, which Kleon held open for them, watching them pass with a look which was far from welcoming but short of malignant.

The small room beyond was hotter by a wide margin, which served to accentuate the odors of animal blood and human sweat. A sleeping pallet took up a quarter of the room, while most of the rest was taken up by jars and amphorae and various implements of the shop-owner's trade.

A tanner in Athens, Kleon had not sprung from any wealthy household, but in his latter years he had acquired something of a reputation as a flaunter of what wealth he was able to amass. To be so reduced could not have been easy on him.

The look he wore as he let the curtain fall and faced his guests was a bitter one; he seemed to expect them to take delight in his misfortune, and for once had no sweetly acidic words instantly at the ready.

"I come in the hope of burying our past differences," Demosthenes opened. "And to take you from this place for a while, if you can stand to part with it."

Kleon snorted, a sound Demosthenes remembered well, and not fondly. "Bah!" he said. "Differences! You mean your fist to my face and my prosecuting you for it? I look back fondly on such things now, reminders of a time when we were free to indulge in our petty squabbles."

The 'squabble' which had precipitated the rift between them was far from petty—the blow had been delivered to prevent Kleon from risking innocent lives in the effort to recapture escaped Spartan prisoners of war. Still, under the current circumstances, Demosthenes thought better of correcting him.

"One day, when our city is restored to us, gods willing, we will return to bickering," Kleon went on. "But for now, in exile, we are as brothers. What is mine is yours." He indicated the cramped space. "As you can see, that is not much."

He turned an eye on Thalassia, and his expression became once more tainted with bitterness.

"This one I remember from Pylos," he said. "The slave whose ransom you made up for from your share of the spoils. I confess I thought you mad, but judging by the tales told of the fight at Eleusis, you got the better end of that deal. The gastraphetes and liquid stone and the trade goods which brought you riches—these were hers, too?" Demosthenes confessed as much. "Some claim she is Pallas herself. She scarcely looks the part, but every schoolboy knows that one's fondness for disguise. So what is she?"

Still taken aback by the speed with which the notoriously vindictive Kleon had offered forgiveness, Demosthenes laughed. "I will not try to explain what she is. Let her, if she cares to. But later, for there will be plenty of time to talk on our voyage to Naupaktos, if you agree to accompany us. Your passage paid, of course."

The demagogue without a *demos* continued to study Thalassia a short while longer, while she stared inscrutably back. Then he frowned behind his beard and said, "That city's one of four or six I heard were sent the terms of an alliance with Sparta." He laughed. "Not unlike the terms we sent to more than a few of the islands in our city's heyday. *Pay tribute or be crushed.* So let me hazard a guess..." Kleon surmised with a smirk, "you desire my help in convincing the Naupaktans to choose being crushed."

"I hope you might find a better way of putting the argument for their ears," Demosthenes said. "And the possibility exists for success." He sent his gaze pointedly to silent, regal Thalassia. "But yes, effectively, that is our aim."

Kleon shrugged ambivalently, studying Thalassia with narrowed eyes. "Athens fell in spite of this one's assistance. What makes you think she can do better by a different city?"

Thalassia's failure to show any intention of answering left Demosthenes to provide one. "I only said success was a possibility. But generally speaking, the failure was more ours than hers. If she had had her way, Athens would have possessed ships to counter those which beat us and better defenses on the frontier as well as at Piraeus. Democracy got in our way, an impediment lacking in Sparta."

"Naupaktos suffers under like burden," Kleon observed.

"The very reason we stand before you. Men's minds must be swayed in favor of war. Even your bitterest enemies admit that no one is better at that than you."

"Especially them," Kleon said, rightly. He looked about him as if weighing the prospect of leaving his current situation. The answer seemed obvious, but was not yet written on his face. He nodded at Thalassia.

"She intends to take the field again at Naupaktos?"

"If need be."

A second later, the newly battle-hungry Thalassia answered for herself, "Yes."

Kleon nodded approvingly before continuing to address his fellow Athenian. "And can she offer some proof that she is more than mortal?" He quickly appended, "Preferably of a kind even a simpleton such as myself might grasp."

Demosthenes thought a moment and suggested, "Thalassia, show him your gash."

Kleon's brow rose while the object of his puzzled gaze raised a hand to her shoulder and unpinned her chiton. With opposite arm holding the fabric to her breast, she turned and let the back of the garment fall away, exposing a deep, gruesome spear-cut. Even covered as it was by a film of dried, translucent mucus, it was obviously a crippling injury.

"Sustained last night as we emptied the jailhouse of Athens," Demosthenes explained. For increased effect, he prodded hard at the edge of the wound with two fingers; Thalassia, of course, showed no outward sign of the pain she did not choose to feel.

Kleon's nose wrinkled. "Well, that's cured my cock of any stiffness she might have imparted to it." While Thalassia restored her dress, he asked, "Does she have armor?

"We left Dekelea with as much as you see now."

The demagogue smiled the broad, wicked grin he had worn often in the assembly of Athens. He stooped and opened a sack set against the wall. Inside was a large object covered by oiled cloth which when pulled back revealed gleaming metal. It was his breastplate, a famously ostentatious and overwrought thing of bronze inlaid with gold and ivory.

"We can scarcely agitate for war without looking the part," he said. "She will need armor. You, as well."

"Does this mean you accept?"

Kleon laughed. "It seems so... *brother*. Of course, I will not face Spartan spears for the sake of Naupaktos. They can have my tongue, but not my life."

Demosthenes offered a hand, which his one-time prosecutor clasped in acceptance of alliance.

"We shall devote the remainder of the day to trying to look the part you have in mind," Demosthenes said. "For which we will need funds. We have a horse we can sell, to start, and then Thalassia here can make up the difference, provided all the gaming tables in Corinth have not opted to ban her already."

3. A walk with a witch

60 days after the fall of Athens (July 423 BCE)

On the day of Agis's return in triumph from Pylos, Styphon gave the king his decision on the proposal presented the day before his departure. Agis took the answer silently, somberly, then walked away and had no contact at all with Styphon until many days later, when Styphon went to him to tell him that a date had been set. They met only one final time before that day arrived.

That day was today, the sixth following the reduction of rebellious Pylos, a day when, if all went well, Sparta was to be freed of a malignant presence.

It began with father accompanying daughter on a walk.

"Thank you for agreeing to this, father," Andrea said, taking Styphon's hand. "I know once you have spoken with Eris, you will understand."

"I have little doubt."

The idea that he meet Eris to discuss his daughter's education had actually been his own, even if he had managed to make it seem as if Andrea had pressured him into it. Were an invitation to have originated with him, the witch might have suspected foul play. The child had acted as go-between, such that Eris would not be lied to directly.

Yet. With luck, if the right questions were not asked, direct deception would not be required.

"If any man on earth can look into her gorgon's eye and withhold a secret, it is an Equal," Agis had offered him days ago, by way of encouragement. "Just act as if you are advancing into battle, which you are in a way, and wear the mask of stone that all Greece dreads seeing over its shield-rims. Keep your heart slow and breath steady."

The advice helped as Eris came into view, waiting for

them on the dusty road leading north out of the city, to the training grounds which were Styphon's purported destination this morning. He and his child's tutor were to speak as he walked there for the day's drills.

She stood on the roadside like an immovable sentinel of Olympus or of the depths, as tall as most mortal men or taller, dressed in a hunter's cloak of deep green that descended from one shoulder to half-cover a plunging chiton which left bare the pale valley between her breasts. Her thin legs were clad from waist to sandal in the nearly skin-tight leggings of softened hide that savages of other lands were said to wear. Her silken hair, which when unbound hung down her back like combed flax, was today woven into a tight single braid which traversed her cloaked breast.

He took note of one aspect of Eris's appearance above all others: she was unarmed.

So was Styphon, but then he was not to be among her many assassins this day. His only task, when the time came, was to get his daughter to safety.

As they drew up to her, the she-daimon smiled her cold smile. Nothing was wrong with the expression itself; it just lacked humanity. Perhaps it was something in her eyes of deep azure, or maybe Styphon's own eyes just imbued everything she did with a monstrous hue. Whatever the reason, it chilled him. He took Agis's advice, imagining her as an enemy phalanx, and shoved the natural fear of things supernatural deep down where it could not be seen.

Andrea, meanwhile, quickened her step at the last second to overtake him. Dipping her head in a shallow bow, she grabbed her tutor's hand and kissed the back of it. Styphon hid his distaste at the display.

Keeping hold of Eris's hand, Andrea turned to stand facing her father.

"Styphon," Eris said in her musical accent of the south of Haides. "I'm glad you came. I will reassure you, I hope, that you and I need not be at odds when it comes to your daughter."

Like her smile, the she-daimon's words struck Styphon as utterly false. In choosing his reply, he understood that he must be honest with her, as far as he was able.

"Let us not waste breath on the pretense we might part this day as friends," he said. "The sight of you all but seizes my limbs with fear. I would know what your intentions are toward her, and if need be, maybe you will hear my objections."

Eris half-smiled—coldly, again—and lifted a thin brow in approval. "You needn't fear me," she said. "Or my intentions. As you, I want what is best for Andrea." She inclined her chin to the north, along the road. "Come, let's walk."

As they did, Eris showed no sign of awareness that it was the road to her potential demise, but then she was only pale, not transparent.

"I somehow doubt many points of agreement exist between us when it comes to what constitutes the best for Andrea," Styphon said. "More importantly, I understand why her welfare is my concern: she is my offspring. But why should it be yours?"

"A fair question. Strange you would ask it, though. Do you despise your blood so much as to think its inheritor of no note to anyone but you? I possess knowledge fit for sharing with students who are sharp of mind and spirit. I see such a student in your Andrea." She put her hand on the head of the subject of their discussion, who walked silently between them. "She embraces the opportunity and proves me right."

"It seems to me that the subject of your tutelage of

Andrea broaches a rather larger question." He knew he risked provoking Eris to anger, but then anger had the power to blind, something which suited a deceiver well—so long as that anger did not give way to violent rage. "Why are you here?" he asked.

"You know that I am here because of *her*," Eris said, circumspectly. "The Wormwhore."

"But why Sparta? I understand we recruited you, and you consented to help us defeat Athens because Geneva is your enemy. But Athens is defeated and Geneva... elsewhere. What purpose remains to you here?"

She clicked her serpent's tongue. "Careful, Styphon. I might think you wish me gone."

"Of course I wish that," Styphon dared to admit. "Would that none of your kind ever came to our world. But being stranded here, surely there are better places for the likes of you than our city."

"Father," Andrea pleaded through clenched teeth. "Please..."

"No, Andrea," Eris said, smoothing the girl's hair. "I will answer. The truth is that I do lack any reason to remain in Sparta. But seeing as I equally lack reason to be elsewhere, it suits me at present to remain. The Whore's pet told me what he genuinely believes to be her purpose here. It is one which I am yet uncertain whether I wish to thwart. It is possible that she has Magdalen's blessing in her mission... or at least that Magdalen knew what the Whore would do. Magdalen knows many things, and works in ways that of necessity remain a mystery to those who do her will. However, the Whore has trapped me here, and so I must end her, in one way or another, eventually. And so, while I have reason to think that her designs keep her in Greece, I too will remain.

"I have no particular need of allies," Eris finished with a

grin lighting her monstrous eyes, "but I must amuse myself in some way in this... wasteland, lest the years be endless."

The she-daimon's flippant tone was perhaps even more telling than any of her galling words. "It would seem," Styphon observed, " that our country, indeed all the world, is to you nothing more than an arena in which your bloody contest, your *pankration*, is to be fought. With even apparent death marking not its end."

Over the head of silent Andrea, Eris shot an amused look. The look belied the witch's next words, which were clearly meant for her pupil's ears:

"Of course not. I admit I aided you at first to serve my own vengeful ends, but I remain here out of... admiration. Perhaps less admiration for what Sparta is now than for what it might become."

She reached over and touched Styphon's shoulder, a surprisingly warm touch under which he managed not to flinch.

"Take my advice, Styphon," she said earnestly. "Remain close to Brasidas, follow him and convince others to do the same, and together we shall make Sparta masters of the world for a thousand years." Her hand fell back to the girl's shoulder. "Your daughter can and will have a prominent place in that future. It is up to her to determine what that place is. I only aim to give her the tools, the abilities, and the knowledge to realize her full potential. You may rest assured there is nothing sinister in what I teach. Science, mathematics, philosophy, survival, and yes, how to defend herself against any adversary, even a grown male."

Eris added, smiling affectionately down on the girl. "Andrea likewise teaches me. You may find it odd for one such as I to say this, but I feel I am a better person on account of knowing her."

It sounded more than odd to Styphon. It would strike him as rather less odd to hear of an eagle bearing off a field mouse to its aerie, only for the two to exchange guest-gifts and part as friends. But his opinion mattered not. What mattered was *time*, and every word Eris spoke ate a little more of the diminishing quantity of it presently separating her from annihilation. The exact place and moment could not be known, but neither could be far now. They had already passed the last parcel of land assigned to an Equal and moved on to low hills and dry, uncultivated prairies where no more habitation was to be seen than the occasional shepherd watching his flock chew tall grass.

Styphon knew it was important that he keep talking, lest Eris fill the opening with some question which might, either deliberately or by chance, force him to speak falsely and risk discovery.

"The tutor's mandate is to instill not only knowledge," Styphon said, as though it mattered, "but also obedience and loyalty to family and state. You can hardly blame me for doubting your own loyalty to our state, and as for family, Andrea has told me that she would disobey my command to stop seeing you, were I to give it. Is that just the willfulness of youth on her part, or is it something you have taught? Perhaps rebellion is to be the norm in this new Sparta which you envision?"

Too knowingly for comfort, Eris laughed. "I see your intent." The heart in Styphon's chest momentarily stopped beating. "You wish to provoke me to anger, thus proving me unfit as a tutor for lack of confidence in my own arguments. It might have worked at one time, but as I said, I have changed for the better."

She leveled a glare at him over Andrea's head. The eyes he met did not, to Styphon's mind, reflect any changed soul, but a cold and inhuman one. Yes, it was possible he saw in them what he wished and expected to see, and that Eris truly had changed, but it mattered not; the trap was set and soon to be sprung, and its success would serve Sparta well no matter what dwelt in the intended victim's heart.

"Maybe you have changed," Styphon conceded, aware that Eris might detect that as a lie of sorts. Rather than giving her time to say so, he quickly observed, "Is it not possible that Geneva has changed, too, since dying by your hand?"

That seemed likely to provoke a response. It did not get an immediate one, but Andrea did look up at him suddenly with some indeterminate expression. Then she faced forward again, leaving something unsaid, it seemed, out of respect for one or both of the two authority figures flanking her.

Moments later, it was Eris who explained the look.

"Father echoes daughter," she said. "Andrea has been arguing that I have nothing to lose by talking to Thalassia. Except my life, potentially, should I let my guard down."

As she was doing now, Styphon silently hoped.

"There is wisdom in the advice." Eris shrugged. "But I cannot at present imagine looking on the Wormwhore's face without seeking to separate it from her body."

As she spoke these words, Styphon glimpsed ahead, coming around a curve from the opposite direction on the same well-worn track which he walked, the sight which he had tried hard until now not to appear to be anticipating. Marching toward them at quick-pace in a neat square, looking not at all out of place on a road used every day for drilling, were thirty-six Equals in full battle gear. Their spear blades and lambda-blazoned shields glowed orange in the sunrise, and if one could make out from this distance the expressionless faces under the rims of their bronze pilos-caps, he would recognize most as belonging to men of Agis's elite, hand-picked royal guard.

Their orders this day included no training exercises, only the assassination, at any cost, of a threat to Sparta.

4. Assault on Eden

Naturally, Eris saw the phalanx, too. Her far-seeing, sea-blue eyes lingered on it while Styphon aimed to keep his own gaze inconspicuously averted. Taking Agis's advice, he tried to adopt the state of battle-calm in which all Spartiates were trained to face the enemy. He also resolved not to let himself fall silent at this critical moment, but to persist in keeping the intended victim distracted until the final moments, when her assassins drew close enough to envelop her and begin the planned butchery.

"You failed to answer my question of loyalty," he said to her, casually enough, he hoped. "You speak of admiration for some new Sparta yet unborn, but I would see my daughter's allegiance given to the Sparta which exists. Not to vague ideas, like a philosopher worships, and surely not to the person of her tutor."

As he finished, Eris's eyes remained fixed on the square of hoplites whose seventy-two heels moving in unison kicked up a thin dust-cloud in the middle distance. Restraining alarm inside his shroud of outer calm, Styphon endeavored to pull her attention back to him.

"Can you assure me your plans include making Andrea a proper citizen, not just some slave dedicated to achieving your vision?"

At last Eris spared him a sidelong look. The look itself, and what Styphon saw in it, encouraged him. She seemed unaware. He needed only hold out less than a minute now before setting to his next task, that of saving Andrea from being cut down alongside her teacher.

"I can assure you that by any standard," Eris said, "under my guidance, Andrea will achieve more than will any child, male or female, yet born in Sparta. And her contribution, unlike that of most of your females, shall not be measured solely by the yield of her womb."

For a moment, the pressure of Styphon's task faded in the face of offense at her remark. More than any city, Sparta valued its women: it wished them to be strong of body, mind, and spirit that they might push their sons and brothers to be better men—and yes, so they might produce offspring who shared those qualities. Dying in childbirth was the only way a Spartan woman could earn the honor of a grave inscribed with her name, as a man would if he fell in battle. For after all, what would Sparta become without a steady supply of sons to defend it? A dead city, perhaps, or worse, a city of slaves to some invader.

If Styphon had worried for a moment (and he had not) that he had chosen wrongly to cast his lot with Agis and the defenders of tradition, Eris had succeeded in destroying his doubt, sealing with her own words the very fate he had helped orchestrate for her, one which was scant seconds away. The formation's front rank of six was hardly five spear-lengths distant and rapidly closing, on a course to trample them.

Was there, in Eris's watchful look, recognition of some of the faces of Agis's loyal men?

"We had best give way," Styphon said, just as he would have were he a bystander and not an accomplice. He set one hand on his daughter's back, between the shoulders, clutching a handful of linen there. "Come, Andrea."

As he spoke those words, Eris's head flicked toward him. Her delicate brows were lowered over sea-blue eyes in a which a ship-tearing storm suddenly raged.

She knew.

Abandoning pretense, Styphon hoisted Andrea bodily into into his arms and ran for both of their lives across the field of grass which flanked the straight road. He kept his head down, not knowing whether Eris was at his heels.

Just seconds into his flight, war cries arose at his back: the phalanx breaking ranks to charge and attempt encirclement of its she-daimon quarry. At least, that was the plan; Styphon did not look over his shoulder to be sure. Were it possible to both see to Andrea's safety and take part in the attack himself, he certainly would, but that was not possible, and so he ran with plodding steps, clutching fifty pounds of stunned child diagonally across his chest. Behind him, the cries of the charge tapered off into the deadly silence of combat, a silence soon broken by a scream.

It was not a scream of fear or pain, nor was it a war cry. It did not even come from the battle now thirty-odd paces behind. Rather it sounded directly in Styphon's ear, and its source was Andrea. He flinched and instinctively squeezed his daughter tighter, even as the scream dragged on and on.

He guessed her intention, strange as it was: to use her voice as weapon, a sharp, shrill one aimed at him. He craned his neck away and continued to run, ignoring her, but he suspected what was to come.

He was right. Pain lanced through his right earlobe as Andrea gnashed it between her teeth. Legs still pumping through the grass, he jerked her body down and away, perhaps along with a chunk of his ear. But he kept his grip on her and barked, *"Be still!* You cannot help her now! It will mean your death!"

"Put me down!" she screamed in answer. Her lean body began to writhe in earnest to escape her father's iron grip. A small, clawed hand soon covered his face, its first two fingers over his eyes, pressing into them, forcing the lids shut and threatening true damage if her demand was not met.

Having not a free hand with which to swat hers away,

Styphon shook his head side-to-side, and he shook Andrea, but failed to thwart her.

Strange that in all the times he had run through this day in his mind, not once had it occurred to him that Andrea might fight him so fiercely. Scream in anger and the rage of betrayal, certainly, and even hate her father afterward, for a time, but she could not have become so separated from her common sense as to think she had any place on the battlefield behind them—other than to be instantly slaughtered.

If so, then he had acted none to soon in detaching her from Eris.

The sharp-nailed fingers applied greater pressure. Running blind, thrusting his head wildly about, Styphon finally lost his footing and careened headlong into the grass. Still he maintained his grip on his squirming burden, even as all his weight landed on his right arm on the rocky soil underneath.

Andrea's fingers left his eyes, by accident or design, but as soon as Styphon opened them on an expanse of cloudy sky, a blow struck his left elbow in just the spot to send arrows of pain lancing to wrist and shoulder. It broke his grip, and a like a caught fish fighting to return to sea, Andrea slipped away.

Styphon lunged in the direction he knew she would be headed: toward Eris and her assassins.

His hand caught her ankle and clamped around it, and she fell. Breaking the fall with her hands, Andrea twisted and lashed out with her free foot at Styphon's face. He grabbed that foot, too, but the sandal came off in his hand, setting the limb free to draw back and renew the attack. Styphon did not wait, but surged forward, letting the blow glance off of his shoulder as on all fours he scrambled up the length of Andrea's body, grabbing her knee, then the belt of her chiton, and finally throwing all of his considerable weight onto her back. His arms sought and found her wrists and pinned them to the earth, into which her fingers dug in the effort to pull free and race to Eris' side.

"Cease this!" Styphon growled in his daughter's ear. "You cannot save her!"

Their heads were side by side, her body pressed to the ground under his. Andrea's gaze was lifted and fixed on the battle underway on the road, and soon, so too was Styphon's.

Eris stood at the center of a shifting, shouting vortex of red cloaks, lambda-blazoned shields and erratically waving spears. Far from being the calm center of this storm, Eris was a frenzy of movement: a pale head, blonde braid trailing, peeking up above a bronze helmet here, shield-rim there. A spear moved with her—no, two—seized from her attackers. They moved quickly, more quickly than the surrounding Equals' blades, and with every swipe a man groaned and a fresh coat of blood painted the polished iron, red droplets spraying the air in graceful arcs. No sound came from her tightly shut lips, but no move of her limbs failed to part a victim's lips in a groan at least of pain, more likely of death.

Before Styphon's eyes, and another pair of black eyes so like his own, one man after another of the king's elite fell under the blade of Eris—one clutching his throat, another a thigh, another missing a right hand, never again to clutch spear. They dropped where they stood or else fell back to let a comrade fill the gap in the sharply-bladed, slowly shrinking, ring-shaped wall of flesh and bronze and leather and iron imprisoning the she-daimon.

Hope was not lost. Some of the fallen, before dying, or limping off to die later, inflicted blows of their own on the victim. However great her powers, however lethal a weapon was in her hands, Eris could not ward off the near-simultaneous onslaught of twenty or more spears. She avoided the thrusts and swipes of most, knocked a few others aside with her pair of stolen shafts, but not a few blades found their mark. The cuts and gashes which those blows inflicted on Eris's white flesh were mortal by any measure. Any measure but hers. Blood had soaked her garment, which now clung red to every curve of the mutilated flesh underneath, yet she fought on with speed and fury undiminished. Despite the cloak of blood, no drop yet touched her face: a grim, expressionless, feminine death-mask of alabaster.

All this Styphon witnessed in the space of a few fast, shallow breaths while pinning his daughter to the ground. Andrea watched, too, offering no further struggle.

For a time, at least, she did not. Then, of a sudden, her limp body came to life underneath him, and Styphon was forced to drag his attention away from the still undecided battle and focus on preventing Andrea from foolishly, suicidally, attempting to join it.

Worm-like, she writhed out from under him and sprang to the feet which had won her the laurels at half a dozen festival races and many times that number unofficially. Knowing he had no hope of catching her once she found her stride, the moment his foot was planted Styphon launched himself into a desperate lunge.

Again, his hand caught Andrea's ankle and again he brought her down. With no concern for bruising the flesh of his flesh, he clamped fingers around the thin leg and dragged her back by it. Her hands clawed clumps of grass, her free foot lashed at his face and connected, but a few seconds of wild struggle put him atop her again, this time with one palm planted on the side of her head, his weight behind it, pressing down into the earth as if to crush her skull.

Were she not his daughter, he might have, so strong was his rage by now at her foolish resistance, fueled by fresh worry that the assassination may fail. When he had seen Eris slay twelve Equals, they had been the ones caught by surprise, and those men had not been decorated champions, as most of Eris's attackers were today.

The feeling in Styphon's breast came near to the battle madness to which most Greeks regularly surrendered but which every Equal was trained to suppress. He suppressed it now, so as not to slay his child. Perhaps sensing how fragile was her young life in her father's hands, or else having had opportunity to reconsider her choice of sides in the sudden conflict sprung upon her, she fell limp. It was not unconsciousness; Styphon's eye was level with hers, and he saw it turn in the direction of the battle, a source of continuing bellows of anger and agony.

Eris, the white-faced, blood-cloaked Beast of Sparta, battled on. She had broken out of the ring of assassins to fight with her back unthreatened, and those Equals who remained standing to challenge her—half or less of the original number —were forced to maneuver around the heaped corpses and near-corpses of their comrades. Apart from a gravely wounded few dragging themselves away, minds clouded by pain, none so far had quit the battle.

None had quit, even though the day was lost. That much was apparent to Styphon, as it must have been to those looking down doom at the points of the she-daimon's spears.

Styphon would shortly gaze up one of those shafts himself, he knew, into the pale face and heartless, alien eyes of death.

Even if he ran, he would die. There was no point now in bearing Andrea away to safety. He would hold her here until the battle, and a girl's opportunity for rash action, had ended. Then he would face his own fate, to be slaughtered on the ground like a hog if that was what Eris decreed.

She was a false goddess, not the sister of Ares whose name she had adopted, but she may as well have been. If the slaughter before him was any indication, this Eris was the God of Sparta now, and her will ruled all.

5. The god of Sparta

Eight Equals remained, fighting on as if victory still were possible. Doubtless each believed it was, and that he would be the one to land the single fatal stroke needed to lay low their strange enemy. They tried. They acted in concert, sharing grunted words and silent signals in an effort to pierce Eris's defenses. She was not untouchable; the ragged flap of flesh hanging from her left bicep, a gash above her right hip and any number of smaller wounds lost to sight in her second skin of blood stood testimony to that. But those had been inflicted when her attackers numbered four times their current strength, and her wounds seemed not to have slowed her down an iota.

Now the advantage was all hers. She did not quite toy with her remaining opponents—now seven, now six—but she might have. The spears in her hands, like living extensions of her arms, stayed in constant motion, but when the time came to kill, as it did every few seconds, she dispatched men with quick, decisive strokes, no more than was needed.

Five left, now four. These victims made no sound, neither in struggle nor in death. All breath was needed to fight. Death sounds, anyway, were for those unprepared for death, and the three Equals yet standing had had plenty of time to come to grips with the impending flight of their shades from rent flesh and broken bone.

Three remained. They shared a silent look. One raised a war cry, in which the others joined, and then all three charged. They knew that as well as Styphon did that it was certain suicide, but at least it was the best kind of suicide: committed with another man's blade held by enemy hand.

Well, this hand was a woman's.

Second best, then.

They fell within instants of each other, two slashed in darting motions of one spear, the third impaled at the end of the second, which Eris released and let fall along with his corpse. It pointed briefly skyward before the weight of its butt-spike sent it toppling, twisting the spasming torso from which its iron drained the last lifeblood.

The fight might have been measured in an easily countable number of heartbeats. In all her battles, Sparta had perhaps never seen the loss of so many of its elite in so short a span.

Eris stood alone on the road of death, surveying the human wreckage scattered by her storm of wrath. Her gaze went to motion in the sparse grass a few yards from her and she walked to the place, casually, raised her spear and brought it down between the shoulder blades of a man struggling to rise. Next she went to another spot and there put another out of his misery.

"Eris!" Andrea called out, her voice distorted by jaw yet pressed hard against the earth. Knowing he was to die, Styphon released his offspring and slowly got to his feet, meeting the freshly drawn stare of the one who was to be his slayer. He would die standing.

In no hurry, bloody Eris walked toward them, butt-spike of her spear stabbing reddened earth with each step until, still a ways off, she raised the weapon and leveled it at Styphon, her stride quickening. By then, Andrea was up and racing toward her tutor as if to share an embrace.

Though it was not aimed at her, the raised spear stopped Andrea, who quickly put her hand on the ash shaft, behind its blade, and blurted, as if in surprise, "No!"

Styphon was surprised, too—not at Eris's intention to skewer him, of course, but that Andrea would elect to interfere.

Eris halted. Over Andrea's head, on which a red ribbon adorned long, disheveled hair, Styphon met and matched the white witch's scorn-filled gaze.

Girl begged slayer of men: "Please, do not kill him. Whatever love I had for him is gone, but he is still my father. Do not make an orphan of me."

Damaged limbs yet pregnant with the promise of slaughter, Eris asked coldly, without a glance spared for her student, "His life belongs to me now. What do you offer in return?"

"Nothing," Andrea said. A bold answer in which Styphon could not help but feel pride. "Except what I have given you already. He deserves death. But if you kill him, I will not forgive you."

Evil eyes on him, Eris seemed to ponder. Styphon watched her in return, idly considering some action against her in this silent interim.

And then his daughter would look the fool, having purchased a life subsequently thrown away. A strange thought, sure, but then the nearness of death could bring strange thoughts.

Finally, Eris withdrew the spear, spun it, and jammed it blade first into the earth, where it remained. "Be a little angel, Andrea," she said, hard gaze still on Styphon, "and run and fetch Brasidas. Send him, alone, to..." She pondered and concluded, "The Satyrs' Ring, in the woods east of here."

"What shall I tell him?"

The death mask of Eris cracked a humorless smile. "I have faith you will convince him of the gravity of the situation."

Andrea nodded, and before departing on a pair of the swiftest feet of her generation, she directed a final, tight-lipped look at her father.

She looked at him as she would a stranger.

She ran off on the road to Sparta. Eris watched her disappear, while Styphon watched Eris, for one did not take one's eyes off a snake coiled to strike.

"She is mine now," the snake said, coming closer, sans spear.

It was a humiliating gesture, confirmation that she considered him no threat at all, probably would not have, even were he armed. Now that she was so close, he saw the extent of her wounds. In addition to the flesh which had been stripped from one arm, her legs were cut in several places to the bone, or close, and a deep cut ran from her collarbone down the side of one breast. They were wounds of a kind one expected to see only on a corpse.

"Do not ever try to reclaim her," Eris said. She spoke in a casual tone, knowing the words themselves constituted threat enough. "I should thank you. I have her in my debt now for sparing you." She chuckled, a sound like melting ice falling to ground. "The funny thing is that I would not have killed you anyway, and not only for Andrea's sake. If it were just that, I probably would have cut your dog-face in half and worried about your daughter's feelings later." She raised a blood-gummed fingertip and drew a line with it down the bridge of his nose, illustrating the cut with something like regret or longing. "I need a witness to what happened here. And anyway, Brasidas wants you alive."

The last remark surprised Styphon, but being surprised already just to remain alive, he gave not much thought to this lesser matter.

Eris gave a groan of annoyance, a decidedly human expression. "You Spartans..." she lamented. "You paint Athenians as liars, and maybe they are, but you are worse. You exert such control of your bodies. You suppress your true reactions, hide your fears, your desires. You become machines, almost. I knew you were hiding something from me today, but not this." She waved a hand at the carnage, the hand which had created it. "I did not suspect your lie was this big." She gave a wry, sidelong smile. "So congratulations. Now come, let us be off before anyone else comes along and forces me to kill him."

She turned away and walked off, a victorious, mutilated ghost, blonde braid slithering down blood-drenched back as she stepped with a serpent's grace over the carcasses of Agis's royal guard. A trio of crows, the vanguard for a larger force sure to come, landed to sample the banquet left for them.

Eris's passage did not disturb the birds, but Styphon's did as he trudged along behind. The birds took briefly to wing and then quickly resettled, finding new sightless eyes at which to peck.

6. Curse of greatness

The so-called Satyrs' Ring was a roughly circular clearing in a forest northeast of Sparta. At its center sat a moss-encrusted boulder whose visible surfaces were crudely engraved with pictograms bearing vague resemblance to men and horned animals. Greeks almost certainly had not made these markings; some other people had in the shadowy time before the sons of Herakles had swept into the Peloponnese, killing or enslaving the earlier inhabitants and erasing most of their mark upon the land. Now there was just this rock in a clearing, and a few other such places. Someone long before Styphon's birth had named the Satyrs' Ring according to what was perhaps the most obvious vision it conjured: that of Pan or some other woodland god piping on the rock whilst the cloven hooves of half-men wildly pounded the forest floor around him.

A number of beaten trails led to the site, and it was on one of these that Styphon arrived in the clearing behind Eris. Immediately the false goddess went to the boulder, stepping over the offerings of beads and bones and amulets intermingled with detritus which lay at its base. She vaulted up onto its flat top, which was level with her shoulders, a near impossible feat for most mortal men. There she sat with legs crossed, enveloped in a crimson cloak pilfered from the dead to replace the soaked garment (almost as red) which she had peeled from her broken body and left behind at the scene of slaughter.

She shrugged the cloak from her left shoulder, baring soft, white flesh that, even had she been uninjured, would have aroused no more interest from Styphon's cock than did the statues of nude Artemis that the white witch's form somewhat resembled.

Eris looked down at the glistening red void on her left upper arm, the chunk of flesh hanging from it by a thick ribbon. "Look what you've done," she said, sighing. She raised the flap and pressed it back into place. "That will take days to heal."

After a lingering, angry glare at Styphon, she found a bottom corner of her stolen cloak and by hand and tooth tore a strip of wool from it. Using her teeth again as aid, she used the strip to bind her arm such that the wayward flesh was held in place. That done, she stared down at her mutilated thighs, which prompted another venom-filled look at the one she held responsible.

"You know," she mused with a half-smile, "Brasidas would not be more than annoyed if I were to kill you." Behind her narrowed eyes, wicked visions danced. "And I doubt he'd be bothered at all if I just hurt you a little. By which I mean *a lot.*"

Covering her half-minced nudity with the cloak, she shrugged off the idea, for which Styphon masked relief.

"Andrea might, though," she reflected. "The trouble is not worth whatever brief pleasure it would bring me. Ironically, your daughter with her fleeting lifespan has helped teach me patience. I am sure the chance will come for me to kill you eventually."

"Put a weapon in my hand," Styphon said. "I will take away your need to wait."

However honest the spirit of the threat in that moment, it was empty, as Eris surely knew: he had stepped over dozens of fallen spears and as many swords to get here, walking at his enemy's back, no less, yet he had passed up the chance to attack. And be cut down.

Eris said condescendingly, "If you are that eager to die, I'll oblige. But not today. Hatch another plot against me, you and *Agis*," with a sneer she identified the plan's originator, "and see what happens."

Styphon turned his back on a malevolent smile from the witch on her ancient, mossy pedestal, and exchanged no further words with her until the polemarch arrived.

* * *

The sound of swift but measured footfalls in the forest was followed by the entrance of Brasidas into the clearing. He stopped at the Ring's edge and regarded the two awaiting him: witch first, then man. Surprisingly, his look was one of cool contemplation, not anger or even urgency. Styphon knew the polemarch as one rarely to act without measured thought (in that, as in many things, Brasidas fit the Spartiate ideal) but even a man of stone could be forgiven for flying into a hot rage on hearing such news as he just had from Andrea. Yet he did not.

He walked closer to Pan's boulder. As Styphon turned to track him, Eris leaped down from her green perch, landing with the lightness of a bird, a red raven.

The three stood arm's length apart, awaiting whomever would speak first. Styphon only knew it would not be he.

It was Brasidas, heavily: "There is no point in crafting lies. We've no choice but to go straight to the ephors from here and tell them all, just as it happened." He directed his shrewd eyes at his fellow mortal. "Styphon, it is your loyalty to a king which brought us here. Will it keep you from doing as I ask?"

"No, polemarch," Styphon replied, almost instinctively, to the man whose trusted aide he had been for a year.

A curt nod, nothing more, and Brasidas turned his attention to the being to whom was due, arguably, at least some measure the current glory in which he stood—a glory he could surely not help but to see threatened by the day's events.

"The girl said you were hurt," he said to Eris.

"Damaged," she corrected. A flick of the cloak exposed her pale, torn flesh long enough to let Brasidas look it up and down in neutral assessment.

"Go to your hideaway," he concluded. "You should not be seen again in town until further notice."

The instruction resembled more in tone a decisive suggestion than it did an order one might give a subordinate. Brasidas might be brave enough to play with fire when it came to Eris, but he was also sharp enough to know his limits. He knew that this fire also played with him.

With a twitch of her thin lips, Eris indicated acceptance.

"We are finished here," Brasidas said next.

The polemarch's behavior since his arrival in the Ring only seconds prior had been a model of Spartan efficiency, in which grave matters were tended to without passion or a wasted word. Thus, in no time, Styphon found himself walking at his superior's side on the return to Sparta, whilst separately the Beast winged her way back to some secret lair, to lick her wounds and await the summons to wreak more destruction.

"You made an error of judgment," Brasidas said mildly as they walked, "choosing Agis's side in the conflict to come. A shame I had no *cousin* to offer you." He looked at Styphon down the bridge of his hawkish nose and smiled a seemingly genuine smile. "But then, it was not relation by marriage that prompted you to action, was it? It was blood. You worry for Andrea."

Styphon let his silence confirm the observation. A well-reared Equal was not generally inclined to admit to worrying about anything.

"If it were in my power, I would give your girl back to you," Brasidas said with an air of honesty. Neither were

Equals inclined to admit that something was not in their power. "I wish I could even tell you that Eris's interest in her was for the best, or at least harmless. But she is not for men to fully understand, much less to control. I have accepted that. She is a weapon, yes, but one which must be wielded carefully, or not at all.

"You see why. Today the weapon was provoked and wielded itself. Now I am left to clean up her mess and a chart a course around thirty-six dead Equals, all with families whose righteous anger will be directed largely at me. I admit, I cannot be sure how it will turn out."

While Styphon listened to the polemarch's frank speech, he recalled what Eris had told him at the scene of slaughter. Brasidas wanted him alive. For what purpose?

* * *

News of the massacre had already reached Sparta by the time of their arrival. There was shouting and chaos and much directionless running, such that the city's normally reserved streets rather resembled a henhouse at feeding time. All knew that some tragedy had struck, but few yet were aware of its cause or extent. Styphon and Brasidas lanced their way through the crowds (the latter forced to brush off several attempts to elicit more information) to the simple, blue-painted structure which served as the office of the ephors.

Two of these highest officials of the city had already convened when Brasidas and Styphon entered the building; two more made their appearances shortly thereafter; while the fifth and last was learned to be away at the hunt.

Brasidas said nothing at all, standing with Styphon at his shoulder until all four available ephors presented themselves, at which time all other men were ordered out and the door shut.

Almost. A hand adorned with an iron ring stopped the

door, and Agis entered, alone and without word. Brasidas did not spare the king a glance, which made it somewhat easier for Agis to cast, as soon as the ephors' gazes allowed, a discreet look at Styphon. In it was not in threat, neither accusation nor recrimination; what it showed, if anything, was a distinct lack of confidence in the outcome of this day. The look said, or so Styphon interpreted it: *You tried. The failure was not yours.*

According to two of the most influential men in Sparta, it was beginning to seem, rightly or wrongly, that Styphon, the once-disgraced son of Pharax, could do no wrong.

The ephors were the only men in Sparta not obliged to descend briefly to one knee in the presence of their king, and so they did not. Styphon knelt, and was surprised to see Brasidas, beside him, remain standing. Perhaps because of the urgent nature of the meeting, the offense went unmentioned, if not unnoticed.

In response to a demand made by the eldest ephor to know what in the Thunderer's name had transpired, Brasidas explained. "One man present—nay, one man alive—was witness to this day's events. I propose that he tell of them first, in his own words, before we assail him with questions."

The proposal meeting with no objection, not even from frowning Agis, Styphon spoke simply, with blank eyes and stony expression, of the trap laid on the road to the training ground and Eris's subsequent slaughter of her would-be assassins, who were mostly members of Agis's personal guard.

By the time his account drew to an end, Agis listened with the set jaw and hard, defiant glare of a man who knew he could not deny his actions, yet would refuse to regret them or call them a crime.

The ephors, after absorbing the witness's story with

reactions varying from anger to disgust to dismay to sagacious composure, posed their questions. Above all, they wished to know precisely whether Agis had been the one to set the plot in motion.

After appearing to be forced to contain himself for a short while, Agis rumbled, "Of course the idea was mine. Sparta must be rid of that blight upon our city." He aimed a finger at unperturbed Brasidas, who spared him not a glance. "She drives us to our doom with black promises whispered in this one's ear. He shapes them into words, and a few slightly impressive deeds, by which to convince even such wise men as yourselves to put our city's fate in his hands. But *his* are not the hands which grip the reins—at least his are those of an Equal—our city is in *her* hands, those of a woman and an outsider, hands which even before today had tasted of Spartiate blood. Now they positively drip with it. Thirty-six of our best went to their graves today, their lives laid down for a noble cause: that of seeing us set free from a man-eating enchantress, a Siren whose false song would lead us to sheer destruction!"

Agis paused to expel a deep breath, which somewhat diminished his fury, but not his conviction.

"I do not envy you lot your decision," he went on. "You have sided with Brasidas of late, and thus with his witch, and it is never easy to admit that one is wrong. But if I may offer my advice as a king of some years to men only just elected to power a few months ago: you had best put vanity aside and think in simpler terms, as do the men waiting outside for you to put their minds at rest. Many of them are kin of the men we are soon to bury with honors. What they will see, if you make the wrong choice, is a torrent of citizen blood spilled and the murderess who spilled it walking free." Agis nodded at the still impassive Brasidas. "And there stands the one who brought her into our midst. He refuses even to look at me because he knows I am right."

It was clear to Styphon, and likely to all, that Brasidas's refusal to give the king his gaze had nothing to do with any such admission; rather, quite the opposite.

Agis waved a hand in the polemarch's direction. "I have said my piece. I leave you now to your deliberations that I might go tend to the more important matter of consoling wives and mothers and counseling sons against taking rash action in pursuit of revenge, in the hope that their leaders will give them the satisfaction they deserve."

Red cape billowing, the Eurypontid king of Sparta stormed out of the meeting place of the ephors who served as the check on his royal power. After a moment spent staring at the oaken door slammed behind him, and perhaps absorbing his advice, the ephors returned their attention to Brasidas. Before any spoke to him, however, the eldest addressed Styphon, thanking him for his testimony and inviting him to leave the chamber.

Styphon obeyed, leaving Brasidas with them, and went outside where he pushed his way through a thronging crowd of men and women wheedling him for answers which they knew he was not free to give. He walked until he was at last alone and then put his back to the nearest wall of sun-warmed plaster, where he sank to the earth.

He heard later in the day, along with the rest of Sparta (following investigation of the scene and the return of the fifth, absent official) the ephorate's official account of what had transpired. Though lacking in detail, it more or less adhered to actual events.

Of more import was their verdict on the parties involved.

Agis, acting as lawful king with the interests of his

people at heart, had done no wrong in attempting to assassinate a foreigner whom he deemed an enemy. Likewise Styphon, his only living accomplice, bore no guilt.

Eris, having killed thirty-six Equals, was inescapably a murderer. A sentence was handed down, the only sentence there could be. *Death*, even if all knew that no lives would be wasted in so foolish an endeavor as attempting to carry it out. In effect, it meant she was no longer a welcome presence in Sparta.

But the ephors could not be seen to hand down no punishment at all, and so Brasidas, as the host and sponsor of the guilty foreigner, in accordance with the nearest precedent, was deemed partly responsible for Eris's actions.

Brasidas would not die, however; he would merely be stripped of his position as polemarch and confined indefinitely to the bounds of Lakonia, not to venture abroad for any purpose, including war.

It was something of a humiliation, but Styphon, when next he saw Brasidas, detected no bitterness in the deposed polemarch. He did not act as a man defeated, though it was possible he merely hid his displeasure well. More likely, Styphon sensed, Brasidas had suggested his own punishment to the ephors, and maybe Eris's too, behind the closed door of the ephorate, and thus was not disappointed with the outcome.

It even occurred to Styphon, in a moment of horror, that perhaps King Agis had all but known that his assassins would be slaughtered, making of the she-daimon a presence which could no longer be tolerated in Sparta.

By now, Styphon had learned that the minds of men like Brasidas and Agis worked in ways that it was far better for lesser men such as himself, unburdened by the curse of greatness, not to understand.

7. Spectacle

The mood in Naupaktos was one of mourning when Demosthenes returned to it. By now, all knew the sad fate of Pylos, defeated by Sparta, ending not only its short-lived freedom but also its existence as a Messenian city. Agis had put to death every male of age in Pylos and loaded the women and children onto ships to be sold abroad. On the heels of that news came word that Argos had capitulated to Spartan demands. The formal end to Argive independence yanked an ancient thorn from the Spartan paw and completed her domination of the Peloponnese.

Three days hence, the vote was to be held on whether Naupaktos would also yield. If the result was as most expected, it would be last vote held by the Naupaktan democracy.

On the voyage from Corinth, Kleon had laid out his plan for rallying the city to war, and on arriving in Naupaktos, they wasted no time in carrying it out.

At dawn, the three conspirators dressed in their new war gear. For Kleon that meant his shining, inlaid breastplate and leg-greaves to match, while the other two had made purchase in Corinth of less extravagant arms and armor. Demosthenes wore a plain breastplate of bronze which had been scrubbed down to mostly remove a layer of tarnish. Its lower chest had been patched, with reasonable skill, to cover a six inch-rent which marked, almost undoubtedly, the site of the wound which had killed its prior owner.

Being a woman, Thalassia had been somewhat more difficult to accommodate. While the panoplies of Amazons like the one she had worn at Eleusis might be common in the collections of men like Alkibiades, they were not easily found in marketplaces, even ones as rich and extensive as that of

Corinth. She had made do, in the end with a stiffened leather corselet onto which thin, rectangular plates of iron had been stitched. It had been made to fit a youth or a man of slender frame and as such made no accommodation for the wearer's breasts, which in Thalassia's case were not anyway of the type to overflow; leaving the uppermost laces in back a touch loose served sufficiently. In lieu of shield, as defense against blades she was not to face this day, she wrapped rawhide strips around her arms, extending up past the elbow. The resulting look was masculine, but few would mistake her for a man, even one barely out of adolescence, if only on account of the naked thighs which bore those subtle differences of shape and tone that could and did betray the owner's sex. Then there were the women's sandals, the high laces of which slithered up shapely calves in dueling spirals to meet in the hollow behind her knee.

And her hair, as ever, gave her away. She was in the process of pulling it back tightly behind her head and fixing it there with a bone fibula when Kleon came up and pulled the fibula's pin from her hand.

"Do not hide your femininity," he said.

Demosthenes scoffed at the idea that Thalassia, who was as likely to adorn herself with 'shiny things' as she was to put one through a hoplite's throat, might ever be guilty of such an aim.

"We wish firstly to attract attention, and secondly to inspire the imaginations of men," Kleon explained melodramatically. "The more exotic the specimen we put before them, the more readily both can be achieved."

To Demosthenes' mind, if ever there was excuse for her to wear her Mark, here it was. And he would have suggested as much, if Thalassia had not, unsurprisingly, been of like mind. Presently she caused the Mark of Magdalen to appear on her cheek and brow.

Kleon, who had not been warned, examined the dark, sinuous lines in wonderment before smiling and proclaiming his judgment: "Yes, yes! Good!"

To this barbaric adornment she added a thick application of kohl, the end product of which were a pair of black-rimmed eyes with irises pale blue like a winter sky, of a kind men might see in nightmares staring back at them from either the gloom on the far shore of Styx, if not on the face of the one who sent them there. To Demosthenes, who felt with reasonable certainty that he would never be subject to a death-glare from those eyes, they held only perverse invitation to activities pleasanter than killing and dying, if just as primal.

As if Thalassia could sense the barest stirrings of arousal as easily as she could lies, which maybe was the case, the eye near the center of her web-like Mark delivered a wink visible only to him.

Dressed thus, swords at hips, halfway equipped for a battle still far off, they went out into the streets of the port, where quickly they drew stares. It was not unexpected, in fact Kleon desired it, such that by the time they reached the agora of Naupaktos by an indirect route they might walk at the head of a gathering cloud of curious onlookers.

It was a risk bordering on folly for fugitives heretofore in hiding to so increase their profile, but they had discussed it the prior night and concluded the risk worthwhile. Open war would erupt soon enough, and so if some few of the Messenians who saw them this day were not true Naupakatans but turncoats looking for pardons from Sparta, so be it. They could hardly have hoped to avoid detection forever, and anyway were that their aim they might be in Italy or Ionia or Egypt by now.

As they made their way like two slowly moving statues

behind their brightly shining guide toward the center of town, following a path not unlike that of water circling a drain, Kleon's intention of attracting a large following became reality. Rather than trusting in men's natural curiosity, the practiced worker of crowds encouraged them with smiles and waves and invitations which revealed nothing of his intent. Owing to his magic, the trio reached the marketplace at the head of a small army. Some were youths and women and slaves, but most looked to be citizen males past the age of majority—wielders of votes, the only audience of import. At the agora, the ranks swelled, since such an army could hardly enter an already crowded market unnoticed.

They ended their march at a place called the Orchard, which at one time in the distant past it had undoubtedly been. Now it was a dusty expanse of gently sloping hillside facing the streets full of vendors where the denizens of Naupaktos were accustomed to hearing speakers of all sorts. While the crowd washed up on the hill like the breakers of a tide, the three who had caused the deluge ascended the stair-like trail etched into the earth by generations of feet to mount the square patch of dirt that was the natural place from which to address this sea of upturned faces. There they formed a triangle, with Kleon standing at its front, and waited in perfect silence until a satisfactory hush settled over his audience.

Then, through the beard he had chosen to keep, since it seemed to be in fashion among the Naupaktans, the demagogue raised his booming voice and addressed the crowd. He appealed to their pride, of course, and their Messenian heritage, likening the ex-slaves to himself, a mere tanner's son raised up by hard work. He spoke of what they had to lose by giving in to Sparta, and how they were a match for any Equal, who were, after all, only mortal men like them.

And lastly, he introduced the man and woman standing

behind him. To many present, their names were already known. One had proven himself among the most capable and effective generals of Athens, Kleon averred, whose city had suffered defeat in spite of, not because of him. Demosthenes' plans would lead Naupaktos to certain victory while denying Sparta the pitched crush of shields which was the only type of fighting in which Equals excelled.

Next Kleon shifted behind Thalassia and set a lean hand on the leather and iron of her shoulder, making her the focus of the crowd's rapt attention, the same it had given Kleon for the duration of his speech.

"And finally, the one at whom you have been trying hard not to stare whilst you listen to me blather. Her true nature I reveal to you now. As educated men, some of you accomplished poets, you will know that bright-winged Selene herself, bringer of light to the night sky, bore fifty daughters with the beautiful shepherd Endymion. Here stands the eldest of that brood, a Titan's blood filling her strong and supple limbs! I present to you Thalassia."

The crowd did not cheer, and Kleon seemed not to expect them to. Many were perhaps unsure yet where they stood, even if they had known when Kleon started, but their gravely contemplative faces seemed to speak to a willingness to hear his arguments and give them due consideration.

"As I said, you are educated men," Kleon went on, flattering them. "As such, I would hardly expect you to accept a bold claim such as I have made without letting your own eyes bear witness. To that end, a demonstration is in order, would you not agree? To show that she has no equal among mortal man, I invite any among you to step forth and test your prowess in battle against hers!"

Thalassia's kohl-blackened eyes betrayed nothing, but Demosthenes caught the flash of a smirk, present for but an instant. They had discussed this on the sea voyage, the idea of putting Thalassia's capabilities on public display that they might inspire confidence in a Naupaktan victory.

The subject of that display had taken an instant liking to the proposal. In past lives and by other names she had been a petty smuggler and then a pilot on the lines which laced together the layers of reality, but only here, as Thalassia, had she discovered her affinity for close combat.

"Let loose against her with murderous rage if you so desire!" Kleon offered. "Try your best to pierce her sweet flesh, while in return she seeks to harm nothing of yours beyond your pride!"

With one hand on Thalassia's shoulder, Kleon used the other to beckon forward any takers. "Come on!" he urged the yet-silent crowd. "Who among you is reckoned the best fighter Naupaktos has to offer?"

Kleon had barely paused the space of a breath before answer came in the form of an unsheathed, upraised sword, the holder of which shortly broke through into the front rank. He was (not surprisingly) a young man, scarcely into adulthood, with smooth chin and short, meticulously groomed dark hair. His chiton hung loosely from a tanned, well-muscled frame.

"Excellent!" Kleon said with a smile. "Clearly you are a lad destined for greatness, regardless of how you fare presently against our Titan-spawn. What name is it that is one day bound to be upon so many tongues?"

"Xenarchos," the youth responded emphatically, as though it should already be known to all. In an admittedly over-swift judgment, Demosthenes decided Xenarchos was like any number of youths he had known in Athens, perhaps a local champion at some sport and likely the head of his class and a troop leader in military training. Perhaps he was as good as he thought he was.

'Endymion's daughter' could have fun with him.

"Clear a space, would you!" Kleon instructed the crowd, which eagerly receded to form a rough semi-circle on the dusty slope under the balcony of earth where perched the goddess and her companions. "Put on a good show!" the demagogue whispered into Thalassia's ear.

Returning no answer, she leaped from the platform into the ring below. The distance was not so great as to prevent a mortal man making the jump, but his legs would have been hard-pressed on landing not to buckle, where hers just barely creased at the knee. Facing her challenger, she drew her sword with like grace and kept it pointed earthward in a pose which showed a sort of unconcerned readiness. Head cocked and slightly bowed, she made eyes at the youth which might as easily have been an invitation to play in some less deadly form than was on offer.

Somewhat less nonchalant, but still clearly underestimating his foe (or trying to convey such), Xenarchos circled with sword raised, observing closely to glean whether his opponent was inclined to strike first or wait.

Within a few beats, Thalassia's intention not to move became clear, and Xenarchos struck. After feinting once to the left, then twice to right, he launched his first attack from the latter direction, an underhanded stroke aimed at Thalassia's left hip, where a hit, if sword point made it under the armored skirts of a fighter's breastplate, would end any battle. It would not have ended this one, but Xenarchos never got to learn that, for his stroke was easily turned aside by a single, swift motion of Thalassia's blade.

Quick on the heels of the parry, his next attack (aimed at her head in proof that he was taking Kleon's instructions to heart) was as easily deflected. So, too, were his next and his next, delivered after another round of circling and feints. Thalassia, for her part, seemed to be defying Kleon, for this was hardly a good show. She had barely moved.

Xenarchos seemed to be done testing her now, and his next attack was a harder one, fueled by anger. It, too, was stopped cold, but now Thalassia was done testing, too, and she struck back. While parrying, she ducked and twisted and brought her hand up in a gentle, open-palmed strike to her opponent's unguarded jaw. The hit rattled him, less literally than in spirit, forcing him to withdraw a step and regroup. Though she might easily have pressed the advantage, Thalassia permitted the youth his breathing space.

He took only one deep breath before launching a fresh assault, this time a frenzy of successive stabs accompanied by a guttural roar. Thalassia knocked them all aside with ease before slipping her empty left hand inside Xenarchos' guard to grasp his sword arm by the wrist. Her whole body followed, and in a smooth, twisting motion, she wound up with her back pressed to his chest, her sword point aimed over her shoulder at her opponent's neck. Just as quickly, she disengaged, leaving all well aware that had she wished it, Xenarchos would now lie dead.

All too aware of that himself, the youth set his mind and blade to saving face. Holding back nothing, he surged forward behind a series of thrusts which Thalassia either nimbly dodged or else parried whilst backpedaling. Then, when the time was right, she delivered another obvious killing stroke which stopped just shy of dealing death.

They battled on thus for another several minutes before Xenarchos at last admitted defeat. Thankfully, he was not so headstrong as to quit in a rage, but was able instead to see the wisdom of yielding amiably. Stepping back abruptly out of a guarded stance, he threw up an open left palm and gave a self-deprecating smile. Accepting his surrender, Thalassia nodded at him, sportsmanlike herself in letting the mask of a barbarian goddess slip long enough to tell him with a look that although he had lost, he had accounted well for himself.

That was when the youth took one final swipe at her. Thalassia blocked it easily and raised a brow in surely-feigned surprise. Xenarchos smiled and shrugged, resuming his former display of cheerful submission.

On the earthen platform above, Kleon applauded, not for the minor goddess of his invention but for the challenger, and he encouraged the crowd to cheer, too. Even as Xenarchos humbly dismissed the ovation, it was apparent that it went some way toward assuaging an ego that could not have failed to be bruised by public defeat.

It was a fine line which Kleon walked, and Thalassia, too, for that matter, between humiliating men and inspiring them.

"A spectacular round!" Kleon declared. "But only the opener. Now that she has warmed up, who else among you would try his hand against this ally sent to us by the Goddess?"

A number of hands were raised by men whose owners began pressing forward to carve paths to the front of the crowd. Most were as young as Xenarchos, in their mid-twenties at most, eager to prove themselves, but not a few were time-tested veterans. Some of the latter Demosthenes recognized from Pylos. Kleon's gaunt, bearded face, meanwhile, showed him to be almost giddy with delight, for the plethora of volunteers hinted that his strategy would reap its intended result.

She fought four more that morning, then three at once for a finale. She put the youths and veterans alike in the dust, then helped them up and raised their arms and presented them to the audience as if they had been the victor. And although she was an outsider putting the cream of Naupaktos to shame, and although all present hoped the next challenger would be the one to beat her, the swelling crowd in the Orchard persisted in adoring her.

She, in turn, appeared to genuinely adore it back. Surely such an experience represented for her, as she had said in Corinth, a pleasant change from the Caliate, where few if any names had been more despised than that of Geneva, the Wormwhore.

As Kleon ended the morning's spectacle with the promise of another show that evening and tomorrow, and more words in favor of war, a familiar voice rose up from the center of the thronging crowd.

"I would try my hand!" It was Agathokles. "Might I have a turn?" he asked into the silence with which his fellow Naupaktans deferred to him. There was no note of humor in his voice. The look of his eyes, too, above his graying beard, was one of disapproval, perhaps even betrayal.

The three conspirators had deliberately failed to inform Agathokles of their intentions to sway the vote, lest he balk at the prospect of such forceful intervention by foreigners in the affairs of his city. Given the dark tidings from Argos and Pylos of the last few days, it was entirely possible that Agathokles himself intended now to support capitulation.

A few words from now from Naupaktos' 'first among equals' could spoil their plans entirely.

BONUS CONTENT:

Join my mailing list *at* www.ironage.space to read Kleon's full speech to the Naupaktans!

8. Defiance

"You honor us!" Kleon said. "By all means!" With a welcoming gesture, he indicated the combat space. "Have at her, general! If anyone can spill her blood, it is you!"

Drawing his sword, throwing off his cloak and putting on an expression of blank determination, Agathokles stepped into the dusty semicircle where waited his opponent. Thalassia watched him silently with sword pointed at the earth, appearing deceptively unready.

On the platform above, Kleon sidled up to Demosthenes. "She must let him cut her," the demagogue said through a corner of his smile, while keeping his eyes on the impending fight. "Do you think she knows?"

"Probably," Demosthenes replied. "If not, you just told her."

Kleon accepted the answer, and with it another manner in which Thalassia was superior to mortal men.

The combat commenced as Agathokles wasted no time with feinting or circling but just made his first thrust. Thalassia knocked it aside effortlessly and followed it with a quick swipe of her own. Even if she intended to spare the Naupaktan leader's pride, she would yet make him work to keep it.

Agathokles dealt with her attack and launched another of his own, which was parried, and they settled into a dance, trading blows which failed to land. For Thalassia the dance was almost a literal one, full of snake-like movements and even a deliberate roll in the dust after which she sprang up to attack from behind. With each successive match, she had given more of a show. Agathokles, thankfully, managed to avoid the too-real beheading which it for a moment seemed she might in fact be prepared to inflict. Shortly after there followed a brief bout of close hand-to-hand grappling in which Thalassia took a knee to the torso then delivered a kick of her own which separated them.

Wisely, Thalassia did not let the fight drag on too long before letting her guard down, lest Agathokles concede before getting his hit in. After a deliberately slow attack of her own was deflected, Thalassia left herself, for the briefest of spans, open to attack from her right. Agathokles' instincts, by now running in something close to the kill-or-be-killed mode of true battle, did not fail him, and he sent his blade into the opening.

Thalassia twisted down and left, but a fraction too late: the blade's edge ran almost the whole length of her right bicep, cutting it. The crowd gasped as one, a few souls cheering, but Thalassia did not cry out, naturally, nor wince or offer any pretense of pain. Springing upright after the evasive maneuver, she paused, as did her opponent who was perhaps stunned by his own success, and she leveled at Agathokles a look of pleasant surprise. Her sword arm, which maintained its grip on the raised weapon, was already half covered with blood that dripped from her elbow to slake the Orchard's dusty earth.

After the passage of a few heartbeats left her convinced that Agathokles did not intend press his advantage, she sent her left hand to the wound and ran fingers over it.

The fingers went to her mouth, where she tasted of the blood before flicking her wrist to send out a volley of red droplets which just missed the first rank of onlookers. Smiling, she swung her sword in a few showy, impractical flourishes meant to demonstrate that she was no worse off before she resumed a defensive posture, inviting fresh attack.

None came. Agathokles relaxed his own stance, put both arms out horizontally to show peaceful intent and bent to wipe his blooded sword blade on a clump of dry grass before returning it to its scabbard of plain rawhide.

Thalassia likewise adopted a casual pose, blood dripping to the ground from untended wound while Agathokles addressed her in a voice loud enough for all to hear.

"Your point is proved!" he said. His tone was carefully neutral. "I have no doubt you would beat me if we fought on. I thank you for permitting me to draw your blood."

The crowd remained silent, apparently sensing that Agathokles, the general they held in high esteem, was not done speaking.

They were right.

* * *

"Countrymen!" he called out. "I have stood here today and heard most of what this outsider said before he offered up this entertainment in which I have just taken part. But the Athenian did not make proper introduction of himself, so let me add what he left out. This man Kleon was known in his city's democracy as a *demagogos*, a derisive term his people coined just for him because he goads the masses with sweet words and half-truths into believing whatever he wishes them to believe. Failing that, he will just get the sense of a crowd's desire and put himself at its front, pretending its ideas were his all along.

"As for the two with him, well, Demosthenes I know to be a man of honor, even if I rather suspect his motives are less patriotic than personal. As for the third, this one who is not bothering to bind an ugly wound, I know her, too, as do many of you. She came with Demosthenes to our city a short while ago, offering the same thing Kleon now is holding out: aid against our common enemy.

"On my own authority as general, I gave them sanctuary and accepted their offer, on the reasoning that no matter what answer one favors giving to Sparta, no one can think it foolish to be prepared for war. Since then, this woman, Thalassia, has advised our engineers, blacksmiths, masons, shipwrights and others—I see not a few of you here today—to build contrivances which might serve in defending our freedom, should we choose that path. Is she the granddaughter of a Titan? Perhaps. I cannot give another explanation for the evidence of our eyes. It scant matters from what source she derives her powers. It is enough to know that she has them, and that she does.

"Yes, beloved Naupaktos, these three outsiders seek to manipulate you for reasons incidental to your welfare. They push you.

"Yet they push you in a proper direction. I agree with them. A demagogue Kleon may be, but the points he makes are no less true for having rolled from silken tongue. And Demosthenes is no less right in his desire to see us fight for the fact that it stems from blood already spilled which he would see avenged. The third of them, for all I know, truly was sent by Athena to aid her beloved city, and having failed in that task would redeem herself by saving ours. I say let her try. Let Demosthenes try. In the darkest of times, as these are, it matters not from what quarter help is offered or what force motivates the givers, so long as the offer is genuine. Knowing these three as I do, I trust in them. I believe in the course they hope to set you on, the course of resistance. I believe that with their help, we can give the Spartans who enslaved our forefathers, and who hold our cousins in bondage still, a fight they will not soon forget. And I believe that we can win, and make our city's name ring synonymous with Honor! Courage! Defiance! Freedom!"

* * *

"Naupaktos!" Agathokles finished, clenched fist held

high.

The crowd bellowed it back at him. *"Death to Sparta!"* someone cried out amid the cheers that followed, and others echoed the sentiment.

From his spot halfway up the slope between bleeding Thalassia and the earthen platform on which stood her accomplices, Agathokles cast up a resentful look at the latter, as if to chastise them for having taken action without him and at the same time claim credit, much deserved, for dramatically increasing the odds that their venture would succeed.

* * *

Endymion's daughter performed twice daily for the remaining two days before the citizen assembly of Naupaktos was set to vote on the demands of Sparta. Of course, while the citizens' eyes feasted on that spectacle in the agora, their ears were subject to Kleon's winged words, which showed clear signs of having their intended effect.

Thalassia played her role to a perfection that seemed due less to innate skill than to her own enjoyment of the attention. Whilst rarely speaking, she played with the crowd, worked it, teased it, defeated its champions with ease, yet never lost its affection. By the third day, she had amassed a heap of gifts and tokens given to her by women, men, and children alike, large enough to fill a large trunk. That same evening, in her final performance, she took on six men simultaneously, the most she felt she could face while still ensuring no harm to any. That match, which she fought with a staff in place of sword, produced her first and only accidental injury: an elbow to the face which left her spitting blood. The crowd cheered, and she laughed it off and went on to win.

"Why can't we just keep doing this?" she asked after the show. "I think I want to live here."

The following dawn marked assembly day. While

Demosthenes and Thalassia walked the nearby coastline, surveying it with an eye for defense, stopping once on a secluded beach to pass some time in a less practical way, the male citizen body of the Naupaktan democracy debated the very existence of Naupakos as a free city. Arguments were made and heard all morning, through the afternoon, and nearly to the setting of the sun before ballots were cast.

The result was brought by messenger to the two outsiders.

By a wide margin, it had been decided that when a Spartan herald came demanding reply to the order of submission, he would be denied an audience.

When next the Spartans came, they would come for war.

9. ...considering

In the half-month after the vote, normal life in Naupaktos was all but suspended as the efforts of nearly every man, and not a few women, were directed toward the construction of defenses. Limestone was cut and smashed and mixed with sand and gravel and water according to Thalassia's instructions to produce large quantities of liquid stone. Even the building of ships, a thing for which Naupaktos was renowned, was halted that the timber might be used to build frameworks into which the stone might be poured to give it form while it set.

By such means the existing walls of Naupaktos were strengthened and new ones built along the coast, the front from which invasion must almost certainly come given the difficulty of the inland terrain on all sides. Well underway all along that coastline was a network of small, well-placed forts, simple gray boxes sized to hold ten men or fewer. Dug well into the earth, the structures protruded barely half the height of a man and had in place of windows only a slit running the length of the structure, no greater in height than what a bowman needed to fire with some accuracy at the terrain below.

Some of those archers would wield their own bows, but plenty, when the day came, would be equipped with superior weapons being made by Naupaktan craftsmen: shield-piercing gastraphetes and its lighter cousin, the *khiasmon,* or cross-bow.

Engineers, meanwhile, were building even larger mechanical bows to be wheeled up onto the clifftops overlooking the sea from where they might launch at any fleet which came into range shafts the size of small trees tipped with fire or keel-shearing lead.

This day, Demosthenes rode the coast inspecting the incomplete defenses of Naupaktos with an attacker's eye, looking for weaknesses which might be exploited. If fortune was with them, the invaders would come overconfident and be taken by surprise, but such assumptions were not safe; Sparta had no shortage of loyal Helots who looked and spoke just like Naupaktans, and were in fact their kin, an abundant source of spies who might even now be helping to build the defenses. Never mind the fact that much of the construction was of necessity being done in plain view of the large number of ships which passed every day through the Gulf of Corinth.

Already they had uncovered spies, or rather Thalassia had with her sharp eyes and innate ability to perceive deception. One suspect had been arrested, and under somewhat forceful interrogation had given up the identities of three accomplices who were subsequently captured and confirmed as agents of Sparta. All four were Messenians, and since it was the habit of Naupaktans to be lenient with their brethren, the spies presently waited out the conflict in chains instead of facing execution.

Surely there were more. Thalassia made regular rounds among the men engaged in the city's preparations in the effort to detect them, while all who possessed knowledge that was particularly sensitive were made to swear oaths in her presence.

Though the bulk of their time was given to the Naupaktos' defense, Demosthenes never allowed Thalassia to forget, or rather pretend to forget, his greater purpose. Not far from this coast, in rows of amphorae inside a cavern fit to serve as home to any withered sea-hag, she cultivated a great many varieties of fungus. For the sake of his health, Thalassia said, it was not wise for Demosthenes even to visit the place. He merely took her word for it, without doubt or reservation, that the time was not far off when her plague could be tested.

Today she rode the coast just seaward of Demosthenes, matching his leisurely pace on her own mount. Here by the shore, a breeze alleviated the heat of summer which made the city streets cloying these days. Fortunately, they spent little time there, for if the coming battle touched the city, it would likely mean Naupaktos was already lost.

Now Demosthenes stared down the track at an unfinished stretch of wall meant to block off a break in the cliffs where the land instead rose gently from shore to heights. He halted his mount as the germ of an idea struck him.

He pointed down the coast at an inlet where the sea lapped a sandy shore on which triremes might beach without much difficulty. Drawing up beside him, Thalassia turned to follow his gaze from beneath the drawn hood of the black cloak for which she had no need except perhaps to shield her hair, in which she took as much pride as any Spartiate male.

"Those men working on that unfinished fort and stretch of wall down there," Demosthenes said. "What if we had them simply lay down their tools today, leaving the scaffolds and materials in place?"

He needed explain no more of the idea; Thalassia understood. When she turned her pale eyes back upon him, they bestowed credit.

"Not bad," she said, "...considering your origins."

"Origins?"

"When I came to this place, I never guessed I would find someone who..." She pondered, then resumed, "who was not just a means to an end. Someone who could know what you know, see what you've seen and..."

Demosthenes felt sure that her pause was an affectation; she already knew what would come next.

"...not run away," she finished. "Or hack me up and

bury me under a rock when you had the chance."

"We are not speaking of defensive walls, are we?"

She shot him a bemused glare. "Maybe not entirely." Aiming her hooded gaze back down at the beach, she said, "It's an excellent idea. They will see the unfinished wall and land their ships there. And we'll be waiting. I should have thought of it."

"Once in a while, I have a good idea of my own."

"You have many good ideas."

The compliment creased Demosthenes' brow. "You've turned kind again. And mistaken me for some other man whose ego is in constant need of stroking. Alkibiades, perhaps."

Thalassia scoffed. "Go *stroke* yourself, Athenian. See if I ever compliment you again. Anything impressive you'll ever do is down to my influence anyway."

"There's my Jenna," Demosthenes remarked of this Thalassia whom he knew better and, if he was honest, felt more at ease around. This creature was not kind or reflective but playfully arrogant—and with better cause for arrogance than any hundred swaggering fools one could find among the *kaloi kagathoi* of Athens.

Rather than answering, Thalassia gave him the frown of one constantly forced to humor an imbecile.

10. Glorious duties

In the days following the failed attack on Eris, Styphon found himself the object of silent stares from his countrymen. They seemed unsure what to make of him. On one hand, he had participated in what most must see as a courageous effort against a creature universally feared—a good thing for Sparta.

On the other hand, he had lived. Every Spartan boy knew the tale of Orthryades, sole survivor of a battle with the Argives, who had killed himself in shame for having been the only one denied the honor of sacrificing his life for Sparta.

By the fifth day, minds were made up: the looks were largely ones of respect, accompanied by words to match.

Then, today, Agis had come to him with some rather momentous words of his own, ones which Styphon was shortly to share with Hippolyta, assuming Agis had not done him the dishonor of speaking first to his wife.

On his approach up the hill to the door of his home, Styphon received no greeting, which struck him as odd. Typically Hippolyta would see or hear him and appear with a wave, a smile, a kiss. His heart froze, then pounded harder in sudden apprehension, mind filling with visions of walls painted with blood, floor strewn with the limbs of butchered corpses, the vengeance of a wronged she-daimon.

He had his war-gear with him: spear in one hand, shield on his back, breastplate and helmet in a sack of oilcloth. Crouching, he set them down as silently as he could, keeping only the short sword at his hip, fingers tight around its handle. Breath held, he cautiously approached the door, pushed it open just far enough, stopping short of the point where he knew it would issue a familiar squeak, and he slipped through.

The megaron, formerly the modest dwelling's one and

only room, stood empty. The hearth fire smoldered. No blood. No vengeance, unless Eris's vengeance was to begin with a kidnapping.

Then a sound: a quiet moan, from behind the curtain which separated megaron from marital chamber, old construction from new.

He knew the moan as Hippolyta's.

He stepped to the curtain, keeping hand yet on sword even as trepidation began to release its tight grip on his chest. He peered through a gap between curtain and door frame and confirmed it: no danger, no vengeance. Not today.

There was only his wife, consummate huntress, in his bed with their slave, the hunted, both naked, grinding thigh to thigh, sex to sex, limbs so entangled that the Thracian's freckles became the quickest way to assign any one an owner. A few seconds' silent observation told Styphon that his wife was on bottom at present, Eurydike atop her, gyrating in the constant, fluid motion which had given rise to Hippolyta's moan. The Thracian's back was to him, while Hippolyta's reclining posture would have let her see the watcher had she been looking for one, which she was not. She was too busy climbing toward release.

Her climax was near, Styphon could see in the fluttering of his bride's eyes, the way she chewed her lower lip, the whisper of her irregular, panting breaths.

He watched for a short time, with no thought given to interrupting, as Hippolyta came, and Eurydike collapsed on top of her and rolled to one side for a post-coital embrace. It was then, as ecstasy faded and bodies and eyes began to shift, that Styphon carefully backed away, removing himself from the gap and backpedaling stealthily toward the door.

He had already accepted Hippolyta's sexual pursuit of the girl as part of her character and a feature of the feminine world in which she was raised. Having now witnessed proof of the hunt's success, he accepted it still. It was perhaps not the most convenient of arrangements, having his new wife's state-owned concubine dwell under his roof and share his bed, but as far as inconveniences went, this was a mild one. He had his life, all his limbs, and even his honor, which for quite some time had been in question. If his wife, whom he loved and who loved him, wanted to part the skinny legs of the timid little Thracian bitch on a regular basis, so be it, so long as both lived up to their other responsibilities inside and outside the household.

Styphon's responsibilities, of course, lay primarily outside. He had new ones now, of which he intended to tell his wife, once he had finished doing her the perhaps unnecessary favor of sneaking back out of his house to spare her any awkwardness. Not that she was likely to have felt any, he sensed, since it seemed doubtful that Hippolyta had an intention to hide the liaison from him.

Perhaps he was doing the slave the bigger favor. Though he did not know her well by any means, Eurydike did not strike him as one to consider Hippolyta's attentions an honor.

Outside, Styphon picked up his gear, making sure it rattled, then walked to the door as if he had just ascended the hill. On his arrival, the two females (both wearing a sheen of sweat in addition to hastily and incompletely donned garments) emerged from the bedroom. Hippolyta, smiling widely, greeted him with an embrace and a long and far more sensual kiss than usual, while Eurydike slinked off to the hearth with mussed red hair over downturned face.

A certain glow in Hippolyta's expression, a mischievous glint in her eye, held promise that she would in fact share news of her conquest with Styphon when they had a private moment. But for now, it was Styphon's turn to share good news, news that actually had import outside these walls.

"Agis has invited me to join the royal guard," he announced. "Naturally, I accepted."

He did not bother to spoil the mood by mentioning the well-known reason that there were vacancies in that elite body.

In an instant, Hippolyta's air of self-satisfaction fled her, and her features lit anew with genuine surprise and delight of the kind only to be shown in Sparta behind closed doors and among close confederates. She flung arms around his chest and squeezed, as if to lift him and whirl him around despite being smaller than he by half.

"That is wonderful!" she exclaimed.

There was more, and when his wife had detached from him, Styphon gave it: "I leave with Agis in ten days to conquer Naupaktos."

"They will bow before you," she said, an expression of honest belief, not empty platitude. "Who could fail to?" She kissed his neck. "The ten days will be busy. Or the nights, at least."

Smiling, she said no more, did not need to. There had yet been no signs of a child sprouting in Hippolyta's womb, making it imperative that as much seed as possible be sown there between now and his departure.

It was no light responsibility to the Spartan state, this obligation, but neither was it an unpleasant one.

Head hung, Eurydike breezed past them and out the door carrying an empty basket to be filled with vegetables. When the slave was gone, Styphon said dully, "Congratulations to you, as well."

Knowing his wife, or so he believed, Styphon rather expected the smirk of a conqueror. He got instead a strange, distant look, which quickly vanished to be replaced by averted eyes and a tight smile of near-embarrassment.

He shrugged it off. One could only know a woman so well.

"You saw, did you?" Hippolyta looked up, and there was the smirk. She jabbed her husband's chest with a finger. "I will not have you being jealous," she warned. "You are my husband, and all I truly need." Her hand found his genitals through the linen of his chiton, and then his hand. Before he had a chance to say anything, which he would not have, she said, "No point in waiting."

He walked with her to a bed still warm with woman-love and commenced his glorious duty.

Ten days later, the preparations made, he marched north from Sparta with Agis and the royal guard. Eight hundred other Equals went with them, with as many Helots to carry their gear. In Arkadia, the force joined with two thousand further troops gathered from elsewhere in the Peloponnese.

Wayward Naupaktos was to be brought to heel.

11. The Battle of Naupaktos

100 days after the fall of Athens (September 423 BCE)

Near the end of the sailing season, the Spartan fleet came. It rounded the Peloponnese and beached at Panormos, across the narrow straits from Naupaktos. The ships were triremes, Naupaktan observers reported back, not the sleek, oarless vessels that had taken Athens, nor some new, yet unseen design, but beaked, square-sailed triremes like those which had cut the sea for generations.

Perhaps the newer ships had been deemed unsuitable for use this near to winter, or at all in a landing which was sure to be contested. But it did beg the question of whether some less revolutionary thinker than Brasidas were not in charge of this invasion.

The same observers reported back that the Spartan hulls were empty, or laden only with supplies. A day later, the troops arrived by land, likely sparing their stomachs a rough ride on wind-tossed seas. The next evening, their campfires dotted the night on the rugged north coast of the Peloponnese across the strait from Naupaktos. Alert Naupaktan watchmen manning the barricades and forts along the coast captured or killed half a dozen Helots and an Arkadian trying to slip ashore on missions of reconnaissance.

That evening, it was learned that King Agis commanded the Spartan force. The following dawn the Spartan ships, now numbering more than thirty owing to the contributions of allies, rowed east and put ashore near Panormos for the loading of the invasion force. The main architects of Naupaktos' defense waited tensely together on the heights to see what course the ships would set when they began their crossing. The two architects were armed and armored and ready to spill blood themselves this day, even if the shorter-lived and more fragile of them had reservations regarding the other. While they waited to see where the ships would go, he voiced them.

"This is not your fight," Demosthenes said to the other.

"No more or less than it is yours," Thalassia countered meditatively, keen eyes on the far shore.

The sky was gray, storm looming, dangerous to sail, but none on this side of the waves dared believe a few clouds would deter the new hegemons of Hellas from seeing their will imposed.

"It is a battle for men to decide," he said, then quickly clarified: "Mortals."

She took her gaze from the distance. Her 'warpaint', the Mark of Magdalen, was like a spider with too many legs devouring her right eye. Demosthenes had let her paint him, too: a few strokes of oiled ashes around his own eye in crude imitation of hers. It was meaningless, he knew, and emphasized his bond with alien Thalassia in a way that made the heart yearn for simpler times, times when he could appeal to Pallas or Apollo for a blessing in battle and be halfway sure of receiving it. But now that he doubted those gods, or rather knew them to be false, what harm was there in adopting another empty ritual to replace the prayers used by most men to instill courage before battle?

The one whose mark he bore held his eyes for a while and said, "Just say it. You want me safe because you'd miss me."

Demosthenes scoffed. "You have ruined me for any other company in this world, so yes," he freely admitted. "Yes, I would miss you."

"And you're not even lying," she said, and knew. "I've grown on you. Like a... never mind. I'll be safe. Now shut up." She gestured at the waters. "There's killing to do."

* * *

By mid-morning the Spartan triremes, their decks clogged with marines, pushed off from the white beaches of the far shore. Within a few minutes their course became clear to the owner of the pale, superhuman eyes which observed them from the cliffs. She reported the good news to the one beside her, who evidently would miss her if she were to die.

The ships' intended landing point was the one hoped for: that small stretch of coastline where the defenses appeared not yet to be complete, and where moreover the beach was smooth and sandy, had proven too enticing for Agis.

The fortifications in that spot were in fact unfinished, but in their place were other, hidden defenses, including six hundred Naupaktans waiting out of sight to challenge whatever number of invaders succeeded in setting foot on the beach.

At Demosthenes' word, the morning's diffuse sunlight flashed off mirrors of highly polished bronze, telling men up and down the coast that the time had come. Runners followed the light, just in case. Wherever the signal was seen, Naupaktans flew into action, goading oxen out of sheds on the heights overlooking the sea and leading them the short distance to the cliff's edge, each team hauling behind them either a two-wheeled platform or a heavy wagon. On each platform was mounted a horizontal bow with a span greater than the height of most men; each wagon was filled with the shafts which the bows were designed to launch.

At twelve sites chosen well in advance, the crews detached the oxen, aimed the great *ballistae* out over the channel, locked their wheels, turned the cranks of wood and iron which tensed their thick bowstrings, and they waited. The men had been trained in the weapons' use, mostly on the inland hills with trees or logs as targets, and they were eager now to test their skills. Their targets this day would be in motion, but the great distance put the Naupaktan crews out of danger and meant they could take their time and fire at will, missing ten times for every hit if need be.

The bolts which would rain down on the ships making the crossing would at first be tipped with lead. Descending from such a great height, the leaden projectiles would smash their way through the deck and hull of any ship unlucky enough to be struck, the shaft then lancing to the channel bottom with ship soon to follow. Later, when the invasion fleet drew closer, other bolts would be loaded, ones fitted with clay pots filled with a viscous, pitch-like liquid that could set fire to any ship's timbers, its crew, or even, if the shot missed, make the waves themselves burn.

Demosthenes had used the stuff himself to burn the siege engines of the Spartan invasion force on Skiron's road as it made its way to Attica. Back then, his small force of raiders had been slaughtered afterward by Eden, and the loss of his siege engines had proven no impediment to Brasidas. The conquest of Athens had come by sea in the form of Sparta's new navy of faster and more maneuverable ships, those which seemed absent this day.

Instead, trireme oars slapped the waves rhythmically to the faint, shrill sound of piping, while above, on the cliffs, patient ballista crews waited while the enemy's vessels maneuvered into a loose agglomeration, then poured on the speed, plying cold, dark currents on a gently curving line to their intended landing point.

Into a trap.

A single, Cyclopean bow loosed a lead-tipped bolt. It vanished into the waves, well short, perhaps even unnoticed. A few brief words of recrimination were shouted, then more waiting.

Minutes later, another shot, another miss. It fell between hulls, harmlessly, but well inside the amorphous collection of thirty-odd ships. The rest of the twelve ballista crews took it as their cue and followed suit, raining bolts down from the heights onto the clustered ships far below, which looked but for their white wakes as if they barely moved at all. The pipes which timed the rowers' strokes were easily audible by now, and so too were the cries of alarm, the barked orders of trierarchs, even if the words themselves were lost in the wind and crash of surf. Evidently they urged calm and no change of course, for the invasion fleet rowed on undeterred as every bolt of the first volley missed. Likely the Spartans believed this the worst they would encounter until they set foot on the beach, as had been the case in many battles past. The arrows were rather larger, but still only harassment, no deterrent.

Fresh bolts were plucked from the wagons by two men each and set in place on the stocks of the great bows, whose coiled sinew strings were pulled tight by men straining against the handles of sturdy cranks. Aims were adjusted, wind was gauged, and as each crew became ready, second shots were loosed.

One of the first was a hit, holing a forward deck. From the cliffs a cheer went up, while the wind carried shouts of the stricken ship's crew, whose oars lost time. Then the oars stopped altogether, the hull listed, and black specks which were her crew and the marines she carried, then more who were the oarsmen emerging by the dozen from below deck, spilled out into the sea or clung to the wreck. The fighters among them were almost sure to die, dragged down by the weight of their war-gear.

The third volley crippled another ship near the formation's head, forcing others behind to take evasive action. A fourth tore through the hull of one ship and sheared the steering oar from another.

Still, the remaining ships plowed on toward the beach they hoped to storm, the beach on which Demosthenes stood while the barrage continued, round after round lancing down, unabated and unanswered. It would not destroy the invasion fleet—not even close—only diminish it, but that suited the designs of the two architects, who meant for the fleet to press on, unable to know that the worst was yet to come.

As the remaining ships rowed nearer the beach in moderate disarray, leaving behind a half dozen triremes and their hundreds of occupants flailing in the waves or vanished under them, the rain of massive bolts tapered off. The weapons would be retargeted now, their leaden projectiles swapped for incendiary ones.

But even before that fiery rain came, the invaders were to face another obstacle.

The ships scudded on, beaked hulls splitting the sea, white foam filling their angry, painted eyes. They neared the beach on which they meant to land and disembark the eager marines presently singing war chants on their decks. It was the beach above which the defensive walls had been left incomplete, in irresistible invitation to any straightforward-thinking invader, as King Agis was by all accounts.

Brasidas might well have attacked by some other route, and stood a chance of winning.

Standing on a rock with a commanding view, Demosthenes waited for the first of the ships to pass a certain wooden buoy with a bright green flag fluttering on its top. When that mark was reached, he spun and hoisted his spear and cried shoreward, "Heave!"

At three locations not far from him, at the inland ends of six small channels dug in the sand all the way to shore and lined with set liquid stone, oxen were goaded to motion.

Affixed to the beasts' yokes were thick, tarred ropes, and the ropes sat in the channels which went out into the sea, and in that sea, beneath the water's surface, at the ends of those ropes and anchored in place by great cubes of stone, were the trunks of three massive trees lain horizontally. Set into the stripped trunks were tall bars of iron, made by the melting down of a great many objects, such that the resulting construction somewhat resembled the comb of a Titan, its handle of raw wood, its tines of iron. The six ropes were affixed to these three combs such that when pulled, the ropes caused caused the trunk to rotate, sending the iron bars, heretofore lying flat on the sea bed, into an upright position.

Thus did the invading fleet of Sparta and her allies, rowing at speed for the shore, witness appear suddenly between them and the beach, with no time left to steer away or back water, a regular array of iron posts spaced such that a trireme could not pass between any two.

The crashing of wooden hulls, sharp snapping of oars, and cries of alarm filled the air as the first several ships struck the barriers. Prows or sterns were propelled up and out of the water, keels exposed, while other ships spun sidewise like toys, depending on how they struck. Scant seconds later, the sounds of chaos intensified as the vessels following immediately behind collided with the arrested ones to fore, their bronze-sheathed rams doing the very job for which they were built: holing hulls underneath the waterline. Yet the hulls holed today were not those of enemy ships; they held brothers and comrades.

The swiftly realized result was a packed line of triremes, hardly any two facing the same direction, some slowly sinking, others capsized.

Not every enemy ship became embroiled; those farthest back were able to steer clear, and some ships of the van had already been sailing west of the traps and avoided the bars. For those not so lucky, a fresh assault waited; it commenced with no need for word of command from Demosthenes. On the heights, the ballistae, their aim adjusted and projectiles changed, let loose once more.

The new shafts fell upon the closely packed enemy hulls like the fire-arrows of Apollo himself. Where they struck, fire spread in bright tendrils of orange, setting alight decks and oars and men, and filling the sea winds with a thick, black smoke and screams of agony. The soft, waterlogged pine of the hull and deck did not burn well, but the black burning ooze was its own fuel.

More than half the fleet stood shattered, sinking, burning, but some credit was due to the stricken mariners; only three ships, the contribution of one allied city or another according to their fluttering standards, turned prows and beat oars for the far shore. One trireme flying the red lambda even pressed on with fires burning on its deck, its crew racing up from below with filled bilge buckets in an effort to extinguish the persistent blaze.

Waves of the acrid smell produced by the liquid fire reached shore and stung Demosthenes' eyes. He wiped them and continued to watch with a bitter smile fighting to curl his lip.

Here was the start of his vengeance, proof that one man... give or take.. could smash a city.

The start. This was but the start...

He directed a look at the other party responsible for the death this day, standing geared for war down at the base of the rock on which he stood. Thalassia detected his satisfaction, of course, but the look inhabiting her own pale eyes was darker. It warned him: This is but the start.

Demosthenes climbed down to the sand and shared no

words with her as he went to join the Naupaktan force positioned out of sight, ready to spill down onto the beach to contest the landing.

He arrived to hear Agathokles delivering to them final words of exhortation.

"These Spartans come thinking they will face an army of slaves!" he cried. "Men of weak will, craven heart, broken spirit! They think they have nothing to fear, that they are as giants at whose thunderous footfalls on our shore we must tremble and run. But look out there! Those are *men* going to the sea god! Listen! Those screams are wrenched from *men's* throats! Inhale! That stench on the wind is that of *men's* flesh burning. They are no giants, no gods. They are men just like us! The difference is that we fight this day for our liberty, for our existence as a free people, for the very lives and dignity of our wives and mothers, while they fight only so that when they march home, their mothers won't spit in their faces and their wives won't snap their thighs shut for a season!"

A chorus of light laughter arose behind the dune, briefly subsuming the song of waves and wind and screams and beating oars. A little laughter was a good thing before battle, so long as laughter did not come at the expense of lust for victory, for glory, for blood.

To feed the latter, Agathokles loosed a roar. "For Naupaktos!" he cried, unsheathing his sword and raising it. His men echoed back the same invocation. Likewise the next: "For Messenia!" And the last: "For Pylos!"

Turning, sword in hand, red helmet-crest whipping behind him, heels kicking up sand, Agathokles ran toward the beach. As one, six hundred of his countrymen and one Athenian followed.

* * *

On a hill on the channel's southern shore, standing at his

king's side, Styphon watched the sea fill with fire, with the helpless hulks of sinking ships and the bodies of doomed men whose bones would never rest in cold earth, their shades consigned to drift on the tides. He watched in silence, now and then glancing at Agis, who likewise kept his mouth shut apart from a few terse commands delivered to his aides. Many of the commands were for silence, and so the cluster of Spartiates surrounding the king just looked on, with no words spoken or action taken to aid their countrymen, specks in the distance, who had embarked short hours ago with the invasion force led by Agis's own half-brother Agesilaus. What aid could be offered, anyway, by mere men, and ones lacking ships at that?

Only the gods could be of assistance now, but even the individual arguably best equipped to beseech them was silent, a small, black-shrouded figure standing well apart from the Equals in their red cloaks, leaning on his tall staff, encompassing hood drawn over his hairless head.

He was Agis's seer, the so-called Minoan, Phaistos. This dawn, he had cut open a calf and declared the day a propitious one for the success of a seaborne assault. Agis, being no fool, did not make military decisions strictly on the advice of a soothsayer, but he did put great stock in the Minoan's communication with gods and spirits—and likely would again, in spite of the apparent disaster unfolding.

"Leave me," Agis said to the men around him as the rain of destructive bolts from the opposing cliffs subsided. The surviving third or so of the invasion fleet beat steadily onward toward the beach they were meant to storm. "Not you," he added to Styphon, who had been about to depart with others. He turned instead and reported to Agis's right hand.

Phaistos evidently was likewise exempted from the order to disperse, for he remained a black shadow a few paces off, probably out of earshot unless the meandering sea wind turned just so. But then, Agis did not seem to care if his seer heard the words he shared privately with Styphon once the green hill was bare of Equals.

"You have met her," he said.

It was not a question, and there was no need either to speak her name. All who had watched from this hill knew who must be here in Naupaktos: the other deathless one, Eris's enemy, the sea-bitch Thalassia.

"Do you think she might help us?"

This truly *was* a question. The king's eyes were fixed hawk-like on the far shore, as if he might pick her form out from here.

Help us what? Styphon wondered for all of half a second before understanding dawned: help us to do what earth-born men had failed to do. Kill Eris.

"It is... possible," Styphon said after a moment's inconclusive thought. "I met her only once, before her association with Demosthenes."

"That is more than any other Equal can say. Living ones anyway." Agis flashed annoyance. "Come on, man, it's no time to keep your lips in check. You have knowledge shared by no other. Use it for king and country. Give your honest opinion, even if it is not what I wish to hear."

Styphon's mind reached back two years, to Sphakteria, where he had consigned his countrymen to chains. He visited those memories infrequently on account of the shame they inspired.

"Before aligning with Demosthenes and Athens, she offered her services to Sparta," Styphon observed presently. "I cannot imagine her loyalty is great, either to man or city. Like Eris, she has her own agenda, whatever it may be." He joined his king in squinting at the far shore. "She and Demosthenes were still together, last I knew, in Attica. Perhaps she is here, but I would not discount the possibility that what we witness today is only her influence, through Demosthenes."

"She is here," the king said with certainty. "Of course you recall the incident at the jail of Athens last month. You were present for the burial of those killed. And the assassination of our tyrant there, whatever his name was."

"Aye," Styphon said.

"That was her. And him."

This came as news to Styphon, but in retrospect, it had crossed his mind, on hearing of it, how unlikely it seemed that the feeble Athenian resistance he had known during his time in Athens should be able to achieve such a feat as the massacre of twenty-four Equals.

"Does Brasidas know?" Styphon asked.

"No doubt. He has his agents, as I have mine, and the ephors have theirs. And Brasidas was still polemarch then." He waved his hand with its iron ring. "It seems clear we must fail this day, but we may not need leave empty-handed."

It seemed to Styphon that Agis was reacting rather philosophically to his defeat, but then, it was the way of Spartiates never to give way either to impotent rage or to despair. Surely he considered, as he stared out over the Gulf, into the distant haze of black smoke, how to make the most of a defeat. This, too, was the Spartan way, and surely the way of wise kings.

"They remain in league together against Sparta, those two," Agis remarked. "But I wonder if the right offer might not persuade one or both to give up that fight."

Into the pause which followed, Styphon cleared his throat. "Sire," he began, "with utmost respect and apologies if I overstep, any truce which leaves Naupaktos with its freedom will... or I should say *might*... meet with extreme opposition back home. Again, with all respect, it could mean..."

"Exile?" Agis finished for him with a smile.

"Yes, Sire."

"Worry not. You will not offer them a truce."

Agis's words took a moment to sink in. Then Styphon blurted, "I?"

"Who better than one who has spoken to her previously and lived to tell it?"

"Sire, if what you have in mind is persuading her to kill Eris for us," Styphon pointed out, knowing it was not enough to dissuade the king, "what exactly is it within our power to offer her in return? It will not be freedom for Naupaktos, which it seems anyway she already has every chance of winning. On top of that, she is Demosthenes' ally, and he despises us and wants vengeance. I cannot imagine he would have an interest in aught but killing as many of us as possible."

Remarkably, wickedly, Agis smiled. "You are an Equal without equal, but you would scarcely survive a day as a king. The reward offered will not be for the sea-bitch at all, but for that very Demosthenes who despises us so. I dare say there is one man upon whom he desires vengeance more than any other."

Styphon had thought he could no longer be shocked, but not for the first time in the present conversation, he found himself proved wrong, if he correctly understood Agis's proposal.

Worse, it seemed Styphon would shortly be charged with presenting that proposal in person to a man whose wife, heavy with child, had been slaughtered while Styphon stood by. A man who had, by all appearances, just orchestrated the defeat of an invasion. A man whose closest ally was every bit as much an unstoppable force as was Eris, whose terrible fury he had witnessed first-hand.

Agis turned to him, set a hand on his shoulder, and said quite casually, "Go find a boat with two oars and cross to Naupaktos. By the time you arrive, the fighting should be finished. Find sea-bitch, find Demosthenes, and put my proposal to them. Offer in return anything they desire which is within reason, short of guarantees for Naupaktos, plus that one unreasonable thing. And see that they accept."

"Yes, Sire," Styphon said dutifully, heavily.

Privately, he knew this was far from the first time that an Equal had undertaken a mission which he personally found unwise to the point of absurdity. Neither would it be the first time, or the last, that an Equal had marched knowingly to his own likely death by a king's command.

A good thing, then, that Spartans were not raised to be lovers of life.

12. Beachhead

The first Spartan trireme to hit the beach was within seconds swarmed by defenders. Demosthenes was there among them, knee-deep in seawater that lapped at the tops of his greaves. Thalassia was not beside him, but satisfying her own urge to kill among another group of Naupaktans. He would not fight this day watched over by a higher power, but like any other man, with his life in his own hands.

Charging into the surf in the front line, round shield raised to keep it clear of waves working to shove him back, he was among the first to meet the enemy and first to spill blood in an overhand spear-thrust which took an Equal in the jaw. The blade no sooner escaped that's man's flesh than it found rest in his neighbor's neck. Both splashed down, to float or sink, Demosthenes did not stop to see; he only saw the gap created by their absence, and he waded into it behind his shield.

A wave shoved him back: the benevolent finger of the sea god, some believer might say, for just ahead of him two Equals converged, and the spear of one whipped past Demosthenes' ear, spraying it with cold droplets. Unbalanced, Demosthenes fell back, legs leaden in the deep water, footing unsure in the shifting sand, but he struck back anyway. He missed once, then drove the point of his spear under the waterline, where it met resistance in his target's groin. New blood clouded the water.

The second, meanwhile, trudged forward, posing a challenge which Demosthenes met by charging under a spear thrust to smash the man in the face with the bowl of his shield. As the man fell, Demosthenes struck him twice more about the head and neck with the hoplon's rim, causing his opponent's spear to fall loose and slice water, after which he was easily dispatched.

All around, Equals leaping from the deck came down into death, skewered or sliced by spears, then finished off in the surf if they still lived. Demosthenes himself killed four more thus, surrendering to the battle delirium which took away one's zeal for life and replaced it with lust for the blood of enemies. It was often better suppressed, but today Demosthenes found little will to do so. Today he wished only to kill, and kill he did.

During the frenzy, Demosthenes grasped that the ship had disgorged rather too many fighters. One or more banks of oars had been manned by light infantry, swordsmen ready to storm the beach behind the hoplites after lending their arms as rowers. These were not Equals but more probably, like the mariners, *mothakes*, Spartan cousins of less pure blood and accordingly lower social standing.

Equals they were not, but neither were they cowards. They died alongside their step-brothers to become warm corpses tossed by cold, red waves. By the time only defenders remained on their feet, bodies bobbed in the surf like driftwood or lay beached in dark puddles on the sand.

Victory ascertained, the Naupaktans around Demosthenes sent up a brief cheer in which he did not participate. A few feet from him, a Naupaktan was bleeding into the sea from a wound at his hip. Wading over, Demosthenes lent him a shoulder for support for the walk to shore while sounds of battle continued to echo in the air over the crash of waves.

Once they had passed the hulk of the defeated trireme in their landward trudge, he was able to look down the shore and see how the fight had gone elsewhere. Three more of the invaders' ships had been emptied; a fourth had been capsized by grapples and lay on its side, half submerged. Several other ships had successfully backed water, oars beating reverse rhythm in a very un-Spartan retreat.

They would not get far; so declared the three white triangles glinting in the sun south of them on the Channel. These were sails, and they hung from the masts of new, oarless vessels freshly built in the renowned shipyards of Naupaktos. Aboard the three ships, each twice the size of a trireme, were a hundred swordsmen and archers waiting to board the enemy vessels if they surrendered, and put fire to them if they did not.

On land, up the shore from Demosthenes, a contingent of Equals and light infantry, perhaps fifty men, had managed to battle its way onto the beach, leaving the damp sand behind them littered with the bodies of fallen Naupaktans. More Naupaktans, having repelled opponents in their own sections, presently raced over to avenge the dead. But spelling more certain doom for the attackers than any of those defenders was the lone figure already standing in their path, unhelmed with a short sword in either hand.

That Thalassia's arms and bare thighs were clean of blood said she had not killed yet this day. But for the weapons, greaves, and corselet of leather and bronze, she might have been attending a festival drama, for she shared in common with Spartiates the odd habit of grooming her hair before a battle. But where they merely combed out their characteristic long locks, she pinned or braided or otherwise formed it into whatever shape she might find pleasing that day. One might think her reason might be to give her victims a remarkable sight to carry with them into death, but one who thought such of Thalassia did not know her.

She did not do it for them at all, but only for her own amusement.

Today her loose waves were straightened and oiled and

pinned up on one side while left to fall free on the other. Scarcely a strand was out of place now as she strode down the sand and became first to engage the band of fifty which had broken through. They must have known they were doomed, or something like it, for the invaders at the fore slowed in their swift advance, causing the loose formation to bunch up briefly before the attackers overcame their hesitation and resumed their headlong run.

They did not all engage Thalassia, of course; only the unluckiest near the center did, while those on the left and right sped past, flowing around her in a stream of brined leather and bronze. But in the spot where she stood, the loose-knit formation may as well have struck a temple column for all that she shifted.

That was the only way in which she resembled marble; her twin blades moved in swift arcs, and invaders groaned as their blood flew then spotted the sand.

Having safely deposited on higher ground the wounded Naupaktan hanging on his shoulder, Demosthenes raced toward that breakthrough, where by now scores of Naupaktans had joined Thalassia in putting a stop to the hopeless venture.

Too late he arrived at the crush of bodies. Before he could find any enemy to kill, a cheer went up. Demosthenes worked his way through the crowd to learn that the remaining invaders had thrown down first their arms and then their bodies onto the sand in supplication. The allies and Spartan cousins among them had, at least. By the look of it, no Equals had betrayed their city's code by surrendering.

Elsewhere on the beach, perhaps a dozen wounded Equals had survived to be captured. In the absence of the helms and lambda-blazoned shields now littering the beach, they were easily picked out by their long hair. While other, more numerous prisoners willingly sat docile under threat of Naupaktan blades, several of the disarmed Equals continued to wrestle with captors who struggled to keep them pinned down.

Demosthenes had more than half a mind to stalk over and grant those Spartans the death for which they longed, but it suited both Naupaktos and his own designs to take as many prisoners as possible today. Even now, the Naupaktan navy was pulling a great many more of them from the sea or from the sinking and burning hulks of triremes. Others combed the shore and found enemies, conscious and not, face down in the sand, clinging to rocks, half-drowned, mostly unarmed, almost entirely drained of fighting spirit.

As the morning wore on, the beach became filled with prisoners seated in the hot sand, bound hand and foot and separated into clusters by citizenship. The most important category, held in the smallest groups lest they entertain thoughts of mass escape, were the Equals: sixty-eight of them, by current count. Of *mothakes*, the Spartan cousins whose blood was too impure to grant them full citizenship, there were about twice that number, plus about the same again each of Spartan allies and Helot rowers.

The Naupaktan dead were tallied and recorded, too, and put at just twenty-nine.

Just past noon, when his path crossed that of Agathokles, Demosthenes hailed the Naupaktan leader and his aides and stood in conference with them on the sands.

"I would claim half of the *mothakes* and twenty Equals as my prisoners," Demosthenes said after the exchange of niceties. "I think that fair."

Agathokles' expression bespoke reluctance. "It is a difficult proposal even to consider, good friend, when you will not tell me your purpose in wanting them. I do not suppose you have changed your thinking on that matter?"

"No. The lives of the defeated lie by rights in the hands of the victors. Your hand would not have been victorious this day without my considerable aid."

He did not mention the aid of the other standing a pace behind him; but then, he knew Thalassia scarcely minded whether men other than himself gave her the considerable credit she was due.

Demosthenes added, "I should think the custody of a handful of men who might as easily have drowned or burned this morning is a small price to ask in return."

"Aye, it is," Agathokles conceded, if less than genuinely. "The step-brothers, I should think, pose little difficulty. You may have thirty or so of them. But the Spartiates..." He scratched his beard uncomfortably. "You know better than anyone their value as hostages. Sparta might hesitate to launch a fresh assault knowing that the throats of seventy Equals would be cut before battle even was joined. Agis might be persuaded to discuss terms."

"He might," Demosthenes agreed, taking his turn to speak less than genuinely. "Yet if he is, I find it unlikely that fifty throats will differ from seventy in that regard. Or sixty, for I will accept ten Equals. But I must have them, and they will be no part of any treaties or exchanges. Where Sparta is concerned, they simply will no longer exist."

Agathokles bowed his head heavily, perhaps attempting to imagine his friend's dark purpose, then sighed in the same manner before tersely delivering his decision. "Very well. Take your ten." He sighed again, and there was a trace of sadness in his eyes on this momentous day of victory for his beloved city.

"If I may," Thalassia interjected, addressing Agathokles. "Will the Helot prisoners be given their freedom?"

Looking to her, Agathokles brightened. He got on well with her, as most humans tended to, so long as she lacked cause to end their lives.

"They will be offered the choice to become Naupaktans, yes. But most will elect to return to Messenia, where their labor provides not only for Sparta but also their own wives and mothers and sons. They would not abandon family for the sake of freedom."

"May I assist in screening them? We would not wish to welcome potential spies into our midst."

"Naturally," Agathokles agreed, far more readily than he had to Demosthenes' request. "I am greatly obliged for your concern, and your service."

Just as Thalassia received the leader's gratitude with a nod and smile, a man on the beach cried out, "A craft approaches!"

Demosthenes, with Thalassia, the Naupaktan leader and his entourage, descended the beach and looked out to sea to spy upon the waves a two-oared boat, the single occupant of which—by his dress, an Equal—evidently had battled strong currents to row across the strait. Attached to the prow was a laurel-wrapped herald's wand which obliged the Naupaktan navy to let him pass.

The boat's approach was slow, but Demosthenes made sure that when the time came, he stood with Agathokles and other officials of the Naupaktan democracy on the stretch of coast on which the craft was set to land.

Thalassia stood there, too. Her eyes being what they were, she was first to recognize the lone Equal at the oars. She whispered his name into Demosthenes' ear.

Styphon.

13. Kill the messenger

The sound of the name ignited in Demosthenes a white-knuckled hatred which he quickly fought to suppress in favor of calculation. If he showed his intentions too soon, he might lose his chance to kill a man who had stood by and watched the murder of Laonome.

He did not consult Thalassia, verbally or otherwise, for he knew with certainty that she would back him in whatever action he took. In a series of seemingly casual movements, he began steadily to maneuver closer to the water line. To attack Styphon, he would need to be first to reach him as his craft approached the shore. The Naupaktans surely would try to interfere: not only was an assault on a herald a desecration of sacred law, they would hope he came bearing some offer from Agis.

When Demosthenes judged the boat was close enough, well before any of the gathered Naupaktans had thought of going forward to meet it, he charged headlong into the shallows. The breaking waves and shifting, wet sand underfoot, combined to slow him to a trudging crawl, but no more or less than it would slow any who pursued him. Heedless of such impediments, gaze fixed firmly on the flat-nosed profile of his target, recognizable when Styphon cast a glance over his shoulder at the shore, Demosthenes pushed on relentlessly.

Grasping his intent, Naupaktans cried urgently from shore, and there followed splashing footfalls as some number of them entered the sea to stop the Athenian guest from ruining whatever chance might exist for a negotiated peace. Demosthenes did not worry, for he was not alone. They would be prevented from reaching him in time.

He was nearly shoulder-deep when he drew close

enough to lunge at the side of the craft, narrowly dodging an oar-stroke. With hate-fueled strength infusing water-heavy, battle-weary arms, he grabbed the craft's topstrake and pulled. He roared, a primal sound which reverberated off the nearby cliffs. The boat rocked, oars flew off time, Styphon slipped from the bench, and Demosthenes, reaching out, seized a handful of long, damp hair. With all his weight, he used the locks to pull Styphon overboard and into the cold waters which were to serve as both site and instrument of the Equal's death.

Demosthenes' sandals found footing on the sea floor, and he shifted his grip from the ends of his victim's hair to the scalp while his other hand restrained a wrist. Downward he pushed, locking his elbow to hold Styphon's head under some three feet of water. Styphon thrashed with his free arm and both legs, but impeded by the water, even those blows which landed could scarcely be felt.

Having never drowned a man, Demosthenes knew not how long it would take. Voices and splashing that grew steadily louder behind him suggested he would shortly have to contend with Naupaktan intervention, barring interference on his behalf. Maintaining the firm grip which denied Styphon breath, he spun to face the shore in time to witness the hoped-for arrival.

Feet away, well ahead of five or six onrushing Naupaktans, Thalassia exploded from the waves like brine-born Thetis herself to bar their path. A toss of her long hair sent up a rain of seawater, and she leveled twin blades at the surprised Naupaktans to ensure there could be no misunderstanding: they were not to pass.

Confident in her protection, Demosthenes carefully shifted his grip on Styphon to renew downward pressure. A storm of bubbles broke the dark surface of the water, which seemed to Demosthenes a likely sign of impending death.

His gaze was downward on the barely visible form of his victim when Thalassia, having backed closer to him while continuing to ward off Naupaktans who were wise in their reluctance to face her.

She spoke just loudly enough for him and no other to hear.

"Let him go," she urged. It was no demand, but an emphatic suggestion.

Demosthenes ignored her, and intended to continue to do so until it was too late.

She backed closer, until their shoulders touched, leaned her head to his and spoke in soothing tones: "Naupaktos needs him. We may need him one day. Trust me."

"*He watched!*" Demosthenes returned, not looking at her. "He needs to die!"

"He will. Another day. Please."

Thalassia had spent some days with Styphon on Sphakteria before coming into Demosthenes' 'possession' as a spoil. Later, she had tutored Styphon's daughter Andrea. Maybe she felt some misguided fondness toward the man or simply did not wish to see Andrea orphaned. Yet there was nothing pleading about her tone, no emotion in the entreaty. Only calculation.

"Will you stop me?" The Equal had all but ceased struggling.

Thalassia kept swords on the Naupaktans, who had gathered in a loose semicircle in the rib-deep water. "No," she pledged. "Nor will I let them stop you. I only ask you to take my advice. I may have been wrong a time or two. Usually I'm not."

Demosthenes laughed.

At Amphipolis, she had urged him to kill Brasidas when

he had the chance. Partly out of spite, he had refused. Had he only listened...

On her advice, he had met Laonome.

Lifting his hands, he released Styphon, who floated gently to the surface. Without releasing either of her swords, Thalassia lifted Styphon's insensate form under one arm and forcefully addressed the Naupaktans: "I can save him! Make way!"

The request was likely unnecessary, as no Naupaktan was in a hurry to put himself in her path. Dragging Styphon behind her, she made haste for the beach. Demosthenes trudged behind as quickly as he could, keeping one eye on the Naupaktans whom he halfway suspected might make some move on him now that his defender was occupied.

They did not, and Demosthenes came ashore sopping wet behind Thalassia and her burden, which she laid out on the sand, discarding her weapons. Tired from sprinting against the tide, Demosthenes sank to his knees and watched Thalassia pry Styphon's mouth wide open and kiss him. She did so repeatedly, deeply, and for quite some time while a gathering crowd of Naupaktans looked on in silence.

Demosthenes stared, too, and was perhaps even more confused than the rest: where the Naupaktans took Thalassia for some type of enchantress, a woman whose kiss might well possess some life-giving power, he knew with near certainty that this was not the case.

While his own racing heartbeat slowed, and Styphon's chest rose and fell, Demosthenes began slowly to comprehend: she was breathing into him, breathing *for* him, forcing air into his frame with each touch of her lips. After a short while, the inanimate corpse of the drowned Spartiate jerked to life, sputtering and coughing, and Thalassia, in success, fell back onto haunches.

In the minutes following, Styphon returned to a groggy awareness and was half-dragged away by the Naupaktans, perhaps to deny his would-be executioner a chance to change his mind. Agathokles, before following the aggrieved Spartan herald away, leveled at Demosthenes a gaze which promised the matter was not closed and forgiveness not guaranteed.

Grievous as was his offense, Demosthenes was not detained or otherwise accosted, perhaps out of fear of Thalassia, perhaps in acknowledgment of his role in the day's victory, or even simply because no one wished to sully a momentous day with squabbling.

Instead, not much later, Demosthenes found himself sitting alone on the beach, wet and exhausted, beside his fellow vagabond.

"It was purely curative," she said.

"Hmm?" Demosthenes replied absently. "Oh, the kiss. Yes, I know."

"He is in my debt," she said, clearly speaking of Styphon. "From Sphakteria. I made him pledge to do me a favor one day in return for removing Andrea from Sparta for him."

"He owes you double now. Somehow I doubt either debt will be repaid. I would not pay them if I were him."

"Thankfully, you aren't. He might be useful to us. And to Naupaktos. If not, we just kill him later."

Staring across the gently lapping surf, Demosthenes changed the subject, wishing to banish Styphon from mind. "Why did you volunteer to question the captured Helots?" he asked. "I know it is more than a simple service to Naupaktos."

Her pale eyes lit, perfect teeth showing in a flashed grin. "A weapon like your *fungulus* needs what we sophisticated killers of the future call a *delivery system*. I think we might just have found ours."

* * *

For some amount of time, Demosthenes slept lightly in the sand, head resting on the arm of Thalassia. Not long, evidently, for the sun yet shone and Thalassia's brined hair was still damp when a pair of Naupaktans came for them. They delivered their message from Agathokles brusquely.

"The Spartan herald insists he will speak only with you two."

They accompanied the Naupaktans silently to the civil building where the Spartan envoy was being housed in semi-captivity. Before any meeting with him, they found themselves before a displeased Agathokles.

"He would you see you both and no other," Agathokles said ruefully. "In private. Given your indefensible act today, I considered sending him away. But that would make us appear uninterested in talking, and that we are not."

Now and then as he spoke, Agathokles flicked an angry glance Thalassia's way, as if for the sake of including her, but he spared most of his scorn for Demosthenes, in whose direction he raised a lecturing finger.

"I shall give him what he wants, but heed well: on entering that room you represent Naupaktos. Our interests come before all else, and our interest is in a lasting peace that preserves our independence. *Not* the slaughter of every Equal who comes into our sight."

The last sounded almost a joke, but understandably was not.

Agathokles gave a final, stern glare before adding an instruction which likewise should have been made in jest.

"Leave your weapons with the guards."

With that, he removed himself from their presence. Demosthenes was of half a mind to call out an apology, but he kept silent. Even if the words were not empty, were they to be spoken in haste, unaccompanied by actions, they could only be perceived as such. A better time for attempting to heal the rift with Agathokles would come after he had heard whatever rot it was that Styphon intended shortly to vomit forth.

To that end, Demosthenes surrendered his arms to the Naupaktans, as did Thalassia (for all the emptiness of such a gesture from her) and entered the small, windowless room in which the recently un-murdered Equal stood waiting.

14. Herald

Styphon ensured that the stony look he had worn while standing alone in the room changed not one bit on the entry of the two to whom he was due to deliver King Agis's ill-conceived request.

One of the two who entered had, a few short hours ago, tried to kill him. From what the Naupaktans said, he had succeeded. The second, the deadlier by any reckoning and one whose proximity made his flesh crawl only slightly less than did that of Eris, had reputedly saved his life—dragged his shade back from the underworld with a kiss, if the same easily duped Naupaktans were to be believed.

Styphon looked at them now as though none of this had transpired, indeed as though he had never met either. They shut the door behind them, and Styphon spoke first, forgoing niceties which would have no place regardless.

"The Eurypontid king of Sparta, his majesty Agis, desires to employ your services," he said flatly.

Neither of the two laughed, a reaction for which even a Spartiate could have forgiven them. The witch Thalassia, damp-haired as if fresh from a bath in Acheron, her home, came closest, with mild amusement lighting her pale daimon-eyes. Demosthenes, for his part, wore on his face the white-lipped disgust one might expect given his undiplomatic actions on the beach. The man's distaste was palpable enough that Styphon put his body on alert for a fresh assault. This time he would repel it—at least until the witch stepped in to save her Athenian thrall.

It was the witch who answered, while Demosthenes remained unable or unwilling to part his grinding jaw. All she said, in a neutral tone, was, "Go on."

Styphon was pleased to oblige: the sooner he could

deliver his message, hear an answer, and leave, the better.

"Agis would see the plague of Eris's presence removed from Sparta," he said. "Permanently. He believes that if anyone can help him achieve that aim"—he set his gaze firmly on Thalassia—"it is you."

The look which came over Thalassia's features was one of interest, perhaps satisfaction. Demosthenes turned his head aside, staring at a corner of the plaster floor. He had come intending to keep his ears and mind tightly shut, Styphon surmised.

The witch continued to speak for both.

"You sound as if you do not agree with your king," she observed. "Are you still Brasidas's man?"

"I am my own man," Styphon returned confidently. He kept in mind, and would with every answer he gave, that his present company was, like Eris, able to instantly discern truth from lies.

"Why did Brasidas not lead this attack?" Thalassia asked next, as her companion continued to silently seethe.

"That is an internal affair of the Spartan state," Styphon evaded. "And moreover, no concern of mine."

"He overstepped, didn't he?"

Styphon gave no reply, but Thalassia's smirk suggested that was answer enough.

"What did she do?" she pressed.

Chilled by the accuracy of the witch's insight, Styphon sealed his lips tighter still.

Abandoning that line of inquiry, Thalassia asked next, "What does Agis offer in return for our *services*?"

Now Styphon forced his lips apart, as much as it pained him to speak what he must.

"When the witch is dealt with," he said, "Agis will deliver Brasidas, that he might face... *justice*."

There. It was done. He had just offered up as payment to a foreigner the life of his countryman, his superior, a man he was bred to respect. It could not but be a sin, even if mitigated by the fact that his king had put him up to it.

Demosthenes glared at Styphon briefly, then fumed blankly at the wall, leaving once more his witch to do the talking.

"You have our interest," she declared. "But we have other aims than vengeance on one man. What of Naupaktos?"

"It must fall. Not today, perhaps, but another."

An Equal who returned home in defeat would meet with temporary scorn, Styphon knew; one who returned having let defeat strip him of his resolve for victory would bear a lifelong stain. After such a defeat as today's, Agis could not entertain offering the enemy peace in any form. The ephors would only void it and then exile its broken author.

"Should the two of you persist in confounding our efforts to take the city, Agis's offer will be rescinded."

Thalassia breathed a little laugh. "Will it, now? If I were to destroy Eden... pardon, *Eris*... what exactly would prevent me from taking Brasidas next? And Agis, for that matter?"

Styphon leveled a look of defiance at the woman-thing. "You are not invincible. Men can harm you. Kill you. When we found Eris, she was imprisoned such that only our help allowed her to escape. *Men* did that to her. And I lately saw with my own eyes grisly wounds inflicted on her at the hands of men."

"And in both cases, how many died in doing Eris harm?" Thalassia asked knowingly. "Never mind. Internal affairs of the Spartan state, surely."

"Eris may yet be in a weakened state," Styphon pressed on. "If you intend to accept, your chances of success are increased if you leave forthwith."

"*If* we were to accept," she said, "then you possess something else which must be turned over. Some*one*, rather, by the name of Eurydike. If she lives."

"She does, and she is treated well," Styphon answered, with no fear of being judged a liar. "My wife and daughter are fond of her."

Hippolyta might protest the loss of the slave she had gone to the trouble of seducing, but she could not rightly protest a decision made in the best interests of Sparta.

Thalassia's brows rose in mild surprise. "Wife?" she echoed. "Congratulations. Consider your life my wedding gift."

Ignoring the remark, Styphon added, "You may have Alkibiades, too, in the bargain. You would do Sparta a favor."

"He has made himself at home in Sparta, I see."

"Made himself the witch's plaything." Styphon's eyes went to Demosthenes, who yet gave the conversation his shoulder, but listened attentively, to be sure.

"I must have your reply."

"We hold sixty Equals prisoner," Thalassia said. "If Agis cares to have them back, he could send them up against Eris. A few might survive."

"I will carry to him a list of the prisoners' names. I am not empowered to negotiate their release. However, be assured that the presence of hostages will no more save Naupaktos than it did Athens."

Indeed, not even the captured Equals' families would consider the lives of a few dozen citizens worth letting an upstart town of Helot-descended fishermen and treecutters humiliate Sparta more than it already had. However effete were Athenians, at least they had proved over the course of generations to be a worthy adversary. Not so this place. Freedom for Naupaktos would set an example for cities all over Greece—or worse, for Helots in very heart of the Peloponnese. Were the defeat this day to go unanswered, the preeminence Sparta had gained just a hundred days ago with Athens' defeat would be all but erased.

But such thoughts were not for the enemy's ears.

"It will be some time before you can mount another attack," Thalassia correctly observed. "Much can happen."

"Indeed," Styphon agreed. After a moment's thought, he added: "Such as Eris gaining knowledge of her hated enemy's whereabouts and taking action on her own. Would it not be better for you to—"

"If I need advice from a worthless mound of shit," Demosthenes at last interrupted, whirling to face Styphon. His wide brown eyes were harder and fiercer than Styphon remembered them in the two prior instances in as many years that they had stood this close. For some reason, his right eye was surrounded by faded black smears.

"We have heard your king's offer," Demosthenes seethed. "It is rejected. Our offer in return is that Agis soon can *die* along with all of his subjects, including you and your new broodmare. I neither need nor wish to have Brasidas handed to me. When I am ready, I will take him!" The Athenian bared his teeth in a sneer. "We are finished here. If I stay another moment, I am liable to try and finish what I started in the sea today."

He turned and started for the door.

"Spartiates do not beg, preener, but now that we stand on dry ground, I would very much like you to try."

Demosthenes paused in the door and said after a brief silence: "You will beg, Spartiate. You all will."

Thalassia watched her servant depart before drawing a step closer to Styphon.

"Tell your king that although Demosthenes rejects the

offer, I find it... worthy of further consideration. In the meantime, do not forget what you owe me."

"I leave no debt unpaid," Styphon asserted. "Only know that there are limits, witch. I will not betray other oaths to keep my pledge to you."

"I would not ask it."

"What is it you desire?"

"Nothing yet." She gave a gentle toss of her head. "But the day will come."

With a parting smile, she opened the door and slipped out between the shoulders of two Naupaktan officials who eyed her with suspicion as she passed.

Credit was due them, then: it was not only Spartans who felt ambivalent about surrendering the reins of their state into the silken palm of a witch.

15. Elegant

Swiftly upon storming out of the interview with Styphon, before his angry steps had taken him far, Demosthenes felt the staying grip of Agathokles on his arm. He let it stop him and turned to face the Naupaktan leader.

"What did he say?"

"Not much of use," Demosthenes reported.

"I prefer to judge that for myself."

Rage already begun to cool, Demosthenes met squarely the Naupaktan's frustrated glare and said earnestly, "Accept my apology. Your generosity deserves better than my rash behavior today."

The words were at least partly born of genuine regret, but a certain awareness was present that as a rootless fugitive, he could scarcely afford to lose the good will of his prime benefactor.

"No harm was done in the end," Agathokles said hurriedly. Absent was the smile he regularly had worn in the past when addressing his friend. "You have my forgiveness, freely given. But if you would care to earn it anyway, inform me of what was said in that room."

As Thalassia silently joined them, Demosthenes did so, leaving nothing out.

"So their witch is causing them civil strife," Agathokles observed. Reserving his smile for Thalassia, he said to her by way of apology, "To use a term which the ignorant might wrongly use to describe your kind. The longer the leaders of Sparta fight among themselves, the better for our city, I would think. I am pleased you declined to help them put swift end to it. It could not have been an easy choice, given the reward on offer."

It had not been hard at all, but it scarcely hurt to let the other think what he wished.

"I wonder if Agis might not be more willing to negotiate than he lets on. If not, perhaps he will become so when he learns from Styphon that one of the hostages is his own brother." The Naupaktan's eyes flashed proudly. "Agesilaus commanded their fleet. A fishing boat netted him clinging to the wreck of his ship."

"I know the name," Thalassia announced, drawing both men's attention. "In the future now averted, in which this war would have ended a generation from now, Agesilaus would be king after his brother, to reign for forty years."

The declaration raised four brows. Demosthenes had no doubt in the truth of it, but Agathokles might well have been more skeptical.

"King, hmm?" he intoned. "A good one?"

"Not the worst. By most accounts, it was not entirely his fault that Sparta was irrelevant by the end of his reign."

"Perhaps he ought to be removed from the succession," Demosthenes suggested, half idly. "Any bargain you strike using the hostages will grant you peace for but a short time. Thus would it have been for Athens, barring... witches. You may as well chain the prisoners to a trireme in the channel and set it alight."

The commander-in-chief of the army of Naupaktos bowed his head pensively. "I have never been the kind of man to condemn prisoners-of-war to death," he said. "I hope not to become him." He frowned at Demosthenes. "Would that you had escaped that fate. No, none of the prisoners will be harmed, least of all the one most valuable. It weighs heavily enough on me turning a share of them over to you, knowing..."

Agathokles thought better of finishing, shook his head and smiled sadly.

"At any rate," he resumed, "even if there exists scant cause for hope, I shall persist a while longer in clinging to it. Some measure of peace might be bought, even if it is temporary."

Nodding, Demosthenes conceded, "You are a better leader of men than I. I hope you are right."

With kind words of parting, they took their leaves.

By day's end, ten Equals and thirty of the so-called 'step-brothers' whose blood was not pure enough to grant them Spartan citizenship had been transferred into the custody of Demosthenes and sat chained in the hulls of two beached enemy triremes, guarded by a few Naupaktan volunteers.

Nearby was Thalassia's dank witch's den, where soon she would be ready to begin preparing meals for the forty prisoners. She had ever been a terrible cook, or had chosen to be one, since Thalassia could excel at anything she set her mind to, but these meals were sure to be her worst.

They would be the diners' deaths, and not accidentally.

At dusk, Demosthenes sat with her and a jar of wine outside the cavern mouth, looking out over the strait separating the Gulf of Corinth to the east from the Gulf of Patras to the west. On the opposite shore, smoke had begun to rise from the cooking fires of the Spartan camp. Styphon would be there by now, reporting to his king.

"You should eat and rest," Thalassia said.

"I was thinking we might row across in the night and kill Agis."

She laughed. "I'm up for it. But..."

"But what?" Demosthenes said testily.

"Even if his offer was not acceptable in its present form —"

"Or any form."

"Agis is a counter to Brasidas's influence in Sparta," she

calmly continued. "He commands loyal followers, some of whom we can infer have died trying to kill Eden. It behooves us to keep our options open. And seem like reasonable people, even if one or more of us is not."

Demosthenes growled into the mouth of his wine jar, but accepted her logic. "'Behooves'?"

"It means it would be to our adv—"

"I know what it means, sea hag. Every month you talk more like a sophist."

"It's called *going native*. I like the way you fucking primitives talk. It's elegant. I'm going to be elegant from now on."

Demosthenes turned to see pale eyes shining with false sincerity, and he laughed, and so did she. He asked, "Is there such a thing as filthy elegance?"

She shrugged. "Is now."

He lowered the wine to the ground and his head onto her shoulder. "Do you know more unwritten plays?"

"Many."

"Tell me one."

* * *

Damp and briny from sea-spray, arms leaden from pulling oars on his fruitless round trip across the strait, Styphon made his way on foot to the Spartan encampment— which unlike that of the allied contingents lacked tents or shelters of any kind. There he found Agis among a cluster of officers seated on some rocks overlooking the gulf, throwing knucklebones in a subdued, stakeless game meant only to serve as a moment's distraction from the day's devastation. On noting Styphon's return, Agis made the current throw his last and cordially dismissed the gathering.

As he had earlier in the day, Styphon stood alone with the king and Phaistos the Minoan, his silent seer. The latter sat on the earth, gazing wide-eyed over the waters as though in a trance.

While Styphon dipped to one knee in line with protocol, Agis asked him, "Their answer?"

Rising, Styphon likewise wasted no words. "No. Demosthenes is adamant. The witch less so."

Consternation briefly showed on Agis's face, then quickly faded. "Worth the trying anyway." His reflective manner betrayed no sign that he begrudged Styphon his failure. "Three hundred and twenty Equals lost to us today," he lamented. "Two hundred and eighty more are encamped here, plus five hundred step-brothers and Arkadians. Phaistos tells me the portents bode well for a fresh attack tonight, under darkness, landing well east of Naupaktos in whatever craft we can assemble, then marching overland to appear below the city by dawn. What do you make of that plan, Styphon?"

In truth, he was somewhat confused by it, for in his final talk with Agis before venturing across the channel, the king had told him a second attack would not be possible.

Suddenly, Styphon understood what Agis had done. They had used the same manner of deception on Andrea, letting her believe a lie in order that she might pass it unwittingly to Eris under a cloak of truth.

Had he known a second attack was possible, Styphon could have—would have—given the secret away to Thalassia.

"It could work," Styphon said tentatively. He only thought: *if* Naupaktos had no more tricks in store, and *if* the sea-bitch chose not to take up arms against them personally.

Agis laughed. "It is not only these witches who can smell untruths, friend. You can say it: we would stand almost no chance of success. Which is not to say it is not worth considering. I am forced to decide: is it better to return home after one failure or two? Would the second be viewed as tenacity or foolhardiness?" He shrugged, showing that he expected no answer from his present company. He asked abruptly, "Is that the list of prisoners in your hand?"

Styphon surrendered the folded slip of parchment to his king. As Agis unfolded it, Styphon elected to let him hear quickly aloud, rather than discover by reading, the one name certain to stand out to him.

"They have Agesilaus, sire."

Scowling, Agis perused the list, eyes stopping halfway down, where Styphon knew was located the name just spoken. His gaze grew distant, moving through the parchment and perhaps delving into the past to retrieve some vision of his half-brother from yesterday or a thousand yesterdays ago.

He blinked and was present on the hill again.

"A shame," he said. "A good man. Would have a made a good king, had that been Fate's plan."

"He may yet be restored to freedom," Styphon observed.

"Yes," Agis agreed without really agreeing. "He may. But not in any bargain to be struck with by us or any Equal. On that, the ephors are clear and unanimous."

He sighed heavily and shoved the list back into Styphon's palm. "Come," he said. "You are as literate as any man here. Help me compose a reply that completely ignores the fact that our side just lost."

* * *

Every Spartan presently alive has celebrated the deaths of a thousand brothers, went the message sent back by Agis the following dawn in the hands of a second herald who was not even an Equal.

That morning, the army of Agis army broke camp to march home in defeat.

Sparta would be back, the folk of Naupaktos knew, but that worry was for another day. This day, laughter rang out over Naupaktos.

Mostly laughter. Men had been lost, and so there were those who wept or wailed. But most laughed.

PART 4

SPARTA

1. Beaten

They trudged home in gray-faced shame, fewer than half in number than they had been on leaving just eight days prior, on what most had taken for an easy conquest, a repeat of Pylos. Not a word was uttered of defeat on the march; all were too busy preparing for the humiliation of their homecoming, for the inevitable taunting by friends and brothers, the dutiful scorn of mothers and wives. That those coming home had not even seen true combat, not been given the chance to die, only deepened their sense of failure.

Agis's spirits seemed higher to Styphon than they rightfully should have been, given that he was surely to bear the brunt of blame. He was a king, of course, of divine lineage and subject to different rules than mere citizens. Mechanisms were in place to dethrone or exile a king deemed unworthy, but a single defeat generally did not cost a king his throne.

Generally, it did not. But as had just been demonstrated at great cost at Naupaktos, times had changed. Opinion was divided within the bodies that ruled Sparta, ruling even over her kings, as to whether Sparta would change, too. Agis might escape serious punishment, but the sort of failure he had just overseen might well change enough minds, it seemed to Styphon, to tip the balance in favor of adaptation and innovation—back in favor of Brasidas.

Perhaps that concern did weigh on Agis's mind, but he did not let it show that Styphon could tell. Even when the official messenger of the ephorate came out on the broad road to meet the broken army before it had passed the inscribed stones marking the boundary of the unwalled city, Agis appeared light of heart.

"Off to the crucifixion post," the king joked straight-faced.

This was a double exaggeration, for in the unthinkable event that he paid for this failure with his life, his execution would not take a form reserved for slaves and thieves.

Where Agis's path was to diverge from that of the column, Styphon moved with the rest of the king's guard to accompany Agis. But the king raised a hand.

"What good does it do me to bring witnesses to my censure?" he asked. "No, go home to your own judges and take whatever beating they have in store."

Some Equals smirked. It was every wife's and mother's duty to make husband or son suffer on return from defeat, but it was also an unspoken truth that behind closed doors, most doors anyway, reunions were a joyous thing whatever the outcome of battle. Styphon knew it would be thus with Hippolyta, who might derive some pleasure from letting a neighbor or two overhear her berating him, only to clamp thighs around him shortly thereafter. If not during.

And so as Agis struck off alone with the ephorate's man, Styphon picked his own path home among the other returnees. Wearier from the long march home than they would have been from the same march following victory, they shambled like a listless wave breaking on the rocks of Sparta and dispersed among its broad streets in search of respite which might at least make the next day seem a little brighter.

Styphon's world brightened before he reached his door, for Hippolyta had come to the property's edge to meet him. She gave a misty-eyed look of consolation and set a gentle hand on his cheek.

"I intended to spit on you and call you a spineless half-man, but count yourself lucky. I cannot bring myself to do it." She set her cheek on his chest, and they embraced before she walked him inside. Something bubbling in a pot on the hearth filled the megaron with a savory aroma. Hippolyta went and stirred it, regarding the pot's contents with a strange, almost vacant look.

The look was what reminded Styphon that it was odd that his wife would prepare a meal, much less alone, without Eurydike or at least Andrea in attendance. Their absence and Hippolyta's distraction, he felt certain, were not unconnected.

He asked, "What is wrong?"

In Hippolyta's answering look, he sensed gratitude for the attention offered to her concerns, whatever they were, on such a dismal day as this. "Eurydike," she said. "I sent her on an errand hours ago, and she has yet to return."

Styphon frowned. Here was just what he had feared when it came to his wife's affection for Eurydike. A shame he could not have broken them up sooner, before Hippolyta was forced to learn, as she was now, that 'affection' shown by a slave was only ever self-serving.

Sensing his very thought, Hippolyta said fervently, "She has *not* run away."

With a shrug, Styphon conceded that she could be right. Eurydike had run afoul at least once in her tenure in Sparta of the law allowing for slaves to be punished as any citizen saw fit. Someone would return her, if not today, then tomorrow.

"Where is Andrea?" he asked, ready to leave the matter behind.

"She rarely shows her face here," Hippolyta said distractedly. "When she does, I plead with her to stay, but she only vanishes again."

She crossed from the hearth to where Styphon had just lowered weary bones to the floor of hard-packed earth. His wife knelt and set a hand on a forearm still glazed with sweat and trail dust.

"Please help me find her," Hippolyta asked with eyes downcast in embarrassment, for either or both of the inconvenient timing of the request or the womanly sentiment behind it.

After the defeat and the long march, it surely was an inconvenience. But what was a spouse if not someone to daily inconvenience?

He took her hand, kissed its knuckle, and together they rose. By the time he stood, Hippolyta was meeting his eyes and girlishly smiling. "Thank you," she said, nuzzling him. "What woman is luckier than I? I promise to repay you later."

"If you can keep me awake," Styphon half-joked.

His wife had changed, he noted, as Hippolyta carefully removed the pot from the fire and then together they left the house. Marriage had tamed the one whose cousin called her *theria*, wild girl. It was not an unwelcome change. What, after all, was the purpose of marriage if not to tame?

They walked arm-in-arm, Styphon treating the search as a pleasant walk down country lanes. It resembled those walks by the Eurotas they had taken during their courtship, and on another day, when he had not already walked endless *stadia*, he might have enjoyed it more. Even still, the feeling of his wife's hand as it stroked his arm in affection, of her cheek on his shoulder as she made a convincing display of being unworried, succeeded in dragging his spirits up from the depths. He had not returned from his latest deployment a hero, but in someone's eyes at least, he still was one.

The day's light fading, they followed the path that Eurydike would have taken on her errand, the fetching of a jar of honey from a nearby farm.

Three quarters of the the way there, they found her.

It was Styphon who spotted her, off to one side of the road: just a pile of red curls barely visible through tall yellow grass.

"There," he said, gesturing. He scowled, for his first

thought was that the girl had fallen asleep. He was wrong.

Racing through the grass to reach the spot ahead of him, Hippolyta shrieked and fell to both knees. Styphon came up behind and saw what she saw.

Eurydike's green eyes were open, and there was life in them, but barely. One half of her jaw was swollen and purple, the eye on the same side likewise. Half-dried blood from her nose coated split lips. Finger-shaped bruises encircled her neck above the thin iron ring of her slave collar.

She was naked, her torn and bloodied chiton snagged on the twigs of a nearby shrub. More dark bruises stained her thighs, back, and arms, and a bite mark marred the side of one freckled breast. Beside her, a honey jar was smashed on the ground, ants swarming in a black mass over its former contents.

It was clear to Styphon, to anyone: she had been beaten, raped, and left behind without regard for whether she lived or died. One man might have done it to her, but instinct told Styphon it had been more. Probably Spartiate boys, a pack of under-twenties coming back from a day's hard training. Such acts by them were not uncommon, and even if it was technically a crime to damage communal property without provocation, only rarely was any effort put toward catching the culprits.

Tears streamed down Hippolyta's cheeks as she clung to Eurydike's unresponsive form, kissing her bruised face, brushing hair from her eyes, begging her to move or speak. But the slave did neither. There was sight in Eurydike's eyes and a flicker of life in her limbs, but the will to live was absent.

"I will kill them!" Hippolyta hissed, cradling Eurydike's head to her breast. "I will slaughter whoever did this to you!"

Styphon knelt behind his wife, setting a hand on her

shoulder. "Be calm," he urged.

Hippolyta shrugged him away. "I will not! Go! Find who did this!"

"They are long gone. We will never know. We can only —"

"If you are a *man*, you will find and kill them! If you won't, I will!"

Styphon forgave her the outburst, persisting calmly, "We must tend to her injuries. I will carry her."

With a last kiss on the slave's forehead, Hippolyta let Eurydike be hoisted into her husband's arms, where she was borne as one might bear a sleeping child to bed. Hippolyta wept as they walked in the direction of their home, holding Eurydike's limp hand which, like all her limbs, fell wherever it may. She was a dead weight in Styphon's arms, a living corpse.

Styphon's mind was less on the slave's welfare than that of his wife. As they walked, he voiced his concerns, knowing they were likely to win him only antipathy.

"It is unhealthy to have such strong feelings for a slave," he ventured.

Hippolyta answered with an icy silence which was impossible for anyone, even a man, to misinterpret. He could take his fucking opinions with him across the Styx.

2. Trial

They took Eurydike home and laid her on Styphon's own bed. While Hippolyta warmed water with which to clean her, Styphon went to fetch the district's slave-healer.

"Not the one who serves Helots," Hippolyta admonished him with a glare that promised consequences if she was ignored. "She will have the same care I would. Lie to the man if you must."

Without argument, he went and did as asked, racing to the healer's home and dragging him from dinner with a few words which conveniently omitted that the party in need of urgent care was a mere slave.

The old man appeared a trifle annoyed on learning the truth, thinking perhaps that he might have finished his dinner first, or even bid Styphon take his request to the proper place. But given that his summoners were the king's cousin and a member of the royal guard, the healer set to work applying poultices and bindings to his conscious but catatonic patient, enlisting a teary-eyed Hippolyta as assistant.

The work had but begun when Styphon glanced out his open door to see a cloaked figure making haste up the trail. Going closer, he recognized the man as the very messenger who had earlier fetched Agis to the ephorate.

Now Styphon was summoned to the same place, the messenger informed. Wondering what the purpose might be (for the summons declined to specify), Styphon stuck his head into the bedchamber and announced his departure to the no one who was listening, and then set off.

By the time he arrived at the unadorned timber structure which housed the ephorate, Styphon had concluded, based on nothing more than his own reason, that he was to give the ephors some testimony relating to the defeat at Naupaktos.

On being ushered into the meeting place, Styphon was thus not particularly surprised to find its walls lined with what appeared at first glance to be all twenty-eight members of the council of elders. A joint session of the council and ephorate was typical procedure for certain matters of import.

He was slightly more surprised to see Brasidas in attendance, standing close to the center of the room, facing the ephors on their low platform.

True surprise came when Styphon noticed two women in the chamber. Even had they been Spartan women, which they were not, they should have been barred from this place. They stood not far from Brasidas, and Styphon recognized both.

Aspasia was one. The other was one of the two Athenian wives whom Aspasia had helped him procure in fulfillment of Agis's request during the king's stay in Athens. Aspasia looked at ease, the other woman far less so, her face downcast.

Apart from hers, all eyes in the room, some forty pairs, all told, were fixed on Styphon as he entered. By chance or will, Styphon found himself meeting, alternately, two gazes: those of Agis, whose face was ashen with checked anger, and of Brasidas, who barely restrained a wicked smile. The two stood apart in the center of the ring of observers.

Styphon came to stand before the ephors' platform and barely managed to feel that the proceedings had the sense of a trial before the chief ephor, a man not yet forty, addressed him.

"Styphon, Pharax's son," the ephor said, "you have been called to deliver testimony. You will swear an oath by Zeus to speak only the truth."

Hesitating only long enough to wet lips, Styphon recited the well-known formula inviting doom upon himself and his bloodline should he speak falsely.

"Is it true that while in Athens shortly before the taking of Dekelea, you were recruited by Agis to obtain for him a pair of Athenian citizen females for the purpose of obtaining from them sexual gratification?"

"It is," Styphon answered mechanically. He looked only at the questioner, avoiding the gazes of Brasidas and Agis, although he felt them, particularly the latter, whose confidence he was betraying.

What choice was there?

"Did you succeed in delivering said females?"

By now Styphon slipped into a familiar mode of soldierly obedience, surrendering control of his lips, which replied, "Yes, ephor."

The ephor indicated the woman shrinking at Aspasia's side. "Is this one of them?"

"It is."

A second magistrate took over the questioning. "Did you join Agis in the sport which followed?"

"I did." Since it had not been asked, he did not volunteer that Agis had insisted; best he not appear to be disavowing responsibility for his actions.

"With one woman or both?"

Styphon took a fresh look at the Athenian female and glimpsed her face long enough, before she put it to Aspasia's shoulder in shame, to be certain of his answer. "Mostly the other one."

"Did you achieve release?"

Beyond surprise by now, Styphon answered in short order: "I did."

"How many times?"

Styphon cast his mind back briefly and returned with honest answer: "Once."

"Where?"

Styphon swallowed, started to speak, then asked what was meant, lest his answer of 'the megaron of Nikias' set the room to laughter.

"I mean where was your seed deposited," the ephor explained humorlessly.

Just as stiffly, Styphon gave the true answer.

"Then you planted no seed in this woman's womb?"

Realization dawned on Styphon, stealing his voice for an instant. He studied the Athenian again and saw for the first time that she kept one hand resting constantly on an abdomen the roundness of which was rather a mismatch for her slender build.

The Athenian was with child, and Brasidas aimed to prove—

"Did you witness Agis enter this woman?" the ephor inquired.

The purpose, if not import, of his testimony becoming clear, Styphon at last spared looks for prosecutor and accused. Both gazed back expectantly, one showing no cracks in a hawklike mask of supreme confidence, the other, with a trace of desperation, urging the witness to give the hoped-for answer.

But the answer for which Agis hoped was a lie.

Styphon had done much for Agis and been well rewarded. The young king was a friend, perhaps not an entirely genuine one, but close. A better one than Brasidas, to be sure.

Perhaps a better man and better friend to Agis than Styphon was could stand before the supreme authorities of the Spartan state, under oath, and tell a lie on his behalf. But Styphon was not a better man than himself. He was no ideal citizen, either, but he knew that here, in this place, under these eyes, truth was his only option.

"I did," he confessed.

With his next question, the ephor reached, for all purposes, the interrogation's climax. "Did you witness him planting his seed within her?"

The room tensed in utter silence, anticipating Styphon's reply. Like many a man before him, he disappointed.

"I cannot say for certain." This was the truth, and Styphon was glad that his knowledge stopped where it did.

The air in the chamber warmed with forty released breaths. The ephor who had asked the question frowned. The presiding magistrate asked his colleagues, "Are there any further questions for this witness?" There were none, and so the ephor went on, "Is there anything more the witness would like to add?" A swift, grateful negative. "The witness is dismissed."

Turning to leave, Styphon caught an empty stare from Agis, a look of slender hopes dashed more than ill will to the dasher. Neither did Styphon in turn bear ill will toward the king whom he had followed now through one successful venture, the capture of Dekelea, and two catastrophes.

He bore no ill will toward Brasidas, either, whatever their differences when it came to Eris. If he felt anything, it was only frustration that Sparta could not simply remain whole, as it had always been, instead of descending into the kind of civil strife, faction set against faction, which had reduced other cities to graveyards. The day had not yet come when Equal slaughtered Equal, and it was not yet imminent if Styphon was any fit judge, but such a day seemed to him to loom just out of sight, past the horizon on this path which Sparta currently tread.

There must be another path, some middle path, by which unity could be preserved. After today, Agis surely would not be the one to find it. Perhaps Brasidas would.

If anyone stood a chance, it was him. Styphon wondered if he had not erred after all in letting his allegiance to Brasidas flag. Not that the lapse seemed to have harmed Brasidas any; on the contrary, things could scarcely have gone better for the ex-polemarch had he planned it all himself.

Which perhaps he had. Styphon did not wish to know.

Glad to let the wheels of government turn without him, Styphon exited the ephorate into a brazier-lit autumn twilight. A small crowd of perhaps twenty men stood gathered outside the door. Most of them surely had little inkling what was transpiring inside, knowing only that it was something of great import. As small crowds tended to do, it was growing. Styphon was the target of hopeful stares, but questions were withheld on the correct assumption he would not risk punishment by preempting official announcements.

One man did address Styphon, though, after calling out his name and breaking away from the crowd to accost him.

"My sympathies, friend," Alkibiades said with unwarranted familiarity. "I was dismayed to hear of the defeat at Naupaktos. You will have to tell me about it."

"Ask someone else," Styphon growled at the Athenian. He turned away from the man, who only maneuvered to compensate.

"Is it true?" the preener pestered, his voice low. "The way the fleet was destroyed? It was *them*, wasn't it? Demosthenes and Thalassia."

Styphon answered with a sneer meant to tell Alkibiades that his company was undesired.

Unsurprisingly, and doubtless deliberately, the Athenian failed to take the point.

He whispered casually near Styphon's ear: "I know what is going on in there. If you told me what I wanted to know, I could tell you."

"I was in there."

"True. But I wonder if you know Spartan law better than I do. Do you know, for example, what can be done to a king found to have fathered a child on a foreign woman?"

Styphon looked over to see Alkibiades' arms folded casually, his lips twisted in a smug half-smile aimed at the ephorate door which was also the focus of every gaze present.

No longer a participant but just another Equal in a crowd, Styphon had little better to do than indulge the preener.

"There is no child," Styphon said, for only the Athenian to hear. "Not yet."

"True. And it might have been dealt with in a certain distasteful way. Quietly. Without recourse to a trial. But it was not, was it?"

Styphon knew just what the other meant. The extraordinary session presently underway would not be happening at all if the outcome were in much doubt.

"Unless it is that rare occasion on which my instincts are wrong, Brasidas has a majority lined up. Your little provocation of Her Frostiness might have forced him and his supporters into a tactical retreat, but evidently they're back. Sooner than I would have thought. Best not to waste the momentum of the disaster Agis just oversaw at Naupaktos, I suppose." He shrugged and nudged Styphon. "No offense."

Offense, of course, was taken, but since Alkibiades virtually exhaled offense, Styphon had grown used to it by now.

"I've told you what I know," the Athenian went on. "Or think I know. Your turn. They were there, in Naupaktos, weren't they?"

Styphon let his answer double as mockery. "Your vaunted instincts do not fail you. What clued you in? The giant fucking fire-arrows?"

"For one," Alkibiades returned, unperturbed. "Is it known for certain both of them were there? Not just one or the other? I would like to know they're alright, if you can forgive my concern for enemies of Sparta. They were my friends not long ago."

The question gave Styphon enough pause to let the Athenian deduce the answer himself.

"You saw them?" Alkibiades said in hushed awe. "How? That means you crossed the straits, but not in battle. Agis must have sent you. As herald, right? Star-girl has a soft spot for you because you named her and gave her a cloak when she washed up, or something. She lived with me for a year, and told me about those days. What did you say to them? What did they say?" He scoffed at himself. "You won't tell me. Never mind. But tell me one thing..." He leaned close, hand on the back of Styphon's neck. "Did they ask about me?"

Whatever this preener's shortcomings, and they were considerable, Styphon at this moment could no longer deny the man's claims to a superhuman level of instinct. How else had he gathered what he had just gathered from literally nothing?

"They did not," Styphon was glad to answer. In fact, he had been the one to bring up the preener's name.

Alkibiades exhaled a sigh of disappointment. "You're sure? I thought I would have made more of an impression on her."

"Go make an impression elsewhere," Styphon said curtly, tossing his head.

Alkibiades laughed. "Yes, the ugly do seem to be immune to my charms. No offense."

Styphon growled, which earned him a pat on the shoulder, intended as placating.

"I shall visit you tomorrow, Styphon," the Athenian threatened. "Likely with some good news. For me, at least." His bright eyes gleamed with secrets. "Goodbye for now, friend."

Alkibiades fell away to resume his former position, nearer the sealed door of the ephorate. Thankfully, none of the many Spartiates present took the Athenian's lead in attempting to strike up conversation, and Styphon was left alone.

The better part of an hour passed. The crowd swelled as passersby joined and those who had heard word arrived deliberately to add their bodies and quiet speculation.

At last, the door flew open. It was Agis who appeared. He stood in the door frame for a moment with head high, looking rather older than his thirty years. Styphon knew the look. It was dignity in defeat.

With one glance each to left and right at the suddenly silent sea of faces before him, Agis waded in, knowing that sea would part before him, and it did. He left through the narrow channel, heading for his home. No word was breathed in his wake.

Next emerged the five ephors and twenty-eight elders, who filled a space rapidly cleared for them just outside the door. The ephors stood in a line at center, while the twenty-eight white and gray-haired elders massed in two wings to left and right.

No, not all of the elders formed up: a dozen or so struck off, one behind the other, penetrating the crowd as Agis had, looks of subdued anger on their wizened faces.

Last out of the ephorate (apart from the women, who evidently were to remain within for now) was Brasidas, who rounded the assembly of officials and took a spot facing them at the front of the crowd.

The chief ephor, occupying the center spot among his colleagues, delivered at last the pronouncement so eagerly awaited:

"Charges were brought forth against Agis," he announced, "son of Archidamus, that he did, contrary to Spartan law as it applies to kings, sire a child on a woman who is not a Spartan citizen. Having heard the testimony and seen evidence with its own eyes, this panel, by a vote of twenty-two to eleven, declares that Agis is guilty of the infraction. By a vote of eighteen to eleven, with four abstentions, the penalty hereby laid down, effective with the coming dawn, is that Agis, son of Archidamus, should be dismissed into exile."

The audience persisted in its silence, surely as much because no one quite knew what to say as because the ephor clearly was not yet finished.

"As there is no heir of age present in Sparta who might reasonably claim the throne, by our laws a regent must be appointed. This body has voted to install in that capacity Brasidas, whose former rank of polemarch is hereby restored and all restrictions on his movement rescinded."

The chief ephor scanned the crowd once more with narrow, hard eyes which dared any to protest. Though the announcement doubtless had put a chill into the hearts of some, none raised his voice in dissent. The exile of kings was not a commonplace occurrence, but hardly an unthinkable one. Agis's co-king Pleistoanax had, after all, only lately been recalled from his own exile—purely to satisfy an oracle, and for no greater purpose than to sit in his home, unliked and untrusted, barely listened to, reigning over few but his family. Even if their blood carried a spark of the divine, the kings of Sparta were men.

The act of banishment itself therefore was no great shock

to the Equals gathered round. But with both thrones of the dual monarchy now effectively suspended, what put looks of bewilderment onto the faces of many of those listening was a sense of uncertainty, shared by Styphon, as to whether the gods, or Fate, would continue to look kindly on a Sparta which had rendered itself kingless.

They could set aside their doubts, Styphon knew, if reassured by a strong voice, an iron hand. Equals were born and bred to take orders, to relish them, and what blood was in the giver's veins ultimately mattered less than his outward qualities.

Brasidas had such qualities. But would Sparta follow him into uncharted realms... or, rather, realms known only to a witch, a she-daimon, a slayer of Equals?

The answer would soon be learned. Styphon only hoped that he would be among those to learn it, for it occurred to him that this moment of Brasidas's triumph might also be the moment at which Styphon outlived his usefulness, having borne witness against Agis and helped depose him.

After a moment's silence, the chief ephor recited the formulaic ending, "It has been decided, and so let it be for the greater glory of Lakedaimon."

Immediately, the ephor to the chief's right bellowed a salute: "Hail the regent!"

The crowd, which by now numbered well over a hundred, wasted no time in repeating. The ephor led the refrain through ten, twenty more iterations, each greater than the last in volume and fervor: *"Hail the regent! Hail the regent! Hail the regent!"*

Only when the chant had gone on for some time did Brasidas acknowledge the acclaim, a smile on his lips, the satisfaction in his shrewd eyes of ambition fulfilled.

With proclamations made, formality faded. Elders and

ephors and plain citizens intermingled in an atmosphere of high spirits and hope for the future. Already the defeat at Naupaktos and the exile of a king seemed distant things. The sun's next passage would light a new Sparta.

Hail the regent.

Styphon eyed the crowd with suspicion, fearing that the new regent's first, unofficial act of office might well be to dispatch a handful of his most loyal men to dispose of an asset no longer required — a disloyal one, at that.

But he found no glaring eyes set upon him with ill intent. What he did manage to notice was the emergence from the ephorate of Aspasia and the impregnated Athenian, the latter sticking close behind the former and looking as though she would rather sink into the earth than walk upon it, if given that choice. He saw movement near the two women, and it was Alkibiades, reaching them and falling to one knee before Aspasia, clasping her hand in both of his and kissing it.

The sight spawned a realization in Styphon, one he would have made earlier had he not been so focused on more pressing matters. Aspasia had been the consort of Perikles, the Athenian statesman to whom Alkibiades had been ward. It would make her something like a step-mother to him, and judging by the greeting they presently shared, their relationship was one of affection.

Styphon lacked a mind for conspiracy, but he began to see the shape of one before him. Brasidas had watched the King's path with his hawk's eyes and positioned himself to deliver the killing stroke. His accomplices were, to greater or lesser extents, Eris, Alkibiades, Aspasia.

And Styphon, unwittingly, from the very day Agis had arrived at Athens.

Sparta was no nation of sycophants like Athens was, but wherever politics existed, there inevitably was favor to be curried from powerful men—hence the large number of Equals presently converging on Brasidas to offer their congratulations, heartfelt or half-hearted. Watching them, Styphon wondered whether he should not press in among them and offer the same, along with an apology. To do so would amount to acknowledging his betrayal and throwing himself on the new regent's mercy.

He pictured doing it, and pride forced him to walk the other way. Even if Brasidas possessed the quality of mercy, Eris (whatever she may say about Andrea's influence having softened her) did not, and it was she to whom he had given the most direct offense.

Alone, as the crowd in front of the ephorate grew in size and Helots went about its perimeter hanging street lamps to stave off darkness, Styphon began the walk home in near certainty that his remaining hours were numbered.

3. Night visitor

Styphon spent the night alone on a pallet in his megaron, his place beside Hippolyta in the bed in the recently built addition being occupied by the slave-girl with whom, the evidence did more than suggest, his wife had fallen in love.

Eurydike, whom he suspected did not reciprocate her mistress's feelings, would make a full physical recovery, the healer predicted. What happened to her mind was up to the gods. She had yet to speak, and her green eyes seemed barely to see what was laid before them.

Earlier in the night, on his return from the ephorate, Styphon had wrenched Hippolyta from the slave's side long enough to inform her of her cousin's exile. In spite of her distracted state, the import of the news did not escape her. She knew what it meant for her husband's safety, if not her own. She had kissed him and held him close and assured him with sincere but empty words that all would be well. She invited him to take a third of his bed, an offer he declined with a kiss on the salty skin of a brow burdened this day with too many woes.

Styphon sank surprisingly easily into sleep—and emerged from it just as easily with sword in hand, ready to strike at whatever had just woken him.

He saw nothing at first in the pitch darkness and heard no further sounds. Tense seconds later, when his vision had settled, he set down his weapon. It had been aimed at nothing. The nocturnal visitor, his daughter, sat in a different location entirely, staring at him with calm eyes blacker than than the night itself. Styphon was uncertain what noise had woken him, but he sensed that Andrea had made it deliberately just for that purpose.

That rather implied a wish to speak with him, but she

only stared.

Styphon lowered himself back onto to his pallet, setting sword back into a place where he might easily grab it to engage in a futile fight for his life if assassins came. He shut his eyes, but sleep did not come. Still, Andrea sat and stared.

"Forgive me," he said to her after a while, spontaneously. If he could not supplicate himself to Brasidas, he could at least to her. "I acted in error." He might have said more, but chose to see if the fewest possible words would suffice.

"You only say so because of Agis's exile," Andrea said placidly, coldly.

She was right. Had Agis triumphed in his political struggle with Brasidas, there would have been no apologies made. Or, for that matter, if the attempt to destroy Eris had succeeded. But those things had not transpired, and here he was in a position of weakness, making a weak gesture. It did not even escape him that his daughter might be the only thing preventing Eris from killing him. He had to acknowledge the possibility that any feelings he had toward his daughter from this moment forth were self-serving.

Sighing, he abandoned the attempt to win back something like respect from his daughter. "At least accept my gratitude," he said. "For saving my life."

She had not, of course. Not really, not directly. He had lived mostly because Brasidas had wished for him to live a while longer, to help achieve the exile of Agis. Styphon hoped that Eris had not yet imparted to her young disciple the gift of truth-sense.

"You are my father." Andrea spoke the words bitterly, as if disliking their taste. "It means something. Even if I do not know exactly what." Her hands, resting in her lap, toyed with something. A ribbon. Gray in this light, but he knew its color:

red.

Rather than lecture his strange daughter on the deep and unbreakable nature of blood-ties, Styphon demurred. After some silence, morbid curiosity got the better of him and he asked, "Does Eris intend to kill me?"

"*Eden,*" Andrea corrected. "Her name is Eden. She has left Lakonia for now on an errand. But when she comes back, you will be safe. I won a promise from her. But before you thank me, hear what the promise was. If Fate does not beat me to it, *I* shall be the one to decide when you die."

Hearing such words from his daughter's lips, spoken in a voice barely above a whisper out of respect for the women sleeping a room away, prompted first a chill, then righteous anger. Aided by the dark, Styphon let neither show. He said, lightly, when rage was checked, "Then my life is in your hands."

"No. It is in your own," the child countered. "I want my father to live. You happen to be him. You would have to do something unspeakable to make me wish you dead. Eden and I both trust that you learn well enough from your mistakes never to make another attempt on her life."

"I will never even think it," Styphon agreed.

It was probably true. Even if was not, it was what needed to be said.

With hardly a sound, the shadow which was Andrea reclined on her little-used pallet, and she must have slept, for she did not speak again in the long minutes which lapsed before Styphon himself again succumbed to sleep.

* * *

Dawn brought no change in Eurydike's condition; she yet declined to speak or even move significantly under her own power. A Helot was enlisted to take over the slave's chores while Andrea sat at her friend's bedside with a bearing cooler and more reserved than Hippolyta's—or of almost any full-grown woman, for that matter.

The girl kissed Eurydike's forehead, smoothed the red hair around it which was yet full of grass stems and burrs, and she made a solemn pledge: "The men who did this to you will pay. I will see to it."

Styphon saw his wife's eyes light briefly with pleasure on that promise, so similar to her own yet far more worrisome. Were circumstances such that he was the supreme authority under his own roof, Styphon would have scolded both females for entertaining such mad ideas. But the feeling that one's life hung by a slender thread easily slashed in the night by any number of parties on account of a wrong word or deed could have a powerful staying effect on tongue and hand.

Following her swearing of vengeance, Andrea got up and left as if to get that very task underway. Perhaps that was the case, though she said nothing of her destination and Styphon elected not to ask.

Not long afterward, when Styphon had taken breakfast and convinced Hippolyta to eat the food prepared by Eurydike's Helot replacement, Alkibiades maddeningly kept his promise of the prior day by appearing at the door.

Shortly upon entering the megaron, Alkibiades saw through the half-open curtain into the bedchamber where battered Eurydike lay staring blankly. The smile which had begun to crease his fine features instantly faded, and he ran to her, leaping onto the bed, gripping her limp body close, burying his maned head in the crook of her neck. Finding her unresponsive, he called, "*Little Red!* What have they done to you? Who did this?"

"The *who* is unknown," Hippolyta answered for her slave-love. "The *what* is the rape and near-killing of a woman incapable of defending herself."

An anguished look came over Alkibiades on hearing this, and he planted tender kisses on the Thracian's face and hand. "Can she not speak?"

"She chooses not to," Styphon answered.

"And I came with such good news," Alkibiades said. "She would have been delighted." He put his bright eyes on Eurydike's near-dead ones and addressed her instead: "Maybe you still will be, if you can hear. I am to return to Athens. In fact, I am going to be its ruler."

The pride in his voice was unmistakable. What was also unmistakable to Styphon was that this was the Athenian's reward from Brasidas for having secured Aspasia's aid, or else the price set by Aspasia for assistance she had volunteered. It hardly mattered which; the result was the same.

"Not ruler in name, perhaps," he said, "but I am to be one of thirty magistrates, the bulk of whom I will have under my thumb in no time." He went on, leaning close to his unresponsive audience, "I asked Brasidas if I could take you with me, and he said *yes*." The Athenian turned now toward the master of the house. "If Styphon allows it."

Suddenly Styphon found himself the target of two stares: one pleading, the other full of worry—and the threat of retaliation if a wrong answer was given.

In Naupaktos, he had been prepared to promise Eurydike to Thalassia, but today there was only one reply. Even if it would be better for all parties present—not least Hippolyta—if Eurydike were to depart with the preener, Styphon could scarcely do that to his wife. She would not soon forgive him for taking away the object of her misguided affections. One day, she would see reason, or maybe just grow out of her foolish crush.

Today was not that day.

"No," Styphon declared. "She stays." When Alkibiades' mouth flew open in protest, he added firmly, with open palm uplifted: "I will entertain no arguments."

Hippolyta smiled, a small triumph among defeats.

With a sigh, Alkibiades accepted the verdict. "At least I know she is well cared for," he said sincerely to Hippolyta.

The compliment earned the vanquished party a glimmer of pity from the victor.

Alkibiades rose from the bed, smiled and shifted his attention to Styphon, even though it was Hippolyta whom he addressed.

"And I, in turn, shall take good care of your husband," he said, and laughed. "Oh, yes! In my concern for Red, I forgot to mention it..."

It was abundantly clear Alkibiades had forgotten nothing, but just devised on the spot this overly dramatic means of delivering his message.

Why did all Athenians think themselves actors?

"I asked Brasidas whether my good friend Styphon might be the one to escort me and my step-mother home," Alkibiades said, causing Styphon's stomach to bubble. "And he agreed! He said you *deserved* just such an honor, in fact."

Styphon suddenly found a hairless, well-sculpted arm draped over his shoulders.

The loss of Eurydike seemed already to be behind Alkibiades as he exclaimed, "We sail for Athens as soon as arrangements can be made, my friend!"

4. Turtle

They had spent the morning walking east, to the place where the river Mornos emerged from the hills to the north and flowed across a wide, flat plain into the sea. The river was where, if all went to plan, the next battle for Naupaktos would be fought.

Brasidas (or whomever commanded) seemed most likely to land his troops on beaches well east of the river, past where it was practical to extend the city defenses, and march west. The invaders would therefore be forced to cross the Mornos, which thus seemed the logical place to attempt to repel them.

They sat for a while marking up Thalassia's exquisite maps with notes on where obstacles might be constructed, ballistae secreted and troops drawn up, and then, near noon, started back to the city.

They reached the landward side of the sheer cliffs where one day, not as long ago as it seemed, they had leaped together into the sea and one had emerged a new man. The cliff's face was not visible, rather only the long, grassy slope leading up to where the land fell away and the sea was just a gentle roar beyond. Demosthenes was looking in that direction when Thalassia's hand clamped onto his shoulder, forcing him to halt.

The move took him by surprise. His head whipped around to question her, but what he found stilled his tongue, if not his heart.

It did not show in her features, only her pale eyes, but Demosthenes knew: Thalassia, the first or second most powerful being who presently walked the earth, was afraid. Instinctively, even before he followed her gaze, he knew what could be the only cause.

Not what but *who*. It was the reason they almost never

went unarmed these days. After the battle, their presence in Naupaktos would be known to all, including...

Eden crouched atop a boulder ahead, far enough away that Demosthenes' mortal eyes might have missed her were it not for rays of the noonday sun flashing brightly on long hair so blonde it was nearly white. The cut of Eden's compact silhouette said she was armored, and her pose was that of a siren or harpy ready to swoop upon her next unsuspecting meal.

She saw them, of course, had been waiting for them, but remained in place. So did Thalassia, fingers tight on Demosthenes' collarbone.

"Do not fight her!" he urged. The words were scarcely louder than air through his teeth, for he knew Eden's senses were no less sharp than her rival's.

"She wants to talk," Thalassia said. She also kept her voice low, but likely intended for Eden to overhear. "If not, there would be blood already."

As she spoke, her eyes naturally did not leave the distant figure, which straightened and leaped down from the rock, raising open palms.

"Get away," Thalassia said calmly in Demosthenes' ear.

"No." He pretended the same calm, if less perfectly.

Thalassia forewent him the insult of arguing. Instead she clutched a handful of chiton at Demosthenes' chest, leading him to think, briefly, she might pick him up and throw him, as she had done at least once in the past. But she only leaned close and whispered a forceful instruction: "The instant anything happens, leave by the way we did the first time I brought you here."

Demosthenes nodded acceptance, and they separated for the walk up the grassy slope by the sea toward their enemy, Thalassia's killer, toward malice made pale flesh.

When they had gone about halfway, Eden addressed them in her voice that was like frozen silk and still accented with an alien lilt.

She had not 'gone native' quite so fully as Thalassia.

"You would keep your weapons when I have none?" she asked as if offended.

Thalassia stopped. So did Demosthenes, and when she removed her two swords from their scabbards and tossed them into the high grass, he reluctantly followed suit.

Disarmed, they resumed their approach. As he walked, Demosthenes felt a strange calm descend, setting right his erratic breath and racing heart. It was no lack of fear, certainly, for he did not trust Eden's intentions and knew well that death might be imminent. And no longer did he despise life so much as not to care whether it ended or not.

What, then? It was an opportunity sensed, perhaps. Here in front of him was the foremost obstacle to the attainment of his vengeance. However great the chance was that Eden might destroy both him and Thalassia before this encounter ended, there was a smaller one that Eden might be the one who wound up dead.

Or so he wished to, and let himself, believe.

Thalassia stopped a good two spear-lengths from Eden, a distance Demosthenes guessed must mark the inner limit of either's ability to react to the other's sudden assault. He halted in the same spot.

Eden did not quite smile, but there was some dark satisfaction apparent in her eyes of deep blue. Possibly it was the satisfaction of watching a trap begin to close on unsuspecting prey, a thought which made Demosthenes aware of every foot separating his hand from his discarded blade.

If it had been a mistake to disarm, it was an

uncorrectable one. There was naught to do now but hear what the white witch had to say.

Eden yet stood watching them with a curious look when Thalassia claimed the first words of the meeting.

"Kicked out of Sparta?" she asked.

The dormant smile emerged on Eden's almost bloodless lips. No other lines appeared in her delicate, frost-graven features. "They are mildly annoyed with me," she said. "But I have not come here for their sake. Only to have a word with the coward and traitor Geneva."

Geneva, not *Wormwhore*. Had Eden softened?

"I know you didn't come to vaguely insult me over things that happened long ago," Thalassia said.

"True," the other conceded. "I come on account of an otherwise bright girl who suffers a soft spot for you."

"An errand for an eleven-year old," Thalassia observed. "Interesting."

"One must entertain oneself in this wasteland." Her features ticked to indicate Demosthenes, whose blood briefly chilled accordingly. "Something I needn't tell you."

When her gaze returned to Thalassia, Eden spoke some flowing syllables in a tongue unknown.

"In Greek," Thalassia demanded.

Eden's smirked at the only earth-born present, becoming once more comprehensible as she resumed. "Andrea desires for me to make peace with you. Foolish child. Dreamer. But I was, too, at her age."

Thalassia returned, "Dreamers are right sometimes."

"Indeed. And so here I stand, willing to offer a second chance—or would it be third, or fourth? I have lost track. So let us try and make peace."

For a moment, just a moment, a Demosthenes emerged from darkness who yet believed that goodness and honesty could exist in the world, willing to believe that her offer was genuine. But the other quickly choked the life from that poor soul, leaving in command the scarred one who trusted only himself and one other.

"Peace is yours for the asking," Thalassia said. "It's a big planet. We need never cross each other's paths."

"Tsk, it's not quite so easy as that," Eden chided. "First, I must understand why you came here. Why you *trapped* us here." The accusation dripped with acid. "A while ago, your plaything told me you meant to unmake the Worm. He did not lie, but that only means it is what *he* believes. Is it true?"

The truth-sense possessed by both women was of no use in this exchange; the star-born could lie to one another with the same ease with which humans did among themselves.

Thalassia opted not to lie.

"It is. This is the layer, the planet, of his birth. He cannot be directly destroyed, since the universe won't allow it. But if enough change is made here, then perhaps he can be... averted."

"Did Magdalen send you on this mission?"

"I learned of the possibility, and the location of this layer, while I was with him. And when she forgave me, I told her all. But no... Magdalen did not send me."

Eden scoffed. "And why is that, I wonder? If your aim had any possibility of success, she would have known, and acted. She would not have sent *you*, surely, but some other. Or simply obliterated this world."

"I can't speak for Magdalen," Thalassia said. "I came here on my own out of hatred. He used me against all of you, and when I became inconvenient, when I was no longer of any use, he abandoned me. I knew in that moment, it was what he always intended."

Thalassia spoke the words not with anger but sadness.

Rarely did this side of her emerge. Was it genuine or but a tactic?

"But you did *not* come on your own!" Eden grated. "You brought me, and you brought Lyka!"

"I'm sorry," Thalassia said loudly, and to Demosthenes' ears, sincerely. "I am truly sorry that I stranded you both here. If there had been another way, I would not have. Maybe there *was* a better way, and I let hatred blind me to it. Probably. But it can't be undone, and I am deeply sorry."

From the look in Eden's alien eyes, she gave the copious apologies little value. It seemed her thoughts were elsewhere.

She confirmed it. "Before your time and mine, the heretics in the war that split the Caliate said that Magdalen and the Worm were two aspects of the same being," she said. "That to destroy the Worm was to destroy Magdalen. In fact, to destroy... *everything*. It is for this reason, they said, that he cannot be killed. It is the universe acting out of self-preservation. If that is true, do you think the universe will allow your idiotic plans to succeed? He will simply be born in another time, another place, and continue to exist! Are you a heretic, Geneva?"

Thalassia shook her head, but in exasperation rather than any negative. "No," she answered. "Yes. I don't know. The truth is I want no part of it anymore. The Caliate. Malcolm. Magdalen's Plan. I want out. I'm happy here. I want to stay. I've run out of hatred. I don't hate you. I want you to be happy."

"*You* want! *You* want!" Eden roared, her face twisted. "Your sole concern, then as now! You think I can be happy *here*? What I want is the Caliate! The Plan! You took them from me! For all I know, your actions will obliterate them and uncreate all of us!" Snakelike, Eden's white arm rose and she pounded a clenched fist into a boulder, sending chips of stone flying and staining the rock with blood. "You fucking bitch! I don't know whether I should kill you or help you!"

"You could step aside," Thalassia said. "Join Lyka in Nadir. Or go elsewhere."

"Join Lyka, sleeping until the sun burns out! Or go where? I don't want another chunk of wasteland!" She hissed through clenched, ivory teeth: "I want the *universe* back!"

"I'm sorry I took it from you," Thalassia said, sounding truly penitent. "If you still feel you need to destroy me, I understand. But I will not let you."

Eden aimed a finger at Demosthenes, inspiring in him an involuntary pang of terror. "Maybe I should take away your *toy*."

Thalassia glanced at Demosthenes with a calm look which made his fear evaporate.

Then she said to Eden, also calmly: "Then you would truly learn the meaning of vengeance."

In the silent moment that followed, while Eden seethed, Demosthenes risked speaking for the first time.

"There need not be war between us."

Eden creased her brow at him, while Thalassia kept her gaze on the enemy whom she did not hate.

"If you care nothing for Sparta," Demosthenes ventured, "then merely step aside while we destroy it."

Eden chuckled darkly. "How cute. Your pet turtle thinks it can contribute."

"Is the one whose word sent you here also a pet?" Demosthenes returned. The remark earned him a look from Thalassia advising caution.

"One makes do with what is available," Eden said. The words in no way had the flavor of a lie, but here she stood, conversing with her enemy at the urging of 'what was available.'

"Andrea is why she cannot give us Sparta now," Thalassia declared with confidence.

"You have your pet. I have mine. But make no mistake: I would burn the girl in a heartbeat if it could put me in a hardliner."

Thalassia shrugged and spoke a string of incomprehensible words in the tongue of the star-born.

"That's rude of you, Geneva," Eden said with a playfully malevolent smile. "It was you who insisted on Greek. Allow me to translate for him. She says, *'If one wishes to keep a pet at one's heel, it helps first to render it rootless.'*" Eden raised a blonde brow. "But worry not, tiny turtle. She only wishes to plant an idea in my head, an effort which would have been all too transparent if spoken for you to hear."

"If you came to talk peace between us," Thalassia said, "I give it. You need only accept. Unless you want a hug, or you came for some other reason, it sounds as if we are done."

"Yes..." Eden concurred. "Yes, we are done. You have given me food for thought, Wormwhore and tiny turtle." She looked at them anew, and present in her eyes again, unmistakable, was the malice of the Eden of old.

"She's going to try to kill us now," Thalassia said. "Run."

Demosthenes' reply came instinctively: "Only if you do."

"Kill you?" Eden said. "No..." Her hands moved to her torso and, from somewhere, produced two small blades. "Well, yes."

"Run, idiot," Thalassia hissed, planting a hand on Demosthenes' chest and shoving as Eden lunged.

Trusting in her to follow, Demosthenes faced the direction of the cliffs and set his legs to pumping in breakneck flight. A moment later, when he risked looking, he found Thalassia running just behind him, surely holding back her unnatural speed to match his pace. Past her, he saw Eden racing toward them, gaining.

"Don't look!" Thalassia commanded.

Ahead loomed land's end: a jagged, grassy line above which stood an expanse of sky, below which lay—nothing but wind and sea.

Nearing the edge, Demosthenes gave a command of his own: "No heroics. You come with me."

Thalassia's attention was on their pursuer as she ran sidewise so as not to fully give Eden her back. "I know!" she roared, and she flew past Demosthenes, grabbing his arm to half-drag him behind her as Eden closed the gap in steady strides, ethereal wisps of flaxen hair a gorgon's crown in the sea wind. She was on them now, mere seconds from striking distance.

Even so, Demosthenes could not help but stop at the threshold between earth and sky. He was human, with human fears.

His companion was not. Thalassia hesitated not an instant, but just jumped, giving Demosthenes scarcely an eyeblink in which to realize that her iron grip was still upon his arm.

* * *

Stomach lurched, breath seized, and heart stopped as the firmament vanished from under to be replaced by nothing but the sea far below. Thalassia's grip on him lent reassurance— but not even a being as powerful as she could slow his descent, soften his predestined meeting with the waves, or still the currents that would fight to drag him under.

He had made this very leap once before, throwing caution to the sea winds at a time when he had not thought life not worth living. Now, he jumped to save that life.

In the first instants of weightlessness, his eyes had been focused (to his stomach's detriment) downward, on his destination. Now, falling, as he felt Thalassia's grip leave his arm, he craned his head back to learn that their escape had been too narrow.

Eden, reaching the edge half a step behind, had thrown herself or rather sprung arrow-like into the void after them, headfirst and on course to collide with Thalassia, who twisted mid-air to meet the attack. They met, wrestled, and blood flew, Eden's blade plunging into Thalassia somewhere between breast and hip. Thalassia's hands, meanwhile, went claw-like for her enemy's face. One thumb found an eye and pushed. Eden clamped ivory thighs around Thalassia's waist, locking them in a terminal embrace as both fell.

He saw no more. The imminent impact of his fragile body had to be his first concern, and turning his gaze to the frothing sea, he prepared for it. Seconds later, the waves at the base of the cliffs exploded around him with bone-jarring, limb-shattering force. All thought was wrenched from his mind as flesh took command in the battle to live, to find air and breathe again in the hard crush of enveloping, liquid chaos. Tossed like a storm-blown leaf for what seemed an endless time, he kicked and flailed, seeking sanctuary that the sea-god denied.

He fought thus until it seemed his head would burst open and skull slip loose from its embrace, and when he could fight no longer, he bid goodbye to life, surrendering it unto sea and Fate.

* * *

He awoke, slowly, to pain. Rocks scraped his chest and cheek, and his arm was taut with such tension as to tear loose from its socket. He was glad at least to know he was alive; the pain told him that much.

His last memories, ones of watery death, flooded back. Eyes, when he opened them, told him more. He lay face-down

377

on a beach of pebbles, onto which surface, he managed to surmise, he had just been dragged by the wrist.

He coughed, gulping precious air. His body begged him to let consciousness flee once more.

But there was yet to be learned the outcome of a vicious battle on which much depended—if indeed it did not still rage in the sea that presently lapped his calves, or on the cold shore kissing his cheek.

With difficulty, he moved his head and saw the sandaled foot of a woman.

Its skin was pale.

He lifted his gaze to look upon his rescuer, seated on the pebbles just upslope of him.

Eden's face was covered with shallow scratches. Triumph shone in her unnaturally blue eyes.

"Wormwhore got away, turtle," she taunted. "But I have a feeling she will come for you."

5. Omega's men

Two dawns after the exile of Agis, the ship *Sorrowful Wind* set sail from Sparta's port. It was a freshly built vessel designed for speed, close in size to a trireme but with triangular rather than square sails affixed by complicated rigging to its twin masts. The ship was of a type called a *delphine*, and Sparta possessed ten of them now in her new navy, with as many intensively trained crews of step-brothers to sail them. Warships dubbed *skolopendrai* were also being purpose-built and crewed to replace the modified triremes which had conquered Athens.

The voyagers on *Sorrowful Wind*, Styphon among them, were on no mission of war. Neither was it a mission of peace exactly. It was a matter of imperial administration which sent this sleek ship north on a one-day voyage which on a trireme would have taken two.

A new tyrant was to be installed in a conquered city, the same city which until this year had ruled the very seas over which the *Wind* now flew. The city was Athens, and her tyrant-in-waiting was Alkibiades, until lately a prisoner-of-war. The Athenian had, by the mercy of all the gods, refrained from pestering Styphon for nearly the whole of the voyage. Instead he spent most of his time with his two countrywomen from Agis's trial: Aspasia, the courtesan Alkibiades called step-mother, and the young widow whose womb was swelling with a child that the elders of Sparta had decided to believe belonged to Agis. Myrinne was her name, and she seemed in better spirits now, not least because of the affections Alkibiades bestowed upon her with un-brotherly interest.

It came as a mild surprise to Styphon that the girl was being allowed to return to her home with a royal child in her womb, bastard or no. A potential reason for that decision was, of course, the widely known but unspoken possibility that the child was not Agis's at all. (In Styphon's unformed, entirely masculine opinion, Myrinne seemed rather too round to have been impregnated so recently.) Sure, the child would be half-blooded and therefore have no claim even to citizenship, much less a throne; but who could ever know what choices might be faced by generations to come? When a throne was judged better filled than left cold, half-legitimate blood was warmer by half than none at all.

Perhaps that explained Alkibiades' interest in Myrinne. Certainly he was clever enough to be thinking ten or twenty years into his future. And if he was not, then the middle-aged brothel mistress whispering in his ear unquestionably was.

Brasidas had such foresight, too, and maybe it was he who saw reason to stash the child away in Athens in the care of an Athenian traitor.

Let them all scheme. Styphon was grateful that his own mind failed to function in such a manner. He was content to live in the moment.

If only Fate would consent to make his moments duller.

Now, as Attica came into sight over the prow of *Sorrowful Wind*, was one of those moments which Fate was more accustomed to handing him.

Piraeus, the port of Athens, stood aflame.

* * *

"Looks as though I've arrived just in time."

The ambiguity of this statement by Alkibiades as he came alongside Styphon on the deck forced the latter to wonder just what was meant. Given that it appeared a rebellion might be underway, had Alkibiades arrived in time to suppress it or support it?

"If I suspect at any time that you intend to betray us,"

Styphon was glad to take the opportunity to point out, "I am fully authorized to kill you."

Alkibiades grinned. "No worries, friend," he reassured. "I will not lie: I wish my city stood where yours does now. But that is not how the bones fell. I am finished fighting Fate. It's better to be on her side, and from all I've seen, Fate stands with Sparta."

Though nothing had been said to alter Styphon's near-certainty that this Athenian's loyalties were a dynamic thing, subject to change at any moment, he offered no argument, only scowled at the smoke rising skyward from the port which had been their destination.

But no longer: the captain, with Styphon's consent, gave his crew new orders to moor *Sorrowful Wind* at the fishermen's jetties a short way up the coast from Piraeus. It was one disadvantage of these new vessels that they could not, as triremes could, put to shore almost any place where the waves broke gently on a smooth slope. In fact, Styphon had learned from crewmen, the new ships were built from different, harder woods, and spent their lives in water rather than ever being dragged ashore at all.

That fact caused a second drawback about which it was best not to think: unlike buoyant galleys, these new ships, if their hulls were holed at all, would quickly vanish into the depths.

As the sun sank, *Sorrowful Wind* dropped anchor some two miles from Piraeus. Styphon, the three Athenians, the ship's crew, and thirty-six Spartiates under arms went ashore alongside fishermen and their full nets. The odd-looking sails had not gone unnoticed from afar, which meant three relieved looking sycophants of the tyranny were there waiting. Speaking over one another, they scrambled to explain what had transpired whilst simultaneously attempting to divest themselves of all blame.

Styphon absorbed what was relevant, which was that Athenian rebels had seized and barricaded the port. He interrupted their squawking to ask the rebels' numbers. *No one knew.* Were they Omega's men? *Had to be.* Was Omega with them in Piraeus? *Unknown.* What had been tried so far to retake the town?

Little. The tyrants lacked enough men they trusted to kill their countrymen rather than join them. There was a loose cordon of Athenians and Scythians along the port's mostly-demolished walls, and nothing more. The small Spartan garrison had refused to leave Athens, lest the seizure of Piraeus prove to be a deliberate diversion.

Save us, these officials begged, and there was one fresh arrival in particular who was more than happy to oblige them.

Alkibiades, who had listened intently to every word, abruptly demanded, "What remains of the citizen cavalry?"

The oligarchs gave him looks that ranged from skepticism to disgust.

"Answer," Styphon said in a voice of authority.

"Maybe twenty that can be called upon," one official offered.

"And trusted," added a second.

"Get me forty," Alkibiades commanded. "Tell them the request comes from me and that I want them here tonight. Round up as many mounted Scythians as you can, too."

The three men looked to one another, complaints and curses caught in their throats by the presence of Styphon, who yet again felt forced to compel an answer by asking them, "What is your objection?"

In a trio of glances, they elected a spokesman, who replied, "He has no authority."

Styphon produced a folded bit of parchment and thrust

it into that sycophant's hands. "He has been appointed to your council. Is that enough? On top of that, my Equals do not clean up your messes or fight rabble. This man is presently your only hope. He may be a braying ass and a libertine, but he very nearly has the brains and bravery to back up his own opinion of himself."

Alkibiades flashed Styphon a sidelong smile of gratitude which went unreciprocated.

Looking as though they regretted having come to beg help, the trio of humbled officials did as requested while Styphon's men made camp for the night. The women, Aspasia and Myrinne, bid Alkibiades warm goodbyes (the latter's looking decidedly less than final), politely thanked Styphon and the ship's captain for their service, then shared an ox-cart to Athens with a fisherman and his catch.

When the females were gone, Alkibiades shouldered up to Styphon and said, "Thank you."

"For what?"

"Your trust."

"Trust?" Styphon gave the preener a rare gift: a laugh. "I do not trust you one iota, Athenian. I just believe you are marginally more competent than those other traitors. Not to mention that if you put down this rebellion, I look good. If you fail, I can do the job for you and still look good." He wiped all trace of humor from his rough features, which was not difficult. "And if it turns out you are up to no good, I get to kill you. Whatever happens, I win."

The Athenian gave a puzzled smirk, then another of his accursed grins. "One of these days, my friend," he said, "I will get you to admit how much you love me."

Styphon growled.

* * *

As the evening wore on, horsemen arrived from Athens,

alone and in small groups, so that by the time full darkness came, there were in the camp almost twenty riders of Athens' famed citizen cavalry. Alkibiades greeted every man of them by name and gave him an embrace, and all sat and laughed and dined together.

It stood to reason that these cavalrymen were ones who had chosen not to make a last stand at Dekelea with Demosthenes and Alkibiades. They were, by most practical definitions, and certainly the by Spartan one, cowards, men who had turned and fled home before the battle for their city had begun. Their comrades captured at Dekelea probably had been pardoned by now, but even if their arms had not been confiscated, the present Spartan-installed oligarchs of Athens surely could not count them as reliable.

If Alkibiades considered these men cowards (which it seemed to Styphon he must), he did not allow it to show, a feat which lent weight to the preener's boast that he would soon rule Athens. The danger for any conqueror who employed such a charismatic man was, of course, that sooner or later he might decide he needs no help ruling. But that was a worry for ephors and regents, not a mere soldier sent on the errand of installing him.

Dawn brought more cavalry, bringing the total near to thirty, along with a platoon of twelve mounted Scythians, the barbarians who had served, both before and after the conquest, as the police force of Athens. In the early hours of morning, this assembled column of man and horse, a brightly armored Alkibiades at its head astride a white charger fetched for him, advanced along to coast toward rebel-controlled Piraeus. Styphon accompanied the column with three-quarters of his men, the rest having been left behind to guard *Sorrowful Wind*, itself a treasure since the design was a state secret.

The silent port, ringed by the remains of the walls its Spartan conquerors had ordered demolished, was shrouded in a haze of smoke and morning mist. The Spartiates went as far as the wall, and there took up position to augment the existing cordon of club-wielding Scythian police, foreign mercenaries and Athenian anti-democrats.

"You know what happens if you join this rebellion," Styphon warned Alkibiades in front of the single doorless city gate which remained in the tyranny's control.

"Indeed I do," Alkibiades answered from atop his mount. "If I joined the rebels, Athens would shortly be liberated. And remain so for a while, until you conquered us again. But since I still enjoy drawing breath, I will not do that."

With that nonsense uttered and a few final instructions to the men appointed as his lieutenants, Alkibiades led the body of cavalry down the stone-paved street into mist. The slow, echoing clatter of hooves grew distant and irregular until there was near silence again.

Not for long. There soon arose the angry shouts of men, the whinnies of horses, bursts of galloping hoofbeats on unseen streets, crashes of falling wood and metal. Arms did clash, but rarely, and rarer still were screams or groans of pain. Whatever was transpiring inside shrouded Piraeus, no pitched battle was underway.

Some twenty minutes after the entry of the cavalry, the first bloodied group of rebels tried to slip out through a gap in the broken wall only to kneel in surrender when confronted by the tyrants' men.

Similar scenes were repeated elsewhere in the cordon, rebels in scattered bands being driven out of the port, in many cases with horsemen on their heels. Once the fleeing rebels were rounded up, the riders turned and rode back into town in search of more rabble to run down.

Within an hour, the hunt was finished. Alkibiades was among the last of the riders to emerge. He rode up to Styphon and the tyrants, thrust into the earth the lance he was wielding with its blade upturned, like a staff or club, and he dismounted. The flock of oligarchs, today some fifteen in number, hitched up their chitons and ran over in time to hear Alkibiades report, not over-boastfully: "Piraeus is ours."

The tyrants momentarily were at a loss, but a quick decision was made by some few, with others following suit, to heap praise upon the savior they must now see as certain to lead a wing of their oligarchy, if he did not seize the reins of state entirely as the preener himself believed and intended.

Alkibiades brushed a sweat-soaked curl from one eye and surveyed the line of kneeling, sitting and standing prisoners, all with hands bound behind their backs and ankles fastened with hobbling cords. Half were sullen, with blank eyes; others looked defiant.

"That man there led them," Alkibiades said, aiming a finger at one of the captives. "His name is Thrasybulus. But I suspect you will find he has lately been called *Omega*."

The oligarchs and their Athenian supporters as one leveled stares at the man in question. The venom-filled eyes staring out from stony features at Alkibiades, his accuser, all but proved the accusation true.

"I am ashamed ever to have called you friend, *filth!*" spat the leader of the broken resistance. "If someone had told me when we were children what you would grow up to become, I would have killed you back then. I may not get to give you the coward's death you deserve, *traitor*, but I pray to Zeus Almighty that someone will—and soon! May you die at the hands of a *true* Athenian. One whom you think you trust!"

Appearing unimpressed by the tirade, and even less

alarmed by the curse, the newly anointed tyrant turned his back on his childhood friend Thrasybulus and addressed his colleagues of the oligarchy.

"You will find that only three rebels were killed," he reported. "Most have bloody noses. We used no more force than was necessary. None of our own fell. Now what say we get ourselves to Athens?"

Abruptly, Alkibiades whirled and set a hand on either side of Styphon's face (forcing the latter to suppress native instincts of self-defense), swooped in and planted a kiss on unyielding Spartiate lips. Then, throwing his head back, the Athenian roared exultantly into the sky, as if to serve notice to the very gods.

"I am home!"

6. Elean

Every city had a number of inns not far from port in which mercenaries rested briefly between terms of employment, if they were lucky, or if they were not, where they sat and soaked themselves in wine while awaiting one. The man from Elis fell somewhere in between. He was not old, but enough past his prime that by the end of a long day's march he walked leaning heavily on his spear. As such, he chose to employ himself only enough to keep his belly full and have a few extra coins left over for gambling or the whore-temples of Corinth.

His present residence was a boarding house by the harbor of Patras on the northern coast of the Peloponnese, but time was running out: if he spent funds on nothing else, he could keep a roof over his head for just four more days.

On this as every morning, he entered the boarding house's megaron early to learn whether any new leaflets had been tacked overnight to the board where hiring notices were posted. As most mornings, it was empty. He sighed and turned to begin pondering whether to spend a quarter of his earthly wealth on a jar of wine when he found himself startled by the sudden presence in front of him of a woman who seemed to have materialized from nowhere.

She wore a black winter cloak and had the complexion of a Persian, a tone of flesh the Elean knew well, for he had spent many a year making corpses of Persian males by day and rubbing against their females by night.

This one was cheerless, with blue eyes that chilled.

"Sorry, mum," the Elean said. "Didn't see you there."

"You seek work?" she asked.

The Elean brightened, stood taller, forgot about wine.

"Yes!" he answered enthusiastically, then thought better

and added, "Well, I could take it or leave it, depending on the pay."

Her cold expression did not crack. This particular Persian female was not as warm as the ones he remembered.

"I have a note which needs to reach a girl living in Sparta. Deliver it and return to me in Naupaktos before the next Spartan attack, and you will earn three more of these."

A hand appeared from within her cloak. In its palm rested a disc of gold the sight of which briefly stole the Elean's breath. An Athenian gold stater, if he was not mistaken. Instinctively he reached for it, but the Persian closed her fingers around it and offered instead her other hand, which contained a small canvas pouch which presumably the message she meant for him to deliver.

"May I open it?"

"If you wish."

The Elean loosened the string binding the pouch, which weighed very little, and spilled its contents into his open palm. "Some stone tiles," he observed. "With letters on them. How is that a message?"

"This girl is clever. It will take her but a minute to solve, and she will know from whom it came. We were close once. It is a plea. I hope her heart remains soft enough that she will not ignore it."

"What's her name?"

The Persian reached out and turned the pouch, revealing the answer, which the Elean read aloud. He enjoyed showing off that he was literate; most men who fought for coin were not.

"Andrea... Styphonides. If I go to Sparta asking around about a young girl, seems likely I might attract the wrong kind of attention."

"Shall I employ another messenger?"

"No! No. I'll manage it. Somehow."

"Good. Not to tell you how you do your job, but you might claim you found the item and wish to return it."

The Elean nodded. "Yes... I might just. Now, as for the payment?"

The Persian surrendered the gold stater, which the Elean clutched tightly.

"Tell me, do you intend to take that and never see me again?" Her pale eyes penetrated him.

"No, ma'am," the Elean answered. "Why settle for a quarter of a fortune when the whole thing could be had for taking a long walk?"

She nodded her satisfaction with the reply. "Ask the girl the name of she whose eyes are as twin eclipses. To claim the remainder of your payment, you must have the correct answer when you return to me. Lest your honest nature fail you. You understand."

"Aye," the Elean said, taking no offense. He had not yet contemplated just waiting a few days and then returning pretending to have delivered the message, but it was not a course he would have ruled out.

"Do you have a horse?"

"No, ma'am."

"But you can ride?"

"Well enough."

She produced several silver coins and set them in his palm. "Acquire one. Haste is essential."

The Elean tucked the coins and pouch of tiles into a hidden pocket behind his scabbard where he was sure not to lose them.

"Must be an important message."

"Life or death," the Persian said, and departed as silently as a shade.

7. The gift of Eris

110 days after the fall of Athens (September 423 BCE)

He entered Sparta a prisoner, wrists bound tightly behind his back, a rope around his neck tethering him to the horse ahead. On the horse was his captor, Eden, who had brought him nearly the entire length of the Peloponnese from north to south. By the time they crossed the inscribed boundary markers of the unwalled city, they led a crowd of men, women, and children speaking in hushed whispers.

They must all have known Eden, or Eris; she was likely the reason for their lowered voices. But at least one among them correctly identified her prisoner, for he heard it sharply whispered.

"Demosthenes!"

They continued thus, the procession growing longer, until they reached an open public space at the foot of the high acropolis of Sparta, a sight on which Demosthenes had before never laid eyes. Few living Athenians had. If they did, it was only in this way, as prisoners. Atop the heights sat the city's only brightly painted structures, its temples. Even still, they were plainly built, resembling the shadows cast by their ornate Athenian counterparts.

Eden reined her horse and yanked the rope, sending Demosthenes to his knees. Quickly, out of the many Spartans and slaves filling the public square in the shadow of those temples, Demosthenes' gaze found one man standing in the doorway of a boxlike structure of wood and plaster. Slowly, as Eden slid from her mount and stood next to it, the Equal came forward.

Demosthenes had tested his bonds many times already, and so did not bother doing so again. But he flexed his jaw, preparatory to biting out the throat of Brasidas should he come near enough.

Wisely, Brasidas did not. Halting well beyond the reach of Demosthenes' tether, he put hand to breast, bowed his head and declared loudly, "Dread Eris, you honor Sparta with your gift. A man directly and indirectly responsible for the deaths, most by ignominious means, of a great many Equals. Their wives and sons and mothers are deeply in your debt. It will help heal their broken hearts to watch Demosthenes pay for his crimes against our state."

As Brasidas spoke, Demosthenes could not bear to look upon the face of the man who had slain Laonome and be powerless to destroy him. Their next meeting was not meant to have been like this.

Brasidas began to clap and gestured at Eden, standing with a look of antipathy, as one who only tolerates those around her. The crowd took Brasidas's meaning and granted her their thunderous applause, celebrating by extension the promised punishment of her 'gift.'

Waving them to silence, Brasidas took another step forward and lowered himself into a crouch. He yet was too distant for Demosthenes to reach in a single lunge, but the soft hollow of his neck was lower to the ground, at least.

"Demosthenes," Brasidas said in a low voice. "I will have you know that I do regret killing your wife. It was a... lapse of discipline. Had I a chance to do it over again, I would not repeat the error. I wonder, do you feel the same about your actions? Torture. Assassination. Gods know what else."

Demosthenes only set his jaw, longing for some chance, any chance...

"It matters not. My better judgment bids me arrange for your immediate execution. But..." He stood, feet wide apart, hands clasped in front of him. "The same good fortune which put Geneva in your service... or you in hers..." He smiled.

"...works in your favor today. Come the dawn, I leave Sparta to undertake the task in which Agis failed, the reduction of Naupaktos. Geneva may be there, and if I am to use your welfare as currency, I need to tell her that you yet live. And should I be forced to do so to her face, I will in fact need to *believe* that to be true.

"*If* she is there, and if she cares for you, she will not take the field in defense of Naupaktos. And in the event she comes here, instead, to rescue you, Eris will be on hand to keep you safely awaiting the imposition of justice." Brasidas set hand to rough jaw. "That poses a dilemma, does it not? The Spartan people are eager to see you pay, while I require you to live until my return."

Within seconds, his mock deliberation came to an end, and he declared, "Fortunately, I believe a solution can be found in something which our two cities share in common. You Athenians, I know from my tenure there, favor the same manner of execution for criminals that we often use, albeit not on your fellow generals. It is a method which may be easily prolonged and avoids the imposition of blood guilt if the accused is innocent, for no blood is spilled." He raised a brow. "Not to suggest there is any such doubt in your case."

Brasidas lifted his arms and once more addressed the crowd.

"To trial with Demosthenes!" he called out. "And then... to the *stauros!*"

8. Slave

Only at one time in her life before now had she cared so little whether she lived or died.

The prior time had been many years ago, in her native Thrace, when her sister had been thrown off a mountain by slavers for becoming too sick to be worth carrying the long way to the slave markets.

A silent ghost, as though she had been the one to die, the survivor had made it to market, to be traded more than once. At some point the slavers had given her a new name, a Greek one for Greek owners.

Eurydike.

She did not remain long a ghost. When shock wore off, she took to spitting and biting and cursing, half in the unspoken hope it would prompt someone would set her free of the flesh she felt guilty for continuing to inhabit when her sister did not.

Instead, her behavior had only ensured that no master wanted her. Months later, in Athens, the Thessalian broker into whose possession she had fallen pledged that he would not be leaving the city burdened by her. He gave her one more day to fetch a price, and if she did not, he would gift her to the mines, to be used there (if she was of any use) until she died.

With the stark choice between life and death made suddenly real, she had chosen life, and at market that day she had pleaded with customers to take her. The Thessalian had responded by gagging her while he talked his buyers into costlier merchandise.

Then Demosthenes had come, with his kind eyes, looking to buy, and demanded her gag be removed. He had heard her plea, ignored the slaver's up-sell and taken her into his home.

It soon become *her* home. Not just a roof, but a place where she could heal. Maybe he did not love her exactly, nor she him, but they enjoyed each other's company. Yes, she was still a slave and still had to earn her keep with work, but who in this world did not? Demosthenes was no harsh master, at least. Far from it. It had taken him half a year to start fucking her. Even then, it had been her suggestion. Not quite calculation, a means to make him like her more, but almost. He was not unattractive, and once healed sufficiently of heart and mind, she had found herself able to feel such things as desire and enjoyment.

She began to feel contentment, or at least grow into her new slave-self, Eurydike, putting the past and its burden of pain behind, even if they were never forgotten.

Then Demosthenes had brought Thalassia into their home with her dark, goddess-like beauty and secrets darker still. When childish jealousy wore off, Eurydike realized she had found a friend and ally. Almost a sister, even if none could ever begin to replace the true sister she had lost.

Then Demosthenes had taken a wife. Again there was jealousy, but with Thalassia's help she stifled it and found Laonome a welcome addition to her life. The child Laonome carried was a source of eager anticipation.

Then, chaos: Spartans overrunning Athens, an attempt at flight, she and Laonome taken prisoner for no other reason than that they were dear to a man who had caused Sparta difficulty.

To make Demosthenes yield, Laonome had been slaughtered before her husband's eyes, and Eurydike, having failed to give her life in exchange for that more valuable one, had gone to a new master.

Now she dwelt in that master's house in Sparta, a place where slaves were slaves.

Styphon was not cruel, but neither did he care one bit about her.

His wife did, and Eurydike had to count herself lucky for that, even if she did not return the affection, nor enjoy serving in a woman's bed. But because there was no other choice, she helped Hippolyta to think what she wanted to think, see what she wanted to see. It made life easier.

Andrea made life easier, too. They had been fast friends in Athens and remained so here. Now Andrea spent most of her time with the blood-chilling pale bitch who was called Eris, but surely could not in truth be that goddess.

Alkibiades was in Sparta, too. He had fucked everything in Athens, including her, on numerous occasions, and she was fond of him, but being near him, it turned out, only made Eurydike feel more sick with loss.

Life in Sparta thus was not as terrible as it might have been... but on balance it was not worth living.

Partly responsible for that was a vanishing hope, held for a while, that Demosthenes was coming for her. That he cared. Maybe he was dead. How much longer could she wait, she had wondered for a time, before finally accepting that this was how life was to be now. There was no going back.

The old feeling returned that life and death were one and the same. If faced with the choice between them again, she suspected, she would not choose life, as she had before.

One day, the choice came. Six young Equals crossed her path, surrounding her and insisting that she fuck them all then and there. She made her choice quickly to fight. She was already Hippolyta's whore; she would not be all of Sparta's.

If they killed her, they killed her.

She had no chance, of course. Once they had subdued her, and beaten her, done what they wished, and left her on the roadside, she wanted to call them back to finish the job.

Instead she blacked out, and when she awoke, they were gone. And so she just silently wished for no one to find her, that she might be left to die there in that spot, in peace.

But she had been found and taken back to that house which was no home where she persisted in hoping that her injuries were enough to kill her, that she might only linger for a few days and then succumb.

Days passed. Denial could not last. Against her wishes, she survived. Eventually, she resumed her duties, sullenly, speaking rarely and only when obedience required, to give curt answers to questions or commands. She was dead within, if not without.

She identified to Andrea, at the girl's insistence, four of the six perpetrators of the assault. The faces of the last two Eurydike felt herself unlikely ever to recall, to the extent she even wished to, for her visions of the assault were primarily ones of grass and dirt and the bottoms of sandals and the freckled backs of her own forearms as she raised them to defend her face.

But Andrea said she could learn for herself the identities of the final two. All six were to meet with fatal accidents in the coming year, but that was not to say that one or two, before succumbing to misfortune, could not be interrogated...

Hippolyta kissed her slave's face often and treated her tenderly, begging her to respond to her affections. It was all Eurydike could do not to pounce on the conceited bitch, choke the life and baseless vanity from her. Such a course would surely see a slave condemned to death, and for that reason she did not rule it out. When she did again make the choice to die, that might be the way.

One thing held her back. A persistent, silver thread of hope in her heart which even now refused to be cut.

The hope that he might still come for her. Her time here

had only *felt* like an eternity. In fact, it had been but a season, give or take. Demosthenes might still come.

The darker part of her heart, the knife-wielding part which had as yet failed to sever the last thread of brightness, said *no*. Never. He had chosen Thalassia. She was more important to him, that false friend. She was no sister, but a selfish, scheming bitch, just like the blond one. Thalassia had caused all of this, wrecked her world and left her here in misery. Thalassia had twisted Demosthenes' mind and taken him away, and he was hers now, ruled by her, wherever he was, persuaded not to risk his life for the piece of Thracian meat that had drawn his baths and warmed his bed for a while.

As Eurydike resumed her slave duties, blank-eyed, she felt these things as though they were truth, yet still, despite herself, she hoped. The silver thread held fast, and at its end, above an abyss, hung her faint desire to live.

Some number of numbing days after the attack, Eurydike was bearing water from the spring up the hill to Styphon's house when Andrea ran to her. The girl, who was only half a friend now, spending most of her time with Eris, took one of the two water pots and addressed Eurydike in a way that suggested she believed what she had to say was of some importance, a prospect Eurydike found doubtful in the extreme.

"There is something you must see," Andrea said.

Eurydike, as was her habit since her failure to die, said nothing. They reached the house and poured the water into its cistern. Hippolyta was away. She had duties of her own, managing Helots in the fields of Styphon's holding.

"Come with me," Andrea said.

Again, Eurydike said nothing. Andrea was a citizen and therefore to be obeyed, and so Eurydike followed her in silence to the public space which passed for the center of Sparta. It was a feeble joke compared to the smallest of marketplaces of Athens, just as the acropolis behind it was a crude imitation of the marble-crowned grandeur of its Athenian counterpart. Andrea led her there, past lines of busy Helots whose faces did not betray, as Eurydike's did, the crushing weight of their burdens, perhaps because they had been born into them. They passed Spartiate children tumbling together in the dust or swinging sticks in violent games.

They went to the platform where speeches were given, announcements made and, on occasion, some prominent criminal or prisoner of little interest to a Thracian expatriate was publicly executed by some means or another. Eurydike had passed the platform often enough. Just to one side of it, three thick posts rose up from the earth, about eight feet tall. She knew the purpose of the posts, for she had walked by them while men (and once a woman) were chained to them to be left until their deaths from starvation or exposure. Although the *stauros* was also used to execute criminals in Athens, there she had not had occasion to witness it.

Sparta possessed more stakes than just these three, but most were in less well-traveled places where the odors of suffering and death could pose no nuisance. These three particular posts in the meeting place were reserved for victims of special note, ones whose humiliation and slow deaths were causes for civic pride. A day prior, and for a few days before that, Eurydike had walked past and seen affixed to the *stauros* an Athenian unknown to her but identified by a placard which she had managed, if barely, to read, sounding out the letters in her head.

She was a poor student, but Thalassia and Andrea, whatever their other flaws, had been good teachers.

The name on the placard had been Thrasybulus.

This day, until they reached the execution site, with its Spartiate guard in full panoply, and Andrea pointed in the direction of the posts, Eurydike had had no inkling that this was the girl's intended destination. Following Andrea's arm and black-eyed gaze, Eurydike saw some other unfortunate, not Thrasybulus, currently dying on display. He was fastened to the posts by wrists above his head, as well as his chest, both ankles, and neck—but not with rope, as was typical. Instead this man was bound with heavy iron chains. He wore a ragged chiton, and the greasy locks of his untrimmed hair fell down and obscured the features of his hung head. The hair was brown. No—a lighter shade, but heavily grimed.

It was hair she would know anywhere. She had washed it half a thousand times. His limbs, too, resembled the ones that she had bathed, even if they were harder and darker now.

Even as her eyes caught the first letter on the placard, a *delta*, her breath halted and the fire of recognition blazed a path from eyes to heart.

As if sensing the attention, the chained man raised his head and looked straight at her.

There were those kind, brown doe-eyes which had saved her from the mines. In them there appeared affection and pleasure, and Demosthenes smiled, just barely, as much as one condemned to death was able. It was a smile devoid of hope, as if only to say: *I am glad to see you one last time before I die.*

As she laid eyes upon the very face she had longed to see, that silver thread of hope in her heart abruptly snapped.

Demosthenes could not save her, for he was a prisoner himself, alone and far from home, surrounded by enemies and helpless.

He shook his head at her, warning her away, but such warning was unneeded. She took no step in his direction, felt no such urge.

"We can help him," Andrea whispered in her ear.

Keeping her customary silence, Eurydike turned her back and left the square.

9. Deliverance

Styphon had been instructed to remain in Athens, alone, until new orders came, standing at the preener's shoulder to show the city that he had Sparta's full backing.

Days came and went with no messenger from Sparta.

It was hard to tell whether Alkibiades even needed his support. Within a matter of days, with no heads cracked (aside from those of the rebels), he seemed to be comfortably in charge of the ruling council and thus the city. No one needed to be told to listen to him; they wanted to.

Before long, Styphon found himself the recipient of an invitation.

"If you are still in the city in a month," the tyrant prattled, "and I hope you will be, you must attend my wedding to Myrinne. Since you Equals don't have weddings, it will be a novel experience for you."

Styphon began to pray harder that new orders would come.

Just a day later, they were answered. He was to trek to Corinth, there to take command of a new *enomoty* of thirty-five hoplites.

Hoplites, the orders said. Not Equals. Strange. It could not mean Corinthians, surely, for allied cities commanded their own contributions in battle.

Brief reflection brought an answer. *Helots.*

Years prior, at Amphipolis, a force of Helots granted freedom in exchange for their service had taken part in that battle. By all accounts, it had not been due to any fault in their skill or bravery that they had suffered defeat by Demosthenes; on the contrary, they had stood fast and been loyal unto death, acquitting themselves well. Arming and training them had been Brasidas's idea then, and since the defeat of Athens and the growth of his influence, he had spoken of repeating and expanding the experiment, and even of phasing out Helotry altogether in favor of importing slaves from conquered foreign lands.

According to Eris, who knew the future, it was a formula that worked. Not only that, Sparta could shed its omnipresent fear of a Helot rebellion.

Naupaktans were ex-Helots themselves, of the same Messenian stock, and so perhaps Brasidas saw value in testing his idea again there. If freed Helots proved themselves of value in a battle against their own cousins, then they could be trusted on any battlefield. It would be unlike Brasidas, too, to miss the perverse symmetry of pitting ex-slaves against one another: one group fighting to keep freedom already achieved, the other to earn it.

The posting as a commander of Helots fell somewhere between compliment and insult, but in the sense that Styphon was still alive and considered of any use at all by Brasidas, it scarcely mattered which. It meant a swift exit from Athens, and that was enough. It was thus with joy in his breast (and possibly in his black eyes) that he went, after having packed all his gear and supplies for the cross-country hike, to inform Alkibiades.

His 'dear friend,' by now the fully entrenched ruler of Athens, embraced him, kissed his cheeks and swore that their paths would cross again. As he left without looking back, Styphon prayed the opposite.

Hard winds whipped off of the sea as he followed the coast to Corinth. They penetrated the crimson cloak wrapped around him and the chlamys of undyed wool draped over it, but the cold failed to dent Styphon's mood. Not only did he have native discipline to call upon to fight the elements, there was also an excitement not felt since he was a younger man.

Before Pylos. Before Thalassia and Eris. Before imprisonment and disgrace in Athens and his return to favor under Brasidas and then Agis.

Before being caught up in plots and assassinations.

This was where he wanted to be. Simply following orders, doing the duty to which he had been born, looking forward to battle without wondering whether he was being used. He even had a wife again back home, sending warm thoughts from afar and awaiting his return.

Maybe it would not last, but for now at least, he felt like a soldier again, not a pawn or a schemer or anyone's dog.

If he was to be given command of Helots, he would do his best to be sure it was those Helots who won the coming battle. Firstly because those were his orders, and secondly, because victory in battle served the interests, clearly and unequivocally, of all Spartans—not just those of one man, and certainly not those of a she-daimon.

On the road to Corinth, Styphon decided there would be no more schemes. No more deviation from the straight and true path of obedience. No more credence given to whispers in his ear from witches or kings. No more independent action taken on behalf of self or family. What best served self and family was whatever best served Sparta.

By the gods, he would be, as he once had been, a faithful servant of his city.

Such a pledge, he knew, was easier to make than to keep. But he would try. That was all that any man, even a Spartan Equal, could do.

10. Bright Eyes

The first hours on the *stauros* were endless. At first, Demosthenes' mind swam with thoughts; he could not stop them coming, and with them came feeling of rage and regret and longing and despair. Tears came, and he could not wipe them away, just as he could do nothing about the itching and pains and aches that came and went on every part of his flesh. His skull pounded for lack of water.

Before the end of the first day, it was only oblivion for which he longed. Thought ended, and he made of himself an animal: a gelding in its stall, an ox in its stockade, a donkey hobbled by the roadside, only staring with eyes that betrayed no glimmer of interest in what the future held.

Time became a single moment which never ended, nothing separating one hour from the next, and he hung, increasingly in pain, with eyes either shut or open; it hardly mattered which. Night came, and he slept and woke, slept and woke a hundred times.

The sky brightened, and the smell of baking bread set his skull to pounding harder.

He opened his eyes and found before them a face he well knew.

He managed a smile that cracked dry lips. Once, yesterday, an Equal had given him water, just enough to ensure he lived until Brasidas returned.

"*Bright eyes...*" Demosthenes croaked. His old name for her, in Athens.

Once, her green eyes had been bright. But no longer. Neither did her speckled face show even a trace of a smile, sad or otherwise. His own smile quickly faded as Eurydike stared —blankly, dully.

"Andrea asked me to help her free you," she said. Her

voice was as dull as her eyes. "I told her I would not. You never came for me. I waited for you. When I heard you were alive, I *knew* you would come. Or send *her*. But you never did. Neither of you. You were kind to me, but I know now that I was to you just what I am here. Nothing. An object to be discarded when it ceases to be of use. Or *amusing*, as I was to you.

"And so even though Andrea is the one person in the world whose affection for me is true, I told her *no*. Even though my life has no value, I will not risk it for you, as you refused to risk yours to help me. When I saw you here, I realized why it was I still clung to hope that I would see you again. Not so you could save me, but to do this."

Pursing her lips tightly, Eurydike spat. Small, warm droplets peppered Demosthenes face.

"If she were here, know that Laonome would do the same."

Turning, she shambled away, past the red-cloaked Spartiate sentries and into the square, where she vanished among the citizens and slaves freshly risen from their beds to greet a new dawn.

11. The second battle of Naupaktos

(i) The army of revenge

On reporting in Corinth, Styphon began immediately to drill with the thirty-five Helots whom he was to command. They were not as capable as Spartiates bred from birth for battle, but they were motivated, disciplined, and readily trainable. Anyway, they did not have to be good enough to stand against Equals, only other Greeks. At the end of three days with them, Styphon was convinced they could.

A total of a hundred and forty-four helot soldiers were present in Corinth awaiting the attack on Naupaktos. So were twice as many Equals, who treated their Helot counterparts with just slightly more contempt than would be shown toward fresh, untested Equals abroad on their first deployment.

More than they spoke of the Helots, Styphon's fellow citizens spoke of some new weapon which was to be employed against Naupaktos. None knew what it was, only that it was exceptionally dangerous. Most figured it was some new siege engine, while others guessed, half-joking, that tigers (or maybe goats) had been trained for war and fitted with iron jaws, armored hides, and scythes for tails. All knew it was surely the work of Eris, who was also the focus of other news from Sparta which reached Styphon's ears in Corinth: the witch had entered Sparta with Demosthenes in tow as her prisoner.

The development brought Styphon some personal satisfaction, but far more importantly it raised the possibility that the coming invasion would not run afoul of Thalassia. With Demosthenes prisoner, it seemed likely that his protector was dead—for now, at least. Barring that, she might be headed to Sparta to rescue her lover, or whatever he was.

Styphon also learned in Corinth, by means of slipped tongues and half-mentions, that some of the Equals present, mostly drawn from units reckoned most loyal to Brasidas, had been recipients of special training. Having been in Brasidas' confidence for a few seasons, it was not hard for Styphon to guess that these men were meant to form the core of Brasidas's transformed Spartan army, one which was not dependent on the cohesion of a phalanx, but could fight equally well in mountains and forests and marshlands as it could on level plains. With the eastern seas virtually ruled already by the new navy, such a transformation would give Sparta the world.

Hearing of such grand plans, Styphon could not help but feel excluded. Had he not put his faith in Agis—

But then, he *wanted* to be left out of grand plans, he reminded himself. Today, leading a few dozen freed slaves would serve as sufficient opportunity for glory. He had learned the hard way that too much glory could be a heavy burden.

Two days after Styphon's arrival, Brasidas came at the head of the last of the troops who were to participate in the assault. The ships came, too, from the east, landing at Corinth's port on the Saronic Gulf, so that they remained always in friendly waters—the only other option being a course which took them directly past Naupaktos. It must have been for that very reason that the ships were shallow-keeled triremes, which could be hauled overland across the isthmus, and not the new breed which never left water.

Styphon and his Helots, like every man of the army in Corinth, lent their backs to the task of dragging the ships and their cargo from port to port. Among the latter were a large number of plain, sturdy amphorae which were treated with extra care, tended only by those men, mostly Helot slaves, who had arrived with them. It was on this trek that Styphon saw Brasidas for the first time since the trial of Agis. The polemarch was no horseman, but he rode one up the length of the caravan, informally inspecting his army on the wide, flat road over the isthmus.

Brasidas rode up alongside Styphon, who sweated despite the winter's chill beneath the thick tow-rope which stretched over his bent back to the trireme rumbling behind on its timber rollers.

"Are you pleased with your new posting?" Brasidas asked.

"As I said in the past," Styphon answered, "it is not my place to be pleased or displeased."

The polemarch let out a sharp laugh. "A safe answer," he said jovially, "even if it is a load of shit."

His mount twisted as if to veer off the road. With a faint frown, Brasidas jerked the reins to bring it back in line.

"I want to tell you that your past is just that," he went on. "Agis used you. I used you. That is the end of it. Look forward now, not back. Your future will be what you make of it." He laughed through his teeth. "Unless you are not careful, in which case it will be what Eris makes of it."

Brasidas rode off up the lumbering column, leaving Styphon to throw his shoulder against the tow-rope with a renewed sense of purpose. This simple reassurance from Brasidas, rightly or wrongly, held more meaning to him than any promotion in rank or commendation from the elders.

The warning about Eris was worrying, but no surprise. Almost involuntarily, as the polemarch departed, Styphon cast looks in every direction in search of a telltale glint of sunlight on golden hair, but found nothing. If she was in Corinth, or any place where this army would pass, she likely would not be seen. The knowledge she had given Brasidas had been of unquestionable value to him in his ascent to regent, and it served him still, but as a physical presence, Eris almost had to be reckoned a liability. Even before her slaughter of thirty-six elite Spartiates, she had been only been tolerated. It probably would serve Brasidas best for her to remain far from Naupaktos during the attack, lest he come to appear as her puppet. He could not be unaware that powerful men in Sparta, as anywhere, tended to fall more quickly than they had risen.

* * *

The ships and men reached the port of Corinth on the west coast of the isthmus, and the next day before dawn they took to oar on the Corinthian gulf. Sailing season was over and the waves high, but by hugging the coast the fleet made land as intended on a beach just east of Naupaktan territory, in Phokis, where the people had for years already been docile Spartan allies. They were met there by a dozen members of the elite Arkadian light infantry, the Skiritai, who had been sent ahead by land days earlier to perform reconnaissance. They reported, Styphon heard third-hand, that the Naupaktan defenses only began (as expected) at the river Mornos.

Landing unopposed, the invasion force disembarked and drew up into formations along plans drilled in Corinth. Katapeltai and rams and towers rolled down ramps from triremes modified to carry them and then were unlimbered on the beach. Unloaded, too, with great care, were those mysterious amphorae which all present suspected by know must comprise the new weapon expected to make its debut at Naupaktos. Unlike the machines, the amphorae did not remain long on the beach; they were removed to some location unseen, away from the main body of troops.

When the forces were arrayed, less than an hour after

landing, Brasidas, in all his war gear apart from helmet, climbed onto a rocky projection that put him ten feet above the sea of bronze-clad heads, upright spears, red cloaks, and lambda-blazoned shields. In all, twelve hundred men stood on the sands, half of them Equals, the rest Helots and Arkadians and others.

From the rock above, Brasidas addressed them:

"Brothers, friends, cousins!" he said. "You already know why we are here. To teach a city the lesson that no one sinks our ships and kills our men without paying dearly. You need no fiery words from me to set your blood burning for retribution. What I stand here to offer you instead is a choice. You have all heard the talk of a new weapon to be employed today. The talk is true, but I shall be honest with you. Like stones and arrows, it is what any man of honor would call a coward's weapon.

"I count myself an honorable man, and count every man here the same. Our city is an island of honor in a vast sea that teems with base creatures lacking in spine and unable to do harm without aid of dart and stinger and paralyzing venom. Virtue is the most blessed of possessions, but alas, it is no shield against the scorpion's sting. We, I believe, as men of honor, face a choice. We can let the edges of our island slowly recede until it is swallowed by the surrounding sea of ignominy. Or we who are virtue's defenders can fight to push the edges outward, using whatever means are needed, to secure for all men a brighter future.

"I confess that I have brought with us a coward's weapon such as that which our enemies might have used against us. Nay, one which they would not have hesitated to use, were it theirs and not ours. This weapon can help to give us Naupaktos with little blood shed—beyond that already lost under Agis's command. I would not dare suggest that even a single man here is unwilling to spill his blood today, to lose a limb or an eye or his life. No, we are not cowards! But there will come better days to shed our blood, and better places than this wretched little town. Your noble blood and strong arms will see no shortage of fighting so long as I am regent!

"*Regent*," Brasidas scoffed at himself. "I dislike the sound of it. Call me *polemarch*, for that is what I am, your leader in war. At the front, fighting by your side, giving my life if need be to spare yours. Because every life here is essential to winning for Sparta far greater glory than we can possibly win here today. Naupaktos is not worth your blood, or your lives, and that is why I would have us today resort to methods we rightly despise.

"However, I am no emperor, ruling by fiat without regard for what others think. And so, in a moment, I will put the choice to you whether we march forth and test our virtue against the waiting defenses of an enemy who is ready for us ... or swat them like the shit-feasting flies they are. I have told you where my mind lies, but the final decision I hand to you, and I will gladly abide by it."

Brasidas fell silent, and for the space of a few breaking waves, the water on the shore was the only sound.

"*Use it!*" someone cried out from the ranks of the Spartiates. Possibly, but not necessarily, he was a plant. Surely, he was one of Brasidas's confidantes.

Then more cries went up, echoed and repeated until all were shouting:

They are dogs, not men! They are not worth our blood! Our spears are too good for them!

A smile splitting his hawkish features, Brasidas urged them back to silence with an upraised palm. "The right choice!" he exclaimed. "But before we march, I would speak to you briefly of witches!"

"Brasidas!" A bellowing voice, resounding off the rocks, soaring over the crash of surf.

All eyes flew upward in search of its source, which was swiftly found. High on the rocks, the figure stood upright, defiant, wanting to be seen. It was clad from head to toe in dull leather and bright bronze, with no skin visible but for a face partly obscured by the cheek pieces of an Attic-style helmet. At its hips hung two sheathed blades, but its right hand held one of those weapons which Brasidas had just decried as fit for cowards, a cross-bow.

The tall figure might have been that of a slender male, but it was not. There was only one fighter who would dare to appear alone in front of this army, and it was no man. It was the very thing about which Brasidas had been about to speak.

A witch, armed for battle.

12.The second battle of Naupaktos

(ii) The breath of the Hydra

As if to extinguish doubt, Thalassia yanked off her helm. Sea wind raised hair like a black banner hoisted by the hordes of Erebos. It had been cropped since Styphon had seen her last. Perhaps she had given up Demosthenes for dead and was in mourning. But then, she had worn it even shorter on the day his men had first dragged her corpse from the sea on Sphakteria, the black day she had sprung to life to begin meddling in the affairs of men.

Would that he had ordered her hacked into a thousand parts and every morsel fed to the sea birds. But how could he have known?

On his lower perch opposite her, Brasidas stood fast, calling out, "Bowmen, *draw!*" while three of his loyal men clambered up the rocks to cover the regent's body fully with their bowl-shaped shields. Brasidas made no move to dissuade them.

"Any man who fires an arrow gets one back in the eye!" Thalassia admonished. "I come to warn you. You will not win this battle. Every one of you will die."

Brasidas cackled. "Name a battle before which the losers did not make that very boast!"

"In fact, I lie," the witch returned. "I will not kill *you*, Brasidas, because your life belongs to *him*."

"Ha! The man of whom you speak is my prisoner. For the moment, he lives. You know I speak truly. Stand against us this day, and he dies!"

"He died on the same day you doomed your city!" Thalassia shouted back, and next addressed the whole army: "Cross this river, and I will kill every man of you, just as I have already killed the men who carried these gifts you brought for Naupaktos." She bent and picked up from an unseen place behind her a clay pot—one of the very same which had been so carefully transported alongside the invasion force.

"Shall we open them now?" Raising the pot, she casually tossed it down from the rocks toward the massed men standing below.

Above the rims of his protectors' shields, Brasidas's jaw fell open and eyes went wide in an expression which Styphon had never seen upon the polemarch's face, and indeed was rarely to be seen on the face of any Equal.

It was fear.

"Do not breathe the gas!" Brasidas screamed. "Move away! Do not breathe! Distribute the cloths! *The cloths! Cover your faces!*"

The clay pot shattered on the rocky beach at the feet of the army of' revenge, and from its broken shards billowed forth a faintly yellowish fog

Leaping from his perch in a direction opposite the cloud, Brasidas continued to cry out urgent warnings to the army he had kept too long in the dark. Now, as another pot smashed in another location, and another, and yellow gas spread in wispy tendrils, ordered ranks descended into chaos. At once, every man tried to run from the nearest impact only to have another pot land in front of him, sending him in a different direction, where he collided with another fighter doing the same.

Where the yellow cloud enveloped the faces of men, they collapsed in a fit of retching, unable to rise, barely able to crawl over their comrades likewise afflicted.

Styphon and his formation were among those fortunate enough to be far from the initial impacts. However, he had little doubt of Thalassia's ability to cast pots over greater distances than this, and so he did not stand idle but barked orders at his Helots. True to his assessment of their ability, they pivoted, keeping formation, their faces stony, and moved east in an orderly advance, putting their backs to the chaos. Other surrounding formations did the same.

Then the death groans began, rising up over the hacking coughs. Styphon looked back to see through a yellow haze that the witch had begun firing her cross-bow down into the mass of crawling soldiers, loading and loosing and reloading time and again.

Styphon knew without needing to see that not a single bolt failed to steal a man's life.

While his unit fast-marched to relative safety, a scrambling slave handed Styphon a handful of small squares of sackcloth which were filthy with what looked like soot. Gathering their intended purpose, Styphon halted his men to distribute the cloths among them.

"Breathe through the cloth!" he commanded, putting one over his nose and mouth.

None too soon, for more pots were sailing up into the air and falling further east, and these too were followed by a barrage of bolts from Thalassia's cross-bow. Styphon's unit presently stood out of range of that weapon, or so Styphon judged, but fingers of yellow mist drifted on the wind in their direction. To be safe, he moved his men further back rather than rely fully on the supposed protection of the cloths.

Back at the site of the attack, through a yellow haze, Styphon saw the tiny figure of the witch vanish behind the rocks. She had cast down upon the army at least a dozen pots and fired many times that number of bolts.

She was given no pursuit, of course. She had already promised to be waiting beyond the river Mornos, if they yet dared to cross it.

The sounds of men gagging and retching and moaning en masse persisted. Perhaps the gaseous weapon had not been lethal, but only a choking mist. That was odd for an invention of Eris.

Before the wind had fully diffused the yellow clouds hanging over the broken army of revenge, the men around Styphon had a name for it.

Hydra's Breath.

13. The frogs

Another endless day passed, a day of physical anguish and mental decay, a day made harder by something Eurydike had instilled in him. Not guilt, although there was that. She had given him a new cause for *hope*. Andrea wished to help him.

But on the *stauros*, Demosthenes had found, it was easier to be hopeless.

Another night fell, and once more he slept intermittently, drifting in and out of consciousness.

Somewhere in between the two, he began to hear frogs croaking loudly and deeply. He had heard the sound of frogs in the nights prior, but it had been distant then, surely from the woods beyond the city limits. Now the frogs seemed much closer.

He felt rather than heard gentle movement behind him. Something brushed one of his hands, or so he imagined; secured above his head, they were all but numb.

"Andrea?" he risked whispering.

"Shh," a hushed voice returned. "Yes. Do not move. I must take care. This substance I use will eat iron but also flesh."

Remaining still posed no difficulty for Demosthenes; to do otherwise was hardly possible.

While waiting, he grasped the meaning of the frog sound. Andrea had brought them to mask any sounds that might be heard by the sentries in the square.

Some seconds later, Demosthenes' arms became suddenly heavy. They would have fallen if not for Andrea's small arm wrapped around them, softer and lower than the iron manacles that yet encircled his wrists and which might have rattled had she not prevented it.

Next came the rustling of a cloak and more movement as Andrea climbed down. His savior whispered from behind, presumably while working on the remainder of his bonds, "I am sorry about your wife. Brasidas should not have done that."

With strength he did not have, Demosthenes raised his arms again over his head, in case one or more of the sentries had keen eyes or chose to check on him as they sometimes did. "Is that why you wish to help me?" he breathed back at the girl.

"No. Geneva sent a message. Just two words. I could not ignore them."

Demosthenes could not suppress a faint smile on his cracked lips.

The chain encircling his neck fell loose and was quietly removed. "If only you understood the living nightmare our world might become," Andrea whispered. "The things Eden can make, or worse, teach men to make... This liquid I use, in another form, could become an odorless, colorless vapor which if breathed, would melt a man from the inside. Geneva could make such weapons if she chose. But she is content here. I wish for Eden to be content, too."

The pressure on Demosthenes' ankles eased, and for the first time in two days he moved his legs, just slightly. Only the chains encircling his chest remained.

"But you cannot deceive her..." Demosthenes observed.

"Deceive? You mean when it comes to my affection? I need not. She is a sad and beautiful creature. My fondest hope is one day to see the sights that she has seen." A brief silence, then, "Magdalen allows each agent of the Caliate, in the course of her service, to recruit one member. I will be Eden's."

"Then it is she who deceives you."

"Careful," the girl returned sharply. "I think what you

419

mean to say is *thank you.*"

"Yes... thank you," Demosthenes amended. "Will she not be angry when she learns of this?"

"It is Brasidas who wants you here," Andrea said. "I am confident she prefers me over him. Help keep the chains silent."

Demosthenes lowered his hands to the chains which for two days had dug into his ribs. Seconds later they fell loose, clinking lightly into the cloaking veil of frog noise, and he and his savior lowered them to the ground.

He was free. Weak of limb, but free. Small hands reached up and threw a black cloak over his shoulders that he might become, as was she, one with the night. Taking his hand, Andrea led him a few steps, looking all around. At her signal, Demosthenes moved behind her in a crouch along the edge of the faintly torchlit square and into the first alleyway which presented itself. From there she led him, sticking to shadows, to to the outskirts of the unwalled collection of towns that was Sparta.

The frog sound faded, then increased again as they entered a wooded grove where at last they halted—mercifully, for Demosthenes' body everywhere ached, even if he would gladly have walked ten *stadia* to ensure he kept his freedom.

Andrea guided him to a fallen trunk, where he sat and accepted from her a skin half filled with water.

He drained it and asked, "What next?"

"I shall return home. I advise you to get as far from here as possible. North and east will give the lowest likelihood of discovery. I..." she began to add, and hesitated. "I asked Eurydike to meet us here and escape with you. She refused."

"That does not surprise," Demosthenes said sadly. "She came to me."

"I know."

"The man I once was deserved her loyalty and affection. I am no longer him."

"I know," Andrea said again. "I must—"

"I would be disappointed in you, Andrea," came a chilling, familiar voice through the darkness, "were I not so proud."

Soundlessly, Eden appeared and took a seat on the trunk. Instinctively, Demosthenes flew to his feet, stumbling in the underbrush on weak legs before recovering. He did not run; even were he in full health, there was little point.

"And I am touched by your kind words, as well," Eden continued. "Of course I prefer you over Brasidas. That fact is beyond question."

In the darkness, Andrea's expression was unreadable, but her manner was subdued, as any child caught by parent or tutor in a misdeed.

"This act, and your success in it, only deepen my affection for you," Eden said to her. "But I wonder if you would have done the same tonight if you knew that the man you rescued does not only want the life of Brasidas for his revenge. Will you tell her, turtle, or shall I?"

Demosthenes did not bother to answer, directing his racing thoughts instead toward salvaging his seemingly aborted flight to freedom.

"In Naupaktos," Eden resumed, "I discovered a cave, much like the place where I create my own... *nightmares*. It was Geneva's, and within it she was developing a means of poisoning Sparta's grain supply. He would see you dead, along with every woman and child of Sparta, as payment for his wife and child. Ask him to deny it."

Andrea's black eyes fixed on Demosthenes, flashing starlight.

"I did lay such a plan," he hastily confessed. "But ample time remains to see it averted."

"And will you?" Eden asked. "Avert it?"

Demosthenes knew Eden's reason for asking this; he had chosen his own words carefully.

"Yes," he answered her. "If I go free, I will abandon that course."

"He lies," Eden declared with evident satisfaction.

"I do not lie," Demosthenes insisted. "I shall keep my word."

"Say it as many times as you like, turtle. It will be a lie every time. Your heart's hatred is too powerful to be bargained away, even in return for your own life." She addressed silent, confused Andrea: "He would see Sparta destroyed. He said as much to me."

"And did you not say to me that you would let Andrea *burn* if that were the price of escaping this world?" Demosthenes argued in desperate tones.

Eden chuckled. "Am I more likely to have spoken truly with you than with her? Andrea knows the truth. If I escape this world, it will be *with* her." Still seated on the trunk, Eden clasped the girl's hand. "Enough blathering. We can kill him now. Brasidas needs only *think* Demosthenes alive. It need not be reality."

"No," Andrea quickly declared, to Demosthenes' great relief.

"Why not?" Eden scoffed. Releasing Andrea's hand, she produced a small pouch, which she upturned, spilling some small tiles of clay or stone onto the forest floor. "Because of this?"

The girl answered glumly, "Yes. Because of that. I have lived among Spartans and Athenians. Both peoples, for the most part, are petty, and thoughtless, and ignorant. But they are people. Not monsters. Monsters are made. Brasidas is one. Here in this clearing, there are two. The one who sent that message is not. And I want with all my heart not to be one."

In the darkness Andrea sniffled, betraying invisible tears. She laid a small hand on Eden's cheek.

"We can love monsters," Andrea said. "We can follow them down paths we would rather not travel, becoming as beasts ourselves. But if we are strong and determined, we can choose instead to show the monsters a better way."

Eden's hand rose and settled atop the small one on Eden's cheek, a gesture which laid bare a truth now undeniable: the monster truly held affection for the girl.

The revelation inspired in Demosthenes no pity for the witch, only the girl. In so many ways Andrea was wise and clever, but in this one thing she was utterly foolish.

Just as her cleverness had proven useful, so now did her foolishness.

The starlit hands separated, and Andrea shakily sighed. "Given his intentions, I cannot let Demosthenes go free. But neither do I think it just for him to die. Yet."

A shrill, resonant note split the night: a horn blown in alarm. The cause might be anything, but the greatest likelihood was the discovery of a suddenly empty execution stake.

Take him," Andrea concluded. "Keep him for now. Safely, if you care for me. Feed him."

Silence. Though less than pleased with the verdict, Demosthenes dared not protest lest a bad outcome turn worse.

He would live a while longer.

"Go," Eden said gently to the girl. "Get home."

"*You* are my home," Andrea swiftly returned. Then, to Demosthenes, "If I regret this, you will find one day that my claws are sharp."

She left the clearing, joining the night.

Eden rose from her seat and gave her captive a warning sneer. "Not a word from you, turtle. There are a hundred ways I could hurt you without leaving a mark."

14. The second battle of Naupaktos

(iii) Black witchery

Ninety men lay dead, most Equals. Those who had breathed the yellow mist were not among the fatalities, so long as they had not suffered a bolt in the back while lying prone. After their fits of choking faded, they remained in a weakened state, their breaths shallow, lungs burning. They were not fit to fight, even if many yet wished to.

Brasidas confirmed it: the Hydra's Breath was not meant to kill men, only steal the fight from their limbs.

Late in the day, with mountains to the right and sea to the left, the regrouped and diminished army of revenge marched until the rough terrain broke and a flat expanse of grassland spread out ahead, checkered with empty fields of harvested crops. For all who saw it, some relief accompanied the sight, for it meant the choicest spots for ambush now lay behind. The witch had implied no further resistance until the river, but those were the words of a witch and a sworn enemy, scarcely to be trusted.

Around the time they reached the plain, riders of the Skiritai returned from the river Mornos ahead and imparted to Brasidas some news which Styphon was not privileged to hear. Whatever it was, it seemed not to please him. Styphon thought he overheard in their report the word *aichmolotoi*, prisoners.

A short time later, when the march to the Mornos was complete, Styphon saw what the riders had seen.

The river at this spot was fordable absent other obstacles, stretching some forty feet from bank to bank and moving in a gentle current toward the sea. But today the river was not absent other obstacles. Near the midpoint between near bank and far, a barrier had been erected of wooden stakes, roughly half a hundred, each jutting up from the water's surface exactly the height of a man.

It was easy to tell that the stakes were the height of a man because affixed to each one was the lifeless body of one.

All wore the red cloaks of Equals, and on their lifeless left arms were the lambda-blazoned shields of Sparta. No man doubted, no man could, that here were the prisoners taken in Agis's failed assault.

A thousand prayers went up from the orderly phalanxes of the halted army, and then almost as many curses from the Equals looking upon the desecrated corpses of their executed brothers.

The curses abruptly ceased when from between the center-most stakes, their executioner waded into view. Clad in the black armor of leather and bronze which covered all her limbs, cropped hair tied tightly back, Thalassia wielded not her customary twin swords—they hung at her hip—but two large-headed axes such as the tree-cutters of Naupaktos surely used to harvest timber for their shipyards. Tree-cutters, though, swung them two handed; Thalassia stood waist-deep in the waters with one ax resting on either shoulder.

There was no mistaking what she meant for her harvest to be.

One of her two eyes which burned coldly with malice was encircled by the fine, web-like tracery which served her as the black witch's war-paint.

She stood there, flanked by corpses, in the river Mornos, waiting, unafraid of missiles which Brasidas did not order loosed because they would only further desecrate the flesh of the dead Equals.

"The Skiritai saw no sign of a defending army!" Brasidas addressed his force. "The coward Naupaktans have fled! We battle *only* the witch this day! She cannot stand against us all!"

While Brasidas spoke, a light commotion arose from somewhere in the lines, and by the time the polemarch finished, an angry Corinthian general in black-crested helm had pushed his way through the ranks.

"My men leave now, Brasidas! Corinthians shall not this day sacrifice themselves to a spawn of darkness so she might —"

Brasidas cut the general short by grabbing the upper rim of his breastplate and drawing him in, baring clenched teeth.

He remained thus for a few heartbeats, then shoved the Corinthian back, saying, "Go, then, and take your feeble whores! They are useless anyway! But your choice will not be forgotten!"

"*Bah!*" the Corinthian answered, and pushed his way back to his city's contribution, calling out orders to break from the army and march east, for home, where their flesh and shades were safe from witchery.

"*She is flesh like us!*" Brasidas screamed to the rest, his face red as spittle flew between the cheek pieces of his helm. "We can destroy her! We are *fortunate*, for there is more glory in sending this creature back to Erebos than in crushing an army of slaves! *Full advance!*"

The trumpeter sounded that order's clarion note, and before it faded it was drowned out by the bellowing war cries of a thousand men. On other days, in other battles than this, Equals went to war chanting inspiring words by the poet Tyrtaeos. But today was not such a day, and this not such a battle.

As Styphon raised hoplon and spear, shoulder to shoulder with Helots likewise armed, and strode forward in even strides, he welcomed the battle-calm which the great Founder Lykurgos intended. If his life was to be lost this day in service to Sparta, it was a right and fitting fate.

Styphon was not among the first to enter the water and begin wading toward the barrier of flesh and timber. But he did see, over the shoulders and shield rims ahead of him, the figure of Thalassia turning and retreating behind that grim wall, and she walked along it, axes striking in swift, sharp strokes at the back side of each stake she passed, as if to sever something hidden there.

The sight threatened to pierce Styphon's battle-calm. There would be more witchery to come before any clash of arms, he knew. Yet there was no path but forward. Those who thought otherwise had already fled, leaving not a man present who would heed any call to delay the advance

Styphon's and the Helots' sandals had just sloshed on the near bank by the time the first Equals, waist-deep, reached the wall of death and unhesitatingly dared to cross it by angling their shields to fit between the posts and brushing past the lifeless legs of the fallen. The war-cries were gone from their lips by now.

Thalassia, having spent the time of the army's crossing moving north to the furthest extent of the barrier, behind it, chopping whatever it was she chopped, now waded to the far shore to begin retracing her path on dry land.

Nearing the wall himself, as river water enveloped genitals which recoiled from its chill, Styphon glanced down on the water's surface and noted it was alive with rainbows; some slick film coated the gently rippling surface. He drew a sharp breath in alarm, for he knew of a sudden what the witch had planned.

"Out of the water!" he yelled, and he quickened his stride, lifting knees high to fight the water's resistance.

He set a hand on one of the stakes, using it to push himself forward, and his fingers found a cut rope, the mechanism by which some substance had been released from containers at the bases of the stakes. His foot struck one now on his way past.

Passing the wall, Styphon saw the witch on the far bank. She had donned a bronze helm that cast her face into shadow. Raising a burning torch, she drew back and cast it up and out over the heads of the Equals who even now mounted the far bank at a run with spears lowered to charge her.

As the torch flew, she restored her second ax to the briefly emptied hand, and with fresh cries from the mouths of the attackers, battle was joined.

But Styphon could not witness the clash of arms, the certain deaths of those Equals, for his eyes were on the flame as it descended from the twilit sky and met the water five spear-lengths upstream from him.

Where the flame touched the water, instead of vanishing in a hiss of smoke, it burst to new life and roared and spread like the bright fingers of Apollo. He saw, at the edge of his vision as he trudged for the far shore, one and then another of the staked corpses become swiftly immolated, as if they had already been treated with pitch or other inflammable substance, which surely they had. Sudden heat warmed Styphon's arm. He heard screams of pain, the roar of more stakes and more corpses catching alight, the pop of blazing wood, and the hot wind carried on it the odor of burning hair, which in an army of Equals was a plentiful thing.

15. The second battle of Naupaktos

(iiii) Thalassia's day of glory

Styphon pressed forward, the water becoming shallower. A tongue of fire crept up from behind and seared his thigh. Without stopping, he splashed water on it with his shield, but to little effect since it was the water itself which burned. Ignoring the pain, he trudged on while the roar of flame and the screams of the men behind him caught in the conflagration soared to deafening. Ahead and to the north lay the immediate destination of all those thus far to have set foot on the far bank, the focal point of the incipient clash.

Past ash spear and round hoplon, over the helms of his comrades, Styphon glimpsed a pair of swift moving tree-cutters' axes, trailing dark blood that glistened thicker with each stroke as necks were severed and breastplates split. But any final groans which passed their lips as they died were lost in the screams of burning men and the roar of the flaming river as the bank began to fill with cloying smoke that stank of roasting flesh.

The army of revenge had come to assault a city of slaves and found itself charging instead across the burning waters of Phlegethon into the scything blades of its deathless guardian, a creature with no other purpose but to reap their souls.

The reaper's ax clove an Equal's skull, then lodged in another's breast, and she let its handle go and drew a sword to replace it. As Styphon made haste toward the fray alongside his Helots, the invaders first out of the river, many burned but undeterred, began to encircle the witch.

Hoisting spear overhead, Styphon led his men toward a place behind the witch where he could plainly see that bodies were needed to complete the encirclement. But before they could plug that gap, black-clad Thalassia spun and quickly dispatched the few men behind her, clearing a path by which she escaped. Halting her flight on a rise not far away, she turned and flung her second ax, which buried itself in the face of an Equal who added silently to the high pile of Spartan corpses he had just been surmounting to give pursuit.

Before drawing the second of her short swords, Thalassia paused long enough to tug off her helmet, which itself became a weapon as she hurled it at her onrushing enemies. It dealt a man a glancing blow to the head, but he pushed on.

"Come, you men!" Styphon cried out to his Helot hoplites. "It is our turn for glory!"

And battle was joined anew, with the witch standing fast before a fresh tide of fighters whose shields were interlocked, their spears the teeth of a fearsome beast such as to strike terror into any foe. Any but this one. To her, the deadly ash spear-shafts were as broomsticks, batted aside as she plunged into the shield wall, dipping sword tips into the necks of the men who carried them, each death given no more attention that was needed to inflict it. Styphon, his own lambda-blazoned hoplon locked with those of Helots at either shoulder, joined the crush of men waiting for their turns to die.

Thalassia slew another two men, or five, or nine, and then there she was, within reach of Styphon's spear. Loosing a roar, he thrust its long blade at her bare face. She dodged, and her pale daimon's eyes caught his, even as her limbs persisted in the work of killing. Her lip curled in a look of—something.

There was a gash in her neck, pouring red blood onto black leather. Some price had been been exacted, at least.

She moved away from Styphon; she never stopped moving, striking first at one quarter, then another, ever thwarting encirclement. Neither did Styphon stop. He raced toward her, as every man did, stepping over the bodies of the fallen, eyes peering over shield rim, spear ready to carve inhuman flesh. In this manner Styphon approached the witch, foregoing war-cry since her back was to him, for the moment. It would not be for long, he knew. His comrades noted it, too, and all sped their steps to take advantage.

As Styphon put his shoulder and all his strength into a downward blow, she spun and dodged his thrust, along with those of three Helots, and she sent her body low to the ground, adder-like. Then up she rose, right in front of them, behind the blades of their spears, and her swords poked holes in the necks of the two men flanking Styphon.

For an instant, her icy, angry eyes found Styphon's. There was no joy in them now, none of light he had seen in them when had come to Naupaktos as herald for Agis. No, here was a black eagle eyeing a mouse. *Here is what I truly am capable of,* her look said to Styphon in that breathless instant. *This is the fury you unleashed upon your world on that day you failed to destroy me, when I was helpless and naked and at your mercy!*

Even as Styphon's mind accepted a deserved death, his war-bred body refused, opening its fingers to release spear-shaft and trade it for short sword. Long before he could bring the blade to bear, either he would be dead or Thalassia gone from his reach. But that mattered none.

While the two Helots sank gurgling into oblivion on either side of him, Thalassia winced. Not in pain, for she felt none as far as Styphon knew; she winced in annoyance, and as his body of its own accord drew his sword, he saw why, and it sent thoughts of death from his mind.

From behind, two men had lodged spear blades deep in her torso.

"Fucking fuck," she muttered, and whirling she sent the shades of those two heroes to the same bleak halls which were every man's fate.

Hope swelling behind his shield and in sword arm, Styphon drew back to hack at the supple, already sliced neck exposed beneath her tied hair, even as past her, to the north, he glimpsed a sight to inspire hope greater still.

The mass of men caught behind the fire and not in it, a number greater than those who had made it across, had finished marching around the flames and presently raced at speed to lend fresh aid to the mere twenty or so who remained battling Thalassia.

Hesitating none at the sight of the onrushing lambdas, or for any other cause, Styphon brought his blade sweeping down in a man-cleaving arc.

Blade cleaved neither man nor witch of Erebos, for Thalassia did as she had done a thousand times in the preceding minutes, maneuvering out of harm's way as if her attacker was submerged in honey whilst she moved through air. She kicked Styphon's knee out from under him, sending him to the earth, where she stepped upon the hand holding his sword. While standing thus, in two fluid moves she slew two more Helots.

If he had not known before, Styphon knew now, kneeling helpless before her, surrounded by the bodies of all the Helots under his command: she was deliberately letting him live.

Of those who had made it across the Mornos, but a handful survived, and they now kept their distance, electing to await the imminent arrival of reinforcements. There was no shame in that, only wisdom.

Keeping sword and eyes upon those men, her sandaled foot yet crushing Styphon's fingers, Thalassia knelt low.

"You live for one reason," she said with some urgency. "You owe me. It will take me at least a day to heal. When I reach Sparta, if he is alive, your debt will be discharged. If he has died, from any cause..." Without removing her gaze or right-hand sword-point from her enemies, Thalassia sent her second blade down to graze the nape of Styphon's neck, and she hissed: "... then you will die. But not before you watch your new *broodmare* go to hell before you. Do you understand that, you witless fuck?"

"Aye," Styphon answered quietly.

The sandal rose from his hand, then seconds later descended on his cheek, driving his head into moist dirt. When the weight left him, Styphon restored his grip on his sword and scrambled to one knee, looking all around.

To the south and west, he spied a black form in the distance, running, a swift Atalanta melting into the distance.

The witch had retreated from the field.

In any battle of men, victory was said to belong to the side which remained on the battlefield when the fighting was done.

This evening, on the bank of a river that burned, there were few living who would agree.

* * *

By day's end, the shattered remnants of the army of revenge had marched to the walls of Naupaktos. It came as no surprise that the city stood silent and empty. Scouts had reported as much. The port of Naupaktos, likewise, stood empty of ships and men. By sea and by land, the inhabitants had fled, up the coast, into the woods—it mattered not where, for there could be no pursuit nor even occupation of the conquered city by an army so broken as theirs.

By fire and iron and arrow, the witch had slaughtered at least five hundred. More than half that number were Equals.

A great many more were barely fit to complete the march to Naupaktos owing to the effects of the Hydra's Breath.

Brasidas had been burned at the Mornos. The left half of his face was bright pink and blistered, and much of the arm on that side was wrapped in bandages that covered skinless flesh which seeped. The look on the polemarch's rough, damaged features as he led his men through the city gate in a mockery of victory was a haunted one.

"Tear it down," he commanded in a dull voice, not his usual bark. "Burn. Destroy. Work through the night until morning when we depart. Leave them no homes to which to return."

With no ardor, the men set to carrying out his order. Styphon lent his back to pulling down the city walls; no easy task, and one which could not be accomplished in a day. But significant damage could be done. It was ever the way of things what took years to build could be all but wrecked in a day.

Brasidas, stripped to loincloth, lent his own back to the same task, and lent his anger, too, working with tightly clenched jaw and eyes that no longer appeared dull but burned with bitterness.

In the evening, he paused in his labors to hear an aide report, "They emptied the granaries, polemarch. All but one, which it seems they tried to burn. But it did not catch, and the grain is—"

"Set the slaves to making barley cakes from it," Brasidas instructed the man dismissively.

"Aye, sir."

Overhearing, Styphon found himself strangely bothered by the exchange. A few moments later, he realized why.

"Polemarch," he called out immediately. He was not one quick to speak—few Equals were—nor was he eager to address Brasidas, but in this there was no choice. "Perhaps any grain to which *she* has had access is best left untouched."

Brasidas looked over at him and scowled, not in annoyance or contempt, by the look of it, but rather consternation at having missed the possibility himself. Sighing, he called out to the departing aide, who returned.

"Feed the first batch of cakes to some slaves. If they greet the dawn no worse off, we will have our provisions."

"Yes, polemarch."

Issuing a throaty growl, Brasidas resumed his labors, as Styphon already had.

"So Styphon," the polemarch said as he put his good shoulder into helping reposition a siege engine. The great *katapeltai,* unneeded in attacking the city, had been adapted for the demolishing of its walls from within. "Seeing as you are such a font of good advice, and you find yourself without a unit, I suppose you must become my lieutenant once again. It is to my credit that I kept you alive, even when I wondered what reason there could be."

Styphon's reply was suitably laconic: "Thank you, polemarch." Yet his mind continued forming words which needed saying, and he addressed Brasidas anew: "Polemarch, the witch spoke to me during the battle."

"You mean the battle in which she might have killed you ten times over, but chose not to?" He scoffed. "Spared by two witches, by Demosthenes, by me. I wonder whether such good fortune will last you a lifetime, or if you are not exhausting a lifetime's worth in a season. What shall happen when you face the foe who fails to show you mercy?"

Ignoring the insult, Styphon reported, as was his duty: "She told me she planned to come to Sparta. Soon."

This silenced Brasidas for a time. Styphon deliberately failed to look upon his leader's face, for he knew there would be fear there, at least for a instant. He cared not to witness that.

"Then we must hasten home to face our fates," Brasidas said at length. "When the ships of the new navy come tomorrow, *delphines* and *scolopendrai*, you and I must be aboard the swiftest."

"If she has not sunk them already," Styphon advised.

"*Yes...*" the scarred, defeated polemarch grated. "*If she has not sunk them.*"

16. Among better folk

Next morning, the fleet sent to meet the 'victorious' forces at Naupaktos was late, turning thoughts of its destruction from idle fears into very real ones. As the morning wore on, the army took its breakfast of barley-cakes, for the slaves who had tested them seemed to have suffered none. Styphon found himself untroubled by hunger and so instead set to readying neighborhoods to be put to the torch.

Hours later, triangular sails appeared round the strait: three *delphines* and two larger *scolopendrai*. As it turned out, one of the latter would carry to Sparta nothing but corpses for burial, many of them blackened and unrecognizable.

Styphon embarked with Brasidas and his picked men on a sleek *delphine,* the same, in fact, which had borne him to Athens many days prior, *Sorrowful Wind*. Without awaiting the loading of corpses and war engines, *Wind* departed Naupaktos alone to round the western coast of the Peloponnese in a swift return to Sparta's port of Gytheio. The remainder of the fleet would embark with the following dawn, leaving behind them a city and port ablaze.

As they passed Patras, Styphon thought he glimpsed a dark figure watching from atop high rocks. But then it was gone, and he put it to his imagination.

They sailed all day, Brasidas hounding the crew for greater speed. The *Wind* passed Pylos, a town of shades laid waste by Agis as punishment for its having followed Demosthenes and thrown off of Spartan rule. It was also where, two years prior, the age of witchery had begun with the entrance into this world of the unnatural being whom the Equals besieged on Sphakteria had named Thalassia, the *thing from the sea*.

From afar, Styphon looked upon the rugged island, its

forests still scarred by fire from the long-ago battle. He was glad when the place left his sight.

It became clear that *Sorrowful Wind* would fail to make Gytheio before full night, owing to their late embarkation. From conversations with sailors in the past, Styphon had learned that the new breed of ships were meant to be sailed through the night, unlike galleys; it was the sailors who refused. Brasidas knew this, too, of course, and had some harsh words for the step-brother captain, even as he accepted the delay. The rounding of the many rocky fingers of the peninsula's southern coast was treacherous enough in daylight this time of year. Neither was careening overland at full gallop in blackest night an option for Equals who were not ashamed of their aversion to riding.

And so they put in at Pedasos, a town which Sparta generations ago had cleared of Messenians and given to the more trustworthy Nauplians, who had sided with Sparta against Argos. There they rested, and dined again on the barley cakes from Naupaktos. Styphon considered eating but found himself unable on account of suspicions which he could not name. Secretly, so none noticed, he discarded his share uneaten. The next morning *Sorrowful Wind* moored at Gytheio, where Brasidas wasted no time going ashore and announcing to their waiting countrymen that victory had come at dire cost on account of witchery against which Sparta herself must soon be defended.

As he spoke, Brasidas yielded every so often to a shallow cough. A number of Equals had developed such coughs overnight. They attributed it to the chill of the sea wind.

One of Sparta's five ephors, the elected officials who were a check on the power of kings—and regents—was among those meeting the ship at Gytheio. This man, a supporter of Brasidas, whispered to him some news to which the polemarch reacted with tight-lipped fury.

"Horses," Brasidas growled. "Get us horses. We make haste to Sparta. Styphon, come! This matter concerns you."

The regent declined to elaborate. They rode at speed, and an hour later Brasidas and Styphon and several of Brasidas's men reined their mounts in what served as Sparta's center.

"Bring them out!" the regent yelled at two Equals standing sentry as he leaped to the ground. "Bring out those responsible for freeing Demosthenes!"

Styphon dismounted and set to waiting and wondering while Brasidas shared private words with the elders and ephors who hastened to meet him.

He wondered who was shortly to be brought forth. Brasidas's words haunted: *This concerns you.* He whispered prayers that those words did not have the meaning he thought they might.

Minutes later, from the direction of the windowless complex in which accused men awaited their trials or executions, a pair of red-cloaked Equals came flanking two prisoners in chains. One was a girl, the other hardly out of girlhood.

His prayers were for naught: the accused were Andrea and Eurydike.

The slave was almost entirely supported by the arm of her escort, feet dragging and head hung in the semi-living state which Eurydike had occupied since the attack upon her.

Styphon's daughter walked erect and with black eyes defiant.

He would expect no less.

The guards halted in the square as Brasidas separated from the ephors to move nearer to Styphon. Eurydike sank into a heap in the dust.

"I am told they both confess to having acted alone in freeing the condemned," Brasidas informed Styphon. "Clearly, a citizen's word carries the weight of truth whenever it differs from that of a slave. However..."

Brasidas let that word hang. Styphon knew well what hung from it: to accept Andrea's confession was to impose a sentence of death upon her.

"Given the circumstances," Brasidas resumed after a pause to cough, "it might be judicious to accept the confession of the Thrassa, who after all was the concubine of Demosthenes. We might simply execute her and be done with the matter, that we might get on to preparing a defense of our city. However... Andrea is your daughter, and both dwell in your home, where you are lord. I yield to you."

"I freed Demosthenes, father." Andrea spoke calmly but emphatically. "Your wife has given sworn testimony that Eurydike was at home with her all night. They refuse to listen. I will face justice, not her. Eris will confirm my story. Even now, Demosthenes is in her custody."

Speechless, Styphon looked upon the two females before him, glad at least that Hippolyta was not present.

"He must be returned," Styphon said, half-heartedly. He had, after all, in Naupaktos staked his life and Hippolyta's on delaying Demosthenes' execution, something which it seemed his daughter and Eris had done for him.

"Demosthenes' fate will not be decided by the regent," Andrea declared.

"Styphon," Brasidas said, frowning, "I urge you to control your offspring."

"I... shall," Styphon answered, though he had no certainty that such was within the realm of possibility.

"*Styphon!*"

This, the cry of a woman, drove Styphon still deeper into

uncertainty and despair. Hippolyta pushed her way past the gathered crowd in the square to throw herself against her husband, clutching at his breastplate.

"End this madness! Eurydike was with me, the whole of the night, in my bed!"

Men and women all around chuckled and whispered. Styphon's face burned.

He clutched his huntress wife's wrist and growled at her, "Silence."

"Perhaps I had best handle this, after all..." Brasidas suggested, taunted.

"No, polemarch. I—"

"Father," Andrea addressed Styphon anew. "If either of us is harmed, Eris will—"

"*Silence!*" he demanded of that one.

Then, Hippolyta again: "Styphon, you must—"

He shoved her away. "Quiet, woman."

All around him were females, instructing, threatening, owning. Daughter, wife, Eris, Thalassia.

In a voice barely above a whisper, for he did not wish it to fall on Hippolyta's ears, Styphon delivered his verdict to the regent.

"The slave is guilty," he said. "My wife had best be restrained, lest she put herself at risk."

"Excellent." Coughing, Brasidas waved over Eurydike's guard before commanding two other Equals to seize Hippolyta, who screamed in protest, seeing what was to occur.

"As master of your house, would you do the deed?" Brasidas asked loudly, publicly, of Styphon. "By the blade, for the sake of expedience, unless you fear blood-guilt. If you prefer, another can—"

To any well-raised Equal, there was but one answer,

which Styphon gave: "I shall do it."

"*No!*" Hippolyta shrieked, struggling violently against her captors.

But Eurydike made no struggle as she was led to a place in front of Styphon.

"Father, you make a grave mistake," Andrea pleaded, her calm facade showing cracks. She bit her lip and seemed to fight a desire to rush forward in some futile effort to save her friend.

"Fucking *trembler!*" Hippolyta cried. "You are not even a man! *I'll cut your craven seed from my womb!*"

"I *am* a man," Styphon muttered.

Eurydike was deposited in a pile before him, her thin, freckled limbs encircled by irons, copper-colored curls matted. She showed her first clear sign of comprehension by dragging herself to her knees and facing away from Styphon with head raised, that his blade might be set upon her neck.

Styphon drew his sword. All those around him were silent, all but Hippolyta who had given up on escape and fell to begging instead. A hundred pairs of eyes rested on Styphon, the eyes of all Sparta as he laid the tip of his blade in the hollow between neck and collarbone, just inside the dull iron ring of her slave-collar.

"You wish to die, girl?" Styphon whispered down his sword.

The Thracian craned her neck to look up at him. Her green eyes, sunken and red-rimmed, held no light.

"No," she said. "I wish to live. Far from Hellas, among better folk." She hung her head again and breathed a sharp, nervous breath. "But since no god will ever grant me that wish, I beg of you... make it swift."

As she whispered prayers to those cruel gods in her native Thracian, Styphon looked down on the head of this slave who had dwelt in his home for a season. She was friend to his daughter, object of his wife's misplaced affection. She had done little to earn the fate handed down to her.

His anger was at other females than this pathetic one... but this was the one kneeling before him, whose punishment by his hand was not only possible but demanded, sanctioned.

It could be no other way than this.

Firming up his grip on her collar, Styphon drove his blade deep, scraping the collarbone, slicing through the girl's Thracian heart. She tensed and whimpered then sighed out her shade while Hippolyta screamed. The deed done, Styphon released the iron collar. The body of Eurydike slid down the length of his wet blade and settled to the dusty earth, her short life finished.

* * *

"Let me go to her, you animals!" Hippolyta cried, twisting to escape the iron grips of the two Equals holding her. Tears coated her cheeks, but her rage of moments ago had melted into grief. Styphon, sword slick with Eurydike's blood, caught the eyes of her captors and silently gave them leave to release her. He was not their commander, but he was nominal master of the one in their custody.

The two let go and Hippolyta flew forward, falling onto her hands before scrambling to the new corpse at Styphon's feet. Dragging limp Eurydike into her lap, Hippolyta cradled the slave, kissing her brow in a display which stirred in Styphon feelings of pity, not for Hippolyta's loss, but for her weakness. He felt the sting of humiliation, too, for the emotional display reflected poorly on him.

Over that regrettable spectacle, he looked at his daughter, who stood more as a Spartan girl ought to, glaring hard-eyed and hard-hearted, a look which Styphon returned until Brasidas demanded his attention.

"You must go to Eris's lair and bring her here, Styphon," he ordered. "Along with Demosthenes, unless you can convince her to kill him, or do it yourself."

"With respect, polemarch," Styphon objected, "Eris is more likely to kill me than heed me."

"Are you averse to risking death?" Brasidas asked with a smirk.

"No, sir. Even though Thalassia swore to take my life and my wife's if I let Demosthenes die, I would put a blade in his heart now, given the chance. However, I believe my daughter spoke truly. Eris favors her. If she protects Demosthenes at the girl's behest, we may—"

Brasidas raised an open palm for silence, then instructed two Equals to return Andrea to incarceration.

She left willingly, under guard, but not before delivering a warning: "From the sound of you, regent, Geneva and Demosthenes may have already won."

Scowling at her back as she left, Brasidas resumed to Styphon, "Eris must hear our side before the girl's. There is no sense in lying to her, of course, but the facts can be presented in a certain manner which I trust you to find. Her student will face no punishment from us. A mutual enemy approaches. A combined defense benefits all."

The regent fell briefly to a fit of coughing before clapping Styphon on the shoulder and bidding him hoarsely, "Go. I must see that every spear is raised when she comes."

And so, as trumpets sounded the call to arms in defense of an unwalled city which had not come under attack for generations, Styphon went alone to the lair of a witch whom he had previously conspired to destroy.

17. Lair of the white witch

The place to which Demosthenes was taken by his captor in the darkness of night was somewhere in the Lakonian countryside. He was no less a prisoner for not being bound; he knew the folly of attempting escape. Even were Eden not many times stronger and faster than any man, her star-born eyes, like Thalassia's, saw by night as well as day.

With a hand gripping the back of his befouled chiton, she guided him through the entrance of some structure and to a corner of its megaron, where she deposited him, less roughly than she might have, onto musty-smelling cushions.

"Sleep," she said. She was a faintly white shape in the darkness, and then not even that as she withdrew.

"May I have water?" Demosthenes did not wish to ask, but days of deprivation left him no choice.

There was no answer, and he settled onto the pillows to pass the remainder of the night, either sleeping or simply laying still. He had just shut his eyes, causing scant difference in the darkness before them, when a faint sloshing sound accompanied by the scent of wet earthenware sent them open again.

He felt around the plaster floor, carefully, and found the pitcher freshly set there, cool to the touch. Righting himself, he drank, stopping briefly, when his throat was wet enough, to utter thanks to the unseen monster which had delivered it.

He neither heard nor saw any more of Eden until first light some hours later, which was also when he first glimpsed his surroundings. The place was a country mansion, barely furnished and unpainted in the Spartan style, but large, with several rooms opening off of the expansive megaron. The plaster was much cracked and the floor uneven, showing it to be an old construction, doubtless dating back many generations.

As he drew himself upright, Demosthenes found his eye drawn to an area of dark stains on the floor not far away. It was blood, to be sure, and none too old.

"You imagine terror and cruelty," came the lilting, accented voice of Eden.

She appeared from another room, looking like some barbarian hunter of the far north, dressed in hide leggings, boots, and a loose upper garment of gray cloth over which her long, straight, golden hair flowed.

She walked to where the blood was. "I have been cruel and terrible, yes, but not here. In that spot, I taught Andrea anatomy using corpses. Knowledge useful for healing—and killing."

After shaking the last drops of water from the pitcher into his open mouth, Demosthenes answered. "Geneva taught such lessons to healers in Athens. You two have more in common than not. Including your real enemy."

Eden chuckled softly. "I call you *turtle* as an amusement, but you truly may as well be one. You know nothing and cannot manipulate me. Do not bother trying. Do not even speak of Geneva at all, or the Caliate or any other such matters. You may quickly find your captivity less pleasant."

Calmly accepting the rebuke, Demosthenes asked, "Might I bathe?"

Eden led him to a stream on the bank of which she climbed onto a large rock and sat. Removing his sandals, but not his chiton, which needed washing as much as did his body, Demosthenes waded into the water and submerged himself, heedless of the chill. He spent some minutes thus, surfacing only for air, opening his mouth often and drinking of the water. At length he removed his garment and wrung and thrashed it many times, for it seemed unlikely that Eden had a fresh one to offer.

Whenever he looked over to where Eden sat, he found her position to be utterly unchanged and her azure eyes unseeing, almost glazed. Before he finished, remembering things Thalassia had told him in seasons past, he understood the reason.

Emerging unclothed and hanging his sopping chiton from a branch, Demosthenes chose a spot in the weak morning sun not far from his captor.

"You look upon other worlds, do you not?" he said, knowing Eden could hear him but not whether she would see fit to reply. "Inhabiting some false reality, the world lost to you, perhaps. *Worlds*," he corrected himself. "Not just a vision, but sights and sounds and feelings, a true imitation of reality. Geneva—"

Too late he recalled Eden's prohibition on that subject. But since she remained unresponsive, he pressed on.

"—mentioned such practices, made possible by those augmentations which make you more than human. Were I capable of such, to shape a new world according to my own desires, I cannot be sure I would ever leave it."

Eden emitted a low growl which at first Demosthenes took for the arrival on the banks of some small animal. "You mean the worlds she *stole* from me. Yes, that is where I spend much of my endless days and nights in this wasteland. But be assured I am always present enough to make you regret failing to cease your pointless babble."

Back at the estate, Eden produced a bowl of brown eggs. She asked, "Do you know how to cook these?"

"I can manage."

With that, Eden climbed the ancient ladder to the roof, leaving him alone. She spent most of the day up there, and much of the next, her body utterly still while her mind traversed other realms. Demosthenes rested his own much abused flesh, and when he had rested enough, he began undertaking calisthenics routines remembered from the military training of his youth in Athens. His body was much healed, yet his mind chafed at imprisonment. Even though escape was so unlikely as to be considered impossible, he might have begun considering the attempt were it not for the sure knowledge that the present state of enforced tranquility could not long last.

Death would come. War would come. Chaos would come.

She would come.

Whatever change came first, he would be ready.

It was late on the third day that change did come, announced by a distant horn. Demosthenes did not know the signal's precise meaning, but guessed it to be a call to arms.

Not long after, Eden descended from the roof—by leap rather than ladder. "Someone approaches," she declared. "I think you share my distaste for him."

"Styphon," Demosthenes said when the Equal came into sight down the country trail leading to the house. "Would you stop me from killing him?"

Eden snorted. "A valid question. Let us hear what he has to say, and then decide."

They took up positions on the trail, where Styphon halted his approach a spear-length from them. The Equal's expression, although controlled, subtly betrayed his fear of the witch. He gave a glance at Demosthenes, nearly his killer in Naupaktos, but otherwise paid him no heed.

"Lady Eris, Brasidas summons you to Sparta, along with his prisoner," Styphon announced.

Eden returned, "He summons me, does he?"

"Might we speak outside the presence of the prisoner?"

"The prisoner asked my leave to kill you, and I did not tell him no. Do not test me."

"Even if I did not have the advantage of being armed, I would welcome his attack," Styphon said, throwing Demosthenes a bitter look. "Geneva comes. For him. For you. For all of us. We stand a greater chance of repelling her by—"

Styphon ceased speaking in the face of laughter from both of those whom he addressed.

They soon stopped, and Demosthenes was quickest to speak. "Apologies, sack of goat-shit, but I rarely have occasion to laugh anymore. The impending destruction of Sparta is quite a good one."

"She will be stopped," the sack of shit asserted.

"You imply that we need each other," Eden said by way of explaining her own laughter, "when the truth is more one-sided. I've made no secret to Brasidas that I aid Sparta only insofar as it serves my ends, or at least does not run counter to them. I am no longer sure that is the case."

"Will you come and tell Brasidas as much?" Styphon asked. "And hand over his prisoner?"

Eden did not answer, asking instead, "Where is your daughter?"

"Safe," he replied.

"Where?"

"Imprisoned for the crime of aiding in this one's escape." He aimed his dented nose at Demosthenes. "But she is not to be harmed."

"Kill him," Demosthenes urged his captor. "Or hand me a weapon."

"No," the white witch answered disappointingly. "We will accompany him to Sparta. I am bored of spear-fighting and plots and politics. It is time to end them."

18. Between love and slaughter

The three shared no words on their walk to Sparta, and those whom they passed kept their silence, too. Owing to the call-to-arms heard earlier, the latter mainly consisted of women, children, and the ancient. All able-bodied men of sixteen to sixty had answered the summons.

Feeling no fear of the death which shortly could await him, Demosthenes found himself eager. Whatever was to come, there was truth in what Eden had said: in Sparta lay endings. The chain of events begun at Dekelea with Laonome's murder had led to this day, the sun of which would set on Brasidas lying dead, or Demosthenes, or them both. The same might be said of the two star-born interlopers whose conflict had shaped, and been shaped by, the war between two human cities.

Had his path to this day not stripped him of faith in the gods of his people, Demosthenes would have sent prayers to Zeus that he be granted his vengeance and that his enemies might be the ones to fall. But if those gods did exist in some other layer of reality, they were as inaccessible to a mortal man as were his multitude of twins who walked other earths, each wrongly believing himself unique.

Only in this singular world, this one layer, did Demosthenes of Athens presently walk toward Sparta between Eden of the Veta Caliate and an Equal whose city stood threatened by another of Eden's kind. For it was upon this earth and no other that Eden and Geneva dwelt among the people of Hellas, forever changing the destinies not only of those Greeks but of many generations yet unborn, in cities unfounded.

Ahead in Sparta lay endings, but the echoes of this day, and those already past, seemed likely never to end.

451

Inside the unwalled bounds of Sparta proper, Equals in full panoplies of war marched in small formations according to whatever plan had been devised to defend the city from a lone, deathless invader. Other days, Demosthenes would have looked on those Spartiates with rage and contempt, but today he hardly gave them a glance, instead keeping his eyes forward.

The formations of red cloaks and lambda-blazoned hoplons grew larger and denser as the trio approached Sparta's center, and it was there that Demosthenes spied the one he sought. Brasidas was pointing in every direction and shouting orders to various officers subordinate to him in Sparta's labyrinthine chain of command.

As Demosthenes entered what passed in Sparta for a main marketplace, the square in which he had previously hung upon the execution *stauros*, Brasidas paused briefly in directing his troops—to cough.

And Demosthenes could not help it: he laughed.

Not loudly, but perhaps because laughter was a sound not commonly heard in this city even in better times, Brasidas looked over. Or perhaps he had not heard at all but just glimpsed the gold of Eden's hair and pale white of her skin at the corner of his vision. Either way, his sharp gaze found the face of Demosthenes. Immediately, the foremost general of Sparta fell silent, glaring for a few beats before giving one last instruction to an aide and then striding through the crowd.

Demosthenes halted, as did Eden, while Styphon proceeded forward to meet his fellow Equal and stand beside him, facing the two arrivals who were not of Lakonian blood.

"Thank you, Eris," Brasidas addressed the more distantly born of the pair, "for heeding Sparta's call—and returning to us our prisoner, whose execution is overdue."

Smile long faded, with Brasidas so near, Demosthenes

now felt the familiar hatred rise from deep within his flesh, urging him to suicidal attack. But he quelled it, waiting with held breath to learn whether Eden—as unpredictable now as Thalassia had been in her first days in Pylos and Athens—would surrender him.

"His death will have to wait a while longer," Eden said, giving hope. "He is *my* prisoner now, by way of Andrea. Bring the girl out."

Brasidas endeavored to look at ease, and halfway succeeded even if his brow glistened with sweat which could scarcely have been due to the weather. Neither did it seem to have resulted from exertion. He cleared his throat and began, "Styphon must have told you that—"

"Geneva is on her way," Eden finished. "Yes. How fared your assault on Naupaktos, *polemarch?*"

"We razed the city, as we set out to do," he answered. Somewhere in the square, unseen, another man was overcome by a fit of harsh coughing. "If you wish to keep the prisoner, keep him. He is inconsequential. What matters is the destruction of our common enemy. You bested her once and shall again, surely."

"Surely," Eden half-agreed. "I requested the presence of Andrea. Must I ask again?"

"An oversight," sweating Brasidas assured her, and he bade Styphon beside him, "Fetch your girl."

Drawing back a step, Styphon spun and hastened off. Brasidas wiped his brow with wrist, then used the same to stifle a fresh cough while looking up the bridge of his beakish nose at Demosthenes.

"What are you smiling at, Athenian?" he grated when his fit had passed.

"Was I? Apologies." Demosthenes lowered the corners of his lips, but ensured that his eyes remained alight. "Let me hazard a guess, polemarch. Did your army eat of grain you found in Naupaktos? Because I have seen these symptoms in Equals. Alas, I was abducted before learning how long any of them lasted. Not terribly long, I suspect."

The red-rimmed eyes of Brasidas narrowed with rage. "You think I do not know what's been done? You are so small minded, Athenian. You have at hand a weapon unlike any a man could ever craft, and rather than employ it to shape the world, you..." He stopped to cough. "You use it to settle your own petty quarrels, matters to be forgotten in a few years' time. You think I have done what I have for Sparta alone? I must tell my city that, yes, but I have worked for the good of all Greece. Twenty years from now, I would see all its cities united, every Greek a citizen and an Equal, none a slave, united in a Hellenic empire to last a thousand years and spread across the maps which I know Geneva has drawn for you, as Eden has for me. By then, we will have ships to navigate Ocean, and the land across it would be ours, too.

"But you...." He growled. "I kill one woman, one innocent out of the many thousands upon whom you and I and men like us bring suffering every day by our actions, and you would crush that bright future. Would you drag my own wife, my child, out here, if you could, and put them to the sword? You would, I am certain, because we are the same, you and I, with but one difference: I am a man of vision, while you possess the mind of a mere *animal*."

With a final sneer and cough, Brasidas turned at the approach of hulking Styphon and the slight form of Andrea beside him.

As the two drew up, Demosthenes taunted, "It seems to me I wielded my weapon rather better than you did yours. If you can still call her yours."

Andrea, the Spartlet whom it seemed might be a better

wielder of unearthly weapons than her city's regent, regarded the two visitors impassively for a moment before speaking.

"Priests and ephors have spent the last two hours impressing on me the importance of convincing the white witch to stand with Sparta," the girl said. "I let them talk, and asked if they saw any humor in their apparent belief that the fate of their ancient city might rest on the words of an eleven year old girl. They did not." She shrugged. "I am proud of my heritage. With good reason. I have no wish to see Sparta destroyed. It does not deserve destruction, and I will do my part to avert it. But, Eden..." She turned dark, earnest eyes on the witch. "I do not think you should stand with Sparta today."

"Silence, girl!" This from Brasidas. "Styphon, remove her."

"Yes, Styphon," Eden said. "Do try it."

Styphon, making the un-Spartan choice to live rather than obey, made no move.

"Between love"—Andrea's eyes fell on Demosthenes as she spoke this word—"and all-out slaughter, there must be a middle ground. With such power as has fallen into our world, that place is where we have no choice but to dwell." Pleadingly, she addressed Eden: "You need not love your sister. Hate her if you must. But there is room in this world for you both." Then to Demosthenes, "And there is room for Sparta. I have called it my home, and also Athens. In both places I found things to dislike and to admire. It is—"

"*I* am the one," Brasidas interrupted, "who would see all the cities of Greece uni—"

"Shut up," Eden told him calmly, and he did.

"You must live, Demosthenes," Andrea went on, "because if you are killed, then Sparta's only hope for survival will be that Eden can destroy her sister. That would be a terrible outcome. And so I beg you to use your influence on Geneva to see that my city is spared. I know that your vengeance has already begun. Please end it before it slaughters guilty and innocent alike."

Brasidas roared. "Why do we listen to this prattle of a child who knows nothing of the world? When she comes, Geneva will not be talked to! I have seen what she can do when—"

"Draw your sword and silence the child, if you dare," Demosthenes said. "I am not certain I agree with her, but I would hear her out. Perhaps that is why we have philosophers in Athens, and here you have none."

Andrea resumed, "Today I watched my father kill my good friend." Her black eyes moistened. "For a time in Athens, she was my only friend, as I was hers in Sparta."

"Eurydike?" Demosthenes's gaze flew to the man identified as her murderer

Styphon glared back, stone-faced.

"Yes," Andrea confirmed. "Executed for setting you free. Brasidas passed sentence and Styphon carried it out, both knowing that I was to blame, not her. I hate my father for it. He probably deserves to die, as I have already plotted the deaths of others who harmed my friend. But if I am to ask others to show restraint, then I must show it myself."

"I will show none," Demosthenes muttered at Eurydike's killer. The slave had died despising her former master. Not without reason. But it hardly warranted denial of proper vengeance, and he would see it was granted.

"You three stand here and discuss *philosophy* if you must," Brasidas said with disgust. "Come, Styphon, the defense—"

A horn sounded, high and urgent. Then distant shouting:

"She comes! She comes at the head of an *army!"*

19. Reunion

Eyes widening under a scarred brow sheened with sweat, Brasidas raced off barking orders. With a lingering, rueful look at Demosthenes and Eden, and avoiding any glance at his daughter, Styphon ran after the polemarch.

When they were gone, Andrea took two steps closer to her star-born mentor and put out a small hand which clasped the fingers of Eden. The girl looked tired, the witch melancholy.

There was some human in this star-born killer after all, Demosthenes had come to know these past three days, as he had learned of Geneva in years past. The knowledge prompted him to venture a question as they watched armed hoplites all around scramble in what looked like chaos, but surely was not.

"What was your name before it was Eden?"

The witch answered brusquely, still clasping the hand of Andrea: "Shut up, turtle."

Evidently, it had been decided that the most sensible plan to defend Sparta against Thalassia was to concentrate troops at the city's heart, where she would face as many blades as could possibly be brought to bear against her at one time. Any other formulation, any effort to bar her before she entered Sparta, covering every avenue of approach, would see the defenders spread too thinly to stand a chance when she actually came. And so the agora beneath the high acropolis and the main thoroughfares leading to it were jammed with red-caped soldiers as ready as they could be for what was to come.

With an army, the criers had said. But what army could Thalassia have brought? Agathokles and any sizable force of Naupaktans could not possibly have marched this deep into the Peloponnese.

Then again, impossible no longer held the meaning it did some years ago.

After long minutes spent watching the frantic deployment and hearing a cacophony of shouting, Demosthenes remembered that one among them possessed senses far keener than his.

"What are they saying?" he asked Eden.

"It is what they have forever feared, the reason I advised Brasidas long ago that Helotry must end if Sparta is to endure. A neighbor enslaved is an enemy eternally at the door, waiting for such an opportunity as this, a spark such as she evidently has provided." An amused smile twisted Eden's pale lips. "Geneva leads an army of slaves."

Demosthenes laughed. In Naupaktos, they had raised between them the possibility of agitating for such a rebellion. He had rejected as too slow and uncertain a path. But Athens knew, any city knew, from bitter experience how swiftly revolutions could arise to sweep away old orders when the time was right and the right man—or otherwise—was present to stand at its head.

"Andrea, it is time for us to do as we discussed," Eden said softly.

"No." The girl's refusal was emphatic. "I cannot leave my city in this state. I will not."

"You are smarter than that. We will return one day."

"If I leave now, I may have no home to return to."

"She is right, Andrea," Demosthenes said to her, self-servingly. "Go. I will impress on Thalassia that Eden is no longer her enemy and that Sparta should be spared."

"He lies," Eden declared. "On one or both counts."

"I am not."

Not explicitly, at any rate. Surely, though, he meant not

to be bound by any promise made to a little girl and a madwoman.

"That, too, is a lie."

"Enough," Andrea said. "My blood is my blood. I remain."

"Then I remain," Eden said, with penetrating eyes and a wicked sneer at Demosthenes. "And I will forever be Geneva's enemy. It is only a matter of how hotly the fire burns."

Slowly, the ranks of hoplites settled into their final formations, facing roughly west. The square and surrounding streets became a sea of crimson and bronze, bristling with gently waving spear shafts. But for some distant shouting, the soft clatter of neighboring shield rims, and not a few hacking coughs, Sparta fell silent in anticipation of the first direct attack it had suffered in the memory of anyone's great-grandfather.

After listening for a short time, Eden reported: "The slave army is small at present, but growing, as new rebel armies will. Still, it is no match for Sparta's forces. Brasidas insists on fighting, but the ephors have overruled him."

She listened some more to the impossibly distant conversations. Watching her features, Demosthenes saw her brow wrinkle and lip curl in an expression of puzzlement or disbelief.

"No..." she said, as though to herself.

Demosthenes prompted her, "What?"

"It seems that in single-handedly smashing the attack on Naupaktos, Geneva killed nearly three hundred Equals."

Knowing that any display of his true reaction could be dangerous, Demosthenes managed not to laugh out loud or let his eyes light with satisfaction. He only studied Eden's face, which he rather suspected hid her own true reaction to the news. Fear. Or jealousy, perhaps.

"Sparta cannot sustain another loss like that, even in victory," she resumed. "The ephors have agreed to discuss terms with her. To which end *your reunion approaches*, turtle."

Minutes later, her eavesdropping proved accurate when six Equals came with orders that Demosthenes should accompany them.

"I come, too," Andrea insisted. The men scoffed.

"And I," Eden added, silencing them. "He is my prisoner."

The three were escorted west, through the mass of troops, past their front line, and along a short stretch of deserted street until they reached a small band of Equals whose number included the five ephors of Sparta. The officials were geared for war, for they were men of fighting age who could not be spared only because they had been elected for a one-year term.

The band's number also included Brasidas, who on seeing Demosthenes drew his sword and lunged. Demosthenes threw himself out of the path of the attack, the blade grazing his left forearm. He fell onto all fours, but did not stay thus, for here was an opportunity he had long awaited; it had come unexpectedly, but could not be missed. As Brasidas swung his sword into position for a downward stab, Demosthenes exploded toward him, driving his shoulder into the polemarch's legs, grabbing him around the knees and bringing him down before the blade could descend.

Brasidas fell face-down, and in an instant Demosthenes was atop him, knee upon bronze-plated back. While Brasidas struggled, unable to bring sword to bear from the prone position, Demosthenes locked one arm around the head of Laonome's murderer, set the other under his chin and he pulled, throwing all of his weight backward with no other goal than snapping his enemy's neck.

He surely would have, too, had it only been a second later that he was struck on the head from behind and dragged roughly upright. Brasidas's face slammed into the dirt, and he scrambled to his feet with crazed eyes and rage on his soiled, sweating face. He made to lunge again for a second attack on his now-restrained opponent, a certain killing blow which would in turn kill any chance at appeasing the enemy at Sparta's door, granting Brasidas the battle he desired. He would have had his way, but two men, including an ephor, wrapped arms around Brasidas and hurled him back, keeping their grip as he struggled against them.

"Stand down!" the ephor holding him barked. "Brasidas, surrender your blade!"

At length, breath hissing through clenched teeth, Brasidas did as ordered, handing over his sword. His captors released him, and he took swift steps toward Demosthenes, who was yet held fast by a man on either side.

Brasidas drew back a clenched fist and struck Demosthenes full on the left side of his jaw.

Demosthenes tasted blood, which he quickly gathered and spat at Brasidas. It spattered his breastplate. "Your grave can get no deeper," he said with a bloody smile.

Brasidas glared a moment longer, drawing heavy breaths, before his inbred discipline was restored and he turned his back to join the conclave of Equals.

"What is the girl Andrea doing here?" he asked angrily. "She has done enough damage this day."

"The enemy witch has affection for my daughter." This speaker was Styphon, who became the next target of Brasidas's scornful look. "If our goal is to prevent battle, she can be of help."

"*Prevent battle,*" Demosthenes taunted. "What would the Founder say?"

The men holding Demosthenes' arms shook him violently. "Quiet, preener!"

"Andrea will attend," Eden said. It was a declaration, not a suggestion. "As will I."

"Very well," an ephor conceded. Moments later, an embassy detached itself from the Spartan enclave to make its way along the dusty road toward an enemy force rendered all but invisible by woods. Demosthenes, walking freely, was among the embassy, as were Eden and Andrea, two ephors, Styphon, Brasidas, and about twenty more Equals tasked with protecting the rest.

From the hidden enemy line, a lone representative galloped forth on horseback. There could be no mistaking the rider's identity. Long before he saw her face, and she his, Demosthenes smiled, not triumphantly or vindictively, but merely with the pleasure that comes from seeing a friend after too long.

It was better than that, for she was no mere friend.

Thalassia, general of a slave army, wore a corselet of black and bronze, and her arms and legs were black-clad, too, in barbarian fashion. Since their separation, she had cut the hair which it had previously been her eccentricity to fashion elaborately before a battle; now it was bound back tightly and efficiently. Where once she had appeared as some demi-goddess or ancient heroine descended from on high to aid one side or the other in battle, now she looked more like what she was: a visitor from some alien world never glimpsed or imagined by mortals.

Riding behind her on the same horse, gripping her armor with hands bound together at the wrist, was a second, male figure. He wore a soiled chiton, and a sack covered his face.

Reining her mount, Thalassia caught Demosthenes' eye

and answered his smile with a look of joy and relief that was no less intense for all its briefness and subtlety. In a flash it was gone, replaced with the steely mask which every general must wear when meeting the enemy.

The bulk of her attention, though, was plainly on Eden.

After slipping to the ground, Thalassia reached up and roughly grabbed her hooded passenger, depositing him on his knees in front of her. Aiming pale, threatening eyes at the Spartan delegation, she yanked off the sackcloth.

The young prisoner who blinked at the sudden brightness wore a thick, unkempt beard and surely was an Equal, even if his long locks had been crudely hacked off.

"Agesilaus, brother of Agis," Thalassia announced. "Rightful Eurypontid king of Sparta. Want him? You know the price."

"Give up nothing for my—"Agesilaus began, and then was silenced by Thalassia kicking him from behind, sending him face-first into the dust.

"Send him over," she said.

"Though he be exiled, Agis is yet the rightful king," one of the two ephors present yelled. "We have no need of an heir! Our demand is a swift end to armed threats which Sparta would rather not take the time to—"

Thalassia sighed heavily. "You people and your fucking constitutions."

On her horse's rump hung a large satchel, into which she now reached. Her hand emerged holding by long its hair a cleanly severed human head, rather fresh by its complexion. To the sound of not a few stifled gasps, she hurled this toward the Spartan delegation. Bouncing, it rolled to a stop.

"Agis, ex-Eurypontid king of Sparta," Thalassia said. "Little brother was nice enough to tell me where I might find him."

She took from the satchel a severed hand, removed from its stiff finger an iron ring which, stooping, she forced onto the finger of Agesilaus. Drawing one of her two swords, she put its point to the new king's neck.

"Send him over," she repeated icily.

"The Helot rebellion will be called off, and you will make no further moves against Sparta!"

"The rebellion is not mine to call off," she returned. "But I'm happy to kill no more of you than I already have. Send him over."

"She offers us *nothing!*" Brasidas hissed at the two ephors. "Even if she did, she is not to be—"

"Quiet, polemarch."

"This can only be settled by—"

"*Quiet!*"

While the leaders of Sparta bickered thus, Andrea slipped between their red cloaks and ran forward to cross the open space toward Thalassia. Immediately after, Eden stepped in front of Demosthenes and shoved two Equals apart from behind, opening a path. The two turned and glared, but dared not retaliate. Reaching back, Eden grabbed Demosthenes' chiton and dragged him out, marching him along the same path Andrea had taken, safely ignoring the angry muttering of Sparta's leaders.

The girl was already addressing Thalassia with warm words of greeting when they arrived, but Thalassia's wintry eyes went to the two coming up behind.

"Listen to her," Eden demanded coolly of the rival whom she had once cut to ribbons.

"I know what you and Demosthenes intend," Andrea said. "I can stop it. They have seen the illness you gave them. I will tell them its cause, which is proved easily enough. But it need not come to that. Days ago you sent me a simple plea, and I heeded it, as was right. Your friend and mine, Eurydike, paid the price with her life. I now return a simple plea of my own. Leave with what you came for, and spare my city and people. Eden will do you no harm. Your feud with her will be at an end."

Lowering herself to one knee, the girl clasped Thalassia's hand and pressed her lips to the back of it.

Demosthenes had his own answer to Andrea's plea, but he kept his silence awaiting Thalassia's, meanwhile watching Eden for any sign of an imminent, murderous end to her forbearance.

But it was another quarter from which there came burst of sudden motion as the hostage Agesilaus exploded to his feet and broke into a wild run in the direction of Sparta. Eden watched with scant interest, while Demosthenes tensed to give chase until Thalassia put out a hand and said calmly, "Let him go."

Just as well, for Demosthenes remembered that he was unarmed. A spare sheathed sword hung at the back of Thalassia's mount, all but certainly intended for him; he walked a few paces now and drew it.

As her hostage escaped, Thalassia crouched, pulling Andrea into an embrace.

She kissed the girl's face, whispered into her ear, "I'm sorry," then with a sharp whistle, she flung Andrea bodily aside and became a black blur moving in the direction of Eden.

There came the sound of blades drawn, and an impact like that of a javelin striking a bronze-clad shield. Blood flew —whose, it was impossible to tell—as the two became entangled in an ungraceful, black-and-white maelstrom of brutality. No sword-fight; this was murder.

At the same instant, the forest around the road came to

life with the sound of rustling leaves and twanging bowstrings, and the sky filled with bolts and arrows which sped just over Demosthenes' head on course for their true targets: the Spartan delegation. Behind the volley came fighters at full run, screaming, well armed and armored Helots eager to spill the blood of their hereditary masters.

Though caught fully by surprise, Demosthenes hesitated none, and required no time for thought. He knew the reason Thalassia had not warned him, which she might have done with a mere glance: Eden was sure to have caught her signal, too.

Since the cliffs at Naupaktos, he and she had been two parts of the same ruthless machine. His half, even if it was the lesser, needed no instruction. He knew what was to be his part in this plan, which was less a plan than a combination of instinct, preparation, and adaptability.

Of all things which might be accomplished this day, the elimination of Eden was by far the most important. But he was not meant to interfere in that effort, one which easily might cost him his life, or Thalassia's by forcing her to protect him.

No, his role was clear. He was to claim his vengeance.

20. Ruthless machine

Even as the first wave of arrows hammered the Spartans, striking the two attending ephors in the face and neck, Demosthenes set eyes on Brasidas, and he charged, armed but unarmored, hearing from behind him the fierce battle-cries of the onrushing Helot fighters.

More bolts flew from the rebel crossbows, cutting the air near Demosthenes' head, but he heeded them not. He saw only Brasidas, who appeared no less determined to resist despite having being freshly pierced by arrows in the arm and leg. Seizing the sword of a fallen ephor to replace the one stripped from him, the polemarch cried out at the twenty Equals present, *"Forward! Forward! Ignore the slaves! Kill the witches!"*

Under a hail of missiles, the Spartan formation closed ranks, locked its round shields, bellowed defiantly, set its heavy spears, and surged forward.

Having no intention of impaling himself or any interest in battling this armored beast, which likewise held scant interest in him, Demosthenes veered sharply, setting course to outflank it. The one whom he desired—sweating, freshly wounded, and lacking both shield and spear—ran at this formation's rear.

In plenty of time, Demosthenes removed himself from the phalanx's path.

A man on its edge spared him a glance. Demosthenes knew the face well, for it belonged to the Spartan whose death he desired more than any other save Brasidas. Styphon.

A glance was all that Styphon spared him, all he could spare, for he was not at this moment his own man, if a Spartiate ever was, but rather only a small part of a larger organism born and bred to enforce the will of the Spartan state.

So were they all, and the Spartiates had two more urgent threats to face in the form of rebels and witches, which is why a ragged, unarmored, formerly condemned Athenian could maneuver unchallenged to the formation's rear. There, its leader turned, saw his bitter foe, stopped running, and fell into a defensive stance.

Following the example of his other half, Demosthenes slowed not a bit but instead used his blade to bat aside that of Brasidas before slamming bodily into him. The Equal had the advantage of a breastplate, but he also was ill. Already, his breath was heavy from the exertion of the run, and his brow shimmered with plague-sweat.

The two tumbled as one to the ground, striking rapid blows at one another with fist and sword pommel, each all the while struggling to put edge or point of blade to soft flesh. Brasidas was first to succeed, and when Demosthenes drew back a cut arm, the polemarch followed with a sharp headbutt to Demosthenes' face then tried to use the momentum to put himself above his enemy for a killing stroke. But Demosthenes put his injured left arm to good use by grabbing and pushing on a broken arrow shaft lodged in Brasidas's leg.

The Equal grunted in pain, faltering in his assault long enough for Demosthenes to send him back into the dust with a sword hilt to the jaw. Finding his feet, Demosthenes sprang up far more quickly than the polemarch, who was overcome by a wheezing cough.

When Demosthenes came to stand over him, Brasidas swung his blade upward, but the effort was weak and easily deflected. Once it was parried, Demosthenes drove his sword point down into Brasidas's right wrist, causing the fingers to open and the sword to fall free.

Groaning, coughing, face streaked with blood and sweat

and soil, Brasidas wheezed, "End it, Athenian. Do it. Kill the hope of Hellas."

"No," Demosthenes said. He drove his blade down again, slicing the polemarch's ankle, which spouted blood. Then the other, and then both knees. The wounds would not soon cause his death, Demosthenes knew from practice, but Brasidas would not be able leave this spot under his own power. "You don't get to die in battle. You will have no name on your grave."

Gripping the legs of his crippled, writhing, semi-conscious captive, Demosthenes began dragging Brasidas west in the wake of the phalanx which had just passed.

* * *

Running in the front rank of the formation, at its left edge, Styphon watched Demosthenes pass, and he did nothing. The Athenian was irrelevant. Even in the absence of specific orders, Styphon would have known that the final destruction of the two witches was far more vital to the future of Sparta, and here was a rare chance to accomplish it, while they were busy slaughtering each other.

It meant, in all likelihood, that Brasidas was to die. He was wounded and sick, and Demosthenes was not. But even a polemarch's survival was irrelevant to the well-being of Sparta when weighed against the boon of the removal from it of both Eris and Thalassia. No doubt Brasidas himself would understand that.

And so Styphon charged on alongside his brothers. The Helot rebels were ineffectual and could be all but ignored, as Brasidas had commanded. They were swordsmen, not hoplites; a few tried to attack the formation from one side or the other, falling in the attempt, but none were fool enough to stand in its path.

The spindles from enemy bows kept flying, lodging in

shields and stealing the lives of at least two Equals, but spindles could not slow the phalanx's swift, steady advance on its objective, the witches presently butchering each other in a tangle of slender, swiftly moving limbs and bloodied blades.

Near them, on her knees, was Andrea, the daughter who hated him. She was nothing if not clever; surely she possessed the wits needed to move out of the way of a charging phalanx. But the phalanx drew closer and closer, screaming the battle-cry, swatting Helot flies, yet Andrea did not move.

Styphon's lips fell silent as he saw why.

She held both hands tightly across her midsection, where a red stain was slowly spreading. Just feet from the warring witches, fully in the path of the phalanx, Andrea sank to her knees.

A part of Styphon's mind, the bulk of it which was loyal and obedient and loved his city above all things, began instantly to mourn her, a child lost in the achievement of a greater good.

But another part told him that if he only threw aside spear and shield, the added speed would let him reach her in time to remove her from harm's way...

Any attack on the witches was doomed to disaster anyway. Andrea would die for *nothing*.

He ran on, shield high, spear overhead, nearing the point past which there could be no choice. Ahead, blood-soaked Eris seemed to have the upper hand: on top, stabbing downward over and over into her enemy's inhuman flesh.

It was Styphon's body which made the choice, more than his mind. His mind told him to remain in formation, to stay by his brothers and persist at any cost, but instead, he cast off the lambda blazoned hoplon encumbering his left arm, and with his right he threw his heavy spear in the direction of the witches. He knew not whether it struck them, for his eyes were on Andrea as the legs underneath him thrust him harder forward, giving him speed enough to get ahead of the spear blades, several of which would have scalped him had he not held his head low as he crossed in front of them.

It was Andrea who was champion of foot-races, but today it was her father, the font of her fleet blood, who ran, and the laurel to be won was her life.

Crossing nearly the entire width of the phalanx, six shields minus his own, he scooped up his kneeling daughter without missing a stride, squeezing her to his breastplate of stiff leather, just ahead of the spears, and he ran on, beyond the rim of the rightmost shield of the phalanx, rounding it to take him back east, toward Sparta.

The glimpse he had had of her as he swept her into his to arms had shown the bleeding to be extensive. She needed a healer, and he would run until they reached one.

"*Father*..." Andrea said dully, in his arms. "Father... please. P-please don't let me die." For the first time in memory, she sounded her age.

"You will not," he pledged, a promise not his to keep. He could only run.

Clutching her tightly, he sped through the woods toward Sparta, intending to let nothing stop him before he reached a healer. After a few short minutes, he heard over the rush of his own breath and the crunch of dry leaves underfoot a set of unmistakable sounds: the cadence of hundreds of feet hitting the ground in unison while a lone voice set the rhythm with a chanted war-hymn of Tyrtaeos.

Sparta had learned of the treachery and was marching out to meet its enemy. Emerging from the wood onto open plain, Styphon saw the walls of shields moving toward him through tall grass and he adjusted his course to take him through a gap between formations. The soldiers knew him for one of theirs, of course, and so he was allowed to pass, if not unmolested:

"The battle is that way!" Equals called to him mockingly.

"What, did you bring the wrong shield?"

"Ah, it's Styphon! Once a trembler, always a trembler. Men's hearts do not change!"

He paid them no mind and began to cry out, "*Healer!* I need a healer! Swiftly!"

He passed the phalanxes going off to victory or death, or some combination thereof, and continued through the outskirts and into town proper, crying all the way for a healer.

After too long, an elderly man in the cloak of that profession appeared, moving as swiftly as he could, with his young apprentice at his side. Both were half-blooded step-brothers, for no male Equal could have any profession other than war.

Styphon hastened to them and set a faintly gasping Andrea on the ground. Her abdomen and the hands which had clutched it were nothing but slick blood, which also covered Styphon's breastplate and arms.

"You must save her," he said. "She is deeply cut."

"I can see that!" the old man snapped while the youth tore a hole in Andrea's chiton. "I haven't much time for her. There'll be *men* bleeding soon. Bad enough, this disease they brought back from Naupaktos."

Kneeling over her, he poured water from a skin over her flesh, exposing a long slice from which new blood continued to pour. But Styphon only glanced at that; he looked instead upon his daughter's face, for she spoke to him in a breathy voice, repeating over and over, "Hot iron... hot iron... hot iron."

"Do you know of what she speaks?"

"Hmm, what?" the old man asked, perturbed. "Ah,

searing iron... I have heard some use it to stop bleeding. Not tried it myself. No, we'll pack the wound with—"

The youth clapped the old man's shoulder. "No better time to test it, grandfather. I shall heat a blade." He rose and ran off.

A shadow fell over Styphon, and he looked up to see one of the three surviving ephors standing over him.

"What will they find out there, Styphon?" the ephor asked.

Styphon rose and answered, "The Helot army is ineffectual, though they are well armed and harass with spindles. Of the two witches, I cannot say if either yet stands. At minimum, they have done each other great harm. There may never come a better chance than today of destroying them."

"I too pray their time in our world is done," the ephor answered. "But come. You are scant wounded. Your place is —"

Coinciding with the sudden end to the ephor's words, some strong force hammered Styphon from behind, at the small of his back, alongside the spine. Pain and sudden numbness spread there, and he stumbled forward, stopping himself on the shoulder of the stunned ephor.

He heard fast footfalls from behind, and he whirled, a move which caused a fresh burst of pain. Reaching behind him, he learned why: a thick, smooth shaft jutted from his back, and had bumped against the ephor.

A javelin. And having turned, Styphon's eyes fell now upon the huntress who had cast it, running full-speed toward him with hate in her eyes and dagger in hand. He had time barely to raise his arms, and the ephor no time to intervene, before Hippolyta was upon him, blade plunging into his neck.

Twice more it bit before Styphon fell backward, onto the

javelin, which twisted and drove deeper, sending a chill wave throughout his torso and down every limb.

"*Coward!*" Hippolyta screamed, struggling as the ephor seized her knife-wielding arm by the wrist. "*Murderer!* I loved you! And I loved her! Now, thanks to you, I know only hate! Take it with you to Haides!"

Rolling onto his side, javelin in his back, the taste of blood filling his mouth, Styphon looked skyward through a mist which slowly crept in from the edges of his sight. He saw his wife aiming the dagger at her womb, where Styphon's seed was lodged. But the ephor restrained her, aided by two other Equals who ran up.

He shifted his dimming gaze and saw the old healer step over the form of Andrea just as the apprentice returned gripping tongs which held a rod of iron. The youth's mouth and eyes were wide with shock.

"Not me..." Styphon uttered. The words gurgled. "Save... her."

His graying vision found the face of his daughter, which had turned to look back at him with its black eyes. Nearer, he saw the fingers of Andrea's hand, reaching for him. Styphon commanded his own hand to meet and clasp it, but the limb was numb and went nowhere. He could only look, for a few more fleeting moments, on a young face which featured in his fond memories, even if its owner had come to hate him.

There was no hate in her eyes now, though, and Styphon was glad for it as he expelled a final, wet breath and fell backward, spinning, into that bleak, lightless realm where all memory died.

21. Death storm's eye

It had angered Demosthenes to see Styphon race away in the direction of Sparta. Though he dearly wished that Equal dead, he could not consider following him. For one, it was a great enough risk not to have killed Brasidas yet, sparing him for a more fitting death later. To leave him unguarded to chase lesser prey would be utter folly.

A second reason was that the Spartan phalanx had just collided with its two targets, Thalassia and Eden, flowing around and surrounding them. From behind, Demosthenes could see little other than the backs of Equals.

Thalassia would escape. Not unhurt, but she would escape. It was far from certain, but he believed. He had faith.

Eden would not. He hoped.

Perhaps it would be wise, after all, to deal Brasidas a quick death now. Not only was there uncertainty in front, but also behind in the direction of Sparta. Surely reinforcements would not be long in arriving.

Demosthenes slowed and stopped. He wore no armor, held no shield, and was armed only with a short sword to their spears. In such a fight, he could only die.

Swiftly upon surrounding the two star-born combatants, Equals quickly began dying at the hands of one or both, while others died from bolts in the back as Helot bowmen dared venture closer, maneuvering for better shots.

Spear blades rose and fell and swords slashed in a crimson frenzy, but whatever harm the two 'witches' had done each other, whatever their differences, they were not enough.

Within minutes, the last spear fell, and silence and stillness reigned but for the moans and languid movements of the half-dead.

Dragging Brasidas, who was inert—perhaps dead, given his illness—a short distance farther, Demosthenes released the leg of his captive and ran to the site of the carnage, stepping over Spartan corpses until he reached the death-storm's vortex, where hoplites were stacked three deep. There he stopped and pushed fresh bodies and lambda-blazoned shields aside, searching.

He saw movement and found a hand, blood-coated, slender: a woman's hand, reaching up as if from underwater. Clasping it, he rolled a dead Equal, kicked another aside, and uncovered the hand's arm. It was black-clad. Lifting a shield, Demosthenes found the arm's owner's head, likewise attached, and the blood-greased hair on it was dark and cropped and bound back.

Demosthenes blew held breath in elation as he helped Thalassia climb from the human wreckage of the destroyed phalanx. She was covered all over with deep gashes, her torso appearing like a corselet stuffed with freshly butchered meat. Her face was a gore-mask, its left eye split open or missing entirely.

This ghastly apparition laughed. "I must look awful."

"No," Demosthenes argued. "Very elegant."

After accepting help which she may or may not have required to stand, Thalassia set to pushing corpses aside. "We have to find her."

"I have Brasidas," Demosthenes informed her. He looked back to where he had left the polemarch and was glad to find him yet lying there. All around, Helot rebels stood staring in disbelief at the walking corpse which was their rebellion's leader.

"Kill him," Thalassia advised of Brasidas. Having found what she sought, she began wrestling it free.

"Soon," Demosthenes pledged.

The body of Eden was more thoroughly mutilated than Thalassia's. Only in a few patches was her fine hair still golden; the rest was slick with gore. As more of her emerged, Demosthenes saw that her upper and lower halves were very nearly detached. Still, Thalassia took a bronze sword from one of the dead and drove it, without malice, ten or twelve times into her enemy's face.

"They're coming," Thalassia said, heaving Eden's body over her shoulder and rising. She wobbled slightly, one of her thighs being largely shredded. She turned to face one of the cross-bow wielding Helots, a man who appeared somewhat less awestruck than his fellows. He was a man whom Demosthenes had met once or twice, not long ago.

"Antigonos," she addressed him. "As we planned. Melt away. No pitched resistance. Yet. Their end comes soon."

"Aye, *stratega*." Rounding up his comrades, the Helot led them into the woods.

Stratega. Woman general. A made-up nonsense word, until today.

Demosthenes, meanwhile, dragged Brasidas over to Thalassia's horse, which had wandered into the woods to avoid charging phalanxes. Thalassia met him there and slung Eden onto the beast's back before taking Brasidas over her shoulder. The polemarch moaned, proving that there still was some life left in him in spite of fungus and blade.

Demosthenes thought Thalassia would next sling Brasidas onto the horse's back, but instead she kept the burden herself and said to Demosthenes, "Mount up."

Opting not to question the *stratega*, Demosthenes climbed up behind the mutilated corpse. A season prior, it had been Thalassia's body slung in front of him on the desperate flight to Dekelea.

Today he rode at a steady canter, ahead of a distant

Spartan war-chant while Thalassia moved swiftly alongside, carrying Brasidas, keeping up in spite of the butchered leg which caused her no pain. The army soon to arrive would find only its dead brothers and the head of its exiled king.

"Those Equals may have saved me," she observed. "One of them, anyway, who threw his spear during the charge. It hit her and not me."

"Fortunate," Demosthenes remarked. "Andrea was hurt," he added, intending no connection, only to inform. "I saw Styphon carry her away. I regret that he lived. But if he saved her, it is perhaps an acceptable trade."

"Andrea tried to interfere," Thalassia said, her tone one of regret. "I cut her, accidentally."

"She loves Eden."

"I know."

They rode swiftly and in silence for a short while, sometimes on a small trail but more often through forest. Thalassia seemed to know her way.

"You gave them back their king," Demosthenes observed when they were far enough from danger that they could let their pace flag.

"Doesn't matter," Thalassia said. "I fed him well on the way here."

22. Antigonos

Like nearly every living Messenian, whose forefathers long ago were conquered by Sparta, Antigonos had been a slave since birth. He undertook his daily labors not only for the survival and welfare of his family and town, as free men did, but also for the glory of masters to whom his life was worth only as much as the service he rendered. In his twenty-two years, Antigonos had largely avoided direct harsh treatment by his masters, but he had witnessed much of it: cousins given the lash until they nearly died; friends leaving the village at morning only to be found dead by night, sport for young Equals; maidens raped for the same reason. The life of any Helot was ever one of mourning and sorrow and impotent rage.

Antigonos had been present at King Agis's razing of Pylos, the city of Helots which had risen up under Demosthenes and thrown off Spartan rule. It had been a rare source of pride for Messenia.

Agis had emptied it of life, a lesson for any slaves who dared entertain notions of freedom.

The message was effective. Antigonos, and all his fellow shield-bearers—who were little more than pack animals—had returned home broken of spirit.

He and others had heard of the polemarch Brasidas's intention of letting Helots win their freedom on the battlefield, fighting on behalf of the folk who had hunted their brothers and violated their sisters. There was little interest in such an arrangement. Rumors even spread that Brasidas wished to free all Helots, but none believed that. Even if it were true, surely it would be reversed by some later decree. Brasidas, even if he was powerful, was still only one man.

Not long after Pylos, Antigonos had been called up as a

rower and shield-bearer for the King's invasion of yet another city built by slaves who had thrown off the Spartan yoke: Naupaktos, which had been free for at least two generations.

Antigonos went, for he had no choice. And just when he thought his miserable life was to end in the sea, victim to a Spartan defeat the sight of which was almost worth the price of his life, he had been pulled from the water by the victors, his kinsmen the Naupaktans. They had treated him well, sympathetic to the plight of all Messenians.

In Naupaktos, Antigonos had met a strange woman, Eastern in complexion, with blue eyes that saw through him and into his heart. She had put questions to him about Sparta, about his feelings toward his masters and what he would do to get back at them.

What was he willing to do to forever end the domination of Messenia?

He had given the right answers, it would seem, as had thirteen other captured Helots, for he found himself in a group of that size being trained in secret by that strange woman, whose name was Thalassia. She was partner to the Liberator of Pylos himself, Demosthenes, whom the fourteen met once or twice.

Thalassia treated them kindly, like nothing they were used to in a leader. She addressed them all by their names, needing to hear them only once to learn them. She was patient, and she laughed, and made the men wish to work harder to please her. For a while, she trained them in fighting and in deception, and then at last revealed their purpose.

The fourteen were to enter Lakonia and poison the granaries used to supply the messes of the Equals. The illness which the Spartans would contract was fatal and would continue to kill so long as they did not learn the cause of the plague and cease consuming the contaminated grain.

Not only men would be killed, but women and children, too, old and young alike with no distinctions drawn. Helots, too, unavoidably, would die.

After informing them, Thalassia had questioned them again, looking into their hearts as they answered. Were they willing? Would they waver?

All must have met her standard, for their number remained at fourteen. She had chosen well.

Their training continued. And then, a change: Demosthenes was abducted. Thalassia, now smiling not at all, informed them they were to leave sooner than expected and undertake still another task, one which sent their hearts soaring.

Not only were they to poison Sparta's granaries. They would foment a rebellion, bringing arms and armor provided by their cousins the Naupaktans and spreading news across Messenia that Sparta had suffered a second disastrous defeat at Naupaktos, with Equals slain by the hundreds. The defeat had not happened yet, but Thalassia pledged she would make it so, and the fourteen believed in her. Such news would inspire Messenia, helping to convince them that the time was ripe and Sparta was at her weakest.

She taught them new lessons: how to enter a village and find the right supporters who could in turn find others; how to conceal and distribute the smuggled arms; how to convince others to revolt and to do so quietly, secretly, and then move on to repeat the same in another village; and if they failed to spark a truly widespread revolt, how at least to make it *appear* as one.

Dividing into four groups which would follow separate paths to Sparta, they embarked south across the Peloponnese with wagons laden with arms disguised as other cargoes and amphorae full of a thick, deadly, black paste. For now, they bid the one they called *stratega* farewell, but they were to meet her again outside of Sparta, bringing whatever following they had amassed.

Antigonos's group of three met with success in rallying men to the cause, and as they neared Sparta, it came time to fulfill the original purpose for which they had been selected.

In times of peace or war, Equals were not ones to heavily guard their granaries. Lakonia itself, the Spartan homeland, was under no particular threat. At the present time, with heavy losses suffered at Naupaktos and a second attempt on the place underway, there were no sentries at all. Creeping up to the granary at night with deadly amphora in hand, Antigonos mounted the steps to the top of the domed structure of brick and plaster and pulled open the hatch at its top through which grain was poured in by the Helots who harvested and dried it.

Unstoppering the jug, he upended it and let the viscous, foul-smelling paste, which he was careful not to touch, fall down into the hatch in mud-like globs to spread on the kernels within. When it was empty, Antigonos's comrade poured in a sack of fresh grain to cover the poison, and then, carefully, by moonlight, the empty but still dangerous vessel was placed into the grain-sack and the hatch closed. Their purpose discharged, the enemies of Sparta escaped into the night to repeat the feat elsewhere.

The sludge was alive, the *stratega* had told them. In a small amount of time, it would grow and spread, infecting the grain underneath almost invisibly, such that the Helots who scooped kernels from the hopper at the granary's base were unlikely to notice anything amiss. Nor would those to whom they served it find it distasteful.

Victims of the poisoned grain would cough and sweat and grow weaker and weaker by the day, until they died, all the while continuing to eat of the food which harmed them, ignorant of the illness's cause, thinking it to be from gods, not men.

When they had treated three granaries thus, it was time. With almost a hundred men following, they went to the meeting place from which they would threaten Sparta herself.

Antigonos had no children yet. And he would not, he vowed, unless they were to grow up as free men and women.

23. A mad universe

Their destination was a spot in the woods distinctive only for the presence of a second horse, tethered to a tree, from the branches of which hung two packs. Underneath, a sword and cross-bow leaned against the trunk.

Thalassia laid Brasidas down, and Demosthenes dismounted.

"You'd best kill him soon," she advised, "or the fungus will." She pulled butchered Eden from the horse's back, depositing her on the ground, and tethered the beast beside the waiting one. Fetching a knife and returning to Eden's corpse, she knelt to begin fresh butchery.

"Her Seeds?" Demosthenes asked.

"Yes."

"You'll destroy them?"

"Yes. But..."

She drove the knife into Eden's leg and began slicing, searching for the metal spheres which might be embedded anywhere within her enemy's flesh. They contained her mind, her memories, her essence, and any one of them, given time, could become a new Eden.

"But what?"

"I'm sure she's hidden one away in a secret place. As I have. And I'm almost as sure that Andrea knows where."

"You mean we'll need to go back and make her tell us."

Thalassia paused in her bloody task and looked up. "Are you suggesting we torture an eleven year-old girl? One who saved your life?"

"No," Demosthenes said quickly. "No. For all we know, she's dead already."

Dragging unconscious Brasidas to the base of an elm, he left him there briefly while he fetched the cross-bow and two bolts. After loading one, he 'stood' Brasidas up against the bark, raised his limp right arm over his head—and fired a bolt at close range through the wrist, into the wood.

The captive screamed and twisted, but the bolt held while Demosthenes repeated the procedure on Brasidas's left arm. His scream faded into a pulsing, involuntary groan until he opened his eyes and remembered discipline.

"Do you have a spare bowstring?" Demosthenes asked of Thalassia, who persisted in her own bloody endeavor.

"In one of the packs."

Demosthenes found it where she said and brought it with him, along with yet another bolt, to stand once more before Brasidas, who glared with intense hatred from bloodshot eyes which he could but barely open halfway.

"The power which came to us, you and I..." the defeated whispered. His voice was low and hoarse. "We could have shaped the world! I tried. But *you*... you are a small man, Demosthenes. You have no vision. She is *wasted* on you!"

"If by *vision* you mean the desire to control the destinies of others, then you are right, I lack it," Demosthenes answered. "I saw only what was in front of me. My family, my city. I wanted only peace and happiness. You took them from me."

He glanced at Thalassia, who looked up and met the glance knowingly with her undamaged eye. The same words, more or less, had recently passed the lips of the woman presently mutilated.

"I understand why you killed Laonome," Demosthenes went on to his victim, as he passed the bowstring under Brasidas's chin and around the trunk of the elm. "You wished to break me. It worked. I probably would have destroyed myself. But you overlooked at least one thing. Probably many, but this is the most important."

Where the two ends of the bowstring met, Demosthenes wound them many times around the spare cross-bow bolt, which he then twisted until it was snug around the tree and the throat of Brasidas. The result was a garrote, the traditional means used on the *stauros* when a relatively quick death was desired. Its handle was a few inches from the condemned's left ear, so that is where Demosthenes stood.

"She is *not* a weapon," he continued. Brasidas had no choice but to look upon the witch in question. "Neither was Eden. The only one in your city who recognized that was a little girl. That's why you had no say in the future of your city, and *she* did. Well, almost."

He cranked the bolt, and Brasidas began to choke.

"A weapon cannot heal your spirit when it has been broken," Demosthenes said. "A sword cannot put new life into a heart that has died." He turned the bolt again. "When hope is lost and death a breath away, no spear, even had it wings, would ever fly to its wielder and turn defeat into triumph."

Another turn, another choking gurgle.

"A weapon does not console, or confide, or sympathize, or caress, or make one laugh when the hour is blackest. She *is not* a weapon."

Another sharp twist. Brasidas's lower half spasmed.

"Knowing that, *I* have the final say on your city's future. And that is..." Twist. "...that it will have none. A few years from now, there will be no such thing as Equals. Lykurgan law will be a memory. The ones you currently call slaves will dwell in your houses and worship in your temples. Or they will tear th—"

"He died five seconds ago," Thalassia interrupted.

Looking into his victim's eyes, Demosthenes saw that the life was gone from him.

Vengeance was taken.

Releasing the handle of the garrote, Demosthenes walked away from the tree turned execution *stauros* to settle onto the ground beside Thalassia. She paused in her grim work to lay her much-abused head on his shoulder and nuzzle him. He laid his cheek on her bloody scalp and returned the brief gesture, after which she returned to hunting Seeds, of which she had so far extracted two. The engraved spheres of gore-specked black metal sat on a flat rock nearby.

"I'll help." Demosthenes took up a knife and did just that.

By the time Thalassia declared the job finished, as night was beginning to fall, she had found three Seeds in total, Demosthenes responsible for none.

She led them to a nearby lake to wash, taking the Seeds with her, lest they be lost.

"Be glad it's dark," she joked on the shore as she shed her armor. "It's probably best if you don't see me undressed for a few days."

They bathed efficiently in water which felt chill only to one of them, then emerged and dressed in the fresh garments which had been in Thalassia's packs: for Demosthenes, a soft, well-made chiton with blue embroidery at the collar and hem, and for her, a dress of pale green like sea-foam, the color which suited her best and was her favorite. There were dark gray cloaks for them both, which in Thalassia's case served to hide the worst of her injuries.

A glimpse by moonlight told him she was right, as ever she was in most things: her unclothed flesh was a sight he was best spared. She was, at least for now, a corpse that walked.

"If you ask me to *feel* this," she said, "I'll find your least useful part and rip it off."

Once they were dressed, they sat on the lake's edge,

Demosthenes on the side of her that showed him an unmarred profile and a working eye.

"Athens?" she said after a while.

"I suppose. But I do not think I wish to stay and be part of restoring the democracy. They can manage without me. They will have Kleon, after all."

"Alkibiades is chief tyrant there now," Thalassia reported. "He crushed the resistance and got Thrasybulus executed. He worked with Sparta. Will you kill him for it?"

Demosthenes sighed. "I suppose I'll decide when I see him. First we should visit our old blacksmith friends for some arms and armor of good Athenian steel. And after that, I thought... perhaps on to Roma. If you still would see it destroyed."

Thalassia was silent a moment, then smiled. "I suppose I'll decide when I see it. But let's take the long way there, via an island or two. Sandy places with lots of warm, oiled bodies with golden brown skin, and girls who want to braid my hair. No blood or fire or fungus. A few days ago, I massacred more men than I ever thought I was capable of. Really, you should have seen me. I have no regrets and would do it again, but... not soon, if I can help it. It's not what I want. Right now, I want to make friends who won't be killed by the choices I make. I want to sit on beaches and just be *sea-thing* for a while. It will be amazing. I'll invent surfing and bikinis and who knows what else."

"Meaning you will make a spectacle of yourself."

Thalassia scoffed. "Hello, I'm Jenna. Have we met?"

"Merely an observation. Not a complaint," Demosthenes clarified. "I do like to think I have met Jenna... and Geneva, and Thalassia, where most only ever know one."

"And you survived us all. That's as impressive as anything I've done. Legendary. Poets should sing of it. About the islands, you should know that now that I've said it out loud, that's my plan with or without you. But... given all the sweet things you just said about me to the man you were strangling, I want to believe it's *with*."

Looking upon her face, as blue in the moonlight as her wintry eyes were by day, Demosthenes gave his answer.

"We should not pretend the choice is mine. Or yours. We are no longer a choice. Our partnership is the dictate of a mad, mad universe. We deny its will at our peril."

"Pfft, listen to you, Athenian with his fucking philosophy," she mocked in her playful way. "So it's *with*?"

Demosthenes slid closer to her and laid an arm over the cloak which encompassed her damaged flesh. She rested her head on him.

"Your game of island witch could only end in disaster without me along," he said. "You know that."

"And?"

"And... I would miss you. Satisfied?"

"So rarely."

"After Athens," Demosthenes mused aloud, "we'll find a ship from Corinth. We can pay Ammia a visit. If it's friends you want, you could invite her to join us."

"Sweet girl," Thalassia reflected. "Like Eurydike. I'll miss Red. She deserved better from us."

"Yes... It's strange, though. I know I should feel sorrow, but I cannot. When Andrea saved me, she spoke of monsters. Is that what I've become?"

Thalassia made no direct reply, only said after a while, "Some island life will set us right."

"I'm not so sure," Demosthenes protested mildly. "I'm not sure we ought to change. We might be best served by remaining as we are. Whatever the future holds, I do not feel it can include peace for us. Not for long. I thought of you once as madness made flesh. Your madness may have eased somewhat, but I believe that chaos will never be far behind you. Or me, now that the gods have made me your disciple."

Demosthenes could not see the broken face which rested on his shoulder, but he knew it smiled fondly.

"All the better reason to enjoy ourselves while we can," she said. "Then, when chaos comes, we'll face it together. In the meantime, we can set ourselves modest goals, such as not killing Alkibiades, or Ammia, or any of our new island friends. Trust me—" She nudged him with her wet scalp. "—we'll have some fun before the next storm hits. I'll make sure of it."

"Of that," Demosthenes said, "I have not the faintest whisper of doubt."

END

Epilogue One

Chaos comes

60 days after the fall of Athens

"Malcolm..." sighed Sevareem DiRivache, who hated the name her starship captain father had given her. "It's your turn to carry the null-crate."

"It weighs six-and-a-half pounds," Malcolm returned.

"It has sharp corners! It's digging into me. Who makes things with sharp corners? Idiots, that's who."

Sevareem shifted the strap on her shoulder, but the metallic box persisted in poking her in the kidneys. It was not uncomfortable, thanks to neurilace masking any unpleasant sensation that might have resulted, just as it regulated her skin temperature, preventing her from sweating in the summer heat as the pair waded through the tall grass of a meadow. Behind them lay a forest which Sevareem had managed to determine was located somewhere in Northern Europe.

"Will you just take it?" she insisted. "I have a lot of shit in my pack, and you have almost nothing."

"Traveling heavy is your choice," Malcolm lectured. "Have you figured out yet how long we're here?"

"No. Well, yes. Sort of. Do you have any conception of how difficult that calculation is?"

"No. Well, yes. Sort of. Hence, it's your job."

"Asshole..." Sevareem muttered, as she frequently did. "Anyway, the answer is greater than two years, so I have some time. Are you going to take this thing, or what?"

By the time Malcolm answered, "Fine," the overly-angular null-crate was deposited in his arms. Its contents weighed vastly more than six-and a half-pounds and were quite a lot larger than the crate's size would indicate.

Only moments after winning the meaningless victory, Sevareem cursed under her breath and informed Malcolm: "Locals..."

Lacking even the simplest of enhancements to his flesh, muscle, and brain, Malcolm squinted at the faraway treeline across the meadow. He likely saw the six men as little more than dark shapes. With her vision magnified by neurilace optics, Sevareem could practically see their body lice.

"Vikings," she groaned. "I fucking hate Vikings."

"I'm sure they're not Vikings," Malcolm said. Hoisting an arm, he called out in a tongue these folk could not possibly understand, "Hello there! We are peaceful!"

Of an instant, the six alerted and ran in the direction of the two visitors. Malcolm, as was typical in such situations, put on a broad smile and held open palms aloft to show he was unarmed.

Sevareem wore her usual frown and wrapped the fingers of her right hand around the grip of the GiG-97 machine pistol slung on a strap around her neck. She had acquired it several layers ago, named it Emma, and applied a rainbow decal which disappointingly had begun to rub off.

"I'm just gonna shoot them," she said as the 'Vikings' made their way in haste across the meadow.

"No! We've talked about this. Bad Savvy."

"'Bad Savvy,'" Sevareem mimicked. "Am I your dog?"

At a sharply spoken word from the apparent leader, the six locals, clad in garments of stitched hide, halted meters away to brandish a mix of well-used swords and slender spears.

Sevareem sighed. "Fucking Vikings."

Still smiling at them with open hands, Malcolm said, "They're not Vikings. They're... Gauls or Goths or something."

"Vikings, Goths, Huns. They're all the same. Hairy, nasty-smelling monkey-men who want to paw me. I'm a city girl."

"Try a few languages. Tell them we're peaceful."

"We're not."

"Tell them anyway."

"Go fuck yourselves, you brainless rat-fuckers," she told the six in Gaulish, which happened to be one of the seventy-seven languages presently imprinted on her brain. Many were of no relevance to any earth, much less this particular iteration of it. Gaulish was on queue for deletion. Some Vikings she had tolerated long ago in some other layer must have been Gauls.

The men showed no sign of taking offense, so evidently they were not the Gaulish variety of Viking.

"I know you said something nasty," Malcolm correctly surmised. Lacking neurilace, he spoke only a couple of dozen languages, which he knew on account of being very, very old, though he did not look it. As in Sevareem's case, many of the tongues were not of this earth. "I would try Latin myself, but if I recall correctly, chances are if they know Rome, they won't react well."

When Sevareem opened her mouth to speak Latin, ideally provoking them, Malcolm warned her, "*Don't.*"

Sighing, she picked at a peeling edge of Emma's rainbow decal.

Malcolm spoke his own name loudly, gesturing at himself. He pointed at his companion and said, "Sevareem."

"*Sav!*" Sevareem corrected him. "*Sav!* Why do you do that to me every time?"

Ignoring her, Malcolm resumed addressing the Viking-types, now in Middle French: "We would like to travel to your village. Will you take us?"

Whatever they spoke, it was not Middle French or any close relative thereof. Whatever it was, they conversed in it excitedly among themselves while keeping wary eyes and weapons upon the travelers.

"Allow me to translate their conversation," Sevareem meanwhile said aloud to Malcolm. "'The smiling idiot is unarmed. Let us stab him a hundred times and take the pretty little one with the colorful hair—'"

"That's enough."

"'—back to our village and rape her. Then we'll pick lice off each other and—'"

"Enough."

"'—rape her some more.' I'm done."

The lead primitive, an older man whose face was hairier than the rest, began to address Malcolm in angry, aggressive tones. Sevareem took the opportunity to raise Emma and aim it at the man, who ceased speaking. Evidently he was possessed of enough warrior instinct to recognize the thing as a weapon.

Malcolm touched the machine pistol's muzzle and nudged it down. Begrudgingly, Sevareem permitted it.

He smiled again at the leader and said, "We'll just be on our way." Since it hardly mattered, he said it in the spacer tongue which the two had grown accustomed to using between themselves down the layers. "Sorry to have bothered you."

As Malcolm began to step away, the head primitive spoke some words to his comrades, who cautiously began to fan out as if to surround the strangers and prevent their departure.

"Oh, come on," Sevareem complained. "I'm just gonna do it."

"Relax."

The leader spoke more nonsense at Malcolm while one of the others stepped close to Sevareem. One hand pointed its ridiculous bronze weapon at her, while the other reached toward her pack.

"Don't touch my stuff," she warned.

He grabbed it. She yanked it away. He grabbed it again.

"Sav..." Malcolm admonished. His tone said he knew protest was by now pointless.

This time, as she yanked the pack away, Sevareem swung Emma round and squeezed its trigger.

She loved the stuttering sound of Emma's voice, and the weapon spoke in it now as a short burst of projectiles tore through the chest of the offending Viking, or whatever he was.

While Malcolm stood beside her, surely wearing that judgmental look of his, and as the other five primitives cried out in anger and terror, making to attack, Sevareem brought Emma to bear on them all, sweeping it left and right, firing without hesitation.

The five fell quickly in heaps of blood-soaked animal skins.

Sevareem sighed at the bodies, putting off turning to see Malcolm's disapproving look.

"So... that's done," she said at length, rubbing Emma's rainbow decal.

"Give me that," Malcolm said, snatching the slung machine pistol by its muzzle. Sevareem bent her head down and allowed it to be removed.

"We don't need to be friends with people like that," she said by way of explaining herself. "It ends with us living like animals in some hut for much too long. And he touched my pack. What am I supposed to let him touch next? Where does it end? Let's just assume he intended to molest me."

At a swift pace, Malcolm started away from the scene of the massacre on a course slightly altered from what it had been. "Honestly," he said, "I don't know why I keep you around."

Sevareem caught him up. "That's the hundred-and-sixty-seventh time you said that. You know the answer: I'm as useful as I am entertaining, and we're not the least bit attracted to one another."

"That is important."

"Plus, I realized something else, too."

"I know you'll tell me."

"When you keep someone around who's even more of a psycho than you are, you get to look like the sane one while I do nasty things that you would have done yourself anyway. Admit it."

"It's... not completely wrong," Malcolm said as they left the meadow behind. "But in every single layer do you have to kill the first people we meet?"

"I don't *have* to..." Sevareem said. "Look, you have your compulsion, I have mine. So? No harm done. Where are we headed, anyway? I already hate this place."

"You want a city, I'll give you a city. If this earth has a Rome, it should be this way."

"Rome again?" Sevareem groaned. "Didn't go well last time. But it beats mud huts, I guess."

"This time we bear gifts. They'll appreciate what's in this crate. It'll be fun. Just, please, try to make them like you."

"You're joking! I'm vastly more likable than you, *space marine*. It's not even close."

"Go tell that to the Vikings."

Epilogue Two

The Wolves of Eris

There was another name by which they called themselves on their inviolable island stronghold, but to most they were the Wolves of Eris. On this, the last of a desperate hundred-day march through marsh, forest, plain, steppe, and finally mountain, beset at every turn by enemies of all kinds, at the head of the ragged remains of an army the command of which he had but recently inherited, Nausis stood among nine Wolves.

The nine were women, as most of the Wolves were. The small number of males among them were said to have been born on the island. Many of the females were, too, but the tales were well known of young girls, frequently orphans, always willing, being carried off to the island not to be seen again on the mainland for twenty or thirty years, if ever.

Why they were called Wolves was no mystery, for each was a finely honed instrument of death. They appeared on the mainland just often enough to put fear into any who might oppose the Royal House. Their connection to Eris was less clear, since by all accounts the dark goddess whom the Wolves honored above all was one called *Magdalen*.

Some said that the Wolves' warrior-priestess leader, the most feared among them, was none other than the slaughtergod's sister. But standing within inches of her on a snow-dusted mountainside beyond the Scythian plains, and having been near to her for many days of the journey here, Nausis rather doubted that.

Three Wolves had died in getting here, as had many hundreds of soldiers of the empire. The less unlucky comrades of the latter were encamped lower down the mountain, licking frostbitten wounds. By all rights, Nausis should have remained down there with his own kind while the Wolves alone climbed higher on the journey's final leg.

That army which had set out with the Wolves had taken on faith that salvation lay here in these mountains. Those who had laid down their lives had done so not knowing what it was they sought, only that something could be found in these mountains capable of reversing the past season's disastrous defeats. Reluctant to take on mere faith whether the death and suffering of the march had been in vain, Nausis had trailed the Wolves.

Their leader, on seeing him, granted her approval with a smirk, and so he was permitted into their company.

Quite deliberately, Nausis hiked close to her, stumbling more than once over the jagged rocks because he found it hard not to stare. A handful of days ago, he had been nowhere near the command of a force like this. A few deaths had changed that and placed him here, beside a figure known throughout the empire, a woman said to be deathless, having led the Wolves since their foundation a great many generations ago.

She did not look old. Quite the opposite. Her skin was maiden-smooth and the long, straight hair which fell upon the steel shoulders of her dented armor was of a rich brown, lighter when the sun passed through blown wisps of it. Nausis might have thought the legend of her immortality a mere trick had he not seen her fight. It seemed impossible that a girl so young could battle thus, kill thus.

He had also seen her wounded. But instead of killing or permanently incapacitating her, as such wounds as hers surely should have, they had only pained her for a few days. By now, quite impossibly, they were fully healed.

It was no myth, Nausis accepted now. Andrea

Styphonides, warrior-priestess, leader of the Wolves of Eris, feared enforcer of the Royal House to which she was cousin, a woman who looked hardly seventeen, was in truth a deathless being.

"Here," the Styphonides announced, stopping by a steep crag which resembled a great many other steep crags they had passed. "This is the place."

The Wolves and Nausis halted in a loose ring around the Styphonides, who drew a deep breath and cried out, "*Lykaaaaaaa!*"

The syllables carried far, echoing off the rocky slopes.

"Lyka!" she called out again. "I know you are in there! I know you can hear me! Answer!"

No answer came.

"The House I have kept upon the throne for three hundred years has fallen. I seek your help! I would not have come were the need not dire. *Lyka!*"

After a long minute of silence in which no woman, and certainly no man, dared speak, there came a laugh as if from the air or the rocks. It was a brief, soft laugh. A woman's.

"Andrea!" said the invisible laugher "Darling! Such a surprise."

"Please let us in, Lyka. Me, at least, so we can speak. I need your help. I need... Nadir. There are men below in need of food, water and med—"

Another laugh. "You're boring me, dumpling. What do I care if your little house fell down? Build another!"

"Lyka!" Andrea Styphonides yelled. "Stop! What I ask of you is next to nothing! All you need do is allow me to enter and leave again. It costs you—"

"Needy, needy!" the rocks exclaimed. "You really are boring me, sweetness. I shall have to ask you to leave."

"*No!*" the Styphonides cried in rage. "Lyka, I beg of

you!"

"Sorry, duckling. Bye-bye!"

"*Lyka!*" the warrior-priestess screamed. "*Lyka!*"

Again and again she screamed it, but the rocks and the air remained silent.

Then the cried name became a guttural scream as the Styphonides strode to the nearest crag and pounded her fist into it, then drew back and struck it again, repeating the action as if she might crack the stone.

Such a feat, it seemed, was beyond the power even of an immortal. Instead, when she whirled and stalked back toward her Wolves, roaring, the knuckles of her right hand and the stone behind her were smeared with blood. Her course put Nausis directly in her path. Too late he realized she did not intend to stop. Even as he tried to step aside, the warrior-priestess planted palms on his breastplate and shoved, sending him to the ground. Fortunately, that was the end of her attentions. While Nausis scrambled upright, she strode past, proceeding another several steps before putting her back upon a flat boulder and sinking against it with breath hissing through clenched teeth, black eyes wild.

Her Wolves gathering round her on the desolate mountain, all hope lost, the deathless enforcer of House Styphonides sobbed.

WHO ARE MALCOLM AND SAV?

Witness their first meeting aboard a starship in deep space in

"BRING ME THE HEAD OF SHEBA SHEBARI"

Free story exclusively for members of my newsletter.

Get it at
www.ironage.space

Printed in Great Britain
by Amazon